CW00429969

REVENGE OF THE BETRAYER

Book Seven in the Viking Blood and Blade Saga

Peter Gibbons

AUTHOR MAILING LIST

If you enjoy this book, why not join the authors mailing list and receive updates on new books and exciting news. No spam, just information on books. Every sign up will receive a free download of one of Peter Gibbons' historical fiction novels.

Hart er í heimi,   hórdómr mikill
—skeggǫld, skálmǫld —skildir ro klofnir—
vindǫld, vargǫld— áðr verǫld steypiz.
Mun engi maðr ǫðrom þyrma.

It is harsh in the world,   whoredom rife
—an axe age, a sword age —shields are riven—
a wind age, a wolf age—   before the world goes headlong.
No man will have   mercy on another.

- From the Poetic Edda, a collection of Old Norse poems
taken from skaldic poems in the 10th century.

REVENGE OF THE BETRAYER

By Peter Gibbons

ONE

880AD.

Hundr's dead eye leaked a salty tear as the wind whipped across the dunes and scoured his face raw. It was the desolate, powerful wind that the sea god Njorth unleashed to fill ships' sails and crush others beneath the crashing waves of his fury. A wind that seemed to come from nowhere, stretching across the bleak, wave-tipped vastness of the horizon, and it was both cherished and feared by those who dared to venture the treacherous Whale Road. Hundr cuffed the involuntary tear away from his face and dragged a calloused hand beneath his eye patch to knead the aching, puckered flesh of his missing eye. Torches sputtered and danced on the sand a hundred paces away, casting the beachside camp in shifting shadows. The men on the beach drank ale and laughed and roared in drunken celebration. A woman screamed from somewhere in the tangle of ale barrels, bearded faces, and raucous shouting. Moonlight glinted off an axe blade, and the smell of roasting mutton filled Hundr's nose.

The sun had all but dipped beyond the western horizon, and the wind sang as it danced through the tall grass and wildflowers that dotted the small island. The sea slopped and sighed against the shore, lapping at sand and shale. Hundr ran his fingers across the ivory hilt of his sword, Fenristooth, and its touch was smooth and reassuring. He had used the blade countless times, taking many lives in battle and single combat. It rested snugly in a fleece-lined scabbard belted at his waist while his second sword, Battle Fang, was strapped across his back. The raiders at the camp would think themselves lucky and rich. Having plundered the southern lands of the Picts, they had embarked on a short journey north, passing by the Orkney Isles, before settling on this smaller northern island. They had braved the risks of the Whale Road in their shallow draughted warship to bring their blades, daring, and brutality to those not strong enough to protect themselves. Their Jarl, or Earl, would allow his men to revel in drink, rape the slaves they had captured, and fill their bellies with stolen meat before embarking on their journey east to Norway and south to Jutland, the Vik, or wherever it was in Denmark the crew of Vikings made their home.

"How many?" said Hundr to the captive pressed into the coarse grass of the sandbank beside him.

"Three hundred champions," the man replied gruffly. He spoke Norse with a Danish accent, and his golden bearded face twisted into a rictus of hate as he spat a gobbet of white phlegm at Hundr. Sigvarth Trollhands rewarded the captured Dane with a vicious punch to the eye, and the man grunted in pain.

7

"Tell us how many men are in your camp, or I'll cut your ears off," growled Sigvarth.

"Bastards," the man hissed, and then his eyes went wide and white with pain and terror as Sigvarth clamped a firm hand over his mouth, slid a bone-handled knife free of its leather sheath at his belt, and sawed the blade through the man's left earlobe. Dark blood pulsed into the Dane's blonde beard, and he bucked and jolted beneath Sigvarth, who sat on top of his back to keep the prisoner's face pressed against the grass.

"How many?" Hundr asked again.

"Forty men on the beach and six on board ship," the man said through gritted teeth.

"Who is your Jarl?"

"Jarl Fullr War-Raven," the man answered. A smile played at the corners of his mouth as though Hundr should know the name, clearly eager for the one-eyed sea wolf to cross blades with his Jarl and meet his fate against the greater warrior.

Hundr nodded and then glanced at Sigvarth, who grinned before he slit the prisoner's throat. They had captured the man while he was taking a long, ale-stinking piss over the dunes. The Danes had sent the man up the beach to stand watch,a duty he'd performed half-heartedly due to the inhospitable nature of the island – it was low, flat, and relentlessly battered by the brutal sea wind. But despite the perceived safety of their remote island camp, the

8

Danish Jarl would fear another man like himself, a wolf of the sea, approaching unlooked for and unseen to take away his spoils. And he was right in that fear because Hundr was such a man – a formidable killer and the leader of the warship Seaworm and her crew of ruthless warriors.

Hundr stared over his shoulder where his crew crouched in the grass. Their hard eyes glinted back at him like a pack of wolves, and he smiled. There were men to fight and kill on the beach, warriors with axes, spears, knives, and the skill to wield them. A Viking crew were on their way back to Denmark with a ship full of plunder, and Hundr's men were about to take it all away from them with steel and fury. If a man was brave and savage enough, it was easier to do it that way; to prey on the hunters rather than make the treacherous journey south to raid villagers and churls. The Saxons in England had grown adept and learned to retreat behind their stout burh fortresses or trap raiding Vikings within meandering rivers, and if Njorth turned against a man, a coastal squall could drive both ship and crew into the depths. So it was better to hunt the hunters,even though it meant engaging in battle, a prospect most men dreaded but one that Hundr eagerly embraced.

"Let's just charge the bastards," said Bush, the grizzled shipmaster and Hundr's friend. "The smell of that meat is making my belly grumble so loud they'll hear it down the beach."

There wasn't much cunning in what Hundr was about to do. From a claw-like inlet of a neighbouring island, his men had spotted Fullr War-Raven's sail earlier that day, racing north before the wind. She was a *drakkar,* a Viking warship of forty oars with a sleek, long hull which sliced through the surging waves like a blade. Hundr had watched from a distance, tacking into the wind to keep her in sight, until the sun had dipped into an orange-tinged horizon, and his prey had dropped her stone anchor off the coast of the small island. Her men had waded ashore to make camp for the night, and as darkness descended, Hundr had sailed his own warship, the Seaworm, around the island's western side. Crossing its low hills covered in rough grass and hardened soil, he brought seventy men with him, men who wielded shields of linden wood reinforced with iron and adorned with Hundr's distinctive sigil of the one eye. Hundr's warriors came armed with axes, spears, swords and seaxes, and they came to kill.

Hundr was a sea Jarl who owned five warships, with over three hundred men sworn to his service. Hundr promised his warriors rings, adventure, reputation, food, and shelter in exchange for their oath to fight for him. So, every summer, he took to the Whale Road and honoured Odin with the blood of the slain. The rest of his ships sailed east and south in search of plunder. Two raided along the northwest coast of Northumbria, and the other two down the wild cliffs of Strathclota and further south into the cliffs and bays of Ireland. They would reunite before the harvest at their home in Vanylven, Norway, where Hundr's friend Einar was Jarl, and their families would welcome them home, eager for tales of bravery and gifts of amber, ivory, jet, and silver.

Fenristooth scraped across the wooden throat of her scabbard as Hundr drew the blade. With a swift motion, he reached across his shoulder to pull Battle Fang from its sheath and stood, blades held out wide as he turned to face his men. Hundr wore a chainmail brynjar, which protected him from knee to neck. Its riveted links were heavy about his shoulders and shone like rippling seawater in the moonlight.

"I am the Man with the Dog's Name," Hundr said loudly enough for all in his crew to hear. He used the name by which men knew him across the north, a name feared and respected by the fighters and warriors who yearned for reputation and glory. As he spoke, his men clashed their weapons once upon their shields in recognition that their leader was speaking. "You are the crew of the Seaworm, feared men and fighters all. Down there is a crew of brave men with a ship full of plunder. We can take it all from them if we fight them on this beach. When our arms clash and men scream in pain from the blows of our axes, Odin's attention will fall upon us. The betrayer and lord of warriors in Valhalla will welcome new recruits for his Einherjar, and the Valkyrie will ride down from Asgard to carry the glorious fallen to Odin's hall. Do you want to go to Valhalla?" Another clash of weapons on iron shield rims sounded – harder this time, like the ringing of a Christian church bell.

Hundr looked across the hungry faces of his men, at their bright blades and the hard lines of their scarred cheeks and long, braided beards. They began to shout and growl, working themselves up into the fury necessary to charge into battle, to risk death and pain in pursuit of riches, glory, and fame. Hundr didn't care about the noise. They were close enough to the enemy now that the fight upon the sands was inevitable and could not be prevented or avoided by Fullr War-Raven and his crew. "So take everything from them, take your axes to colour with blood and honour the gods, fight for each other and fight for me. Kill these dogs, and we sail home rich and burnished with war fame. For those among us who will die today, we salute you and ask you to save a place for us in Odin's hall. Are you ready to fight?"

Hundr's Viking crew rose from where they crouched in the grassy dunes and clashed their weapons so that the din was like rolling thunder in a winter storm.

"For the Man with the Dog's Name!" bellowed Sigvarth, and Hundr strode across the lip of the dunes and down onto the beach. His leather boots crunched on the tiny stones, and he flexed his fingers around the hilts of his swords. He breathed deeply, and suddenly, an image of his wife Sigrid flashed into his mind, her golden hair falling over her curved shoulders and his twin children cuddled in her arms. Hundr's family awaited him in Vanylven, and the thought of their love and warmth made him pause. They were softness and light, happiness and joy, but

Hundr needed to be cruel and ruthless, so he shook their image from his mind. That was the risk he faced by pursuing glory – if he died and took his place at the feasting benches in Valhalla, he would never see Sigrid or his children again, and that altered the stakes of battle. Now that Hundr had a family, the danger wasn't just the pain of wounds, the infection and sickness that might follow, or death itself; it was also the potential loss of their love.

"Here come the bastards," growled Bush, and his gravelly voice snapped Hundr from his fears. In the flickering torchlight, Fullr War-Raven came to fight and defend his men and their plunder. His crew rose from where they sat on the beach upon driftwood logs or smooth stones. Their laughter had disappeared, replaced by the low rumble of fear and anger. Weapons flashed amongst them, and a big man strode from their midst. He carried a long-handled Dane axe with a wicked bearded blade, and his bald head reflected the camp's torchlight.

"Who are you, and what do you want?" demanded the big man, who Hundr assumed was their leader. Fullr War-Raven himself. The camp crew swayed as they stood, groggy from too much ale and bellies full of roast mutton. There was not a brynjar between them, no armour, and Hundr could only see a handful of shields slung on brawny arms. They had waded ashore from their ship and were so confident in the island's remoteness that they did so only half-prepared. No man wore mail on board ship, for if he fell overboard, its weight would drag him into the murky depths and a death without honour. So, the Seaworm crew faced a band of raiders without armour, and that gave Hundr encouragement.

"We come for your blood and your silver," Hundr said, and his men took up the war cry. Bush blew a low, sonorous note on his curved war horn, and the din of weapons clashing on iron-rimmed shields rolled down the beach like a tidal wave.

Fullr War-Raven's mouth moved as he spoke again, but the roaring and banging drowned out his words. Hundr's heart quickened, the prospect of combat stirring in his chest and the excitement, which could only come from fear, turned over in his belly like churning butter. Hundr's men spread out in a ragged line across the beach. There was no need for a shield wall because Fullr's men were in disarray. They came from their camp in clusters of two or three, with filthy undershirts and baggy striped trews, armed with axes and spears. They were warriors without shields or mail, though some were brave and came to meet Hundr's challenge. Fullr himself strode forwards, unafraid and sweeping his Dane axe in wide circles, bellowing with wild eyes and raving war fury.

Hundr picked up the pace so that his march became a jog. He held his two swords low, and the war din swamped his senses. Fullr War-Raven came at him across the sands, and Hundr's jog turned into an all-out run. Twenty men packed close behind their Jarl, warriors with broad shoulders and thick arms forged to iron hardness by a lifetime at the oar battling against Njorth's sea fury. The Dane axe swept through the air, and Hundr kept on running. He ducked beneath the sweep of the moon-silvered axe blade and rammed Fenristooth's tip into the paunch of a fat-bellied man who came at him from behind the enemy Jarl. Hundr turned and ripped the blade free, and hot blood spilt from the wound to splash over his arm and whet his blade. He dropped to one knee and raised Battle Fang just as the Dane axe hurtled toward him in an overhand sweep. Hundr could not parry the heavy weapon with his sword blade because the weight of the enormous axe would drive his own blade down, and though it might take some of the strength out of the blow, there would still be enough venom in it to carve open his skull like an overripe apple. Instead, Hundr sliced Battle Fang's long blade across the inside of Fullr War-Raven's forearm, causing him to twist away, grunting in pain. Simultaneously, the Danish leader cracked his elbow against the cheekbone below Hundr's dead eye. He had not seen the blow coming from his blind side, and it sent a wave of searing heat through his skull. Hundr cursed and shook the black and white dots from his head.

Hundr rose and stamped on the face of the big-bellied Dane, who rolled screaming in the sand, clutching at his ripped stomach. The battle raged around him, and blood congealed in the sand as men screamed and died in a clash of weapons under a moonlit sky.

Odin, see me. Watch what I do in your name, take the brave to Valhalla and bring me luck. Guide my swords and protect my family.

Hundr lost sight of Fullr amidst the chaotic mass of battling warriors and attacked a short man with a tangle of beard and a roaring maw within it. The man sprinted toward Hundr, brandishing a spear with both hands. He thought that his momentum would carry the point of his spear right through Hundr's mail, bursting the riveted iron rings to carve into his chest and kill him. The man wanted to rip away Hundr's life, and if he died, Hundr would never see his wife or children again. He would never hear their laughter or smell the sweetness of their hair. So, he batted the spear point aside with one sword and slashed the blade of the other across the man's throat so that the edge scraped on gristle and spine.

A Seaworm warrior fell to the beach beside Hundr with an axe buried in his chest, and his killer whirled away to strike his blade at another man's legs, only to meet the furious axe of Sigvarth Trollhands who chopped his weapon into the man's face with a wet thud. The battle had lasted only a few moments before another note blared from Bush's war horn. Men stopped fighting, and weapons fell to their sides as the two opposing forces stepped away from each other. The aftermath was grim. Twenty men lay dead or injured on the beach, and half of Fullr War-Raven's crew had thrown down their weapons to submit themselves before Hundr's mercy. Their Jarl stood in the gap between the two crews, his long-handled axe held at his side, dripping blood into the sand from his wounded forearm. Fullr War-Raven spat at his surrendered warriors in disgust and lifted his mighty blade, pointing it at Hundr.

"They are beaten," piped Bush, dashing to Hundr's side on his bow legs. "There's no need to fight him. We can take what they have and leave them here on the island."

"And men will say that the Man with the Dog's Name refused a challenge and that he is no longer the champion of the Northmen," Hundr replied.

Bush sighed and shook his bald head. "Does that still matter to you? What does it mean to be the Champion of the North?"

Hundr smiled at him. "Nothing," he said and then shrugged. "Everything."

Hundr went to meet War-Raven because the challenge could not be refused. Hundr's men fought for him because of what and who he was. If he shirked this challenge, then another might come from his own crews, so Hundr went to fight. Fullr came at him with the axe, scything it at waist height as though he meant to cut Hundr in half. Hundr leapt backwards, but as he landed, he kicked sand at Fullr, and a wash of it hit the Jarl in the face. He gasped, rubbing at stinging eyes with his left hand. Hundr stepped in and stabbed Fenristooth hard into Fullr War-Raven's chest so that the sword's tip burst through the Jarl's heart. Fullr dropped to the sand, clutching his axe to him as his life seeped away. He held the blade tight because a man could only enter Valhalla if he met his end with a blade in his hand. Hundr did not begrudge Fullr that honour; he was a brave man who had risked everything and lost. Such was the life of a Viking, and Hundr hoped Fullr would take his rightful place in Odin's hall and wait for him there, where they would drink and fight together until Ragnarök at the end of days.

"A barrel of silver, copper and bronze," said Sigvarth after they had herded the surrendered enemy to the end of the beach. "They also have eight slave women and a hull full of wool and pelts on board their ship. Not bad." He rocked his head from side to side with an upside-down smile.

"Bastards would have been rich," remarked Bush with a lopsided grin. He took his naalbinding cap from where he had tucked it into his belt and placed it over his bald pate. "What shall we do with them?" He jerked a thumb at the defeated Vikings, who sat with heads hung low against the dunes.

Hundr gingerly touched the bruising under his dead eye and winced at the pain. "We'll take their ship back to Vanylven with the barrel, pelts and wool. Take six of their biggest men to row the bastard and ten of our own men to crew her. We'll bring the women too and set them free when we get home. The rest of them can stay here on the island."

"Better to have died gloriously in battle than to die here on this Thor-forsaken spit of shale," said Bush.

He stared at the dead, who still lay on the beach in congealed pools of their own blood.

"They won't look so glorious in the morning," Sigvarth tutted, itching his beard. "Not when the crabs are eating them and the gulls peck out their eyeballs."

"What do the dead care? They are in Valhalla. If the survivors aren't found, they'll starve to death and wander Niflheim as wraiths for eternity."

"Who cares about those turds? What did they care for the people they raided and killed? What's all this talk of Valhalla and Niflheim, anyway? We won, and they lost; we live, and they die. That is the way of things." Sigvarth clapped Bush on the shoulder and strode towards a gang of the crew passing around a skin of ale.

"When you get to my age, you think about these things. That's all," said Bush, more to himself than Hundr. Bush's beard was grey and white like an autumn sky, and his lined face was as lined and wizened as old oak.

"As soon as the sun rises, get loaded up, and we make for Vanylven," said Hundr. Which meant home and family. The summer had waned, and there would be no more fighting that year. Hundr stared out at the dark silhouetted sea, foreboding in its vastness, and he allowed his thoughts to slip to Sigrid and his children, envisioning a long winter spent warm and happy in their embrace.

TWO

Einar jerked into wakefulness as a sharp elbow dug into his ribs. He widened his tired eyes and immediately straightened up in his high-backed Jarl's chair. He sat on the top platform in his long hall and turned to see his wife, Hildr, frowning at him.

"Resting my eyes," he whispered and winked at her. "Please, continue." Einar waved a hand at the lugubrious, heavily jowled man before him. He looked nervously at Einar and then at the monstrous, looming figure of Einar's man Amundr beside him. Amundr grunted, and the man shifted his feet and licked his lips.

"As I was saying, Lord Einar," the man spoke up, and his eyes flickered again to Amundr's brynjar and the long spear clutched in his meaty fist. The big man made most people nervous, which was why Einar kept him at his side whenever he heard the complaints and appeals from the people under his care. "Hrafn cut down a swathe of elm and pine from the western hills two moons ago and did not replace the wood with saplings. And, more importantly, he cut more than was his allocation."

"We all share access to the forests, Jari," said Hildr in her soft, understanding voice, her tone a stark contrast from the keening war cry she had unleashed back when Einar first met her as a Valkyrie warrior priestess.

"Yes, Lady Hildr. But we are only permitted to cut the trees allocated to us by Jarl Einar. Hrafn took more than he should have for the roof of his new barn, which means that if I cut my allocation of timber for the roof of my son's new home, then all of Vanylven will be short of wood next year."

"I took only what I was permitted to cut," Hrafn exclaimed. He was a thin man with lank hair hanging to his shoulders. "I don't even know what we are doing here, Lord Einar."

Einar sighed and rubbed the corners of his eyes. "Well, if you cut too much elm, pine or oak, and then Jari here cuts too much, then there will not be enough wood left when we need to repair ships over the winter. And what if I want to build a new ship next summer?"

"You have lots of ships, Jarl Einar," interjected Jari, and then swallowed hard as Amundr snarled at him. "With all due respect, of course."

"We share the woodland between us, Hrafn, as you well know. You cut too much this year and didn't replant saplings. If we all did that, there would be no wood left for our sons and grandsons in a generation's time. So, Hrafn, you will give half of the wood you cut to Jari for his son's roof."

21

"This is an outrage!" Hrafn blurted. He stepped forward to get to the smirking Jari, but in doing so, he came towards the raised dais where Einar sat with Hildr. Einar surged out of his seat, and even at his age, he was still a full head taller than most men and thicker across the chest and shoulder. His hand instinctively reached for the axe hanging from his belt, and the hall, filled to the rafters with folk who had gathered to hear the Jarl's lawgiving, fell silent. All that could be heard was the crackling of the hearth fire and the creak of Amundr's leather boots as he came to Einar's side.

Hrafn flinched and fell back amongst his kin, and he bowed his head to show that he accepted Einar's decision. For Einar had not always been a grey-bearded Jarl with a heavy paunch. He was once Einar the Brawler, feared captain of Ivar the Boneless and Ragnar Lothbrok, and a warrior of reputation known wherever men sailed the Whale Road.

"That's enough for today," said Hildr, rising from her own seat and smiling at the crowd. They returned her smile and dutifully filed out of the hall. Hildr hooked her arm around Einar's and leant into him. He stretched his neck and rolled his shoulders, but he kept his right hand firmly resting on his axe.

"Bloody farmers," Einar grumbled under his breath. Amundr harrumphed behind him to echo Einar's exasperation with men who lived their lives on land, tilling, milking, growing and sowing.

"They are your people, my love," said Hildr. "Without them, we would have nothing to eat, drink or sell. You did well today; they respect your judgement."

"Aye, well. Maybe we should take a ship out into the fjord today. What do you think?" Einar leaned his head over his shoulder towards the hulking warrior.

"Think about what, my lord?" said Amundr in his slow, rumbling voice.

"I said we should take a boat out today."

"Where would we go, Lord Einar?"

"On the fjord."

"Why?"

"Never mind. Make sure there's no trouble between Hrafn and Jari outside."

Amundr clapped a fist to his mailed chest and strode towards the hall doors.

"Amundr is loyal and a great champion," said Hildr, patting Einar's forearm.

"He is those things, but his thought cage is the size of a mouse's arse."

Hildr chuckled, and Einar playfully tickled her midriff. The sound of her laughter filling the air made Einar smile, and it tugged at the scar tissue around his eyes and cheeks. Over at the hall doors, Amundr barked in anger as a tiny figure came barrelling through the half-open doorway. It was a small child, a boy with blonde hair that bounced on his round head as he scampered across the floor rushes on his tiny, wide-set legs. As Amundr turned to go after the toddler, another boy came dashing behind him, giggling and grabbing hold of Amundr's oak trunk leg. The big man reached down, plucked the second child from the ground and lifted him up high. Amundr, champion of Einar's warriors and victor of countless Holmgang duels, giggled like a girl at a summer festival. He peered into the child's ice blue eyes, and his laughter was as deep and rumbling as the lowing of a cow.

"Sigurd, no!" Hildr shouted, and she sprinted from Einar to stop the first child as he ran towards the hall fire.

Einar shook his head and chuckled as the first child ran around Hildr, and she did her best to catch the little bundle of madness. He wore an undyed wool jerkin, and his bare feet slapped on the floor rushes as he ran, laughing so hard that he almost fell. The two boys were Hundr's twin sons, and Einar loved them like they were his own. They were two summers old, and though Einar was Jarl at Vanylven, the place was also Hundr's home. However, during the summer months, Einar's friend was seldom found there. Hundr was a sea Jarl, a Viking raider who spent the summers at sea raiding and fighting with his ships and crews. It was a life Einar had once known well and missed dearly.

Sigrid ran into the hall, her hair a tangled mess and her cheeks flushed red with embarrassment.

"I am sorry, Einar," she said, flustered. She scooped Sigurd up from between Hildr's legs, placed him expertly on her hip, and then took the other child, Hermoth, from Amundr's arms.

"There is nothing to be sorry for," smiled Einar. "Here, give the lads something to eat. Sit with us a while, Sigrid; take a rest." Einar waved to his steward to fetch food and drink for Sigrid and the twins. Sigrid smiled and set the boys down on a feasting bench. She brushed the strands of her golden hair away from her face and blew out her cheeks.

"I can take the boys for a walk, lord," Amundr suggested. "If the lady likes?"

"Thank you. That would be nice. But keep them away from the warriors' practice field," Sigrid said, and Amundr's eyes lit up as though she had rewarded him with a chest of jewels.

"Come on, little bears," Amundr chimed, bending his hulking frame forward and beckoning to the twins. "Let's go down to the water's edge and throw skimmer stones."

The boys whooped for joy and eagerly followed Amundr out of the hall. Einar watched them go and then glanced at Hildr and Sigrid. Sigrid was Hundr's wife, and the two women settled into a conversation about how the boys had grown increasingly rambunctious during their father's absence at sea. Sigrid talked of how Hermoth's teeth were coming through and causing him pain, and Hildr said she might know a remedy involving honey and a plant, the name of which she couldn't quite remember.

"I'll leave you ladies to it," Einar nodded, tucking his thumbs into his belt. They barely noticed he had spoken, and Einar grabbed a wooden mug of ale from his steward as he walked past with a tray of bread, cheese, and ale for Sigrid and Hildr. Einar took a long swig of the frothy ale and placed the empty cup on a bench as he strode out of his hall and into Vanylven's main square. At first, his eyes stung from the sudden transition from the dimly lit hall, illuminated only by the hearth fire, a few rush lights, small shuttered windows on the east and western walls, and whatever light could sneak in through the smoke hole in the roof thatch. Einar winced until his vision cleared to reveal Vanylven's bustling square.

A merchant goaded a donkey-pulled cart and whistled a tune as the goods in his wagon rumbled and rattled across the sunbaked earth. A gap-toothed woman hirpled across his path with her distaff and an armful of rough wool. People stopped to talk, their wool and linen clothing a mix of earthy tones with the occasional splash of red or yellow on a dyed hood or tunic. A man hollered above the chatter from his stall at the square's eastern side, where he sold jewellery made of amber, shells, and carved wood. The light breeze blowing in from Vanylven's fjord whipped smoke from the surrounding buildings, and the smell of fires, cooking vegetables and roasting meat filled Einar's nose. His stomach rumbled, and Einar patted his ever-growing paunch, wondering if he should stop and eat before he wandered down to the water to join Amundr and play with the twins.

Einar turned away from the square into a narrow lane leading down to the quayside, and a line of scraggly chickens ran across his path. They squawked as Einar dodged around their pitter-patter claws. He scrunched his nose at the smell of sheep shit, close and cloying in the tightly-packed press of wattle and daub buildings. A steeply pitched thatched roof dripped old rainwater into a puddle, and Einar was relieved to emerge from the heady smells of Vanylven life onto the quays where three of his ships bobbed, each tied to long jetties that stretched out into the fjord's glassy, eerily still waters. Einar sucked in a deep breath and gazed at the majestic mountains surrounding the water. They rose into the clouds, shrouded by mist, seeming to touch the mighty heights of Asgard itself.

Vanylven folk waved to Einar from the waterside. An old warrior with a scarred face bowed his head, and the people moved out of his way as he wandered through their midst. Einar reached up absentmindedly, touching the scars upon his face, and rolled a stiff shoulder. His hip pained him, and when it was cold, all the old wounds Einar had taken during his life on the frontline of battle ached and throbbed. In the darkness, old faces came to haunt him, the screaming faces of the men he had killed. Souls beyond count. Some had deserved it, some had been enemies, and some he regretted. Einar sighed at that grim thought, but then his mood instantly lifted when he saw Amundr toss a flat stone across the fjord water, and Sigurd clapped his little hands and whooped with joy.

Einar stepped down from the wooden quayside onto the sand which bordered the fjord, where the huge warrior played happily with Hundr's twin sons. Sigurd picked up a rock in two hands, and the thing was the size of his own head. The little boy tottered forward and tossed it into the water's edge, where it fell with a wet plop. Sigurd stamped his foot and crossed his arms because it didn't skim, and Amundr laughed so hard that he rocked backwards.

"You need a little flat one," said Amundr once he had caught his breath. He bent and picked up a small stone the size of his thumb. "Like this." He handed it to Sigurd and helped him position his hand so that he could throw the stone low and level. The boy threw the stone, and it skimmed three times across the water's surface. Sigurd leapt into the air and reached up to Amundr. The burly warrior lifted him, and both embraced each other as if stone skimming was the best thing in all of Midgard. Little Hermoth picked up a stone of his own and attempted to skim it, failing on the first try but persevering until his stone bounced four times across the surface. Amundr ruffled his hair, and Hermoth placed his fists upon his hips like a great conqueror.

Einar smiled at the joyous scene and marvelled at how Amundr, a man he'd witnessed cleave an enemy in two with his war axe and ruthlessly tear out the dying man's heart, could be so gentle and loving to

Hundr's two rascals. Einar's smile faded, however, as he recalled a similar scene from his own past. Long ago, he had once shown another boy how to skim stones on a different beach. That boy had been Finn, the son of Ivar the Boneless, whom Einar had raised as though he were his own son and who, in the end, had betrayed Einar. Only two years prior, Finn had subjected him to imprisonment and torture. Einar strode forward to break away from the melancholy of that unwelcome memory.

"Uncle Einar!" Hermoth chirped as he heard Einar's boots crunching on the sand and stones. "Did you see?"

"I saw," Einar nodded. "I once threw a stone so hard that it skimmed all the way across the fjord and killed a goat on the other side."

"Really?"

"Really. But that was when I was young and the captain of a warship. Then I could have thrown a stone as high as the moon himself."

Hermoth frowned, and Einar helped him to find a new stone to try. As they searched amongst the pebbles, a resounding horn rang out loudly from the fjord barrier, prompting Einar to stand up and investigate. Vanylven's harbour was protected by two long jetties that stretched from either side of the bay, ending in two high timber towers. A rope as thick around as a man's thigh spanned the two towers and barred entry to Vanylven's port. That rope would only be lowered if the tower guard identified a

Vanylven vessel, a friendly visiting ship, or a merchant visitor. So, any hostile ship had to halt before the rope or have her hull crushed to driftwood by its thick coils. Einar hoped it was a merchant ship he had been expecting. A Dane by the name of Halvdan was due to return to Vanylven and collect some surplus fleeces Einar had to sell in exchange for axe heads and iron for his smiths.

The horn blared again, and Einar climbed back onto the wooden jetty and left the twins with Amundr. He strode towards the far end, stepping around a staked and drying fishing net to peer out towards the fjord rope. He knew he could not walk to the long piers thatconnected the shores, forming the fjord bridge. To do that, he would need to ride out of Vanylven's walls and make his way to where they began on either side of the water. Einar stood on the edge of the quay and waited. From that position, he could see between the two towers to where the surrounding hills tapered down pine-covered hillsides into the fjord and sea beyond. He saw only one ship approaching, a fat-bellied *knarr* trading ship rather than the sleek keel of a *drakkar* warship. Einar's eyes weren't what they were, scoured dull by so many years of peering into sun-sharp horizons or squinting into harsh and frost-bitten sea winds, but he watched to see if the ship did indeed belong to Halvdan, the trader, for he would need to have the fleeces brought from a barn deep inside the town.

The merchant ship waddled as her oars bit into the fjord, and sunlight sparkled on the droplets of water cascading from the oar blades. An order shouted from the western tower carried across the water, and the great fjord rope was let loose with a splash and dragged away from the gap so that the ship could enter the harbour. Einar covered his eyes with his hand to shield his vision from the sun. A man stood at the prow, and Einar frowned because it did not look like the tubby frame of Halvdan but rather a hooded figure who seemed exceptionally tall at the prow of the merchant ship. One of Einar's guards leant over the side of the east tower and waved down towards the ship. The prow edged through the gap, and the mysterious man in the bow waved back. Then, in a swift motion, the man reached down, shifting his stance, and the sunlight glinted off iron as he raised a long spear. With serpent-like speed, he hurled it towards the tower. Einar's guard had no time to react before the spear slammed violently into his chest. He toppled backwards into the tower, and Einar's breath caught in his throat.

Suddenly, the merchant ship was alive with men. Voices shouted, and a dozen men leapt over each of the ship's sides to plunge into the fjord. They swam furiously towards the towers. The figure in the bow threw back his hood and raised an axe in one hand and a sword in the other. He was tall, and even from the quayside, Einar could feel his malevolence pulsing across the water. Einar's heart sank, and fear curdled in his gut as more ships raced through the narrow entrance to Vanylven's fjord. Long oars beat from the sleek ships' bows, yet those vessels were not deep-hulled trading *knarrs* but wickedly sleek *drakkar* warships, and Einar counted ten masts hurtling towards Vanylven's open fjord barrier. Heat bloomed in his belly, the fire of fear, for Einar recognised the man in the trader's bow. It was none other than Rollo the Betrayer, a brutal killer – come for vengeance and slaughter.

THREE

Einar drew his axe from the loop at his belt and stared at his approaching enemy. The warning horn blared out three long notes, the signal that Vanylven was under attack, but it was too late. Rollo was through the fjord bridge, and the gap was open. He had fooled the tower guards into believing that the ship was a trader, and now he came for blood. Einar and Hundr had burned Rollo's own settlement in Frankia two years ago. They had killed his warriors, burned his hall, and stolen his silver. Rollo had been away marrying the daughter of a great Frankish duke, and Einar had rued the day. He had wanted to kill Rollo the Betrayer, who had sent assassins to kill Einar and Hundr, and knew that the tall warrior would not let the insult of his burned settlement go unpunished. They were enemies of old, back to the days when Einar and Hundr had helped the King of Norway, Harald Fairhair, win his kingdom. Rollo had fought on the other side in that war, and, in the end, he betrayed his own people to sail away from a blood-soaked battle unscathed. Though he was a Viking, Rollo had risen to become a powerful Duke of the Franks, holding vast swathes of land in the country's northwest where he protected the entry to the river

Seine and barred any Viking fleets from sailing up that river to attack the old and wealthy city of Paris.

Boots pounded on the timber quayside behind him, and Einar turned to see Torsten running towards him. Torsten was a hard man, a warrior of fair fame who had served the last two years as the captain of Vanylven's warriors.

"We are under attack," Torsten called. He arrived in his brynjar, armed with an axe and shield. Einar looked down at himself, at his stomach bulging against his tunic. He hadn't worn his chainmail in over a year, and the axe in his hand was more ceremonial than an actual battle weapon. Its head was carved with runes, and its haft was etched with whorls and writhing dragons.

"Get the men on the shore," said Einar, turning back to glance at Rollo's ship. "Bring them all. There are ten ships in the fjord. That's seven hundred warriors. How many men do we have in Vanylven?"

"Without Hundr's crews, we have one hundred warriors, my lord."

Einar's shoulders dropped. There could be no defence of the town against such overwhelming numbers. "Take half the men and get the people to safety."

"What are you saying, Lord Einar? That we should desert Vanylven?"

Einar turned and snarled at Torsten. "Give me your shield. Take half the men and take the women and children into the hills. Do it now."

The muscles in Torsten's jaw tensed as he chewed over Einar's command. The conflict of Einar's order played out on his broad face: stay and fight next to his lord on the quayside, or follow orders and run with the women and children, saving their lives. Rollo was a pitiless killer, and any women he and his men found in Vanylven would receive no mercy. It would be a bloody ruin of rape and suffering. Torsten nodded. He handed his shield to Einar and then turned and ran back towards the town, shouting orders to his warriors as he went.

Einar glanced at Amundr, relieved to see that the big man had already scooped up Sigurd and Hermoth and was lumbering swiftly towards the town with the two toddlers bouncing in his arms. The swimmers from Rollo's ship had already reached the bridge towers and climbed up the turrets like spiders, knives and axes clenched in their teeth and water dripping from their soaked clothes. There was no way for Einar or his men to saddle horses and race around the fjord to the aid of the tower guards. Those men would have to fight for their lives. If they could win and throw Rollo's warriors back, there was a chance to pull the fjord rope taut and bar entry to the harbour. Yet Einar knew it was a vain hope, and as weapons flashed and men died upon the towers, the futility of it became painfully clear. Each tower had only two men on guard, and they now faced a dozen of Rollo's warriors – odds that meant certain doom.

The jetty beneath Einar's feet trembled as warriors of his own streamed from Vanylven to stand at Einar's side.

"Here, my lord," said Trygve, one of Einar's warriors, as he presented Einar's shimmering brynjar. Einar rested his shield next to his leg, and Trygve helped him pull the heavy coat of mail over his head. Einar grimaced at how snug the armour was around his torso. The thing was heavier than he remembered, but it was reassuring to have the rivetted links protecting his body.

"Are you ready to stand and fight?" Einar called out to his men, and they roared in response. "These bastards have come from Frankia to kill our children, rape our women, and steal our silver. Are you ready to fight for your people?" They roared once more and shook their weapons with fervour.

Across the fjord, Rollo's men had killed the tower guards and were now swimming back to his ship with long, powerful strokes. Behind Einar, cries and screams erupted from Vanylven as folk heard Torsten's orders to take to the hills. The women knew what was coming for them, and panic swamped Vanylven like a wave. Einar set his jaw and hefted his shield and axe. The warriors onboard the *knarr* helped the men in the water aboard, and her oars bit onto the glassy water's surface as Rollo led his men to shore. The first of the *drakkars* swept into the gap between the towers, and the men on board those ships bellowed and roared. Rhythmic war drums pounded in the background, stoking the battle fury of Rollo's warriors, and Rollo himself stood tall and mighty in the trading ship's prow, waving his axe and sword at the defenders.

Each long oar pull brought them closer, and the wait was agonising. The warriors on the quayside shouted and clashed their weapons, but each oar stroke diminished their bravery. The delay was a mind killer, allowing Einar's men to drink in the number of warriors coming to slake their fury with the blood of Vanylven's warriors. There were too many, and the fear of death swirled with the necessity to defend their loved ones as Einar's men pressed onto the shores of Vanylven's fjord.

The ships surged closer, their prows rising from the water, snarling beast heads with painted teeth and glaring eyes seeming to grow so that it appeared that Loki's monster brood descended upon Vanylven just as they would upon Asgard during Ragnarök at the end of days.

"Archers," Einar called, and he raised his axe. A score of bows stretched from the rear ranks, and Einar held his axe for three more oar pulls until he could see the smile on Rollo's handsome face across the water. "Loose!" Einar lowered his axe, and twenty arrows sang over his head. They rose like swallows across the fjord, seeming to pause in midair before slamming with deadly force into the approaching ships. Iron arrowheads thumped into the vessels' timbers to join the booming thrum of war drums, and more arrows flew over Einar's head. Screams of pain came from Rollo's ships as unseen warriors suffered from arrowheads embedded deep in their flesh, tearing at their organs.

"Hold the line here," Einar said, hefting his shield. "The time to kill them is as they come from the ships. Don't let them get a foothold on our shore."

Rollo's ungainly *knarr* headed straight towards the quays flanked by two faster *drakkars*, but Rollo was no fool, and the rest of his fleet split from the front three and rowed towards the broader shoreline along Vanylven's outer palisade. Einar cursed to himself. With the limited force he had stationed inside the town, he couldn't defend the entire coastline, and thus, the men on those ships could easily wade ashore and unleash their blades and murderous hunger on his town unopposed. Then, they would loop around and attack Einar's flanks. His men saw it, too, but said nothing. Einar's best hope was to buy Torsten enough time to get the women and children to safety.

"Make your peace with the gods, boys," said Einar, and he banged his axe on the boss of his shield. "Pray to Odin, ask the ghost lord, the ripper, the battle-screamer, to grant you favour." Einar threw his head back and shouted at the sky. "I ask you, Odin, lord of warriors and betrayer of the slain, grant us favour this day. Let us kill these men who come to slaughter us, and for those of us who die, let us die with honour."

The Vanylven men ferociously bellowed and gnashed their teeth with a menace and madness born of impending death, their fury fueled by the desperate need to protect their loved ones at any cost. Einar wished Hundr were with him, for he was his old, trusted friend and the greatest warrior he had ever known. He wished he had said kinder words to Hildr, and he wished they could have had children together. Einar wished he had killed Rollo when he had the chance, and Einar wished he was ten years younger so he could fight with his old strength and rage.

"A Jarl is just a man," Einar shouted to his men as Rollo's hull crunched into the shore. "Maybe I made a mistake, and I should have had more men on the fjord bridge. Maybe I have failed you, my loyal warriors. But stand with me now and slay our enemies. Let us wade in their blood and kill them with our axes so that they know they come to fight with champions, with Vikings of the Whale Road, and let each of our lives cost them ten of their puny souls. Let them come and die on the blades of heroes!"

The first of Rollo's men jumped into the water, and he wore leather armour and carried a shield emblazoned with a Frankish symbol. The Frank roared his defiance as he waded through the waist-deep fjord water and swiftly died as a Viking axe hurled from the shore thudded into his chest and sent him sinking into the depths. More Franks leapt into the water, and the crew of Rollo's merchant ship heaved on the oars one last time, driving their expendable merchant tub up into the fjord bed, and her hull crunched into the quayside jetty. Timber shivered and smashed under the ship's weight, and a Viking screamed as it crushed his legs to ruin beneath the merchant ship's bows.

Einar raised his shield just in time to catch a spear tossed from the ship. The leaf-shaped point slammed into the linden wood boards, sending a thrumming jar up Einar's arm. He gasped at its force and took a pace backwards. A man with a snarling, bearded face leapt from the bow and crashed into Einar's shield. He kicked Einar backwards and struck out with a short sword, slicing open the chest of the warrior beside Einar. The hot spray of blood splattered across Einar's face, jolting him back to the harsh reality of battle. It had been two years since he had last fought, two years of too much food and ale, of kisses and love with Hildr, of children and warm fires. The ferrous scent of the blood on his face and the knowledge that one of his men had fallen snapped him fully awake. Rollo the Betrayer was at Vanylven and had come to kill. The snarling man hammered his sword into Einar's shield, and the steel rang on the iron boss like the sound of Hel.

Einar bared his teeth, and strength poured into his arms. He was Einar the Brawler, and his people needed him. Einar fiercely shoved his shoulder into the shield, driving the snarling man back. He crouched and crushed the man's toes with the ironshod shield rim, then rose to bury his axe in the man's face. Einar yanked the blade free and tore the man's face from his skull.

"For Vanylven!" he roared. "Fight for Einar the Brawler!"

Another of Rollo's men landed on the jetty, and Einar disembowelled him with a sweep of his axe, leaving the air thick with the smell of blood, offal and dying men's shit. More of the enemy came, yet Einar drove them back with venom and brutal strength. The warriors who had leapt into the fjord had reached the jetty and hacked at the legs of Einar's men so that he had to lead them five paces backwards. They held the enemy there until Rollo the Betrayer himself made the jump from the merchant ship. He landed with a thud on the jetty and rose to his full height, casting off his hooded cloak to reveal his monstrously enormous height and frame, clad in a shining brynjar. Rollo raised his axe and bellowed a war cry in Frankish, which his men took up in a frenzy. Rollo charged at Einar's lines, and they could not hold his power. Einar reeled with shock as Rollo's axe swept a Vanylven man's head from his shoulders.

Men followed Rollo over the side, but these men were not soft-bearded Franks; they were hard-faced war Danes and Norsemen with braided beards, arm rings, lovers of Odin and war. Einar killed the first of them with his axe. The battle for Vanylven had begun, and Einar fiercely fought for Hildr, his people, and his life.

FOUR

"There she is, lord," said Bush, pointing towards a mass of distant haze across the water. "Home."

Hundr clapped him on the back, and the mood aboard the Seaworm changed. The crew had spent a long morning hauling on their oars on a calm, early autumnal sea without enough wind to fill the *drakkar's* sails. The men's purses and sea chests were full of plunder, and their eagerness to return home was palpable. The sight of Vanylven's hills in the distance cast off the grim, backbreaking work at the oars and replaced it with vigorous pulls accompanied by a cheerful song of thanks to Odin and Njorth.

"It was a fine summer," said Hundr, leaning on the tiller. He stood on the steerboard platform, and Bush leant over the side, hanging onto the brace rope with a grin on his lined face. "The men should be happy."

"They're happy – a ship full of silver and tales to tell of battles well fought."

They had sold Fullr War-Raven's captured ship to a young Jarl on the island of Fedje on Norway's west coast. Hundr had put in on the island's north shore for an overnight camp, and the local Jarl had welcomed them with ale and bread. Hundr had told the tale of the fight off the Orkney isles, and the Jarl had been eager to buy the ship, having had to cede two of his recently deceased father's vessels to his brother when taking up their inheritance. He had paid in silver and gold arm rings and a chest of hacksilver, which Hundr had gladly accepted. So, the Seaworm approached Vanylven with a full crew and her bows low in the water, full of plunder and wealth.

"Next year, we should sail east again," said Hundr. "Maybe visit King Bjorn Ironside in Svearland and see if we can't pick off a few ships returning from Miklagard." The trade routes to the great city south of Novgorod were becoming ever more popular with traders. The dangerous rivers, which Hundr had braved before, led to the centre of Midgard and the distant east. Traders who braved the rapids and vicious Pecheneg raiders along the river could return with valuable silk, rich wines, and jewellery to dazzle even the wealthiest of kings.

Bush coughed once and clapped his fist to his chest. He coughed again, and it sounded like claws were raking the shipmaster's insides. Bush let go of the brace and bent over, leaning on the sheer strake to support himself as he descended into a coughing fit, which turned his face puce. Hundr frowned; his old friend had coughed throughout the entire summer, and the bouts of it had become increasingly worse as the months went by. "If I bloody see next summer,"

Bush said, and he spat a gobbet of thick phlegm over the side.

"You should see a healer when we get to port. You sound like you'll cough up your lungs if you carry on like that."

"We'll see. It's nothing a good fire won't fix. Nights spent wet-arsed on foreign beaches don't help either."

Hundr laughed and gave the tiller over to Bush. The smaller man had been the captain of his own ship within Hundr's fleet, a position he had rightfully earned ten times over with his sailing skill and bravery. But Bush had said that he preferred to be the shipmaster of the Seaworm for this year's raiding. It was the position he'd held when Hundr had first joined the Seaworm as a young bail boy many years ago. Einar had been the captain back then, and those days were both distant yet ever-present in Hundr's memories. They had been hard days but great ones full of battle and adventure, and Einar and Bush had made Hundr into the sea Jarl and the man he was today.

"Sail!" came a cry amidships. Hundr wove his way around the sealskin and hemp rigging to where one of the men pointed to a sail cutting through the sea on the light wind.

"I'd know that ship anywhere," called Bush from the tiller. "It's the Wind Elk."

"Ragnhild," Hundr whispered to himself. Ragnhild was another of Hundr's old friends, a Valkyrie warrior priestess who commanded two of Hundr's ships and fought with the heart of a bear. Her second ship must be close by, leaving only two of Hundr's fleet of five ships still at sea unless they were already waiting for him in Vanylven.

"Should we wait?" asked Bush.

"No," said Hundr. "We'll meet Ragnhild in Vanylven." He had waited too long to see his sons and Sigrid and did not wish to wait a heartbeat longer than was necessary before reuniting with his family.

Hundr rhythmically drummed his hand on the sheer strake in time with the oar beats, and the sloping hills around Vanylven came closer. He could make out the evergreen pines and the shadowy rocks dotting the cliffs as mountains rose to the north to circle the fjord in towering slopes. Hundr frowned. At first, he had thought clouds hung low above the hills, but as they grew closer, dark smoke was rising above the terrain surrounding the fjord. It was too much smoke for hearths or cookfires; something was amiss. Hundr moved to the bows and urged the men to row faster. They grumbled at the extra effort, being so close to home. But something wasn't right. Smoke was the signal of destruction and raiding, and Hundr had made many such fires in his time. Yet this was home, where his family and friends lived.

The Seaworm approached the straits where opposing cliffs came together to form the narrow entrance to the Vanylven's fjord. A sense of apprehension rattled in Hundr's chest, the gnawing, stomach-curdling feeling that something was awry. As his men powered the ship towards the open water, their backs to the fjord, Hundr glanced at Bush in the stern, and the old shipmaster returned his gaze with a flat, slack-jawed look. Bush saw it and sensed it, too, yet he remained silent, knowing that voicing his fears would throw the crew off their strokes. Hundr hoped it was nothing more than a barn that had caught fire or a farmer in the hills burning off his fields.

The Seaworm sliced through the waters, the waves splashing against her sweeping prow. As she emerged from the straits, Hundr held his breath as a vision of terror confronted him. His hand instinctively dropped to his waist, but he was not wearing his swords or armour. He wore only a jerkin and trews at sea, and Hundr grasped at the air where Fenristooth's hilt should be. His chest rose and fell with the power of the tide, and a fear like nothing he had ever experienced washed over him. There were enemy warships in Vanylven's harbour. The fjord barrier was breached, and buildings in the west were ablaze. War and pain had come to Vanylven, and Hundr howled at the horror of it like a wounded wolf.

The crew turned on their oar benches at the sound of Hundr's anguished cry and let out desperate shouts of their own as they saw what unfolded in the place that was supposed to be a safe haven for their wives and children.

"Row, row!" shouted Hundr, and he dashed to the oar bench left empty by a long-faced sailor who had raced to the prow to peer, unbelieving, at the devastation in Vanylven. Hundr heaved on the oar, and its blade bit into the water like a knife. He hauled on the shaft and twisted the blade as it came free of the fjord. The men pulled with him, and Hundr's shoulders burned with exertion as he hauled on the oar with all his might to race him closer to Sigrid, Sigurd, and Hermoth.

"Get the weapons!" Bush shouted from the stern, and men ran to the barrels around the mast post where their swords, axes and spears were wrapped in oily fleeces to protect them from the worst of the salty sea air. Sigvarth dropped Hundr's heavy leather belt beside him, and Hundr looked up at the mammoth-chested warrior.

"Whoever it is, lord," said Sigvarth through gritted teeth. "They will suffer if our loved ones have been harmed."

"Leave your brynjars," Hundr roared at the crew as men rose from the benches to pull on chainmail or strap on weapons. The ship canted in the water as more oars were abandoned. "Back to you oars, row for the lives of your families!"

The men followed orders, and Hundr glanced over his shoulder as they came through the open fjord barrier. The towers on either side were empty of guards, yet a dead man hung over the top of the eastern tower, and his blood stained the grey, weather-worn timbers. Hundr hauled again. In ten more strokes, they would be at the shore. Bush guided the tiller at the centre of the enemy ships, and Hundr ground his teeth, wishing that he could summon Thor's strength to get the Seaworm to shore faster.

Ragnhild's Wind Elk sailed into the fjord, and her ship also came under oars now that they entered the sheltered fjord waters. Ragnhild had seen the danger and hurriedly came to Vanylven's aid with her ferocity and her warriors. Between the Seaworm, the Wind Elk, and Ragnhild's second ship, the Wave Eater, a long two hundred warriors came to fight Vanylven's enemies. Hundr pulled again, and his thought cage twisted and turned over who could have brought an army to assault Vanylven. Hundr and Einar had made many enemies over their years of fighting and raiding. They had helped make Harald Fairhair King, and many men had lost lands and bore bloody grudges against the great king of Norway. Then, there were the untold numbers of jarls, lords, warlords, and dukes that Hundr and Einar had fought across the lands of the Saxons, Franks, Irish, and Rus. But one enemy forced his way through Hundr's thoughts, a man he had raided who hated Hundr above all others. Rollo the Betrayer. It had to be him.

"Two more strokes!" Bush called. Hundr pulled again, and the muscles in his back stretched and stung with the effort. He dipped his oar blade once more and felt resistance beneath the sleek hull. Suddenly, a monstrous impact threw Hundr backwards as the Seaworm collided with an enemy ship on Vanylven's quayside. He rolled in the bilge and came up, grasping his sword belt.

"Death to our enemies!" Hundr shouted as he ripped Fenristooth and Battle Fang free of their scabbards. The Seaworm crew took up his cry, their eyes wide with terrified fury, so close now to discovering what awful fate had befallen their loved ones. Hundr took four long strides along the hull and placed his boot on the sheer strake. He had left his brynjar on the Seaworm and leapt across the bows, wearing only his sailing jerkin and holding his shining blades. Hundr landed on decking slick with seawater. He slid to one side and came up with his swords ready. Two enemy warriors prowled across the deck towards him, big men in hard-baked leather breastplates who wore their hair close-cropped to their heads in the Frankish style. More of Hundr's men came over the bows to swarm the enemy ship, and he ran at the two Franks. They raised their spears, sharpened points ready to slice and carve open Hundr's flesh. But Hundr was fast, wicked fast, and he danced between their spears and sliced his swords across the Franks' bellies underneath their breastplates.

Hundr did not wait to see those two men fall, clutching at their opened stomachs. He kept moving, running along the enemy ship where white feathered arrows had embedded themselves in the planking in the earlier fight, and the bilge stank like piss water. He jumped over the low prow and landed heavily on Vanylven's quayside. The last time he had stood on those dark timbers, they had been thronged with townsfolk waving his warriors off with beaming smiles and fond kisses. They had sacrificed a goat to the gods for luck, smearing its blood on the hulls of their ships, and the people had prayed to the gods for strong winds, calm seas and battle luck. Now, Hundr stalked between corpses of men he knew, Einar's men. Lifeless eyes stared glassily up at him, the eyes of men Hundr had drunk ale and feasted with, warriors he had fought beside shoulder to shoulder. But the corpses of their enemies were also thick on the jetty and bore witness to hard fighting, and yet more Franks floated face down in the fjord's shallows.

The smell of burning wood filled the air, and as the Seaworm crew formed up behind Hundr on the jetty, he heard the first screams. They came from deep within the town, and Hundr followed the trail of corpses towards that most terrible of sounds. People he loved, and those dear to his crew, were in grave peril, and that horror clamped Hundr's heart like an icy fist. A dying Frank reached out to Hundr from where he lay in the road, and Hundr stabbed his blade down into the man's throat. There was no time for pity; he had to find his family. The streets were deserted, as though the gods themselves had plucked the people of Vanylven from their daily tasks and whisked them away to their distant halls across the Bifrost bridge.

"Odin, save us," Bush hissed as they stepped around the body of a woman stripped to the waist and left bent over a barrel with her throat cut. Another scream raked across the thatched roofs and winding streets, and Hundr's eye flitted between the snarl of Vanylven's streets and lanes, unsure of which way to find the fight.

"That way," said Sigvarth Trollhands, pointing his axe northwards. Hundr set off at a run again, and he twisted past a blacksmith's forge and a long stable to emerge into a small square where fishermen sold their catch each morning. Enemy warriors thronged the square, armed with spears, each one of them a short-haired Frank. They faced away from Hundr, pushing at one another's backs, clamouring to get at whatever lay beyond the fish sellers' square. Weapons clashed, and men shouted from beyond the press of Franks, and Hundr knew that was where Einar and his warriors fought against Rollo's men. If Einar still lived. It could only be Rollo, the ignoble betrayer who had risen from nothing to become a powerful Duke of the Franks. Memories flashed before Hundr's eye of the previous times he could and should have killed the murderous bastard. Rollo was Hundr's enemy, a man to whom he had once shown pity and had taken into his crew when Rollo had nothing.

Hundr charged into the Franks' rear, and his crew followed. With a mighty thrust, he punched Battle Fang's tip through a man's back, ripping his spine apart, before swiftly whipping Fenristooth's blade across another's hamstrings, leaving the wounded enemies to howl in pain. Sigvarth barrelled into them at full charge, using sheer force to drive a wedge into their midst so that the Seaworm crew could fill the gap with their own flashing blades. There were twenty Franks in that square, and Hundr had cut down four before they could turn and try to fend off the attack. Franks with shields pushed their way through the throng, reacting to Hundr's threat. They carried smaller shields than those used by Norsemen, and each was painted with a yellow sun. An orange banner fluttered above them, mounted on a gilded lance, and the shieldmen held firm against Hundr's warriors.As more Franks surged into the square, they pushed Hundr and his warriors back, pressing them so closely together that Hundr couldn't bring his swords to bear. The weapons were pinned to his sides, and a man with two brown front teeth and stale, garlic-stinking breath shoved his shield into Hundr's chest. He cursed in Frankish, and another behind him lunged a spear point towards Hundr's neck. The press of men held the weapon for a moment, and Hundr bucked, struggling to get free, but his own men shoved forward. The Franks pushed back, and the spear jerked toward Hundr, slicing a nick across his throat. Hundr shook with impotent fury, unable to reach his children or Einar and trapped by his enemies. One more push and the weapon would pierce his throat, and Hundr would die, not knowing if his family had lived or perished.

Hundr gripped his sword blades tight and prepared himself for the pain. He ground his teeth against the cold iron that would tear into his throat and end his life, readying himself for the journey to Valhalla. Then, suddenly, the press of shields and the garlic stench fell away. Hundr heard a high-pitched keening, and he turned and then laughed with mad joy as Ragnhild skillfully darted across a thatched rooftop, shooting arrows into the enemy from her powerful recurved bow. With that, her men joined the fight. Ragnhild had masterfully led them around the square so that six of her archers loosed into the enemy press from the rooftops while the rest of her crews plunged down from side streets. Now that Ragnhild had joined the fray, the battle in the square would rage and boil into a slaughter. A gap opened up, and Hundr immediately twisted away. He ducked and shouldered his way through his own warriors to the rear of the square and down an alleyway. He had to find Sigrid and his children.

Hundr ran through the streets filled with the corpses of the fallen, and his boots splashed in pools of congealed blood. He ran towards the home he shared with Sigrid close to Einar's great hall, hoping to Frigg that she was not there, that there had been time for the women to get out of the town before the Franks had attacked. Hundr burst around a corner, leapt over an upturned milking stool, and dodged past a dead dog whose tongue lolled in the dirt. The battle raged to his left. Blades clashed, shields banged, all accompanied by the shouts of men desperate to kill and survive. Hundr approached his house at a flat run, its red and green painted door frame bringing back a flash of memory from the day he had painted it with the children.

The corpses of four Franks lay outside his door, which was closed. Rollo's marauders had not set this part of the town alight, and Hundr slowed his run to cautious steps. He reached out for the door and swallowed, knowing that inside, his family could be dead and taken from him forever. Hundr pulled the handle, and the door creaked open to reveal dark gloom. He paused, allowing his eyes to adjust, and he grimaced at the overpowering smell that permeated the room – iron-rich blood mixed with the putrid stench of the open bowels of the dead. Hundr entered slowly, swords raised before him, and his foot tripped on something, another dead Frank. There were six dead warriors in his home.

"Sigrid? Sigurd? Hermoth?" he whispered, not daring to hope for a response.

"Lord Hundr?" came a low voice.

"Father!" a child gasped.

Hundr leapt toward the source of the sound, ducking his head around the cured meats that hung from the rafters. Hundr cried for joy as he came upon Amundr kneeling in a dark corner. The huge warrior's face was deathly pale, and two more enemy bodies lay on the floor before him. Hermoth's little face peered over the giant's shoulder, and Hundr laughed as Sigurd ran to him. Hundr bowed his head and clasped his fist to his chest in salute to Amundr. The warrior had killed a dozen men to protect Hundr's children, and that was a debt he could never repay. Amundr rose slowly, and Hundr helped him.

He staggered, so Hundr swung his arm around the big man, who bled from more wounds than Hundr could count.

"Stay with me," he said. Sigurd held Hermoth's hand, and the two children kept close behind Hundr as he led them out of the front door. "Where is Sigrid?"

"Torsten led the women and children into the hills, my lord. But Sigurd and Hermoth were with Einar and me at the fjord's edge, so we couldn't escape in time," replied Amundr. He spoke in halting gasps, grimacing against the cuts and slashes on his body.

Hundr shuffled across the open ground in front of his house and led Amundr and his children behind Einar's hall. The battle for Vanylven raged, but Hundr could not go to the warriors' aid, for he had to get his children to safety. Two men burst from the rear of Einar's hall. They came with jugs of ale in their fists, clenching Einar's silver within a bundled cloak. Hundr charged at them, and both men rapidly died in a welter of sword slashes. After what seemed like an age of supporting Amundr's bulk and bearing the whimpers of his children with terrified apprehension at what might lurk behind the next building, Hundr finally reached Vanylven's landward gate.

Thorgrim, son of Skapti Farsailor, was there, holding his giant double-bladed war axe, and he led a company of ten Vanylven warriors who held the gate.

Thorgrim sent two of his men to help Hundr with Amundr's bulk.

"Thanks to Odin that you are here and alive, my lord," said Thorgrim.

"Did you see Sigrid?" asked Hundr.

"Yes, lord, I saw her. She, Hildr and Torsten led the women and children out of this gate. She is safe and alive."

Hundr clapped Thorgrim on the shoulder and sighed with relief. "And Einar?"

"He fights in the front line against Rollo the Betrayer."

"But he lives?"

"I do not know, Lord Hundr."

"Take Amundr and my children to the forest's edge. I shall go to Einar, and then we will join you there. There can be no defence of Vanylven today. There are too many of the enemy."

"I'll come with you, lord."

Hundr nodded in agreement. With that, Thorgrim ordered his men to do as Hundr asked, and together, they ran back into Vanylven. The battle was easy to find. They followed the screams and the noisy clash of weapons until they reached Vanylven's market square and found Einar and his warriors in a circle surrounded by baying Franks. Their orange banner flowed long, flickering like a dragon's forked tongue in the breeze from its gilded lance. Rollo strode from the ranks. He towered above his men and came with the swagger of a champion.

"Rollo the Betrayer!" Hundr shouted, emerging into the square with Thorgrim at his side. He called out to distract Rollo and lure him away from Einar's men. There were hundreds of Franks crammed into the square, and if they attacked Einar's small force, there would be no victory for the Vanylven warriors. The ground was thick with the fallen, so many dead and wounded, and Hundr went to meet his enemy.

"Dog's Name," said Rollo, spreading his arms wide as though greeting an old friend. "You show yourself at last. I was worried that you were not at home, just as I was not when you burned my hall and killed my men on my wedding day."

"If you've come for me, let's fight together, you and I. Let the others live, and we can settle this between us."

"You'd like that, wouldn't you? Ever the hero. There are no heroes here today, Dog. Just a greater force defeating a weaker one – no champions or tales of single combat. I haven't brought my army north across the sea to fight you alone. I've come to wipe you all out. You and that miserable old bastard, Einar. You are like a pox. Two boils on the arse of Midgard, and I have come to lance you both. So you can join your crusty old friend in his puny shield wall and die together, holding hands like lovers, if you so wish. But you will both die today. I will find your women and whore them to my men. I will take your children and slave them. I'll sell them to Easterners who like to take little ones as concubines. Know that before you die."

Hundr glanced at the vast numbers of warriors at Rollo's back and knew that the Duke was right. He would die. But as that knowing settled in Hundr's thought cage, he felt a tremulous rumble beneath his feet, and then a sound like distant thunder accompanied that rumble as if the mighty Thor himself had come to strike at Vanylven. Two mares suddenly burst into the square from the street across the courtyard, and Rollo leapt back as they charged into the space between him and Einar's men. More horses followed, and then Ragnhild appeared on the back of a white gelding with her loyal crew in tow. The Franks retreated from the churning hooves while Ragnhild's men threw spears into their ranks, and the quiet that had been Rollo's moment of crowing was now a welter of hoofbeats and wounded men.

"Ride!" Ragnhild shouted, her scarred face twisted in desperation. "Ride!"

Einar's men reacted the fastest and seized the manes of loose horses, hauling themselves onto their backs. Ragnhild had emptied Einar's stables and brought his herd charging through the streets of Vanylven to drive a wedge between the Franks and the Vikings. Hundr vaulted himself onto the back of a bay mare, and Thorgrim clambered up behind him. As Hundr caught Einar's eye, a feral desperation marked the Jarl's bloodstained face as he galloped away on horseback. Hundr followed, both of them fleeing their home to escape Rollo's wrath. But the Betrayer had an army, and he would be relentless in his pursuit, determined to hunt them down until they were all dead.

FIVE

Einar grimaced as Hildr bound the wound on his arm with a strip of cloth torn from her dress. She had washed the gash with clean water from a nearby stream, just as she had the six other cuts and wounds upon his body. Sunlight fought through the pine trees in shafts where motes danced, and people shifted like wraiths, moving silently amongst the wounded, fetching water and cloth to aid the injured. Hildr reached down and grabbed a soaking strip of linen from the upturned helmet she was using as a basin. She wrung out the cloth, draining the pink blood-tinted water back into the helmet. Einar flinched, jerking his head away as she dabbed at the gash on his forehead.

"Still, now," Hildr whispered, and she wiped away the crusted blood and tutted as the clean gash became exposed. "We might need to sew this one."

During the battle, a spear point had scraped across Einar's scalp, and the wound had poured blood into his eyes. Of all his injuries, that one hurt the most, even more than the knife wound in his side or the wide slash across his thigh.

"Did someone send for the galdr-woman?" he asked, and Hildr nodded. The galdr-woman was a crone who lived high in the mountains, and she had come to Sigrid's aid two summers prior when she had struggled to birth the twins. The people of Vanylven feared the galdr-woman's power and closeness to the gods, but there was no doubting her skills as a healer. Galdr was the old woman's magic, her knowledge of spells and rune lore, the land and its herbs and fungi, and all of their various purposes ranging from curing ailments like goitres or infections to more malevolent uses like crafting poisons.

Einar shifted his arse on the fallen log; its dampness had seeped through his trews to chill his skin. Vanylven folk thronged the glade, people who had fled the slaughter and now hid deep in the pine forest on a high mountainside.

"So few," Einar murmured, glancing around at the warriors who sat, knelt, or leant against trees, rocks or whatever they could find to prop them up. There wasn't a man amongst them who hadn't taken an injury. They had fought like Odin's Einherjar to keep Rollo's forces away from their women and children as they fled through the landward gate. Many of his men had fallen in the battle, good men. They were husbands, fathers, brothers and warriors, and across the glade, people wept as they flitted from person to person, seeking news of a loved one yet to be found amongst the survivors.

"Jarl Einar," Torsten spoke up. He knelt beside Einar and chewed at the beard below his bottom lip.

"You saved our women and children today, Torsten. Vanylven thanks you," said Einar, and he rested a hand on Torsten's broad shoulder.

"I think Lady Hildr saved herself, my lord. She killed more men with her bow than I did with my axe. Were it not for her and Sigrid's arrows, we might not have made it out of the gate."

"So, what's the tally?"

"We have two dozen left from the Vanylven guard, lord, and you and Amundr. Then, we have the crews of the Seaworm, Wind Elk, and the Wave Eater all guarding the forest's perimeter in case Rollo advances from the town."

"So, two hundred men?"

"Aye, my lord."

Einar sighed because it was not enough to storm the town and take it back. More than half of the hundred warriors who had fought to defend Vanylven were dead. He had lost his lands to an enemy he hated, and his people had lost their homes. It was the end of the temperate weather, and winter would be upon them in a matter of weeks.

"We have three hundred women and children up here in these mountains," said Hildr, as she tossed the bloody linen cloth back into the helmet. She moved a loose strand of hair from her face with the back of a hand stained with blood. "Another hundred or more are dead or captured by the enemy. That's a lot of mouths to feed. We shall need food and water quickly if we are to remain in these hills."

"Torsten, send any able-bodied men in this glade to go hunting and foraging. It will be dark soon, and we must find shelter and food."

"Yes, Lord Einar." Torsten stood and gathered the men, a sorry bunch of limping and shuffling warriors with just as many cuts and bruises as Einar. Einar kissed Hildr, and she helped him rise to his feet. They held each other in a warm embrace. So close were they that no words were required for Hildr to understand how Einar felt responsible for the devastating loss of his town. He had let his people down when he should have protected them. Many had died, and now they were shivering in a mountain forest with no shelter, food, or water. Hildr just held him. She was with him, and Einar knew he had her support.

The sound of approaching horses interrupted the moment, and Hundr and Ragnhild slipped from their mounts to enter the camp.

"They haven't left the town yet," said Hundr as he walked towards Einar. Ragnhild and Hildr clasped forearms in the warrior's grip. They had been warrior priestesses together in the Valkyrie order at Upsala and had grown up side by side, learning blade and bow. They were as close as sisters and both fearsome fighters. "The enemy hasn't marched out of the landward gate yet, I expect, because he fears an ambush in the forest. Rollo has let his men loose inside the walls. They are drinking and eating themselves stupid. Some of our women are still in there, and I shiver to think of their fates."

"Maybe we should attack now," Einar suggested, but he spoke with the half-hearted bravado of the defeated and not with genuine conviction. Neither Einar himself nor any of the other men were fit to fight again that day nor the next. It would be a week before they had recovered enough to mount any sort of fight against Rollo's Franks, and even then, they were massively outnumbered. Einar held his hand up to acknowledge the futility of his suggestion.

"We could press higher into the mountains and head for the caves to the northeast."

"Or march over the mountaintop and look for a place to camp in the next valley," said Ragnhild. She took a drink of cool stream water from Hildr and passed the waterskin to Hundr.

"We could swim out into the harbour and steal back one of our ships," Hundr proposed after he had taken a drink. "Rollo has four of them down there, along with his own."

"But where would we go?" asked Ragnhild. "We would need four of five ships to fit all these people in, and by now, Rollo will have secured the fjord rope."

"The caves will provide shelter, and we can reach there just after nightfall," intoned Einar. He ran a hand along his beard. "Tomorrow, we'll send men into the next valley to make a camp where the women and children can live until we can do something about the bastard betrayer."

"I still have two ships at sea and yet to return. Asbjorn's and Harbard's crews will be enough to make a difference," said Hundr. "They should be returning soon."

"Even with our combined crews, we won't have enough to oust Rollo. He can defend the walls, and the fjord bridge, and ten of his Frankish boats are in the harbour, so he has seven hundred warriors in our home. It will take a bigger force than we can muster to beat him." Einar stared into the lofty green pine branches above him. They would need another four or five hundred men to fight Rollo, yet no such force was at Einar's disposal.

"Do you think he will stay?" asked Hildr.

"He'll stay," Hundr nodded. "Rollo will use Vanylven as a base to hunt us. Even if we make a camp in the next valley, he will march his men over the mountain and slaughter us. We have too many women and children, and we can't have that battle with our families at our backs."

"We can go to King Harald," said Ragnhild firmly. She fixed them all with her one eye, her scarred face challenging and stern. She shifted her shoulders under their questioning looks. "What? He is our King. We fought to make him King of all Norway. Einar is oath-sworn to him, and he holds Vanylven as Harald's Jarl. He must give us men."

"An oath I did not wish to take," Einar blurted tersely, suddenly alarmed when Hundr nodded his head at Ragnhild's suggestion. "Do you think King Harald will welcome me with open arms when I tell him I have lost Vanylven to Rollo? Rollo tried to have him killed, remember? He is as much Harald's enemy as he is ours."

"Rollo fought against Harald in his war to become king, which is all the more reason why Harald should give us men. Do you think he wants a force of seven hundred enemy warriors wintering in his kingdom?" Ragnhild folded her arms across her chest.

"And how do we get to Harald's hall in Avaldsnes? We have no ships, and winter is coming. We can't march our families across the wilds of Norway. How would we feed everybody along the way? It would take us two weeks to march across rivers, fjords, and mountains. Harald might be king of all Norway, but every jarl we encounter on the road would try to steal our silver and weapons. Every landowner would charge us for food and ale. If we steal those things, word will spread faster than an eagle on the wing, and we will find hosts of warriors waiting for us in every valley and village. We must stay and fight with the men we have." Einar waved his arm at the hundreds of folk in the glade and beyond in the trees' shadows. There were too many people to march south to Avaldsnes. It was simply not possible. And even if they could survive the journey, Einar was not sure that Harald would support him. The king was ruthless, and he'd just as easily kill

Einar for losing a valuable part of his kingdom as he would grant him aid.

"I won't let Rollo win," Hundr seethed. His one eye burned with fervour, and he looked at Einar, Hildr and Ragnhild, challenging them to find an answer to their problem. "I can't let him win."

"Well, he has won," said Sigrid. Hundr's wife strode towards where they talked. Her dress was smeared with the blood of the injured she had tended in the glade. "And I remember Rollo when he was a slave in my father's hall on Orkney, and he was a sneaky bastard even then. He has won, but only this day, for there will surely be another. We must fight back for our children and our people."

"We need more warriors," sighed Hundr, and he glanced around the glade to the ragtag band of injured men who followed Torsten slowly into the forest to search for food.

"So, we will march to King Harald in Avaldsnes," Sigrid insisted and clenched her jaw, the muscles beneath her cheeks moving in determination. "Einar will find somewhere safe for our womenfolk to camp with their bairns, and he will harry Rollo until we return with an army to kill the bastard."

"You make it sound so easy," said Einar.

"But it will not be easy, Jarl Einar," replied Sigrid. "Those who stay must fight like bandits from the woodland. They must hit Rollo's men, attack his forces in the forest, kill them when they hunt, and whenever he marches out of our home, those who stay must ambush his men before they reach our camp. It will take a month or more for Hundr and I to return with warriors. By then, the cold will have arrived, and you will be hard-pressed to stay alive. Rollo will not leave until we are all dead, so let us make that as hard for him as we can."

Einar saw the steadfast determination in Sigrid's ice-blue eyes and found a glimmer of hope in her words. Perhaps he could wage a bandits war against Rollo, and perhaps Hundr could persuade Harald to send men and ships to Vanylven. "Very well," Einar said. "I will stay. Hit, run, and hide. Not the way of the drengr, but there is reputation enough in trying to win back a man's home."

"Ragnhild, Bush, Thorgrim, and Sigvarth will come with me," said Hundr. "And I will take twenty men and horses so that we can move with haste."

"You won't leave me here," Sigrid retorted. "I'm coming with you, and so are our children."

"We cannot bring Sigurd and Hermoth…"

Sigrid raised a warning finger to silence Hundr. "Do not tell me what we will or will not do with our children. Did I not give birth to them? Have I not repeatedly stood in the shield wall and proved my valour? King Harald will understand the seriousness of our plea for aid when he sees that you have brought your wife and children to make such a request."

Hundr opened his mouth but thought better of arguing with his wife, and Einar saw that the plan for survival was taking shape, yet it was like a poorly woven fisherman's net with holes large enough for the catch to swim out of.

"So I will stay with Hildr, Torsten, Amundr, and Trygve," said Einar. "We will fight with the men we have, but we must also feed our people until you return, and that, I think, will be harder than fighting Rollo's men. I can call on the farms in the mountains who owe tribute to Vanylven, and we might have to go further out for support. Jarl Ugattr is two days' ride from here, and he might help, even if he is a curmudgeonly old turd." Einar's last encounter with Jarl Ugattr had occurred the previous summer during the collection of tributes for King Harald. They had met briefly, and Ugattr had been as short and belligerent as he always was. His lands were deeper inside Norway's hinterland – a harsh place of thin soil, goats, and dense forests. He was jealous of Einar's coastal home and vividly remembered the former jarl who had met his demise at the hands of Hundr and Einar during the war for Harald's crown.

"So it's settled then," nodded Hundr. "Einar will stay and fight, and we shall find an army."

"Rollo must die," said Einar, and he held up his fist, clenched so hard that his knuckles turned white beneath the blue bruising. "He tried to take everything from us, and he almost succeeded. But we still have our blades and our lives, and that is enough for us to strike the wretched bastard down, trample his corpse into the soil and send his soul screaming to Niflheim."

They all clasped hands, and Hundr went to ready his company for the road.

"Do you really believe we can feed all these people whilst we wait for an army that might not come?" asked Hildr. She fussed at the cut on Einar's head again, which had leaked blood down his face.

"We have to. Whether I believe it or not."

SIX

Hundr rode out from Vanylven with twenty warriors, all mounted on horses used in the escape from Vanylven. They left a forest of thick, dark green pines travelling south and, on the third morning, entered a valley below the range of mountains to Vanylven's eastern border. That night, they camped in a forest where the trees had already shed their leaves, leaving skeletal branches and creeping boughs bare and open to a hard, driving rain that soaked the riders.

Sigrid and Hundr shared the burden of a child each, with either Sigurd or Hermoth propped in front of them in the saddle. The little ones complained of the boredom of the arduous journey and had to stop all too frequently to piss, which slowed the journey to a crawl. As they spent the night in that forest, they used a stinking fisherman's sailcloth, which Bush had purchased from a fjord fishing family for three pieces of hacksilver. The travellers hung the sail across branches, and whilst it provided some respite from the endless rain, the cold bit into their sodden clothes, and sleep was hard to find. Bush coughed throughout that night. At times, it was a wheezing cough behind tight lips as the old shipmaster tried not to annoy his companions, but at others, it erupted into a wracking bark, causing him to double over and clasp a scrap of wool to his mouth and hide whatever fluid emerged from his lips once the bout subsided.

Little Sigurd also began to cough after five days, and a farmer's family took Hundr, Sigrid and the children into their turf-covered home to let the boy sleep by their fire. Sigurd sweated, and Sigrid worried, but he was well enough to continue the journey the next day. Before the company set out again, Hundr had rewarded the farmer with an arm ring for his trouble. Twenty warriors had slept in the farmers' barn and spent two days eating his food and drinking his ale, all on the edge of the upcoming colder months. The farmer had been too afraid to refuse succour to a band of grim-faced warriors bristling with weapons, and Hundr rode away from the farm concerned that the man would no longer have the stores to support his own family through the long, dark months where snow would blanket his farm, casting long shadows over sun-deprived days. A silver arm ring was a mighty price to pay for some thin broth and half a barrel of ale, but Hundr considered the likeliness that he'd need to return on that road with an army at his back if King Harald provided men and no ships, so there would be a need of supplies and places to camp as the cold truly began to bite while Hundr marched north.

After a week on the road, Hundr led his riders along the meander of a fast-flowing river which churned and babbled its way down from the high, snow-topped mountains into a vast western fjord. In a wide sweep of that river was a town where smoke drifted from wooden buildings topped with thatch turned lank and grey from the incessant rain. A line of men waited for Hundr and his company where a grazing pasture sloped down towards the riverbank and the village. They were a week's ride away from Vanylven and halfway into their journey south to Avaldsnes, and so none in Hundr's company knew of the village. It was a small place, existing solely because it sat at the river's ford, which offered ample opportunities for trade and a tithe on merchants and traders who wished to find lodgings during the summer months.

"They don't look friendly," muttered Sigrid, and she had Sigurd hold her reins whilst she unfastened her bow from the back at the rear of her horse's saddle.

"Nor do we," remarked Ragnhild, which Hundr supposed was true. None of them wore brynjars, travelling instead in jerkins and wool cloaks with fur collars to shield themselves from the worst of the chill winds that accompanied the rainstorms. Nevertheless, each had weapons strapped to their saddles: swords, axes, and spears, and all were covered with spare cloaks and fleeces to safeguard them from the rain. Their shields had remained in Vanylven with Einar because it was far too long a journey to carry a heavy iron-shod linden wood shield halfway across Norway.

"Word of our approach must have gotten ahead of us," said Hundr. They had spent nights camping in forests, and Hundr had no doubt that trappers and hunters would have heard their horses from a valley away, so the villagers expected their approach. "I don't imagine these lads are a welcome party."

"Bastards think they outnumber us and want to take our silver," said Thorgrim.

"They want more than that," piped Sigvarth. "They want everything we have. Thirty of the turds are down there, and each one has a spear or an axe. This far inland, there is no king's or jarl's law. They'll pay some tribute to a jarl a couple of days' ride away on the coast somewhere, but he probably leaves them alone. I was born in a place like this, but further north. Grim places, where the brave men join coastal crews and come back every winter to live off their plunder, and the ones who stay till the land or exploit the plight of unfortunate travellers like us."

"Do you think they want to fight?" asked Sigrid.

"No. They think we will see their greater numbers, give them what they want, and ride on without our silver and our weapons. They don't think we'll fight them."

"Then they are fools," scoffed Hundr, and he clicked his tongue to urge his mare onwards. The dead of Vanylven haunted him, and losing to Rollo was like a wasp sting in his mind, persistently burning and itching. His horse cantered across the pasture where a herd of sheep and a few muck-spattered goats grazed near the river. The grass was wet, and Hundr's mount threw up clods of earth from its hooves.

Three men strode forward from the line of villagers. Two wore dark brown leather breastplates, hardened over time and patched here and there with lighter strips to repair damage. They carried spears and axes, which hung at their belts. However, the man in the centre took a pace forward, sporting both a sword and seax at his belt. His black beard was shot through with stark white at the chin, resembling the colour of snow, and he wore a brynjar on which Hundr noticed spots of rust on the links as the man drew closer. He had long black hair tied into a braid and wore a gold hoop in his left ear. Crossing his arms over his chest, he smiled a thick-lipped smile, and his narrow eyes gleamed as he let his gaze wash over Hundr's appearance. He was clearly the village headman, and he licked his lips like a hungry wolf. In Hundr, the headman saw a one-eyed traveller dressed in a journey-stained jerkin and trews, wearing an undyed wool cloak about his shoulders, with only the fox fur trim around the neck showing any indication of his wealth.

Hundr raised his hand to stop his company, who had come to rein in alongside him, and he trotted forward to separate himself from the group so that the headman would know that he was the leader. Hundr let his mare paw at the grass with her foreleg, and she turned in a half circle. All the time, he kept his one eye on the headman.

"Welcome," said the headman. He spread his brawny arms wide, gesturing at the collection of houses, pig pens and barns beside the river. "To pass the river, you must pay a tax."

"We are warriors from the north," Hundr replied. "We just want to cross the ford and will happily pay a reasonable toll. We also need food and ale if you have any to sell."

The headman turned to his men and winked, and they laughed lazily. "Very well. Our price is everything you have. So, get down from your horses and pile up all your silver, knives, those fur-lined cloaks, and whatever else you have of value. Because we are a kind and generous people, you can keep your women, your horses and the clothes on your back."

"Maybe we should take the women too, Fjolnir," said one of the spearmen to the headman's right. He had a long, horse face and a lantern jaw. His tongue flicked out between his missing front teeth. "Not the horrible one with one eye, the golden-haired one. She's whelped that pup there, and maybe the other one, too. But she looks tasty. I'll have her, I think. Keep me warm over the winter; sell her in the summer." The gap-toothed man rubbed his hands together, and the villagers laughed again.

Hundr turned and glanced at Sigrid, whose face was impassive. She just stared at the gap-toothed man with a look as hard as granite. Sigurd sat on the saddle in front of her, and he gawked open-mouthed at the villagers. Hermoth, on the other hand, was further along the line, riding with Bush that day. Hundr leaned forward on his mount. He gently patted the mare's neck and then crossed his arms over her mane. He did it deliberately so that Fjolnir and his men could see his arm rings, glittering silver and gold on both forearms, as a clear sign of a successful and wealthy warrior. It was the first glimpse Fjolnir had of Hundr's true nature, and the headman's eyes narrowed as he noticed them.

"I'll make a bargain with you," said Hundr. "Lay down your weapons, return to your shit-stinking village and bring me whatever cured meat you have hanging from your rafters, a sack of barley and wheat, and ten skins of ale. Do all of that before the sun is above me in the sky, and we will leave this place in peace. I would have paid you, Fjolnir, but seeing as you are a belligerent nugget of shit on a goat's arse, I'll take all of that and cross your ford for nothing."

"You cheeky whoreson," barked Fjolnir, and his hand dropped to rest on his sword hilt. It was a simple thing with a walnut grip, and Hundr leapt from his horse the moment Fjolnir's hand touched the weapon. "You will pay…" Fjolnir began, but he stopped talking and took two steps back as Hundr approached him. "What are you doing? I am Fjolnir Svensson, and I have fought beside the Man with the Dog's Name in Frankia…"

"You are a turd and liar," said Hundr. "I am the Man with the Dog's Name, a killer of jarls and kings, and the Champion of the North. I do not remember fighting beside a nithing like you. I'll fight you here in

77

front of your people, Fjolnir, and when you are dead, your people will let me pass in peace."

Fjolnir gulped. His gaze flitted across Hundr's one eye and the scars upon his face. He glanced again at Hundr's arm rings and knew he had made a terrible mistake.

"Let's not be hasty," Fjolnir stammered, and then Hundr took two quick steps forward and slapped him across the face.

"You touched your sword, and that is an insult. No need to make a hazel rod square, nor for the usual Holmgang rituals." Hundr turned on his heel and marched to his horse. He drew Fenristooth from her scabbard and turned to meet Fjolnir. There was no great honour or reputation in fighting the man, who was clearly a braggart and a liar, but Hundr was a champion and a *drengr,* and that meant he had to defend his honour. He was also still angry and wanted to fight. Although he knew Fjolnir's death would not rid Vanylven of Rollo's presence, news would spread through the valleys that a formidable warrior approached – the renowned Man with the Dog's Name, slayer of Ivar the Boneless and Eystein Longaxe. So, Hundr had to kill one man to avoid trouble for the rest of the journey south, and Fjolnir had earned his place as that man by trying to steal everything from Hundr and his companions. The villagers would have stripped Hundr's men of all their wealth and left Hundr and his family with nothing to face starvation in the bleakness of Norway's mountainous terrain.

Fjolnir stumbled backwards, and the gap-toothed man shoved him. That man would have raped Sigrid all winter, and Hundr pointed his sword first at Fjolnir and then at the gap-toothed man. Fjolnir turned to his men and then back to Hundr. He closed his eyes and raised his face to the sky. Fjolnir realised that his doom was upon him. The Norns had woven the thread of his life into this moment, those three terrible sisters who lived at the foot of Yggdrasil, the great tree which holds up the worlds, spinning the warp and weft of all men's lives. Fjolnir saw that his time had come. Drawing his sword, Fjolnir braced himself, holding his blade low, gritting his teeth, and readying himself to fight.

Hundr rotated his wrist and swept his blade around, twirling the sword, creating a blur of steel before him. The scent of the sheep grease that coated the blade filled his senses. Pausing momentarily, he raised the sword towards the sky in tribute to Odin, then charged toward Fjolnir. The headman gasped and lifted his weapon to parry the blow, but Hundr did not want to score the edge of his sword in such a fight, so he ducked under Fjolnir's weapon and slashed Fenristooth's blade across the headman's knees. Fjolnir cried out in pain and toppled to the earth, scrabbling on his side to rise, but his legs refused to obey. Fjolnir wept, and Hundr stood on his blade, trapping it between his boot and the long, dew-soaked grass. Adjusting the grip on his sword, Hundr brought Fenristooth down underhand so that her tip punched through the rusted rings of Fjolnir's breastplate and drove into his heart. Hundr twisted the blade and dragged it free. He turned in a half circle and brought the blade around to level its blood-soaked point at Fjolnir's men.

The gap-toothed man shouted in defiance, lunging toward Hundr with his spear levelled. However, he met a swift demise as an arrow found its mark in his throat. Hundr turned and nodded his thanks at Sigrid, who spat into the grass and watched with stoic satisfaction as the man who had threatened to capture, enslave and rape her gurgled and choked on her arrow.

"Now," said Hundr. "Bring me what I asked for – unless any other man here wants to fight?"

The villagers backed away slowly at first and then turned to run towards their village. They ran so fast that two of them slipped and fell on the wet grass, and Thorgrim laughed so hard he almost toppled from his horse.

"Bastards thought they were going to rob us," chuckled Sigvarth, shaking his head. "At least now we won't go hungry."

Hundr cleaned his sword on Fjolnir's sleeve, and Sigurd and Hermoth paddled in the ford as the villagers brought out the tribute Hundr had demanded. His company took only what they could carry: a flitch of cured bacon, some goat's milk, cheese and as much wheat and barley as their horses could manage. They left the villagers sullen-faced and weeping over the corpses of their dead warriors but encountered no more trouble from villagers looking to rob them on the road.

The nights grew colder, and Hundr led the company around a foot of high hills and into a hard rain, which lasted for two days. The water poured from the sky as though the clouds had drank the oceans, and it scoured the riders' faces like a whip. Hundr shivered upon his horse and held Hermoth close beneath his cloak as they wound through high passes and roads churned to slippery mud. The company huddled together at night for warmth, and fire came begrudgingly as wet wood spluttered and gave off as much smoke as heat. Bush coughed and groaned in the dark, and little Sigurd came down with another fever. The wheeze in his chest was like wind whistling through a crack in an ancient oak door, and Sigrid cried from sheer helplessness as she cradled his little body while he nestled into her. Hundr would pace in the rain, unable to do anything to help his son but keep the fire burning with damp wood and keep his family as warm as possible.

"What's wrong with Sigurd?" Hermoth would ask, staring with big worried eyes at his twin brother.

"Do not worry, little one, your brother will be fine," Hundr would reply each time. But he cursed Rollo, for he had forced this arduous journey upon Hundr, his men, and his family, and there would have to be a reckoning. Hundr prayed fervently in the darkness to Odin, Thor, Tyr, Freya, and any god who would listen to grant him an opportunity for vengeance. The rain poured, and the wind howled relentlessly each day as Hundr rode further south towards Avaldsnes to ask a brutal war king for help, well aware that Harald Fairhair was not a man known for his kindness. He was a ruthless conqueror, and Hundr needed Harald's army.

SEVEN

"There," said Torsten, pointing down the hillside into the heart of the forest.

"I see them," replied Einar. Shadows moved between the boughs and leaves that turned copper and yellow as the year waned. In the north, autumn quickly became winter, so it was almost a dream, both fleeting and hard to remember. Soon, ice and snow would cover the hills in a silent blanket, and Einar had to finish his woodland camp before the days drew short and winter took its fearsome grip upon the land.

This was the second time Rollo had led men out of Vanylven in search of Einar's people. The first time, Einar's scouts had reported a force massing inside Vanylven's walls, and Einar had led his archers to the forest's edge, where they had loosed so many shafts at the Franks that the advance did not even reach the first tree. The Franks had hastily retreated behind the safety of Vanylven's palisade, abandoning a dozen bleeding corpses heavily punctured with arrows. Each day, Hildr and the Vanylven folk diligently carved and fletched new arrows. They cut yew bows and made sheaves of arrows tipped with wicked arrowheads. The camp collected every trace of metal they could find from their meagre possessions hastily carried away from Vanylven during the chaos of Rollo's assault, and a smith in a thick leather apron melted the scraps in the campfires and forged arrowheads using moulds of sand and clay.

Since that first sally, Rollo had sent large foraging parties out into the forest, hunting and searching for Einar's camp and his scouts. The gruesome discovery of Vanylven men hanging from trees served as a chilling warning to stay clear of the area near the town's walls. So, Einar's men watched from the heights instead, and that was where he stood with Torsten and noticed warriors moving in the darkness amongst the trees, trudging through the bracken and ferns beneath withered, falling leaves.

"Can't tell how many yet, but there could be at least fifty of them," Torsten supposed. He sniffed and cuffed at a running nose. The nights were growing cold, and many of the men had already begun to sniff, sneeze, and cough as the harsh damp weather closed in.

"Well, we must keep away from this rise," said Einar. "They'll reach this spot before midday, so get Amundr and his men and meet me here."

Torsten nodded and went to bring more men. Einar had thirty warriors with him at the top of the valley above Vanylven. Below him, the town stood within the circle of its palisade beyond the swathe of trees, and then beyond the settlement, the fjord glistened like a sheet of twinkling ice where it stretched away and met steep mountainous crags and the narrow passage to the sea. Einar's people had set up home in the next valley, a day's march away from Vanylven and in the heart of a mountainside forest. They had running water from a fast-flowing stream and had built shelters amongst the trees, briars, ferns, gulleys, and rocks. It had been eight days since Rollo's attack, and the shelters had started out as lean-to's made from fallen branches topped with bracken, branches, leaves and earth. The people had shivered and huddled together on chilly nights around small fires, but as the days went by, the shelters became more elaborate, with sturdier buildings emerging. Axes forged for hewing men's heads were used to fell and trim trees, and some women had brought spare dresses, buckets, and cloth with them when they fled Vanylven, so a community was forming beneath the branches. They'd gathered timber for fires, foraged for food in the forest and hunted meat. Yet, it still wasn't enough to feed so many hungry mouths, so Trygve had travelled to Jarl Ugattr with ten men and paid four times the going rate for a wagon of wheat. Einar grimaced at that thought because the wheat was rapidly dwindling, and he would need to send men to the Jarl again. He could only imagine the silver it would cost to secure the food he desperately needed.

The sun poked through dark, rain-heavy clouds, casting gleams of light upon the spears and axe blades deep in the forest below where Rollo's men marched. Einar chewed at his beard as he watched them, and he fingered his axe in its belt loop.

"We'll ambush the bastards," Einar growled. "I'll push down the hill to the east, and when Torsten returns, he and Amundr can come from the west. Hildr, you go at them head-on and take ten of your archers with you."

"Bait?" Hildr said with a raised eyebrow.

"What finer bait could a man wish for than a beauty like you, my love?"

Hildr shook her head and dug her elbow into his ribs. Einar winced – the cuts and bruises from the fight inside Vanylven were still raw and vivid across his body. Einar wore only a leather jerkin, having left his beloved brynjar inside his hall, and he touched at the scab upon his forehead. The galdr-woman had come down from her home in the high crag and helped Einar's people when they'd taken shelter in mountain caves on the night following the battle. She had applied a poultice that stank of stale piss and horseshit to Einar's head, along with the other gashes across his body. He hadn't asked her what was in it because he dared not know the answer, but the stuff worked, and his wounds were healing well. The crone had cast her bones and shaken her black stick carved with runes of power, and she sewed Amundr back together and forced her foul medicines down his neck. The giant feared the galdr-woman's power and sweated like a pig whenever she approached, but she had tended his wounds, and now he was out of his sickbed. One benefit of being driven from his home and forced to live in the woods like a bandit was the shrinking of Einar's belly. A ration of salted pork, thin porridge, and berries will quickly trim a man of any excess fat, and each day, Einar grew leaner and stronger. He stared at the Franks in the woods below him, and he felt agile and hungry and ready to fight for his people.

Amundr reached the hilltop with his men, and the big man clasped his fist to his chest in greeting. Even though he was still limping and had endured numerous cuts and wounds while defending Hundr's children inside Vanylven, he refused to remain at camp when there was more fighting to be done. As the days went by, the astonishing number of Franks he had killed that day increased as folk told the story around campfires, turning Amundr into a living legend amongst the survivors, and rightly so. Einar had watched the galdr-woman sew up a sickening gash on the giant's shoulder, but he was glad of his presence. Morale on the hillside visibly lifted as the men saw Amundr arrive, and they went to him, clapping him on the back or pressing closed fists to their chests in respect.

"Bastards have come out again then, lord?" Amundr said, his broad face flat and his eyes hard.

"Aye, they're in the trees below. We'll flank them and send them screaming back behind their walls. We have to stop them here. If they get out into the mountains, they'll find our camp, and Rollo will march his entire army out of Vanylven to kill us all," Einar replied.

"How many Franks?"

"Maybe fifty."

"I'll meet you down there, kill as many as we can, and then meet on this rise. Don't get embroiled in a shield wall battle. Just hit, kill, and run." Amundr nodded and set off down the hillside, his men trudging after him. "Don't you want to know how many men we have on each flank and how many we have left to guard the camp?" Einar asked.

Amundr turned and thought about that for a second. Then he simply shrugged his boulder shoulders. "Doesn't matter," he said and disappeared into the trees.

"Stay alive, Lord Einar," Torsten implored, following Amundr into the gloom beneath the pine trees.

Einar kissed Hildr on the cheek, holding her to him, and she clasped him tight to her chest. Then he set off down the eastern slope, his boots crunching on the fallen cones and twigs on the forest floor. Trygve marched beside him, and twenty men followed, scrambling down the slope to where Rollo's men came to kill. The woodland stank of damp rot, and the lingering rain from the previous night's downpour sat heavy in the boughs, dripping onto Einar and his men. He led them around to the east, using the sun to show him the way. It was a dim glow, barely visible through the trees and heavy cloud covering, but it showed enough of its position to give Einar his bearings. He went armed with his axe and seax and drew both as he clambered down the steep bank.

Trygve ranged ahead with two warriors. They scampered through the undergrowth to find the enemy whilst Einar kept his men close. It would be easy to lose sight of a man or two in the dense woodland, and the last thing Einar needed was a captured warrior tortured and screaming at the hands of Rollo the Betrayer. Trygve returned, nimbly hopping over a fallen trunk, placing a finger to his lips to quiet Einar. He lowered his hands slowly to indicate that Einar and his men should crouch. Einar dropped onto his haunches, and Trygve signalled to show that Rollo's men were close and to the southwest of Einar's position. Einar concealed himself beneath the creaking branches amongst the rustle and occasional chitter of the forest animals. Birds twittered overhead and flitted between the trees as Einar awaited the men he needed to kill.

The sound of a woman's laughter pealed through the gloom. It was Hildr doing her bit to bait the Franks. She and two other women laughed and joked to the north, out of sight but loud enough to attract attention. Then came the sound of men's voices, low and guttural, a snigger, a cough, and then boots crunching on the rotting forest floor.

"Wait," Einar whispered, and he held up a fist to show his men that he would give the signal to attack. He took deep breaths, preparing himself for the fight to come. Einar was the oldest of his men by far, his hair and beard iron grey and his broad face lined like a sea cliff battered by crashing waves. He had two long creases down each cheek, and his eyes were like flints. He flexed his gnarled hand around the haft of his axe, the leather wrappings soaking up the sweat from his palms.

"We should have brought archers," said Trygve. "Cut the bastards down before they even see us."

"We've flanked them. If we loosed arrows, we'd be as likely to hit Amundr and Torsten's men as the enemy. We'd be shooting blind. Hildr and her fighters will drop a few, and we'll kill the rest with blades."

Trygve grinned at that. He raised his bearded axe blade and kissed its hard, cold edge. Figures moved through the trees ahead, men with short-cropped hair and small shields. Franks. Hildr screamed, yet it was for Einar's benefit rather than a wail of fear at the sight of fifty enemy warriors. A bow twanged, a man shouted in pain, and Hildr had loosed the first of her arrows.

"Attack!" the enemy bellowed. It was a Viking voice calling in a Danish accent. Rollo had sent one or more of his Viking contingent with his Franks, which meant the fighting would be harder because an Odin-worshipping Dane was worth two Franks who worshipped the peace-spouting nailed God.

Einar burst from his crouch into a run. He carried his axe in his right hand and his seax in his left. Trygve ran at his side, teeth bared behind his blonde beard. Ulf, a young Vanylven warrior, surged past Einar, consumed with wild fury and swinging his axe. Einar wanted to call out to him to wait, but it was too late. The Franks appeared suddenly in a gap between the pines, and they turned to stare at Einar's man with open mouths and wide eyes. Ulf crashed into them, burying his axe in a Frank's chest and kicking the man behind him so that he sprawled backwards. The Franks had their shields faced forward towards Hildr's bow and could not react in time to stop Einar's men from slamming into them with vengeful savagery.

Einar cracked his axe blade across the face of a clean-shaven Frank and buried his seax in the guts of another. Taken aback, the Franks cried out in surprise and horror as Amundr and Torsten brought their warriors to slam into the Franks' exposed flank. Blood spilt, dark and red in the deep forest. Weapons clashed, and men died, and the Vanylven warriors fought with the wild fury of men who knew that if they did not win the fight, their loved ones would surely perish. A Frank jabbed a spear at Einar from behind his shield, and Einar hooked his axe over the shield rim, yanking it down and burying the point of his seax in the man's eye. Einar ripped the blade free, and the man fell dead. All around him, the Vanylven warriors ruthlessly hacked and cut at the enemy, and it would surely be a victory to drive Rollo's men back behind their walls.

At that moment, a guttural howl pierced the air, causing a shiver to race across Einar's shoulders. It bellowed and then roared menacingly like a wild animal, and Einar pinpointed the source of that terrible sound. A man shoved his way through the Franks. He was a head shorter than Einar but enormously broad, with shoulders like ale barrels and a neck as thick around as Einar's thigh. The man came bare-chested and wore a bearskin over his head and back, with the bear's maw and razor-sharp teeth hanging over his forehead. He wielded an axe in each hand, and his body was daubed in crusted blood.

"Berserker," Einar cursed to himself. He'd had the displeasure of fighting such men before; they were wild and unpredictable. The enormous man shoulder-barged a Frank out of his path and chopped the edge of his axe into Ulf's back with a sickening crunch. He followed up the blow by slicing his other axe across the top of Ulf's skull, shearing away a slice of flesh and blood-matted hair. It was a terrible injury, and Einar's men fell back at the horror of it.

"I am Kveldulf," the berserker roared, baring his teeth. They were small and brutally flat in his mouth, like granite standing stones. "I am the evening wolf, the bear-wolf. Come and fight with me!"

The Franks gained strength from his presence and fought Einar's men back. Einar quickly found himself bullied backwards by an enemy shield. Kveldulf killed another Vanylven man, and Einar needed to get to him. The berserker was the only Viking amongst that force of enemy warriors, and to kill him would steal their confidence and render them leaderless, running in fear.

Einar dropped to one knee and drove his seax beneath an enemy shield rim, then up into the man's groin so that the hot wash of his blood splashed on

Einar's hand and arm. He drove past the dying man, but another enemy shield collided with his chest, pushing Einar off balance, and the Frank behind it punched the shield boss into Einar's so that he staggered backwards. He kicked the man away, and Trygve surged past him, hacking into the Frank's shield with his axe. Einar's nose bled, and such a blow was a terrible misfortune, for it blinded a man. It inflicted the momentary battle hesitation, the *herfjotur*, war-fetter, sent by Odin to clinch a man in the heat of battle so that a warrior hesitated and died, blade in hand, to join his Einherjar. Odin was ever the betrayer and benefactor of warriors. On one day, he might bestow war luck upon a man; on another, he could bring about *heimhugr,* severance of the mind, which could lead to hesitation in battle and death.

Einar blew blood from his nose and staggered backwards, trying to clear his vision. The clash of blades and the cries of dying men filled the air, and Einar could only discern quick, monochromatic flashes. Desperately, he swung his axe to protect himself from the onslaught. Kveldulf howled again, and Einar shook his head. His eyes cleared for a brief moment to reveal Amundr crashing into the enemy berserker. Then darkness once again overtook his sight. Einar paused, blinked repeatedly, and steadied himself. His eyes cleared, and there was Amundr again amid the press of men. He and Kveldulf swayed back and forth, locked together in a wrestler's grip. Amundr was hugely tall and fearsome, but Kveldulf had thicker, more muscular shoulders and arms. Amundr drove the smaller man down, but Kveldulf snapped at him with his gravestone teeth, and they closed around Amundr's cheek. The giant twisted away in horror, and he picked the berserker up from the ground and tossed him backwards. The Franks groaned, and Einar surged forward, strength flowing into his arms at the sight of Amundr fighting the unhinged warrior.

"Kill!" Einar bellowed as he charged. "Kill them all!" He buried his axe into the thigh of the closest Frank, and then a tall man faced him, a Frank in a shining fish scale brynjar. He had an oiled beard which shone like an otter pelt, and he came at Einar with a bright sword. Einar drove the blade wide and swung his axe at the tall man, missing him by a hair as the man dodged away from the strike. The Frank's sword came at Einar in an overhand blow, but he parried it with his axe blade, and before the Frank could strike again, Einar sliced his seax blade across the man's throat, opening it up so that it smiled like a second mouth. The Frank tottered and clutched at his slit throat before crashing into the undergrowth. That death was too much for the enemy, and they turned and fled, running through the trees like children fleeing a scolding parent. Einar searched quickly for Kveldulf, wanting to kill the berserker there and then and remove him from Midgard forever. But the berserker was nowhere to be seen.

"Vanylven!" Einar's men roared in victory, and they shook their weapons and clapped one another on the back in celebration. Einar dropped his weapons and knelt beside the Frank he had killed. Einar ripped the fish scale brynjar from his corpse, along with a red leather sword belt. They were his now. Einar's possessions won in combat. His men collected the rest of the weapons and armour from the fallen. They seized axes, spears, shields, and breastplates. They also took clothes, boots, hoods and anything of value, leaving Rollo's dead warriors naked and as white as mushrooms on the forest floor.

Einar found Hildr, and they shared a heartfelt embrace. While it was a minor victory, they had successfully driven Rollo's men back away from the mountain, so Einar's camp remained hidden from Rollo's vengeful fury. But the berserker had proven to be a formidable adversary, and if Rollo had more men like that, then the fighting in the forest would be vicious. They would come again, and Einar needed to be ready. He had to protect his people until Hundr returned with an army to throw Rollo out of Vanylven. If he returned at all.

EIGHT

Hundr awoke with frost in his beard on a morning when the sky was as clear and pale as shallow fjord water. He rolled over, kissed Sigrid on the forehead, and slunk out from beneath his blanket. Hundr crept out of his makeshift tent, which was little more than a section of old sailcloth hung over a branch and tied to two adjacent trees. He walked barefoot, for his boots were close to where Sigurd and Hermoth slept on Sigrid's opposite side, and he did not want to wake the children.

Hundr hopped and cursed as the cold, crisp frost bit into his feet on the grass. He took a deep breath of morning air, and it came back out like billowing smoke. Hundr rubbed his hands and tiptoed three steps to the remnants of the campfire, now little more than charcoal, faggots, and a few glowing embers. Throughout the bitter night, they had taken turns keeping watch, and Hundr had taken the first shift, huddling by the fire in a cloak as a thin rain drifted across the hillside to soak him through. Bush had taken the last shift, and Hundr searched the camp for the old shipmaster, whose coughing soon showed him shambling from a copse beyond where the sailcloth tents hung. Bush came clutching an armful of branches for firewood, and he did his best to sink his chin into his shoulder to stifle the worst of his coughing.

"You sound like death warmed up," said Hundr, reaching out to take some of the wood from Bush's arms.

"I bloody feel like it, lad," Bush grumbled, his ruddy cheeks tinged blue by the cold. "My chest's colder than a witch's tit, and this bloody cough keeps me awake all night. Even when I do nod off, I have to wake for three pisses before morning."

"Let's get this fire going again." Hundr set the armful of firewood down and sat on a log that had served as their seating during the previous evening's meal around the fire. He took a stick and stirred the campfire embers until more of the orange, glowing faggots showed themselves. Bush broke up some small twigs, added them to the embers, and then blew into the ashes until the twigs began to smoke and catch flame. They continued adding more twigs until the fire roared to life. Hundr warmed his hands upon it and added thicker branches to the blaze until the warmth pulsed through his body.

"Two more days, and we'll reach the king at Avaldsnes," said Bush. "It's been a bastard of a journey."

"It has. But we have seen little trouble, and we are close now."

"You've given up most of your arm rings to keep us fed and watered, though."

"A small price to pay if Harald will give us the men we need." After the fight on the riverbank, there had been no more attempts at robbery as Hundr's company rode south. Hundr had chopped three of his arm rings into pieces and used the shards as hacksilver to pay for food and ale at farms they came to on the road. It had been two long weeks since they had left Vanylven, and until two days ago, there had been farms with barns or stables where Hundr's riders could sleep and stay warm. The timber or wattle walls and thatch protected them from the increasingly colder conditions. Winter was chasing summer away into a forgotten dream of balmy nights and days at sea aboard the Seaworm. It had been two days since they'd last encountered a farm, during which they had camped in the wilderness while descending from the mountain ranges towards the lowlands. Those lowlands would eventually sweep down into the islands off Norway's west coast, where King Harald made his home. Norway was a country at peace. The wars for Harald Fairhair's overlordship had ceased, and Hundr had not encountered bandits or robber gangs in the mountain passes or around any of the fjords during the long ride south.

"This might be my last journey," Bush uttered quietly. He stared into the flames, which leapt and danced up the branches to send a column of smoke into the pale sky.

"I've heard you say that every winter for the last five years. Yet every summer, you steer our ship safely across the Whale Road and fight with the fury and skill of a man half your age."

"Aye, well. Maybe it's caught up with me now. I'm old, Hundr. I don't know how old, exactly, but old. It's been fifteen summers since you joined the Seaworm crew and another ten since I first sailed with Einar the Brawler, back in the days when we served Ivar and the sons of Ragnar."

"So twenty-five summers since you earned your name being shot by an arrow whilst you were shitting behind a Bush?"

Bush scowled at Hundr as he laughed for the hundredth time at Bush's byname. "This is no laughing matter. What is to become of me? I have no wife or children around to care for me. I could live for another ten years and become older and frailer. Just like old Bolti at Vanylven, a veteran of forgotten shield walls from our grandfather's time. Forced to beg for scraps, sucking soup from stale bread through toothless gums. Is that to be my fate? A beggar reliant on the charity of others for food and warmth?"

"That will not be your fate, old friend. As long as I live, you will be honoured and respected."

"No offence, lad. But what if you don't live? You're always charging into battle with your fancy swords and your reputation, Champion of the North, and all that nonsense. When you and Einar are gone, men will forget me. I'll be another Bolti. I won't let that be my end. My destiny lies in Valhalla, where I will remain young forever. I will feast all night and fight all day until Ragnarök. Blink waits for me there, along with the other friends we have lost on the warriors' road."

"What are you saying?"

Bush leant over to him and placed a veiny hand on Hundr's forearm. He stared deep into Hundr's eyes, and his chin quivered as though the words he was about to impart were the most important of his life. "I must die in battle, Hundr. I must go to Valhalla. Don't let me die as an old beggar or whittled to nothing in my bed by this cursed cough. I want to die with honour."

"But not yet. We need your axe to regain Vanylven. Your fate is your fate, Bush. You know that as well as I do. The Norns have already woven your destiny at the foot of Yggdrasil. Their loom already has the warp and weft of your fate spun and determined. The weave will end only when the final thread is cut, and who can say when that will be? So do not throw your life away when people need you, Bush. I need you. Our crews need you."

Bush smiled sadly at those words. He nodded his head and groaned as he stood. His knees clicked, and he stretched his back. "I need to piss again." Bush trudged off towards the trees, and Hundr watched the bow-legged shipmaster, wondering at the weft of his own fate and when his time would come to journey to the afterlife.

A scream tore through the frosty morning, ripping through the chill air like a scythe. Hundr started. His heart stopped as he stood, but he could not move. He knew that voice; it was Sigrid, but the sound was like something from the underworld, terror-stricken and terrible. Thorgrim burst from his tent, clutching his axe and wearing only his tunic. Bush came running back from the trees, lifting his trews, and Hundr stared at his tent, too afraid to move. That sound could only be a harbinger of something awful, a thing Hundr did not want to see or understand. But then Sigrid came from beneath the sailcloth awning. Pain drew her beautiful face long, and her eyes found Hundr. She stumbled forward, open-mouthed, with tears streaming down her cheeks. One of Hundr's boys was in her arms, but something was dreadfully wrong. The little body was limp, and his arms lolled. His head was tilted, eyes closed, and his face was ghostly pale. It was Sigurd.

Hundr ran to Sigrid, taking the boy from her arms, and he flinched at how cold the boy's body was.

"No, Odin, please, no," Hundr whispered. He held Sigurd to him, but there was no breath in the child. Hundr placed Sigurd on the grass and shook him, but there was nothing. He leaned over and placed his cheek against Sigurd's mouth, but no breath came from his tiny throat. The boy was dead. He had simply gone to sleep and never awoken. He was in the hands of the gods now, and Hundr stood, grief-stricken and silent. He took Sigrid in his arms, and she wailed like the world had ended.

Hermoth, please, not you as well.

Hundr left her and dashed to the tent, yet Hermoth was kneeling up in the blanket, rubbing the sleep from his eyes with his pudgy fingers. Hundr's heart lifted, and he ran back to Sigrid, but she pushed him away.

"Why is my child dead? Why has this happened? We should not have brought you, my Sigurd, my beautiful boy. We have killed you." She crouched over Sigurd's body, shaking, and her grief was like a knife in Hundr's chest. His thought cage turned over and over. He should not have brought the child, but worse than that, Hundr felt a wave of guilt and shame wash over him. He had not spent enough time with his sons since their birth; he hardly knew them. Hundr was always away at sea. Even during the winters, he had not played with them or taken them walking in the forests or out in a faering on the fjord. The time Hundr had spent with Sigurd and Hermoth on the road south had been some of his best days with them. They had talked and laughed, and despite the cold and Sigurd's worsening sickness, he had grown closer to them. But now Sigurd was dead, and Hundr had hardly known the boy. They had bought poultices and harsh brews at farms on the journey, yet they hadn't helped Sigurd's bad chest. He had wheezed through the nights, but Hundr and Sigrid had believed it would pass. Sigurd had been sick before, but he had always recovered.

Hundr stumbled away from Sigrid as Ragnhild, Bush, Thorgrim, and Sigvarth comforted her. Hundr returned to the tent and took Hermoth in his arms, holding the boy tightly. For his twin brother was dead, and Hundr had lost a son. He closed his eyes and rocked with Hermoth pressed close to his chest. Rollo was the father of all that suffering and pain. If Rollo had not brought his ships and warriors to Vanylven, then Sigurd would be warm beside a roaring fire now, playing with the dogs and rolling in the floor rushes. Hundr clenched his teeth. Rollo had killed his son, and vengeance burned in Hundr's heart like the forge of the mighty Völund.

They spent that day building a pyre to burn Sigurd's body and send him to the afterlife with honour, where they hoped Freya would welcome him and care for his soul until Sigrid and Hundr could join him. Sigrid was beyond consolation. She clawed at her face and hacked her golden hair short with a knife. She smeared her face with ashes and wailed to the gods, sometimes cursing their cruelty and then begging them to take care of her dead son. Ragnhild wailed with her, for though she had no love for children nor exhibited any maternal instincts at all, Ragnhild and Sigrid were close, and the Valkyrie priestess cried out to Odin, asking for a blessing for Sigurd, for the boy to pass safely into the world of the dead and for him to leave Midgard with honour.

Hundr took Hermoth into the forest and explained that his brother was dead and his soul had travelled beyond Midgard, but he would be safe and cared for. Hermoth wept and bawled for his dead twin, but Hundr hugged the boy and told him not to worry.

Hundr assured him that Sigurd had gone to Hel but not toNástrǫnd, the dark place for oath breakers and adulterers where the halls are woven with the spines of snakes. Sigurd had crossed the river Gjöll and over theGjallarbrú bridge. He was resting and playing with Odin's son Baldr in a golden hall where they would feast and be happy.Hermoth struggled to understand that his brother was gone forever, so Hundr forced back his own tears and all outward signs of sorrow to not frighten the boy.

Hundr walked with his son and vowed to be closer to him from that day onward. He wanted Hermoth to know his father and what kind of man he was. Hundr's own father had been the Prince of Novgorod, and Hundr, his bastard son, had been born to a Norse concubine. Hundr's father had shunned him, and there had been little talk between them and no love at all. The only gift the Prince had bestowed upon his son was the right to train with the royal weapons master, where Hundr had learned sword, axe, spear and shield. Cold nights spent sleeping in shit-stinking stables had honed an ambition in Hundr, a need to prove his father and half-brothers wrong, to show them he was more than a worthless bastard. That desire had led Hundr to leave Novgorod by himself and to travel the hard roads north where, eventually, Einar took him on as a bail boy aboard the warship Seaworm. Hundr wanted so much more than that for Hermoth. He did not want his son to grow with hate and ambition festering in his heart like a destructive serpent. Those feelings were undoubtedly required for a man to fight his way to becoming a champion of the Northmen and a war Jarl. But such things lost their lustre once a man experienced the joy of loving a woman and the soul-altering miracle of having children. Then, Hundr realised that the truly important things in life were contentment, safety, and a hand to hold in the darkness. Though his desire for glory and reputation still burned bright inside him, Hundr understood that his responsibility was to care for his family. Hundr worried he had neglected the twins and wondered if Sigurd would recognise him in the afterlife if Hundr could visit the realm of the dead from Valhalla.

Hundr and Sigrid lay together the night following the funeral pyre. They held each other in a dark, stony silence. There were no words to be said, nothing that could take the pain of Sigurd's death away. Sigrid had carried the twins in her womb for nine long months, and their birth had almost killed her and the children. Part of her had died with little Sigurd, and she would never recover from his loss, nor would Hundr. Hundr just wanted Sigrid to know that he loved her and that they would live on through the grief and suffering. He did not speak to her of the flame of vengeance torturing his mind. It consumed and burned his grief, feeding on it and growing like a malevolent beast in a dark cave. As he held Sigrid and tried to conjure memories of Sigurd laughing and playing, all Hundr could see in his mind's eye was Rollo.

The remaining journey to Avaldsnes was a silent, grief-filled plod across a land that shifted from bleak, rugged, mountainous terrain to more fertile coastal valleys and meadows. Farms appeared again, and then towns as they reached the coast. Folk pointed southeast along the cliffs and fishing villages when they asked where to find King Harald's seat at Avaldsnes. Off the coast, islands appeared as hazed lumps in the distance. Rain came in drizzling, wind-whipped fogs that cleared to reveal skies the colour of old men's hair. The horses fared better on the short grass fields than the scree of the mountains, but Sigrid was silent and brooding. Hundr rode beside her, but she spoke not a word, not even in the evenings when she would sit with Ragnhild. Hundr would ask Sigrid how she was or if she wanted to rest her horse and take some food, but she would stare at him with tear-filled eyes. Her dishevelled hair stuck out from her head in clumps where she had hacked at it in her grief, and she had not washed the ashes of Sigurd's pyre from her face so that her tears had run through her blackened cheeks to leave rivulets of sorrow upon her skin. Hermoth rode with Thorgrim, and the warrior told the boy stories of the gods and of great heroes as they rode towards Avaldsnes. He kept the boy distracted and apart from his mother, who had descended into a pit of brokenhearted grief and despair.

Hundr and his company reached Avaldsnes on a day when the rain had finally ceased, but a stiff wind scoured the coast, and ships hugged the bays around Avaldsnes island and the mainland.

"Harald was ever a man of deep cunning," said Bush as they waited beyond the Avaldsnes palisade and stared down at the boats in the strait. "This strait is the only safe passage for ships along this part of the coast. Even now, as winter comes, and they have dragged ashore most ships to be scoured and caulked, the coast is thick with masts. A man must go through here to trade northwards, and ships must drop anchor and wait here for fair winds and favourable currents."

"So the king is rich?" asked Sigvarth, picking at a spot of rust on his brynjar. Once the company had descended to the lowlands, they had donned their armour and worn their weapons at their belts or across their shoulders so that men would know that they were warriors of status and reputation, making it clear they were not to be trifled with.

"Rich on taxes from merchants, and rich on tribute from poor bastards like us who live under his rule."

"So let's hope he has enough wealth to afford many warriors, for we need an army to return to Vanylven," said Hundr.

A guard opened an oak door within the gate to Avaldsnes, and Hundr led his company inside. They stabled their horses outside the town at a large farm that spread across what remained of the island beyond the king's fortress. Warriors peered down at Hundr from atop the palisade, their eyes darkened by conical-shaped helmets and their faces hidden by the wooden posts sharpened to points. They passed inside the walls into a bustling square where folk hurried at their business, some with baskets of bread, eggs, or rushes. A woman chased a line of chickens away from where six guards stood before Harald's vast hall.

"That is a hall fit for a king," remarked Sigvarth, his mouth turned down appreciatively.

And so it was. The hall was twice as long as Einar's at Vanylven. It sat upon a raised hill, and timber steps led up to a wide platform where two great pillars of painted wood rose, one topped by a snarling bear and the other with a wolf. They were carved from single oak trunks, thicker around than Hundr's body, and etched with intertwining whorls, dragons, axes and war hammers. Braziers burned before each pillar, and the hall stretched high and wide behind them. Its door was open, vast and cavernous, and above it, two long planks curved upwards to meet above the roof, their ends cut into savage dragons painted blue, red, and green that snapped at each other high above the settlement. On the eastern side, the hall was extended by lower, wattle-walled buildings where the king and his family could live away from the main feasting area and living platforms. They had freshly thatched the roof that summer, so it seemed to shine like a carpet of gold.

"Wait here," barked the guard, and he marched up the steps and disappeared into the king's hall. Hundr waited. Sigrid stood behind him with a hood covering her face. Thorgrim, Bush and Sigvarth all wore chainmail brynjars, as did Hundr, and he wore his two swords, Fenristooth scabbarded at his waist and Battle Fang strapped across his back. Hermoth came from behind Sigrid to stand in front of Hundr's legs, and Hundr placed his hands on his son's shoulders. The boy looked at him, and Hundr winked his good eye with a loving glance. Hermoth smiled.

Moments later, a familiar figure came striding from the hall. He wore a fine tunic of blue-dyed wool and a grey, fur-trimmed cloak. He searched the courtyard, and when his eyes settled on Hundr, he smiled broadly and spread his arms wide.

"Rognvald," whispered Bush. "He looks rich."

"Is he a steward?" asked Thorgrim. He leant upon the long haft of his double-bladed war axe and frowned at Rognvald's courtly appearance. Thorgrim was a barrel-chested, broad-shouldered, thick-bearded Viking warrior, whereas Rognvald appeared the opposite. He hopped down the stairs in his tan, calf-length boots, and his face was soft, framed by a thin beard. His blonde hair was long and tied at the nape of his neck with a strip of leather, and he wore an elaborate, thick silver chain. As he drew closer, he seemed even slighter than Hundr remembered, of average height and build and not a man to stand out in a crowd, and even less so amongst warriors.

"He is the Jarl of Rogaland," said Ragnhild, "cousin and closest advisor to King Harald. And do not mistake his appearance, for he is as fearsome a fighter as I have seen. He is an ulfheðnar and changes into a feral wolf warrior when he goes into battle."

Thorgrim raised an eyebrow and then straightened as Rognvald approached.

"Well met, Jarl Hundr," beamed Rognvald, and he reached to take Hundr's wrist in the warrior's grip. "The famous Man with the Dog's Name. Welcome to Avaldsnes."

"Jarl Rognvald," Hundr said, and he clasped Rognvald's wrist, which was bare of warrior rings. "I have come to speak with King Harald."

"Just so. Follow me." Rognvald inclined his head towards Ragnhild, and she returned the gesture of recognition.

Rognvald led them up the stairs towards the great hall and through its enormous doors. Guards in heavy helmets and green cloaks stood inside the doorway, and they banged iron-shod spear butts onto the paved flooring so that the sound echoed around the great hall like a bell. The inside of the hall was lit by braziers on each roof post, and rush lights hung from the ceiling in iron cages. A great fire burned at the centre, and the smoke escaped through a hole in the thatch so high above Hundr that he could barely see the rafters. Silver birch planking framed the hall's inside so that it shimmered and shone in the firelight, and folk gathered about the hall's edges, where feasting benches had been pushed to the sides, close to the raised platforms where Harald's warriors would sleep. They had scattered fresh rushed across the paved floor, and there were none of the usual smells of old leather, men's sweat, or the stench of horses.

Harald's hall smelled like spring, and Hundr wondered how many servants it took to keep it so.

"You have been well?" asked Rognvald as they strolled through the hall.

"Well enough," Hundr replied, masking the sorrow in his voice and resisting the urge to glance back at Sigrid. "And you?"

"We are preparing for winter, and the stores are heavy with wheat and barley. But there is trouble in the south. This must be your son?" Rognvald reached down and ruffled Hermoth's hair, and the boy rewarded him with a steely glare. Rognvald chuckled. "He has your eyes – or eye," he nodded warmly.

"Yes, this is my son, Hermoth," said Hundr. "Son, this is Jarl Rognvald of Rogaland."

Hermoth bowed his head as Sigrid had taught him. They approached a raised platform on which a vast, intricately carved wooden throne sat beyond a dais strewn with furs. Behind the throne, a row of ten shields hung, some of which Hundr recognised as shields of enemies he had fought alongside Harald during the now legendary battle of Hafrsfjord. Beneath the shields, a long sword rested on a plinth, its blade gleaming, and a banner emblazoned with Harald's wolf sigil hung from its hilt. Hundr recognised the sword also. It was the Yngling blade, a sword forged in ancient times, which Harald had recovered from a *draugr* in a deep howe. That blade had once been stolen, and Hundr had recovered it for King Harald back when he and Einar had won

Vanylven. A man entered from a side door. He marched briskly to the throne, nestled himself within its vastness, and peered along the line of Hundr's warriors before his bright eyes came to rest on Hundr himself.

"Welcome, Jarl Hundr," said King Harald Fairhair. His chestnut brown beard was longer than Hundr remembered and dusted now with silver where once it had been lustrous and thick. He had a long, handsome face and had grown his hair out again so that its thick braid rested on his shoulder. Harald wore a tunic of rich silk beneath a shimmering iron grey fur cloak, and a gold circlet rested upon his weathered brow. Harald had sworn not to cut his hair until he was the king of all Norway, and Hundr had watched Rognvald cut it short after their glorious victory at Hafrsfjord.

"Lord King," Hundr smiled. He clasped a fist to his chest and bowed his head. "You have prospered since last we met, and I am pleased to see you looking so well."

"Your reputation has grown since we last met. You will soon rival Ragnar Lothbrok himself! How long has it been since we fought together shoulder to shoulder? It must be six summers. I have heard tales of your exploits, old friend. The skalds sing of your adventures at hearths across the country, of how you quested for Odin's spear in Novgorod and how you killed another son of Ragnar in Ireland."

"The stories grow more fanciful in the telling, Lord King."

"Then we must hear your version of the legends, and I will have my skald commit them to memory so they can be remembered and retold down the ages."

"Jarl Hundr has brought his son to meet you," Rognvald interjected, and he gestured to Hermoth, who shuffled backwards so that his back was tight to Hundr's legs.

"This is Hermoth," said Hundr.

"It is right to have children, Jarl Hundr, for they are life's joy." Harald leaned forward on his throne and smiled at Hermoth. "I am certain that you will one day become as famous a warrior as your father, boy. When you do, come and see me. There will always be a need for champions at Avaldsnes," Harald intoned, and he fixed Hermoth with a stern gaze.

"Lord King, I have come to you with dire news and a humble request." The King ran his teeth over the beard beneath his bottom lip and nestled back into his throne as Hundr spoke. "Our old enemy, Rollo the Betrayer, has taken Vanylven with an army of Franks, and we seek to reclaim it."

Harald sighed, got up from his throne, and stepped forward with his hands on his hips. "Is Jarl Einar dead?"

"No, Lord King. He stayed behind to harry Rollo whilst I came to you in search of an army."

"An enemy army has taken a foothold in my lands, only a short summer sailing from my home here at Avaldsnes. Einar lost his lands, which he holds in my name, and now he wants me to win it back for him?"

"Rollo came with overwhelming numbers and surprised Einar. He has always been your enemy, my lord. Rollo has not forgiven you nor me for the war we fought against him and his allies. A strike against Vanylven is a blow against you, King Harald, and we cannot leave it unavenged."

"So it is. But what use is a jarl who can't hold on to his own lands?"

Hundr bridled at the scathing comment. He cast a pointed glance at the Yngling blade, making sure that Harald noticed, and then he stared around at the magnificent hall.

"I come to you asking for help, Lord King," said Hundr, and he spoke harshly. "Did I not recover the blade of your ancestors that hangs above you so proudly? Did Einar and I not fight for you at Hafrsfjord, where many men died to secure your reign? Was that famous battle not where Rollo became my enemy? All I ask is that you grant me men to throw the Betrayer out of Vanylven, a fjord in your kingdom. Not only can we put paid to an old enemy, but you'll secure your lands from any further attack. Rollo betrayed Kjotve the Rich at Hafrsfjord, and we saw him do it together. He was allowed to leave that place with ships and his life; he has been a thorn in your side ever since. Did he not send the

Burned Man to kill you? Was it not I who killed the Burned Man and removed that threat forever?"

"All you have spoken is just so, Jarl Hundr. No man here disputes your valour or your deeds. But I cannot simply send an army north. I must keep my warriors here and keep them close, for there is trouble in the south, and my son is caught up in it."

"What trouble?"

"Vikings who fled the great battle of Ethandun in Saxon England are in Saxony, close to the home of the Danes. They have pillaged those lands, and there is a great war there. My son, Erik, is fostered by an old friend of mine, Jarl Ravn Kjartansson. Ravn went to fight alongside the Vikings so recently defeated in England. Rognvald assures me that King Louis of the eastern Franks raises a vast army in Saxony to throw out our Viking brothers and that there is a significant risk that Ravn will perish and my beloved son with him."

"I fought at Ethandun, my lord; it was a terrible shield wall battle. I am truly sorry to hear that your son is in peril. But I need men now, and we can see Rollo dead before midwinter. No army marches in winter, so we can take Rollo by surprise now before he settles in. We can sail north before the weather worsens, and you will have your warriors back to march on Saxony in spring."

"You don't understand. Louis marches on Ravn and the survivors of Ethandun as we speak. He does not wait for spring marching weather. My son is in grave danger; he is heir to the throne of Norway, and I must protect him. I will give you men, Hundr, but first, you must march south and return my son to me. Rognvald will go with you, as will Bavlos the Sami. Then you can take my army north and crush Rollo the Betrayer."

Hundr's shoulders sagged, and he sighed, for there was no other way. He could not take back Vanylven and have his vengeance upon Rollo without King Harald's army.

"Who leads the Vikings in Saxony?" Hundr asked.

"Haesten, the famous warlord."

"I know Haesten." And that statement held true. He was an old friend – renowned for his exploits in England, Frankia, and south to far Ispania and the lands of the Musselmen.

"Good, so you will do this thing for me? You will save my son Erik?"

"I will, Lord King… if you will grant me your army to sail north the moment your son sets foot in this hall."

"It shall be so," said Harald, and then he leant forward and pointed a ringed finger at Hermoth and his eyes glittered. "And your son will stay here with me as a foster son. He will be safe, and I will care for him and raise him as though he were my own."

Hundr bowed his head and swallowed the lump in his throat. Boys often went to live with other families as foster sons to strengthen ties between families, and it was indeed a great honour for Hermoth to live with the King. He would learn the arts of combat, hunting, and the ways of being a nobleman. But Hundr's fingers gripped Hermoth's shoulders tight, for he could not bear to be away from the boy so soon after Sigurd's tragic death. Hundr could feel Sigrid tense up behind him. She pulsed with sorrow and anguish. But to exact his vengeance, Hundr would have to leave his only son in the care of the King and embark on a perilous mission to rescue a Prince from the midst of a raging war.

NINE

The axe haft chopped into the pine log and sent a judder up Einar's arm. He paused, wiping sweat from his brow, and then grabbed the wood axe again. He yanked it free of the timber and struck thrice more until the log creaked and split in two. His shoulders burned, and he was out of breath, but Einar grinned as the log came apart. Another man lifted the axe away to sharpen it to a point and sink it into the ground while a fresh log crashed to the earth at Einar's feet. He looked up to see Amundr staring at him. The big man had another huge log balanced over his left shoulder. His eyes flicked from the wood at Einar's feet and then back to Einar himself, silently questioning why the log had not yet been cut.

"Can you bring them any faster?" said Einar.

"You can have this one as well if you like?" Amundr replied, the sarcasm flying as far over him as a soaring eagle.

Einar shook his head. "Take it over there," he jerked his thumb to where another warrior was also working at splitting logs for the new walls.

"You should rest." Amundr waited for a response. Einar was stripped to the waist, his body dripping with sweat despite the chill morning air. His face was bright red, and he was as out of breath as the winner of last summer's fjord swimming race. Amundr noticed Einar's look of exasperation and stalked off to throw the log at the feet of the next man.

Einar sat on the log and reached for the crock of goat's milk he'd been drinking to break his morning fast. He had ordered the Vanylven fugitives to build a wall around their camp, and the work had begun three days ago. The ring was already half completed, with fifty men cutting trees, splitting logs, and sharpening their tops to points. They trimmed each log to the height of a man and sunk them deep into the earth. It was no stout palisade, but it was better than nothing if Einar had to defend the camp against Rollo's army.

The sound of chopping wood rang around the treetops, and Einar took a long drink of milk. He rose and took up his axe again, but his attention was drawn away by cheerful laughter in the distance. A gang of children played amongst the workers, running and hooting for joy as one tagged another, and they sped off, darting between upright posts. A woman scolded them as they knocked a basket of washing out of her hand. She had been down to the river to wash dirty clothes, and the lot had tumbled into a pile of sawdust.

"You haven't been this slim since you were a prisoner in Ireland," said Hildr. She threw a wool jerkin to Einar and smiled. Einar patted his ever-shrinking belly and flexed his shoulders.

"But they tortured me and fed me rotten gruel. Now I feel as strong as a horse."

"It's been two days since Rollo's men last came from Vanylven. They will probably come again today or tomorrow."

"We have scouts watching the gates; do not worry. And now we have enough forest traps and surprises set to catch a woodland full of game. So the next time they come out, they'll find more than arrows and axes waiting for them."

"Those cursed berserkers killed five of our men in the last skirmish. We can't keep losing men. At this rate, there'll be no warriors left by the time Hundr returns."

"I hate berserkers. Bastards need foul potions to get their courage up."

"Nevertheless, we need to stop them. Quickly. And we only have enough grain to last the week."

Einar cursed and spat. "So we need to pay Jarl Ugattr an extortionate amount of silver for more?"

"Silver we don't have. We can probably scrimp together enough from the arm rings and other trinkets people wore or brought out of Vanylven, but then we have nothing. And even if we buy more from him, he surely doesn't have enough surplus in his stores to feed us through winter."

"We only need enough food to last us until Hundr returns with the army."

"What if he doesn't return?"

"He will."

"Maybe you should go to Ugattr this time and ask him for more than grain. Talk to him, jarl to jarl. You are both oath-sworn to King Harald. If you can be friendly with him, perhaps Ugattr can send us his warriors?"

"Me? Go to beg from that crusty old bag of pig shit? I'd rather eat muck nuts from a sheep's arse."

"You might have to if we don't get more grain."

Einar frowned and pulled on his tunic. "Is there not enough fish in the river or game in the forest? Have we been to every farm on the outskirts of Vanylven and taken their surplus?"

"No, there is not, and yes, we have. Winter is upon us, and even now, we are lucky to catch a dozen fish each day. We would need every hunter to catch something every morning to keep the camp fed. Swallow your pride and go to Ugattr. I'll come with you."

"I'm not going, and that's final. I'd rather starve."

"Really? What about the children? Would you rather have them starve and die in their beds than humble yourself and go to Jarl Ugattr?"

Einar set his jaw, and Hildr blew out her cheeks. "You are impossible." She turned and stormed off, but after five paces, she looked back and wagged a finger at him. "You are our jarl, our leader. Think on that, Einar. Sometimes, your duty must outweigh your pride."

Einar let her go, knowing that she was right. He could have gone after Hildr and told her so, but stubbornness often prevails over good sense in the heat of an argument between husband and wife. Life was simpler back in the days when he was a ship's captain. But even then, he had felt the weight of responsibility upon his shoulders. He had led sixty men and was responsible for their survival, keeping the ship safe and afloat and filling their purses with silver. Einar listened to the sounds of axes chopping and the breeze in the pine boughs, and he remembered sailing across wild seas in the service of Ivar the Boneless. Einar recalled the sea water lashing his face and stinging his eyes, and he remembered the feel of the tiller in his hand, fighting him with all the strength of Njorth as he led his men to distant shores. They were indeed simpler times, but not necessarily happier times. Although Einar was now responsible for the survival of hundreds of lives, and the weight of that pressure was like a boulder upon his back, he had his beloved Hildr and the respect of his people and his warriors.

Suddenly, as if it were sent to Einar from the gods, an idea came to him. It peeked into his thought cage like the edges of a red sun at daybreak and blossomed, warming him with its daring. Maybe his memories of Ivar had stirred the great champion from his mead bench in Valhalla, and the Boneless had sent him a plan worthy of a son of Ragnar. Einar grinned because perhaps there was a way to get food for his people and strike at the Betrayer, who sat like a lord in Einar's hall.

"Are you sure we shouldn't tell Hildr about this?" Amundr asked later that night. The big man sat with his back against a tree trunk next to Einar. He scratched at his beard and pulled at the neckline of his brynjar as though he had to let some heat out of his chest.

"What are you worried about?" said Einar, punching Amundr on the shoulder. "Who is jarl, me or Hildr?"

"You are, but won't she be angry?"

"Never mind if she might be angry or not. I am the leader here, remember? Your oath is to me, not my wife. We've come to get food and kill some of the enemy. They are both good things. When we return with grain and food for the camp, Hildr and the rest of the women will rejoice, and we shall be heroes. So, listen to old Einar and let's steal back some of our own food."

Amundr curled the side of his mouth and stared at Einar through the side of his eyes. Einar tutted, adjusted the coiled rope around his chest and shoulders, and scrambled through the undergrowth to join Torsten at the next tree along. Yellow eyes blinked at him from deep in the undergrowth and disappeared into the darkness. An owl sang its song, distant but haunting, as though a fetch stalked the woodland at nighttime. It was the time of the huldufólk, the hidden people of the night who lived in the darkness, in hollows and crags.

"I don't like being out here at night," muttered Torsten. His usually fierce face was pale, and he licked his lips as he clutched the haft of his axe.

"Thor's balls," sighed Einar. "Not you as well. We are going to attack soon. Pull yourself together. You are supposed to be one of the hard men. What are you frightened of?"

"I'm not frightened." Torsten set his jaw, but his eyes flickered towards the darkness. "The huldufólk live up in the mountains. They will have seen our camp. They might be maddened that we have come into their domain. There could be trolls out there, watching us, waiting to grab us when our backs are turned and eat our heads."

Einar ran a hand down his face. "I'll eat your head if you don't stop this nonsense. The men are listening. That bloody galdr-woman has everybody's heads filled with nonsense. The hidden folk live on the mountain tops, in the places we don't go. And why would a troll come down from the hills so close to Vanylven on this night?"

Everybody knew that elves and thehuldufólk lived in the night. Folk would leave gifts out for them after dark, a bowl of milk or some food, hoping the night creatures would bless them with good fortune. But since Einar's people had made their camp in the forest, those beliefs had grown in importance, fuelled by the galdr-woman and her stories and songs of the gods, spirits and seiðr. The closeness to the trees, glades, boulders, rocks, brooks, holes, bogs, crags, and animals had heightened people's sense of the old world and the magical beings who lived so close yet hidden from sight.

"I'm just saying, that's all." Leaves rustled in the dim light, and Torsten suddenly inhaled sharply, only to relax as Trygve emerged, scampering from behind a bush clutching his bow.

"They had two sentries on the forest side of the gate," said Trygve. "I've killed them both. But there are two men patrolling the fighting platform behind the palisade, and I don't think we can get over the wall without being seen."

"We'll get over. We have to," Einar uttered. He had brought twenty men across the hills after sundown, and Einar would lead them over the walls into Vanylven and steal back as much of the stored grain and food as he could. He knew he could get into the town. Einar had scaled palisade walls before, and now he had the cloak of darkness to cover his attack. The bigger problem was how to carry the food back to camp. They had horses, but three of the older mares had been killed and eaten, and Hundr had taken more on his journey to King Harald. However, Einar needed stealth, so he'd led his men through the forest on foot. They had no wagon, so they'd have to steal baskets inside the walls or find another way to transport the stolen grain and meat back to camp.

"What about once we are inside Vanylven?" asked Torsten.

"Rollo won't expect us to attack. He knows we are in the mountains somewhere because we have killed his men on the half dozen occasions they have sallied out to find us. But Rollo believes we are weak and broken. He has the numbers, and his men are well fed and provisioned by the stores our people have worked so hard to farm and gather throughout the summer. So, his warriors will be asleep in their beds now, and the granary is only twenty paces from the landward gate. We get in, kill the wall guards and any other bastard who gets in our way, and then get out with the food. We do it nice and quiet, and the first thing Rollo will know of it is when he drags his arse out of his scratch pit in the morning and finds his guards dead and his food stolen."

"The men are ready, Lord Einar," said Torsten, his expression resolute as he mastered his fear of the forest creatures.

"Then let's go." Einar led them through the bracken and ferns. He drew his axe and wore his fish scale brynjar beneath a dark cloak, and he pulled its hood over his head as they silently approached Vanylven's walls. All twenty warriors were armed with axes and spears, and four were equipped with bows and quivers of goose-feathered arrows. The forest floor was damp from the frequent rains, concealing the worst of their footfalls in squashed leaf mulch. Einar arrived at the edge of the forest canopy, and an iron brazier burned beyond the east side of the palisade, ten paces along from the forest gate. Its orange glow lit that side of the wall, and two men talked beside its warmth, yet they should have patrolled the length of the wall, which extended east and north until it met the sheer stone cliffs that descended sharply into the fjord water.

"To the west," Einar whispered, waving to his men to follow as he hurried through the forest's edge, uncoiling the sealskin rope from around his shoulders as he went. They had bought the old rigging rope from a farmer south of the camp when Einar had scoured the nearby countryside for surplus food. The man had no grain or meat to spare, but he had provided the rope and sent one of his sons to join Einar's warriors. Einar paused again and waited for ten heartbeats in case the guards had detected their presence. There was no sound save for his men's breathing and the forest's murmur and rustle. Einar ran from the forest towards the wall, stopping with his back against the high staves ten paces from the gate itself. His men followed, dashing like cloaked wraiths from the woods and through the darkness to line up beside him against the wall.

Einar unslung the rope from his shoulders and held out his hand to Trygve, who handed him an axe. During the march over the hill and down the wooded mountainside, Einar had asked his men to check the axes and find the one with the heaviest blade. Each man carried a Viking bearded axe, curved and forged to be as light as possible to make it fast and deadly. But Einar needed a weightier weapon for this night's work. The heaviest was a finely wrought blade, inlaid with runes, and its haft was a hand's length longer than usual. Einar nodded in thanks to Trygve and tied one end of his rope around the weapon's haft. He took two paces from the wall and swung the axe around in increasingly larger loops, letting out the rope as he did so. The blade sang as it flew in wide circles, and Einar swung it faster and faster until it whirred like an arrow on the wing. He carefully gauged the throw and released the axe. It flew up into the darkness, clattered against the wall, and fell back. The weapon landed at Einar's feet, and he had to step back to avoid the blade chopping his toes off.

The warriors against the wall hunched their shoulders and bared their teeth. In the still of the night, the sound of the blade hitting the palisade was as loud as thunder, and they waited for a guard to shout and race along the wall, but nobody came. Einar tried again, swinging the axe by the rope, picking up speed and tossing it higher and harder this time. It soared over the parapet and clattered on the fighting platform beyond. Einar yanked on the rope, and the axe dragged across the wood but found no bite and came hurtling back towards him again.

Einar cursed to himself. He ignored the stares of his warriors as they silently pleaded with him to make the throw work, fearing that if the guards heard them, Rollo's army would come charging out of the gate to slaughter them. He picked up the axe and swung it again, wondering if his plan had been a mistake. Einar thought of Hildr and Jarl Ugattr, and he quietly whispered a prayer to Odin to make his next throw lucky. The axe flew upwards, soaring over the walls and landed on the fighting platform again. Einar yanked the rope savagely. The axe careened backwards, and its blade bit into the timber behind the wall. Einar tugged it, and the axe held.

Lefsi, the shortest and lightest amongst Einar's warband, ran to Einar and took the rope. Einar clapped him on the back, and Lefsi hauled himself up. His spindly legs dangled as he went hand over hand at first, and then, with boots flat against the wall timbers, Lefsi walked himself up to the summit. Once at the top, Lefsi looped the rope around a wall post until it was sturdy, and then Einar pulled himself up. He hauled and walked up the wall, just as Lefsi had done, but after two pulls, his shoulders burned, and his breath became ragged.

I'm too old for this.

Einar's hands sweated, and he grimaced. He peered upwards and let out a sigh of relief as Lefsi reached down with an open palm and helped Einar scramble over the wall.

Einar slumped down and sucked in the crisp night air, cool and refreshing in his chest. The rest of his warband made the climb, and two men had to reach over and help Amundr heave his bulk over the summit. The last man to climb was almost at the top when his hands slipped on the rope and he fell, screaming to the ground. Einar feared that the sound would be heard as far away as Frankia, and he waved to his men to keep low. They waited, yet almost immediately, boots thumped along the fighting platform, striding towards them. Einar dragged the rope from the walls before it was seen and pulled his cloak close around him.

The guard shouted something in Frankish that Einar didn't understand, and then his face came out of the darkness, ten paces along the platform and with a spear held out before him. Einar surged to his feet and swung the rope around just as he had on the ground below. The axe whirred, and Einar released it. The weapon flew through the night and thudded into the guard's chest. Aghast, he stared at the blade in utter surprise, pain not yet registering in his mind. Einar yanked on the rope with all of his strength, and it pulled the guard off his feet. The axe ripped free of his chest, splashing blood and torn flesh on the fighting platform. Although he was getting on, Einar still had the ferocity and anger of his youth, and the fatigue fell from him instantly. Trygve pushed past Einar, moving low like a cat, and he loosed an arrow into the darkness. There was another thud as the arrow struck the second guard. The man groaned ahead where the brazier burned, and Trygve dashed towards the firelight, returning moments later with a bloody knife in his hand.

The warband ran down the wooden stairs which led from the platform into the town, and their boots dashed across the familiar ground inside Vanylven. Einar led them towards the granary – compact barns elevated on wooden supports to ward off pests. Einar formed his men up in a half circle around the structures and sent Torsten and five men to find something in which to carry the precious grain.

Torsten came running with two handcarts. Einar had seen the people of Vanylven use them to carry pottery, clothing, and such on market days. They wouldn't hold much, so Einar waved him off to find more as Trygve took two men to fill the handcarts with grain. It was deep in the night, and above Vanylven, the stars were bright in a clear, cold sky. Einar's breath steamed, mixing with that of his men, and they waited with weapons drawn for any sign of Rollo's warriors. A cat meowed in a distant lane, and Einar thought he could hear a woman's sobs to the north. That hurt him because Rollo had brought no women from Frankia, only warriors. So, any women within Vanylven were the slaves and playthings of Rollo's men, yet they had once been wives, daughters, and mothers under Einar's protection.

Einar fought against the urge to charge into the town, to run to his hall where Rollo slept and butcher the betraying bastard in his sleep. He had fought Rollo before and should have killed him when he had the chance. Torsten returned, this time with baskets and more rope. Einar nodded. They could lash the baskets to the handcarts or their own backs as they made the arduous journey up the hillside and into the next valley back to camp. They filled the carts and

131

baskets as quickly as possible. There was wheat and barley, and Torsten had come across dried fish and smoked pork in his search, and they crammed as much as possible into the baskets. Einar led them back towards the gate, and his heart soared because all he had to do was lift the crutch and remove the crossbeam that held the gate closed, and they would be away before any of Rollo's guards were aware.

At that moment, a man coughed in the distance, and just as Einar wrapped his hands around the heavy beam, a figure emerged from the darkness. He held a spear clumsily in the crook of one arm and rubbed sleep from his eyes with the other. Then, following closely, another man appeared behind him.

"Frigg's tits," Torsten muttered, "they're changing the watch."

Einar ignored the guards, and he and Amundr hefted the beam free, tossing it away from the gate. Einar would have wanted to scout the walls for a night and determine how often Rollo's men changed guard. But there had been no time for that, and he winced as the guards shouted. They pointed at Einar and his warband and shouted the alarm in their Frankish tongue.

Trygve dropped them both with swift arrows, one hitting the first guard in the gut and another tearing through the throat of the second. Einar's men paused and stared at the injured guards, then at each other with mouths agape.

"Go," said Einar. "I'll hold them here." He had opened one half of the gate, and that half was only wide enough for three men to walk abreast, and Einar knew he could defend that space against the foe for long enough for his men to escape into the woods. "Take the food and go."

"The enemy has not yet come. We can all get away," insisted Torsten.

Einar's eyes searched the town, but nobody had yet heeded the guard's call, so Einar nodded and helped them push the carts towards the treeline. They half ran, half stumbled towards the dark, shadowed trees, and then metal clanged in the town behind them. Someone beat a hammer on iron to raise the alarm, and Einar peered over his shoulder to see four men come running from the town bare-chested and groggy from their beds. They came with spears and their shields, and Einar charged at them. He ran without thinking, desperate to strike at the men who had driven his people from their homes. The woman's anguish in the town had done it, and the thought of her suffering at the hands of a yellow-toothed Frank set Einar's fury aflame.

Einar drew his axe from its belt loop, and he struck the first Frank so hard that his axe ploughed through the man's spear parry, ripping through black beard and jaw bone to drive the man to the ground. Amundr came roaring behind him, and he tore one man's face half off with his axe before picking up a second and tossing him back towards the gate. Lefsi charged headlong into the fourth Frank's shield, and they

133

exchanged blows, weapons fiercely clanging together before Amundr dragged the Frank away to slam his axe twice into the enemy's chest.

A figure appeared in the gate, hugely muscled at the shoulders and with an impossibly thick neck. It was Kveldulf, the berserker, and his eyes glittered like those of a wolf in the moonlight. Einar swiftly picked up the shield of a fallen warrior and charged at the gate.

"Bring their fallen warriors!" Einar shouted to Amundr, "Block the gate with their corpses! Trygve, ready your bow to pin them back." Einar charged, and he saw a chance for escape. If they could create a grizzly barricade with the fallen, and if Trygve loosed arrows at any who tried to clamber over the dead, they might keep the enemy at bay for long enough to flee into the forest.

Kveldulf had one foot out of the gate when Einar smashed into him, shield first. The berserker tumbled backwards under the weight of the blow, and Amundr came grunting behind Einar, dragging two dead Franks, which he tossed into the gap. Lefsi came dragging another, and more Franks appeared in the gateway. They jabbed and thrusted with spear points, and Einar held them back with his shield. Amundr shoved at the corpses, dodging around the deadly enemy blades until he had made a corpse fence as high as Einar's waist. It was a grim thing of dangling arms and legs, of blood and lifeless faces, and the Franks shrank back from the horror of it. Lefsi shouted at Einar to move as he dragged the last Frank corpse to toss onto the pile.

As Einar moved aside, his shoulder throbbing from the force of enemy spears hammering into his shield, a mighty howl erupted from inside the gate, and the spears suddenly disappeared. In their place was Kveldulf's snarling face. His head was huge and frightening atop his impossibly broad neck, and before Einar could leap forward, Kveldulf grabbed Lefsi and pulled the little man close. He crashed his slab-like forehead into Lefsi's face and swung his axe to drive Einar and Amundr backwards. The first of Trygve's arrows flew, and one whipped past Kveldulf's face to disappear into the town beyond.

"Lefsi!" Einar called, and Kveldulf grinned at him.

"We must go, lord," Amundr said, grabbing Einar's shoulder. "Lefsi is done for."

More arrows whistled through the darkness, and Kveldulf turned Lefsi around to use his body as a shield. An arrow thumped into Lefsi's chest, and Kveldulf laughed maniacally. Lefsi stared at Einar, his face bloody and his nose mashed to a pulp. His eyes were empty, and there was no anger there. He was small in stature but mighty in heart, and Lefsi knew that his sacrifice would help Einar get enough provisions back to camp to feed the people there for weeks. Einar roared in anger and followed Amundr, scrambling away from the gate.

"Einar the Brawler!" Kveldulf yelled, and Einar glanced over his shoulder just as the berserker hacked his axe into Lefsi's neck. "Run like the whipped dog you are. I'm coming for you, Einar. Your wife will be my whore, and I will piss in your dead throat."

They were just words and slipped across Einar like water across a swan's back, but Lefsi had died, and that tore at Einar's conscience like an axe blade. It had been his plan, his raid, and now Lefsi was dead. Trygve loosed arrow after arrow into the gate, and Kveldulf could not follow. Soon, Einar reached the tree line. He and Amundr helped with the carts and baskets, and they crashed into the undergrowth, fleeing their enemies in the darkness.

"Do they follow?" Einar gasped as Trygve came alongside them and helped Einar heave a cart forward through the bracken.

"Not yet, but they will," said Trygve. "These cursed carts will leave a trail even a child could follow. We will lead them straight to camp."

"Then we must be ready for them."

TEN

King Harald's fleet left Avaldsnes two days after Hundr arrived at the island fortress. Hundr and his company sailed on Rognvald's ship. It was an enormous warship named The Reaver, with room enough for ninety men. Harald had waved them off from the shore with his arm around Hermoth, both him and the boy draped in thick furs. Hundr had waved to his son with a lump in his throat. Harald was a man of his word, and Hundr knew he would indeed treat the boy as if he were his own son. But to part from the lad so soon after the death of Sigurd was a knife to Hundr's heart. Sigrid's desolate weeping heightened the pain. She stood by the prow and stared at Hermoth, tears streaming down her face. Sigrid had not spoken to Hundr since the morning of Sigurd's death. Worse than that, she no longer let Hundr hold her, so neither of them had that warm comfort in which to share their grief. Hundr saw blame in her cold, tear-wet eyes, and though she did not say it, he knew she blamed him for her separation from Hermoth.

Hundr had asked Sigrid to stay with Harald so that she could be close to Hermoth, but she had refused with a vehement shake of her head. There had been blame and sadness in her red-ringed eyes, and on the journey from Avaldsnes south to the Danish coast, Sigrid had remained alone and disconsolate. So uncomfortable was it to be close to such overwhelming sadness even Ragnhild left her alone. Sigrid would stand in the bows, staring out at the heaving waves, and Rognvald's men avoided her, fearing the bad luck of her tortured spirit. On the nights when the fleet anchored in secluded bays, or when the men ventured ashore to find fresh water, she would remain alone on board the ship. Rognvald did not ask Hundr what was wrong with her, and he had likely heard the tale from Bush, Thorgrim, or Sigvarth. The weight of Sigurd's death was like a millstone around Hundr's neck, and Sigrid's mourning tore at him like an eagle's claws, yet the worst of it all was the helplessness, because there seemed little he could do to console his wife, or even share their grief and mourn together.

Rognvald led six warships south, and on the third day, as they reached the northeast coast of Denmark, Rognvald called his leaders together to meet aboard his ship. Bavlos was there, and the little Sami shaman showed no recognition of Hundr or Bush despite having sailed together before the battle of Hafrsfjord. Bavlos wore a thick cloak woven from the furs of different beasts so that its colours shifted and flowed as he hirpled along the deck. The cloak stank and teemed with lice, and the little, dark-faced man cast a handful of bones etched with runes of power and told Rognvald what the Norns had in store for the quest.

One of Rognvald's captains was a big man with flame-red hair named Hrolfr the Mouse, which was ironic as the man laughed and roared with the warriors and was the loudest man Hundr had ever met. There was also Svart the Screamer and Hooknose Ymir. Each led a long hundred warriors, and while Hooknose's curved, beak-like nose was a sure indicator of how he had earned his byname, the origin of Svart's remained a mystery.

Rognvald, Hundr, Svart, Ymir, and Hrolfr sat on opposite rowing benches, facing towards each other as the ship bobbed on the swell and the men took a meal on the aft deck. Bavlos huddled next to Rognvald, shaking a handful of yellowed bones, staring at the sky through his small, flint-like eyes, with only his toe-curled boots poking through the mass of his fur cloak.

"A few more days, and we will be at the mouth of the River Elbe," said Rognvald. He had a handful of small flatbreads and handed one to each of them. "We have enough food and water to get us there, but we will need to find supplies and horses once we make landfall."

"Where shall we find Jarl Ravn?" asked Hrolfr, his voice loud even though the men sat only an arm's length from one another.

"There is an army of Vikings in the lands around Hammaburg. They shouldn't be hard to find."

"Do we know if this King Louis has reached Saxony yet?" asked Hooknose Ymir through a mouthful of bread.

"The last we heard," said Rognvald, "was from a merchant ship that had sailed up the Elbe this summer. They were in the river two weeks ago and said that King Louis had not arrived, but rumours of his advance were the talk of every town on the riverbank. So, he must be close and could even have reached Saxony by now."

"And Louis is King of the East Franks?" asked Hrolfr.

"Just so, and King of Bavaria. He is a powerful man. Haesten's fleet is in the Elbe, so it should provide a secure place to leave our fleet while we march inland. The Vikings have not taken any towns in Saxony, and they advance upon Hammaburg, which would be a great prize. Ravn is with Haesten, and we should have news of their location when we meet the men who guard Haesten's ships."

"Are we going to join their fight?" asked Svart. He was a tall, languid man with long arms and legs, a thin face and a drooping moustache. "There'll be rich pickings in Hammaburg. Christ priests, gold plates, silver, and women."

"Not if we can help it. We are here to find Jarl Ravn and sail home with Prince Erik."

"But if the fighting is already underway?"

"Then we will fight to protect Prince Erik."

"And what of Jarl Haesten?" asked Ymir. "We have all heard of his reputation, but he is our ally. Are we to fight beside him if the Franks attack?"

"Jarl Hundr is friends with Haesten. What can you tell us about him?" asked Rognvald.

Hundr swallowed the last of his bread and cleared his throat. "Haesten is a Viking from the generation of Ragnar Lothbrok. He is old now, for he was not young when I fought alongside him and Bjorn Ironside in Frankia many years ago."

"You fought beside Bjorn Ironside?" asked Ymir, his mouth gaping.

"I did. We led a charge together and killed a great Frankish duke."

"What kind of man is he?"

"Odin's balls, but we aren't here to listen to fireside tales of Bjorn Ironside," said Hrolfr the Mouse. He blew out a gust of air and slapped his knee. "I'm sure Hundr has many fine stories to tell, but all we want to know for now is about Haesten." Hrolfr's brows knitted, and his face flushed as red as his beard. He seemed to like the sound of his own voice and was frustrated that he was not at the heart of the conversation. Hundr had met such men before – men who desire, above all things, to have all eyes focused on them, to be at the centre of all talk, scandal and praise. They were men to be wary of, for if there was no trouble for them to wallow in, they would craft trouble of their own.

"Haesten is cunning and fierce. He was at the famous siege of Paris and had sailed and lost a fleet of ninety warships around the far south coast of Ispania, where the sun burns men's skins black. He held a fortress in Frankia for many years and was one leader of the Great Viking Army in England, which nearly destroyed King Alfred and his kingdom of Wessex. And he is my friend." Hundr could have said more about Haesten, for he was a man Hundr respected. Hundr had first met the old jarl back when Ivar the Boneless pursued him in Frankia, baying for Hundr's blood after Hundr had killed his son. Hakon Ivarsson had taken Hundr's eye and died for that during a rain-soaked battle in a Northumbrian fortress. Hundr admired Haesten, for he had lived the life all Vikings aspire to. He was a warrior who had forged a life of reputation and wealth for himself. He was a warlord, known and feared across the world and would surely have a place at the high feasting tables of Valhalla.

"And what of Ravn?" asked Ymir.

"Ravn is wealthy and a man of war," said Rognvald. "He craves battle and glory and is perhaps the most warlike of all Harald's jarls. He adheres to the old ways, is a stern follower of *drengskapr*, and worships the Aesir with a powerful dedication." Bavlos spat at the mention of the Aesir gods and fumbled with himself beneath his stinking furs. Rognvald chuckled at the Sami, who did not believe in the power of Odin, Thor, Frey, Frigg or Tyr. Bavlos' people worshipped the gods of the sky, water, and trees. They honoured the beasts and the land and prayed to bears, reindeer, wolves, fish, and birds. To Bavlos, the Aesir were trifling gods who fought over women and wealth and were little different to men, whereas his gods were noble and eternal. "Harald hoped Ravn would teach Erik the ways of war, that he would turn him into a *drengr.* But now the Prince is in danger."

"Ravn is certainly a stickler for *drengskapr*," remarked Hrolfr the Mouse. "I have seen him kill two men in Holmgangs with my own eyes. But he is not the most warlike jarl in King Harald's realm. Why, do I myself not raid each summer up and down Ireland and the lands of the Saxons? Do men not tremble when they see my banner of the crossed axes?"

"I'm sure men shit in their pants when they hear you approaching, Lord Hrolfr," said Rognvald dryly, and he held up a hand to quieten Hrolfr when the big man reared up, ready to launch into a tirade of angry bluster. "Harald placed Erik in Ravn's care to turn him into a warrior, which would not happen amongst the courtiers and comforts of Avaldsnes. But Louis of the Franks is not a stripling king. He is a fighter and marches to throw Haesten and Ravn out of Saxony. He brings an army to do it, and if he can separate the Vikings from their ships, Erik will die with Ravn. Erik is the heir to the throne of Norway, and we will fight until our last breath to return Erik to his father."

"So we land in the Elbe," said Hundr, "march to Haesten and Ravn and leave with the Prince?"

"Just so," Rognvald nodded.

"Sounds as easy as shaking silver from a Christ priest," piped Hrolfr, which drew laughter from Ymir and Svart.

"Let us hope so. There will be a full moon tonight, so Bavlos will cast his bones and tell me how his gods augur our quest. If Louis' army has arrived, then we can expect to get drawn into the fighting. We will cut through the Franks to get to Erik if we must."

The captains returned to their ships with the plan clear in their minds, and Hundr pulled himself around and through the rigging, where he found Bush, Thorgrim, and Sigvarth sitting on the steerboard platform, eating a meal of salted pork and cheese.

"We've been lucky not to hit a storm yet," said Bush, frowning up at the sky once Hundr had finished relaying the plan to sail up the Elbe. "This time of year is bad to be at sea. We could wake up tomorrow and find ourselves dragged halfway to Ireland and our sails torn by Njorth's fury."

"Then let us hope Rognvald's little Sami man can keep the storms away with his seiðr," chimed Ragnhild, and she touched the Gungnirspear amulet at her neck for luck.

"Let us also hope that we can get Prince Erik out of Saxony quickly," added Hundr, "because every day we are away means Rollo hunts our people like animals in the forest."

"Will Harald keep his word and give us men?" asked Sigvarth.

"He will."

"Even if we return without his son? Louis and Haesten might have fought the battle already, and what if Prince Erik lies dead in a ditch? If we return with that ill news, will Harald still give us his army?"

"We must trust that he will," Hundr replied, and Sigvarth nodded silently. It was a hard thought, and Hundr wasn't sure that he knew the answer. Hundr had lost a son, and it was beyond painful. Who was to say how the King would react to that news? He could drive Hundr out of Avaldsnes for failing him; he could strip Einar of his jarldom, sail to Vanylven himself in the summer with an army, and place a new man in charge of the fjord and its town. Hundr left them to chew over their destination and what must be done, and he ducked underneath the halyard rope to stand beside Sigrid. She glanced at him and then turned her eyes back to the sea. They were like blue pools in an ocean of blood, so red were the whites of her eyes. She had a cloak and hood pulled tight about her, hiding the mess of her hacked-away hair.

"You should eat," said Hundr, placing his hand on the sheer strake next to hers. Sigrid moved her hand from the ship's timber and drew her arm inside her cloak, pulling it even tighter about her. Hundr struggled for something to say. Sigrid was his wife, and he had loved her since he first laid eyes on her in the hall of her father, Ketil Flatnose, on the island of

Orkney. But the essence of who she was seemed to have died with Sigurd, and whilst Hundr knew that a mother's mourning for her child was a powerful thing, Sigrid needed to begin to heal and recover her senses for the sake of Hermoth more than for her relationship with Hundr.

He stood beside her whilst the crew finished their meal and began the work of bringing the ship about into the wind. The Reaver's shipmaster barked orders, oars lowered, and the crew unfurled the sail as the ship came about. King Harald's wolf sigil growled from the vast woollen sail as the wind caught it, and the *drakkar* surged south. Across the water, Hrolfr the Mouse bellowed at his crew, and the sound rolled across the waves like the blare of a war horn. Hundr waited there, silent, unable to find the words to tell Sigrid that he loved her and that everything would heal with time. The pain of Sigurd's death would dull and soften, but it would never go away, and Hundr wanted Sigrid to talk with him about the happy days in Sigurd's brief life. Hundr wanted to celebrate the light in Sigurd's life and honour him that way, but the words died in his throat because he doubted Sigrid could hear them. She was lost in a world of grief and pain. It had consumed her, and the woman beside him was a husk of the Sigrid she had been before. So, with a heavy heart, Hundr left her there, and a part of him hoped that King Louis and his army were already in Saxony. Battle would take his mind off the tragedy of Sigurd's death and Sigrid's suffering. In battle, Hundr could do what he did best – he could fight and kill, fill his mind with war, and escape the terrible melancholy of his marriage.

Rognvald's fleet reached the River Elbe on a day when the sun shone warmly despite the closeness of winter. The sky was so bright and clear that it was the colour of fjord ice. The moon refused to dip that day, so even though the sun was high and hot in the sky, its shadow hung low in the northwest, and Bavlos howled at its unnerving silver orb. He hunkered in the bilge and crooned to the moon, casting his bones and his sticks, and Rognvald's men gathered about him – not the warship's crew, but the fighters of his ulfheðnar warband, whom Hundr recalled so vividly from the battle at Hafrsfjord. They shed their tunics and jerkins and donned animal skins, the heads of which they draped over their own heads and capered around the deck, barking and growling whilst the strange Sami shaman banged a drum with a long xanthous bone. Rognvald did not join in, but Hundr watched him stare at them from the steerboard platform with a wide smile on his face as he enjoyed their wild ferocity.

"Just like berserkers. I bloody hate them," Bush grumbled, and he helped the crew throw weighted lines over the side to judge the water's depth as they navigated the unfamiliar river. After midday, they came upon Haesten's fleet gathered around a spit of wooded land which sprouted from the river's centre like a long eyot. There were too many ships to count, and all had their mast posts lowered and lay quietly in the calm water between the river island and the river bank. Rognvald ordered his ships to put in, and a grizzled man with one leg greeted him. The man hobbled and used a carved wooden crutch to limp about the riverbank. The Vikings had made a makeshift port on the river where there had once been a small fishing village, just like the longphorts Hundr had seen in Ireland. Haesten's crews had constructed jetties from freshly cut wood and extended the houses where the fisher folk once lived in peace to make barracks and living quarters for the men Haesten had left to guard his precious ships.

"We haven't had a messenger for a few days now," said the one-legged man when Rognvald asked him for news of Haesten. "But last I heard, they were going to besiege Hammaburg. So, best go in that direction. The city is on the river, southwest of here, so follow the water, and you should be there tomorrow. I know little Erik. He's a fierce little troll, that boy is. He already wears an axe at his belt, even though the bloody thing is almost as long as his leg."

Rognvald paid the man a pouch of hacksilver to take care of his ships, and they began the march southwest. Haesten's army had already scoured the riverbank clean of its people, and there was nothing to show for their former existence but the black, charred timbers where villages had once stood, empty pastures where the Vikings had slaughtered sheep and cattle for food, and unharvested fields wild with overripe crops. Rognvald led four hundred men from the river towards Saxony, and without a single horse left in the area, every man marched on foot through the flat and densely forested terrain. They marched towards Hammaburg, which lay on a rocky outcrop where the River Elbe met the River Alster. Just as the one-legged man had promised, they reached Hammaburg the following day, and the turrets of its walled fortress still held strong against the Viking threat because Haesten's vast army was positioned on flatlands to the south. Smoke hung over their tents, dirty and grey, and as Rognvald's warriors approached, there seemed to be no sign of King Louis' army.

"If the Franks aren't here yet," said Bush, rubbing his hand beneath his naalbinding cap. "We could be in and out of there with Prince Erik by tomorrow." Hundr half hoped that was true, that he would have time to feast and talk with Haesten that evening and march away tomorrow with King Harald's son. They would be back in Avaldsnes before the moon changed and then on to Vanylven with an army. But the other half of Hundr's thought cage hoped Louis would appear from the south with battle standards and warriors because his hands itched for battle. He yearned for something to shatter the oppressive shroud of Sigurd's death and Sigrid's worsening mourning trance.

ELEVEN

Hammaburg straddled three islands across the confluence of the Elbe and the Alster. To the north, the land gradually ascended into a long hill that tapered into a wild grass-covered heath nestled between the two wide rivers. The Elbe was vast, as wide as some of the larger rivers Hundr had seen in England, Ireland, and Novgorod. Where the two rivers converged, several large islands divided the waterway as it meandered to merge into a larger single river. The city of Hammaburg sat upon those islands and stretched across the river. This strategic positioning gave the city control over any ships seeking passage, requiring them to pass through a bridge or route regulated by the town. This arrangement allowed Hammaburg to impose taxes on merchants looking to navigate the Elbe, enabling them to sail through Saxony into the lands of the Germans and beyond.

The northeasternmost island was a fortress with a stout palisade and high turrets from which the defenders could easily assault any unfriendly vessels with missiles from the walls. That island was small enough that it was entirely ringed by the palisade, and to assault it, an attacker would need to bring ships close to the walls and clamber up the sheer sides whilst all the time being pelted with rocks, arrows, spears, boiled oil and whatever else the Hammaburgians could toss upon their heads. The fortress was linked to the adjacent, longer island by a sturdy wooden bridge. That extended stretch of land held the town itself, the earth and the wooden-roofed buildings where the inhabitants lived. It, too, was ringed by stout walls and connected to the mainland by a network of bridges. A third fortified structure lay upon the next island in line, and a grand hall with high timber spires like a church of the nailed God sprouted from its centre amongst the huddle of buildings and thatch. The greatest of the fortifications occupied a hill on a jutting corner of the mainland facing north towards Denmark. Its walls were stout, and the hill it stood upon had steep sides, which would be a nightmare to clamber up if a man wanted to attack. A bridge joined the south side of the town to another long, flat and uninhabited stretch that met the mainland on the southern side of the river.

Hundr drank in his surroundings with curious awe. Hammaburg's series of islands and fortresses were so complex that taking the place would necessitate separate assaults on each fortress. It was a daunting prospect that left Hundr shuddering at the sheer number of men required for such a brutal fight.

Haesten had made his camp on the southern side of the river, which was thick with woodland, and to attack the city, he would have to cross the river and

151

its multiple, well-defended islands. Which was, Hundr supposed, why the town had not yet fallen. If Haesten crossed the river and attacked from the north, he could try to storm the hilltop fortress, but should they repel him, Haesten's enemies would push him towards Denmark and away from his precious ships. Haesten was ever a cunning fighter, and so whilst the southern side of the river made for a more complicated attack, it provided him with the opportunity to forage and raid for food across a broad swathe of Saxony and the chance to retreat safely northeast along the river to return to his fleet.

Four riders met Hundr and Rognvald as they marched along the riverbank and led them towards the camp, which was a heaving mass of sailcloth and leather tents. The sound and smell of it drifted on the breeze. Hammers rang, a thousand voices rumbled, shouted, laughed, and sang, and the stink of shit, cooking food, sweat and foulness made Hundr long for the fresh sea air.

"Haesten will greet us warmly," said Hundr as he marched beside Rognvald across a harvested field. "He will want to know why we have come and what we want. Haesten will assume that I have come to join his forces, which I have done before in both Frankia and England."

"Is he favourable towards King Harald?" asked Rognvald, frowning as his boot squelched in a pool of mud.

Hundr shrugged. "I imagine Haesten has no opinion of him as long as Harald does not disturb his plans. But he will be suspicious that you, as Harald's man, have come so far from Norway so late in the year."

"He surely knows that Ravn has fostered Prince Erik, so we shall be honest in our intentions and leave with the boy as soon as the rules of polite guest honour allow."

"And surely Ravn will be insulted that you remove Harald's son from his care? To be the foster father to a prince is a great honour, after all."

"He might be, but he surely knows by now that King Louis marches a great army in this direction. He will understand."

"And if he doesn't?"

"Then we shall make him understand. Ravn cannot turn Prince Erik from foster son to hostage just because we sting his pride."

"Is Ravn a reasonable man?"

Rognvald grinned. "No, he is not. He is a warrior steeped in the old ways. He is quick to temper and always ready to fight. You'll like him."

Hundr doubted that. Suddenly, he could feel his hopes of a quick visit to Haesten and a swift return to the fleet slipping away like sand through his fingers. The scouts led Hundr and Rognvald's men into the camp, and whilst the scouts rode fine horses, Hundr's men were all on foot. A war horn blared to announce their arrival, its song loud and sonorous, and it was quickly followed by the roar of a thousand warrior voices as they shouted to acclaim the new arrivals. More men meant a stronger force with which to fight the King of Frankia. Hundr winced at the sound because it meant that he and Rognvald were now the centre of attention for an entire Viking army.

"Should have brought the banner," tutted Bush from behind Hundr. He spoke of Hundr's sigil of the one eye, which he flew from black banners emblazoned with his white badge so that men knew that the Man with the Dog's Name approached. But there were just as likely to be enemies as friends in the camp – kin or friends of men Hundr had fought against or raided in past years – so he ignored Bush's concern and was content to march into the camp unknown. Hundr slowed his pace, allowing Rognvald to push ahead of him, and the Jarl of Rogaland marched ahead, flanked by Hrolfr the Mouse, Svart the Screamer, and Hooknose Ymir. Thorgrim, Bush, and Sigvarth marched alongside Hundr, and Sigrid came behind him with the rest of Rognvald's crews.

Four dirt tracks facing north, south, east, and west cut the camp into four, and Rognvald's company marched along the road from the west. Warriors came from across Haesten's camp to throng the roadway, excited to see who it was approaching their leaders, the excitement likely breaking the monotony of an army camp where their days were filled with scouting, foraging, digging pits for excrement and filling in old ones, cooking, and practising with weapons when all they wanted to do was fight. Vikings lined the road, staring at the new arrivals with hard eyes and wind-burned faces. There were big men with bushy moustaches, others with plaited beards hung with iron trinkets, and there were shining brynjars, leather armour, axes, spears, helmets, snarls, sneers and challenging stares. Many of the warriors were the grizzled men of Haesten's crews, experienced warriors who had fought for years across countless battlefield raids up and down Frankia and across England. Some of the older fighters would have sailed with Haesten when he sacked Paris and sailed further south than any Northman had before.

Haesten's warriors judged Rognvald and his men. Their hungry eyes pored over armour, weapons, arm rings and stature. They spoke to one another, pointing at a marching man here or a leader there. They singled out those with many arm rings and brynjars as the rich men, the warriors whose prowess and viciousness had earned a warrior's wealth. Hundr saw meaty fingers pointing at his own armour and weapons – his brynjar, two swords, seax, arm rings, and one eye, all of which marked him out as a successful fighter and a man of reputation. A scarred-faced man belched and laughed at something a tall man said, but Hundr ignored them. Haesten's warriors lined the entire pathway, and they were a surging, gossiping, malevolent mass. Every step Hundr took made their presence more oppressive. It was as though they grew taller and closer, boxing him in, and he was shrinking so that their leering faces loomed above and around him. Then, their mass gave way as the mud-slicked path opened into a vast square, and in that square stood Haesten with his hands on his hips, ready to greet his guests.

A big man stood beside Haesten. He wore a brynjar over a red tunic, a red cloak about his shoulders, and a red sword scabbard hung from his belt. He was taller than Haesten, and his beard was trimmed into a point below his chin, while his moustache was curved like a ship's prow. Haesten's face was as blade-sharp as Hundr remembered it, and the severe panes of his cheekbones and forehead gave way to a lopsided grin. He had thinning white hair, shorn short, and it stood up from his head like a brush. He had a thick silver chain about his neck, gold arm rings upon his forearms, and a thick belt studded with silver buttons.

Haesten stared into the approaching warriors, his hard eyes seeking familiarity in their faces. His gaze fixed on the wolf sigil daubed upon the shields carried by Rognvald's men, and his brow creased as his thought cage wondered why warriors had come to him from King Harald Fairhair.

"My lords," the scout spoke as his horse pranced uncomfortably amongst the crowd. He tugged on the reins to stop the beast from turning in a circle. "These men are jarls from Norway and come to you from King Harald Fairhair." He slid from the saddle and pulled his horse away from the scene to avoid any further embarrassment amid the meeting of powerful men.

"Jarl Ravn, Jarl Haesten," Rognvald smiled, and he bowed his head in polite greeting. Rognvald was the only one of the Norwegian noblemen not wearing armour. He wore a plain jerkin and trews with calf-length boots, and only his arm rings marked him out as a powerful lord rather than a courtier or merchant.

"Let me present Jarl Rognvald of Rogaland," said the big man to Haesten. "Along with Jarls Ymir, Svart, and Hrolfr."

"Thank you, Ravn. I am Haesten, and you are most welcome," Haesten intoned, peering over their shoulders so that he could count the number of warriors Rognvald had brought to Saxony. At that moment, Haesten's eyes fell upon Hundr, and his hard face softened into a broad smile.

"Hundr, surely it cannot be you?" he beamed, striding forward.

"It does me good to see you so well, Jarl Haesten," replied Hundr. Haesten strode past Rognvald and spread his arms to greet Hundr in a warm embrace.

"Still alive, I see?"

"Still alive, lord," smiled Hundr. He honoured Haesten with that title, for they were men of equal stature, sea jarls and leaders of men with warships and wealth. But Haesten had been a friend to Hundr when he had needed him most, and whilst there had also been a time where Haesten had shown his ruthless side, Hundr respected him. He held the older man close, and as they pulled apart, he examined his face, which was as cracked with lines and wrinkles as old leather.

"Bush, is that you? Come here, you old boar," Haesten grabbed Bush's forearm in the warrior's grip.

"Well met, Lord Haesten," said Bush, and he laughed, pleased and flattered that the famous warrior would honour him so in front of the gathered army. Haesten noticed Ragnhild amongst the warriors and bowed to her in recognition, and Ragnhild clasped a fist to her breast to honour him in return.

"By all the gods, but we shall feast tonight!" Haesten exclaimed. Hundr had rarely seen him so animated. He was usually calculated and reserved, but that day, he was effusive and unashamedly happy to see Hundr, Bush, and Ragnhild, and it warmed Hundr's heart. He wanted to introduce Sigrid as his wife, as the two had met before in England, but Hundr held back. It was a dishonour to Sigrid, and it soured the fleeting moment of happiness, but he did not have the heart to kill Haesten's mood with the story of Sigrid's evident troubles. Hundr thought of Sigurd and his terrible passing every day, but on the voyage south, he had learned to lock it away in a chest deep within his mind. A chest that he would allow himself to unlock in the dark of night when he lay in his bed. He would think of the joyful child, and his body would shake as he wept for his dead son.

"I apologise, my lords," said Haesten, pulling back to stand beside Ravn. "Greeting old friends can sometimes allow one to run away from oneself. Now, welcome to our army."

"Did Harald send you?" asked Ravn, his face implacable and unmoved by the joyous greetings. Rognvald would not come south on a whim. He was the second most powerful man in all of Norway and did not need to bring his ships and warriors south to raid and conquer Saxony. Rognvald would only have made the journey south on Harald's orders, and then the fact that it was so late in the year made the big jarl even more suspicious of Rognvald.

"Yes, Ravn. I come with Harald's voice and his authority. I will talk with you about the reasons for my visit once I am washed and refreshed, if that is not too much trouble?"

"Of course, we will make you as comfortable as we can," said Haesten after an uncomfortable silence as Ravn held Rognvald's gaze in a silent stare. "We have grown rich this summer in Saxony and hoped to take Hammaburg as our winter quarters. But, as you can see, the place is not so easy to take." He waved his arm towards the island fortresses, which loomed on the opposite side of the river in peaceful defiance of the Viking army.

"Not without losing half of your army," agreed Hundr. He couldn't fathom taking the place, and rarely had he seen fortifications that could be defended so easily. Hundr thought Haesten would do better to find another town in which to make his winter quarters.

"Are you aware, Jarl Haesten," said Rognvald, "that King Louis of the Franks marches an army north to throw you out of Saxony? Sorry to be the bearer of bad news if this is unknown to you."

"Of course, we are aware. Louis will be here within three days. So you have come just in time for battle." Haesten's eyes twinkled, and Hundr saw Rognvald's shoulders visibly slump. They would feast and be made welcome by Haesten and Ravn that evening, which the Norse custom dictated they must do, leaving them no time to take Prince Erik and return to their ships. Three days meant that Haesten's scouts already had eyes on Louis' advance, and to march west along the river with just Rognvald's small company could lead them right into the maw of the Frankish army.

"So we shall feast tonight," Ravn bellowed, shouting so loud that it took Hundr by surprise, and the warriors who thronged the road erupted in cheering and boisterous back-slapping. Ravn leaned forward so Rognvald and Hundr could hear him above the tumult. "Then you can tell me the reason you are here."

"In it up to our bloody necks, again," Bush said into Hundr's ear, and the shipmaster wasn't wrong because Hundr needed to take an army to Vanylven, but now he unwittingly found himself caught up in a war.

They feasted that night on beef, ale, cheese, fish, and boiled vegetables. There was freshly baked bread, butter, and even wine. Haesten was gregarious and happy, and Ravn seated Prince Erik between him and Haesten at the top table, along with Rognvald and Hundr. Hundr sat beside Haesten, where they spoke of old times and lost friends, whilst Rognvald and Erik spent the night in deep discussion. Hundr reckoned Erik to be eight or nine summers old. He had red hair worn long and tied back from his face by a strip of leather. Erik was long-limbed and wore a Viking bearded axe at his belt, and its haft almost dragged across the floor when he walked. The boy had keen, blue eyes and was not daunted when introduced to Hundr. Erik recognised the Man with the Dog's Name; he had heard tales of his adventures and conquests. Ravn railed and banged the table as he and Rognvald spoke, realising that Harald wanted his son brought safely back to Norway. The insult was as plain to see on Ravn's furrowed brow as a turd in a water barrel, and Hundr did not envy Rognvald having to sit beside the angered warlord for a night of drinking and feasting.

The celebration took place in Haesten's tent, a huge woollen sailcloth spread between the boughs of a great tree like a roof without walls. Men had stretched it tight overhead to provide a roof across the forest, keeping Hundr and the revellers dry and warmed by the many fires lit between the crude tables crafted from chopped trunks and logs. Sigrid sat with Ragnhild, Bush, Thorgrim, and Sigvarth at a table of honour close to the top table, but Sigrid ate little and said nothing at all. While talking with Haesten, Hundr saw Ragnhild try to engage her in conversation, but

Sigrid simply stared at her with vacant eyes. Hundr knew that the weight of her tortured soul was something he had to help her with, but she would have to allow him to talk with her if he was to do it.

As Haesten recounted the story of the battle of Ethandun and Guthrum the Unlucky's reconciliation with King Alfred, Hundr remembered that Haesten had been married once and that his wife and baby had died in childbirth. After Haesten had finished his tales, he took a drink of frothy ale from a curved horn, and Hundr edged closer to the old jarl.

"Forgive me for bringing this up," he said, "but I wanted to ask you about when your wife and child passed in Frankia."

Haesten coughed into his horn, shocked at the question. "What of it?" he asked, his face changing suddenly from its jovial half-drunk mirth to its usual hardness.

Hundr raised a hand in apology. "My son died recently, and he was still small. His mother is distraught at his loss, as am I. But we have a living son to care for and our own lives to live. How did you carry on after your loss?"

Haesten cleared his throat and nodded at where Sigrid sat. "I thought I recognised her. She is your woman, no?"

"My wife, Sigrid."

"The daughter of Ketil Flatnose, I remember now. There is no answer, I am afraid, my friend. Grief is not like a mighty fortress to be taken. You cannot come up with a cunning plan to overcome the problem. It is not a cowardly oathman whom you can kill or banish to cut him out of your world. Grief for a loved one never goes away; it remains and lingers like an old wound. It hurts from time to time, and it reminds you of the pain. But it can also remind you to remember the dead and rejoice in their lives. That is all I can say to you. Endure it, use it. But as for your wife," Haesten shrugged his shoulders, "she grew that baby in her womb for nine months. She carried and nursed it, birthed and reared it; for her, the grief is like a part of her own self has died. She will need time and, dare I say, love, which are not things we warriors are apt to give. These are waves crashing on the shores of the mind sea, and for us to keep going, we must navigate them like the most treacherous of waters."

Hundr nodded at that truth and thanked Haesten for his wise counsel. As the evening drew on, they heartily drank, ate and talked of old adventures and heroes, both alive and dead. Later, as Hundr prepared for sleep that night, he brooded on what he could do to help Sigrid recover. Little did he know that he'd have no opportunity to put his plans into action, for the following day, King Louis arrived early, accompanied by his army, and ready to gouge the Vikings from his lands.

TWELVE

Einar scooped up the last of his porridge, running his finger around the edges of the wooden bowl to capture as much of the watery contents as possible.

"How have we eaten so much?" he asked, placing his bowl on the ground and kneading at his stinging eyes.

"There are many mouths to feed," said Hildr, "and it's getting colder now, so there is less game in the forest. We need more grain if we are going to live out here much longer."

"Or we need to take Vanylven back quickly." His earlier question had been rhetorical because Einar knew why the food was running low, even though it had only been a week since his raid on Vanylven's stores. Hildr was right. There were simply too many people to feed each day. He leant forward and warmed his hands on the fire, which now burned constantly inside his recently constructed cabin. The walls were fashioned with pine trunks, trimmed by his shipwrights and neatly fitted to roof beams covered with earth from the forest floor. They had smeared the inside of the walls with a mixture of mud and sawdust to keep the heat in, and the room smelled of dense smoke and fresh pine wood. He coughed and wafted the swirling smoke away from his face. They had not cut a smoke hole in the cabin roof. The space was small, and a hole in the roof would let in too much rain and douse the small fire whenever there was bad weather. So, the smoke escaped the cabin, either by seeping through the roof itself or through the open door.

"Or you can swallow your pride and go to Jarl Ugattr like I said. Ask for food and warriors."

"Why are you saying that to me again? Do we have to discuss this every time we sit down together, woman?"

"Woman?"

"I am not going to Jarl Ugattr." Einar stood and strode the two steps to the cabin doorway. "I am not sure how many more times I can say that."

"Maybe I should go then and take some of the other women with me. I would rather swallow my pride than see our people starve."

Einar ducked under the lintel and left the cabin. Hildr was right again, but Einar had not changed his mind since the last time she had asked him to journey to the next valley. Einar walked through the camp, which was becoming more like a small town every day. The ways between each cabin and tent were now worn pathways or hard-packed frozen ground, and he followed the path which took him around where folk ground wheat into flour. He peered inside at the empty baskets and shook his head. They couldn't live like this much longer, and it would be at least another four, maybe six weeks before the earliest time he expected Hundr to return, or it could be much longer than that.

It was only the middle of the afternoon, and already the sun was dipping towards the tip of the mountain to the west. Soon, the days would grow even shorter and colder, and then his people would really be in trouble. Einar had thought of approaching Vanylven again, of slipping over the walls and slitting Rollo's throat in his sleep. Perhaps that might be enough to persuade his cursed Franks to sail back to Frankia, and then Einar's people could return to their homes and stores of winter food. But his scouts had reported that since the food raid, Rollo's men guarded the entire length of the walls day and night and that their patrols had increased in the forest. Yet they never extended their reach to the tips of the hills and certainly never over the mountain and down into the valley where Einar had made his camp. Einar's men set constant traps in the woodland, such as pits with stakes and logs rigged to crush any intruder's head upon activation, turning the forest into a maze of danger to keep the Franks at bay and away from the mountain.

"What would we give for a warm hall and a night of feasting," said a gruff voice, and Einar turned to find Amundr standing behind him. The big man had an axe over his shoulder, and sweat sheeted his brow.

"Chopping logs again?"

"Yes, lord."

"I'll take my turn later on." The warriors each took shifts, cutting trees and chopping trunks and boughs into firewood. The work and shortage of food had left Einar feeling stronger and trimmer than he had for years. His arms bulged at his brynjar, and his back felt broad and muscular. His bulging belly was all but gone, and all of his men had thinner faces and broader shoulders.

"Shame we don't have a skald with us," said Amundr.

"We won't get many visiting us here, I am afraid." Travelling skalds journeyed between the halls of jarls and lords to tell their tales and sing their songs in return for silver, gifts, and food. They would sing of great warriors or the mischievous adventures of the Aesir and keep folk amused through the long winter nights. "Hildr says you are fully recovered from your wounds now?"

"Aye," Amundr rolled his shoulders and twisted his body at the hip. "That galdr-woman knows her business."

Amundr had taken some deep cuts to his arms and belly during Rollo's assault on Vanylven. He had killed many Franks that day protecting Hundr's children, and his heroism had become a popular tale around the fires. In the absence of a proper skald, the story of Amundr had grown in the telling, and the last

167

time Einar had heard the story, Amundr had killed two dozen Franks.

"So much has changed," Einar spoke softly, staring up at the shifting clouds above the trees. "I had thought my days of fighting and hardship were over. That Hildr and I were at rest, with a fine hall and lands of my own. I had everything I had dreamed of. How the Norns must have laughed at my pride. Perhaps the gods have turned against me?"

"You should talk to the galdr-woman. She is close to the gods."

"What is she going to do? Shake her stick and make my mind sick with mushrooms and piss water just so she can tell me what I already know?"

Amundr chuckled, the sound like rocks tumbling down a mountainside. "She has power. What have you got to lose?"

"Everyone seems to know the best thing to do." Einar ran his hand down his beard and wondered if he was wrong. Perhaps he should summon the old crone to ask her to cast her ancient spells and tell him what the gods had in store for him. And, of course, Hildr was undoubtedly right about Jarl Ugattr, that much he knew.

"Come, let's chop some timber together." Einar clapped Amundr on the shoulder and was about to turn on his heel when a whistling sound overhead stopped him in his tracks.

"Warning arrow," growled Amundr, and he hefted the axe from his shoulder. The scouts Einar had posted around the camp were bowmen who carried quivers of arrows carved so that they emitted a haunting, whistling sound when they flew. One of those arrows had sunk into a large pine trunk at the camp's centre. The people used that tree as a gathering place and hung it with charms and offerings to the gods.

"Get the men together," Einar said, and he ran back along the dirt track towards his cabin. "Attack!" he bellowed as he ran. "We are under attack!"

The camp erupted like a kicked wasp nest. People dashed here and there; men in jerkins ran to their homes to grab weapons, and women with panicked faces scooped up their children and hurried them away from the camp. They had prepared for such an attack, for Einar had always known that it was only a matter of time before Rollo led his forces into the valley. After the food raid on Vanylven, their handcarts had left a trail through the woodland that even a blind man could follow, and now Rollo had negotiated the forest and its traps to finish what he had started.

"How far?" said Torsten, running alongside Einar towards their cabins, which were built next to each other.

"Feathers are white," Einar replied. Their scouts in the forest patrolled the woodland at different distances from the camp. Black raven feathers meant the alarm was within one hundred paces of camp, and white feathered arrows meant the danger was five hundred paces away.

"We have time, then."

"Short enough. I'll join you at the barricade."

Einar ducked into his cabin and bumped into Hildr, who was on her way out. She went armed with her bow, a quiver full of arrows, and an axe in a loop at her belt.

"I'll take the archers to the trees," she said.

Einar grabbed Hildr's arm and pulled her close. "Be careful," he urged. "I love you." She kissed him and sped out of the cabin, calling as she went for her archers to follow her lead. Hildr was a deadly archer and carried her powerful eastern recurved bow. Since they had left Vanylven, Hildr had spent time each day training a force of young women to use bow and arrow, and whilst they were not as skilled as the Valkyrie priestess, they could still send a vicious, iron-tipped shaft into an enemy at close range. Hildr had shown them how to carve a bow from a stave of yew, how to apply tree gum and resin to the bow to strengthen its pull, and how to attach a horn cap at each end for the string.

Einar grabbed his fish scale brynjar, which hung on the back wall, and pulled it over his head. He jumped up and down until its leather lining slipped over his shoulders and down over his body. Einar quickly buckled on his belt, grabbed his axe and seax, and ran to join his men.

"Get them as high as you can," Einar called after an older woman who ushered a gang of teenage girls away from the camp. The woman nodded and picked up the pace. They knew to take the women and children to high caves, just as they had practised and prepared for repeatedly, and by the time Einar reached the camp barricade, the place contained only those who would fight to protect the camp and people who retreated behind the safety of their blades.

"Are we ready?" Einar shouted.

"For Vanylven!" Torsten bellowed, and a line of one hundred men let out a clipped roar in response. They had shields, spears, helmets and axes, and Einar pushed his way to the front to stand beside Amundr and Torsten. Trygve led the left flanks' defence, where a similar force manned the barricade on that side. As they had established the camp and built warmer and more comfortable dwellings, they had also constructed a barricade around it, which they could defend in the event of an enemy attack. It was a chest-high construction of chopped tree trunks, briars, thorns and brush. The timbers were not planted into the ground as deep as palisade timbers, for Einar's men hadn't enough time to cut the vast number of trees required for such a wall. Still, they had made a makeshift ring, laid more posts end over end, and filled the structure with earth and whatever else they could find to build something an enemy would need to clamber over in order to take the camp.

Outside the barricade, Einar and his men had dug a ditch half as deep as a man is tall, spanning the whole perimeter. They had thrown the earth from that ditch up to support the barricade itself. So, a ditch and an earthwork rampart of sorts defended the camp, and Einar said a prayer to Odin that it would be enough. Rollo's men would need to charge into the ditch and climb over the barricade whilst Einar and his warriors hacked at them and battered them with rocks and missiles.

"A black arrow!" came a shout from behind Einar. He had not heard the arrow whistle over his men's shouting, but the enemy was close now. One hundred paces. Einar's heart thumped in his chest, and he clashed his axe and seax together.

"Are you ready to fight?" Einar called, and his men roared back, banging their weapons together until the forest rumbled with their war din.

The trees beyond the barricade shook, and for a moment, Einar thought it was Rollo's men charging, but it was his scouts returning from the forest. They ran across the open ground, where the stumps of cut trees rose like gravestones from the earth. The scouts leapt over the ditch through a barricade section that served as a gate, then dashed inside through a further log gate opened by the warriors to join the defenders.

Then, the first of Rollo's men appeared at the wood's edge. The warrior was bare-chested and daubed with red from head to midriff. It was Kveldulf, the berserker, and he stood alone at the treeline. He wildly shook his axe at Einar's camp and furiously roared his defiance. A line of similarly clad men emerged to stand alongside their leader, and they were all daubed in blood with the crazed eyes and slathering mouths of berserkers driven to madness by whatever potion their *godi*, or holy man, had administered to them.

A tall figure shouldered past Kveldulf to stand in the space between the woods and the camp. He was a head and shoulders taller than any of the berserkers, dressed in shining mail, and he carried a long sword in his right hand and an axe in his left. It was Rollo the Betrayer himself, and the sight of the wretched bastard made Einar's chest burn with pure hatred. Rollo stood there momentarily, staring at the camp, the barricade and the bearded faces beyond it. He laughed and shook his head.

"Look how far you have fallen, Dog's Name. Living in the woods and grubbing for acorns like a pig. Are you ready to die?" Rollo lifted his sword, and his men emerged from the trees. Hundreds of Franks marched past the berserkers to join Rollo, and he pointed his sword towards the camp. Their boots crunched on the twigs and leaves between the tree stumps as they advanced, armed with spears and shields.

"He thinks Hundr is still here?" asked Amundr, an eyebrow raised above his broad face.

"All the more surprise for the lanky bastard when Hundr turns up with an army," said Einar.

The Franks came on in a line, each marching in time with the man to his left and right. They marched through the stumps and picked up their pace as they approached the ditch and barricade. Einar's warriors roared and shouted insults at them, begging them to come and die.

"For Vanylven and Einar the Brawler!" Amundr shouted.

"Einar, Einar, Einar!" the men shouted in unison, and Einar's heart swelled at their acclaim.

Einar could see the whites of the Franks' eyes as they reached the edge of the ditch, their faces full of fear and apprehension. Whilst the defences weren't those of a fortress, it would still require bravery for those men to descend into the mud-slicked ditch and try to haul themselves up the other side, facing the prospect of Viking blades as they grasped and pulled themselves through the mire and over the earth, timber and brambles. Just as the first man was about to scramble into the ditch, an arrow whipped from the trees above and behind Einar to take the Frank in the throat, and the man beside him winced as arterial blood sprayed from the terrible wound, splashing on his face. The injured man fell to his knees, and the Franks roared in anger. They descended into the ditch, and Hildr's archers rained a hail of arrows upon them. The iron arrowheads slammed into the Franks with the sound of meat hitting a chopping block. Some pinged off helmets or armour, and more Franks poured into the ditch, hampering the men in front of them who could not raise their shields to protect their heads from the deadly torrent of white feathered arrows.

Einar peered down at them, clenching his teeth. He was glad to see the bastards die. They shoved and cursed at one another, and arrows continued to ruthlessly thud and rip into them.

"Now," Einar ordered, raising his axe and bringing the weapon down. His men roared again and bent to pick up the hundreds of rocks and stones they had piled up inside the barricade. The Vikings threw their missiles, and the Franks howled in pain as skulls were crushed and bones were broken. A man below Einar screamed in agony and tugged at an arrow which had passed through his cheeks, and then he died as Amundr hurled a monstrous rock over the barricade, crushing the Frank's skull like an egg. The ditch was a churning mass of desperate Franks, and the dead had already begun to void their bowels, so that shit and blood stank and soaked the ditch, making it a place of hellish suffering.

The enemy crawled up the ditch; they scrambled and stamped on their friends' corpses to do so, and Einar shouted his hate at them, poised and ready to strike with his axe. A Frank pulled his way out, only to die with an arrow in his eye, and Einar almost laughed at the peculiar horror of it. Another came behind him, and Torsten lunged with his spear, tearing open the man's face to send him sprawling back into the ditch. More came, and Einar swung his axe over the chest-high barricade to sink its bearded blade into the top of a Frankish skull. He yanked the blade free, and all along the line, his men fought, and Franks died.

At that moment, a tremendous howl went up from behind the enemy lines, and its sound was as though Fenris Wolf had escaped his fetters to loose his fury upon the world at the end of days. A line of warriors ran towards the ditch at full pelt, and they were the bare-chested, blood-soaked berserkers. They came running with wild faces and hurtling limbs, and when they reached the edge of the ditch, they launched themselves across its span, landing on the far side and using the heads and faces of Franks beneath them to kick and push themselves onto the barricade. A heavily muscled berserker with long black hair landed in front of Einar. He dodged Einar's axe, reached over the palisade to grasp a timber, and hauled himself over the barrier. The berserker came up snarling, kicking out with his boots and swinging his axe in wide circles. His beard bubbled with froth from his mouth, and his eyes were so wide that they showed white like a frightened horse.

Einar stepped in, catching the madman's axe with his own, and the two blades clanged together with a force that jarred Einar's arm. Suddenly, Amundr burst past Einar, landing a devastating punch on the berserker's face, and the man fell backwards, dazed by the blow. Amundr stamped on the man's chest and brought his own axe down in a massive swing that began so far behind himself that the axe head touched his spine. The blade swung and came down with a sickening thud to split the berserker's head in two and splattered blood, skull and brains across the barricade.

Another berserker came, and Einar met him as he clambered over, ripping open his unprotected belly with his seax.

"We are holding them," Einar said, and the warriors around him cheered.

"Look, there," called Torsten, pointing his bloody axe to where a company of berserkers had forced their way through the defences and were behind Einar's line of warriors. Kveldulf was there, his monstrous shoulders and huge head unmistakable even in the fog of desperate fighting. There were five of them, and they ran into the camp searching for prey amongst the tents and cabins.

"Hold the line," Einar ordered, and Torsten nodded. His face was grave but strong. Einar followed Kveldulf, and Amundr went with him. They left the screaming, howling horror of the defence to hunt the war-mad berserkers who searched homes for easy prey – for women and children they could butcher to sate their inhuman thirst for blood. Einar ran, blood pulsing around his ears and brain, desperate to stop Kveldulf before he could harm any of his people. Einar hoped the women and children were long gone by now, but there would always be stragglers who hadn't heeded the call to flee.

"There," said Amundr, and he ducked under a line of hemp rope hung with drying clothes and dodged between two tents. Two berserkers grunted and growled there as they emerged from the darkness of a cabin door, and Einar charged at them. They had dragged a young blonde-haired woman from the cabin, and she kicked and screamed as she was hauled out by her hair. The five berserkers capered and whooped, and Einar sprinted. His limbs moved with a litheness he had not felt for years. One berserker came at Einar, all frothing lips and wild fury. He swung his axe, but there was no skill in the attack. It was the type of swing a child would make when first learning to fight, and Einar dug his heels into the earth to stop his run dead, turning beneath the berserker's swinging arm. Einar struck his axe downwards and away from his body so that the blade chopped into the berserker's leg, and he ripped the axe free. The man fell howling, and Einar reared up before the berserker holding the girl. He drove his seax upwards, the wicked tip of the broken-back blade punching through the underside of the man's chin, and he died before he could react. Amundr beat a third enemy to the ground, and the two remaining berserkers backed away, tongues lolling like wolves. Kveldulf emerged from between them, his thick chest heaving and his face twisted in the grin of a madman.

Kveldulf held up his blood-soaked axe and licked the gore from its iron curve. He howled like a dog, charging at Einar, and the attack came in a blur of strength and power. Kveldulf moved like nothing Einar had ever seen before. His shoulders, neck and head were so thick and powerful that each strike of his axe was like a giant hammer, and though Einar parried some and veered away from others, Kveldulf

178

was unstoppable. He bobbed and weaved, ducking low and shuffling his feet so that he came up on Einar's flank and then vanished to reappear on the opposite side. Einar stabbed at Kveldulf with his axe but found only air, and the berserker crowed for joy when he caught hold of Einar's wrist and twisted his seax free so that it clattered to the earth. Kveldulf butted Einar in the nose and threw him to the ground. Einar scrambled, desperate to get to his feet before the killing blow struck, but just as Kveldulf drew his axe back to strike, Amundr came at him, barrelling into the berserker and dragging him to the ground. They rolled, kicked, grabbed, and spat at each other. Each man's muscled arms bulged with the effort as Kveldulf came on top and snapped his teeth at Amundr's face, but the giant tossed him to the side and crashed an elbow into Kveldulf's face.

Kveldulf rolled away, holding a hand to his eye, which had sagged in his face. Einar charged at the berserker, wanting to kill the cursed bastard once and for all, and he swung his axe, but Kveldulf swerved away from it, and then he parried Amundr's axe with his own. The berserker screeched in frustrated anger, baring his teeth at Einar and Amundr. He removed his hand from his eye, revealing shattered bones around the socket so that his face was misshapen and the eye was already swollen. Amundr lunged, and Kveldulf parried with his axe. Einar struck low, slicing Kveldulf's side open, and the berserker snarled and kicked Einar's legs out from under him. Einar rolled in desperate fear and felt the wind of the berserker's axe as it thudded into the ground in the place where his head had been a moment earlier. A horn rang out, shrill and loud.

"Odin grants you luck," Kveldulf said, and he backed away from the fight, "for I would have killed you both." His berserker madness had subsided. Perhaps Amundr had knocked it out of him, or perhaps the potion's strength had worn off.

Einar followed Kveldulf as he skipped through the camp towards the barricade where the fight had raged hardest. He had been so consumed by the brutal combat with Kveldulf that he only then noticed that the sounds of battle had ceased. There was nothing but the creaking sounds of the forest and moans and cries of injured warriors. Einar came around a row of cabins and stopped still. The food stores were on fire, the flames new and small, licking and lapping at the meagre supplies of wheat and barley and the timber building which housed them. Smoke crept out of the open door in curling wisps as the fire took hold.

"No," Einar whispered. For in that building were the food supplies for the entire camp. All of their grain, meat, and dried fish.

"Dog's Name, where are you?" came Rollo's voice, and Einar swallowed his urge to run to the flames and douse them, a sick feeling curdling his stomach, a fear that his warriors were defeated and that Rollo had won the day. If he had, then the Betrayer would surely massacre them all.

"I'll go to Rollo, you try to stem the fire," Einar said, and Amundr nodded. The big man lumbered off to find a water barrel or whatever he could to put the flames out.

Einar marched through the camp, sweating and exhausted from the fight with Kveldulf. He ducked beneath a tent rope and rose to see the Vanylven warriors standing ten paces back from the defences whilst a horde of Franks were positioned on top of the barricade with shields and spears, poised and ready to strike. In the space between the two enemy forces, Rollo stood tall with his sword resting on his shoulder. Trygve stood opposite Rollo, axe in one hand and shield in the other.

"Ah, Einar the Brawler," Rollo drawled cheerfully. He stood amongst the corpses of men slain in the vicious fight but spoke as if he greeted Einar on market day. "Your man here tells me the Dog is not at home, which is a pity."

Einar swallowed hard. Trygve glanced at him, giving a slight shake of his head, and, in a gesture, assured Einar that he had not told Rollo the truth of Hundr's whereabouts. Einar squared his shoulders, raised his chin, and walked confidently to meet his enemy.

"Rollo, you stinking turd. It saddens me to see you alive," said Einar, trying to appear calm while raging internally at the loss of the camp's food and panicking that Amundr could save none of it.

"I think our little skirmish is over for today. It's no fun if the Dog isn't here. What does he call himself again?" Rollo leaned over his shoulder towards Kveldulf, who stood behind him.

"The Champion of the North," Kveldulf sneered, his face a swollen mess around his damaged eye.

"That's it. I want to face the Champion of the North. The man who brought his warriors and burned my home. I've killed a few of your rag-tag warriors here and burned the food you stole from us. I'll come back when the Dog's at home, and we can do this again if you haven't starved or frozen to death by then. First, though, your man here has challenged me to fight. So, I'll give you all something to tell your whoreson leader, Jarl Hundr, about."

Einar stepped forward as Rollo levelled his oversized sword at Trygve, and Rollo winked at Einar, which was almost more than he could bear.

"Fight for what?" Einar asked.

"Your man offered to fight me instead of me allowing my glorious Franks to slaughter your pitiful rabble here. So, I'll kill the son of a whore and then march back to Vanylven, and we'll have ourselves a feast. As I said, I will return when the Dog is here." Rollo smiled and sighed, "There is so much food in Vanylven; I fear most of it will go to waste."

"The only whoreson around here is you. Fight me instead."

"We've fought before, and you are an old man now, Einar. There is no reputation to be gained in killing a greybeard. You keep calling my mother a whore. I am the son of a jarl, and my mother was the daughter of a jarl of the Tronds. I would be a jarl now if your King Harald the warmonger had not usurped my lands to crown himself."

"I met your mother once. She was a comely lass who opened her legs for every ship's captain who came to port. In fact, there's a chance I could even be your father."

Rollo snapped at that insulting lie. He stepped towards Einar, and the tip of his sword flicked upwards, but then he regained control of himself and waved to his men to prepare the fighting square. Without hazel rods or adequate time to make the proper square, Rollo's men made one out of spears.

"Another time, Einar," Rollo chimed, and he beckoned Trygve on to fight.

Einar hurried to Trygve. The warrior stared at him, his sharp features stern and ready to fight. Blood from the battle spattered Trygve's face, and his right arm was cut, bleeding freely. Gore smeared his brynjar, and he shrugged as Einar stared into his eyes.

"I had no choice," Trygve uttered. "The berserkers broke our line, and the Franks were about to overwhelm us. I thought that if I challenged him, it might avert the slaughter."

"You were right," said Einar. "He wants Hundr, not us. But let me fight him. I've fought countless Holmgangs, and I'll kill the bastard."

"I am no stripling new to the shield wall," Trygve replied, which was true. He was a stout warrior of reputation, a skilled front-line fighter, and he had fought countless times. But when Einar was younger, he had been famous for fighting such duels. He had sought them out to burnish his reputation brighter, and whilst he was old now and had lost much of his speed and strength, he still had a few tricks up his sleeve.

Einar inclined his head, sorry that he had insulted his friend. Einar slipped his axe into the loop at his belt, grabbed Trygve's brynjar, and tugged it. It was snug, and its rings were well-fitted. Einar clapped him on the shoulder, stared into his blue eyes, and he nodded. "Kill the bastard," he said. But Einar had fought Rollo before, once in a burning building, and he was not a man to be underestimated. Einar glanced over his shoulder, where smoke still rose from the food stores, and he nodded again at Trygve. Arguing any longer would only delay their urgent need to save as much food as possible.

Trygve banged his axe on the iron rim of his shield and stepped into the square. The two armies were silent. Rollo swung his sword around in two wide sweeps, and its oversized blade sang through the air to make a magical sound – as if the steel sliced through the very wind itself. Rollo looked up at the sky and frowned, but the sun was now out of sight, and darkness crept across the camp.

Suddenly, Rollo burst into a flat run across the square. He sprinted as though he had decided that night was approaching, and he missed his fire. Rollo's long legs covered the fighting square in four long strides, and as Trygve raised his shield, Rollo leapt into the air and brought his mighty sword down in a monstrous stroke. He held the blade in two hands, and it flashed over his head like an eagle's wing on a summer morning. The edge battered Trygve's shield, and the boss buckled under the force, as did the iron-shod rim. Linden wood cracked and shivered, and Trygve was forced down to his knees. Rollo landed and leapt backwards, readying his sword to strike again, and Trygve's shield was smashed to ruin. It hung from his arm, and Einar noticed that the force of Rollo's blow had broken Trygve's forearm. The shield sagged to the earth, and Trygve glanced at Einar, holding his gaze for a heartbeat. There was so much in that look: many years of enduring friendship and comradeship, fear that death was near, and hope that the gates of Valhalla would open for him. Einar felt a lump in his throat, and he swallowed it, killing off the un-warriorlike emotion.

Einar wanted to run to Trygve, to attack Rollo and save his friend from the inevitable end, but he could not. They fought a Holmgang, albeit without the usual ritual, but the laws of *drengskapr* forbade Einar to intervene, so he rooted himself to the spot and braced himself. Rollo surged forward, and with two hands, he stabbed the point of his sword towards Trygve's body. Trygve brought his axe up to parry the blow, but it was like a twig dropped into a raging river, and Rollo's blade continued on its terrible, slicing path, carving into Trygve's chest. The sword point smashed through the riveted links of Trygve's chainmail brynjar and into the flesh and bone beyond. Rollo grunted, driving the sword in further, and his Franks raucously cheered and roared. Trygve gasped and coughed a gout of black blood into his beard.

Rollo kept hold of his sword and dragged the hilt towards the ground, leaning into it like a farmer at a plough with all the strength in his giant frame. The blade tore Trygve's torso open like it was a sack of offal. His insides slopped onto the ground, steaming and grizzly, and Rollo ripped his blade free, skipping away so that the foulness would not mark his boots. He turned the sword to Einar and laughed as he flicked Trygve's blood off the blade. Trygve toppled forward so that his dead body slumped over his spilt insides, and Einar thanked Odin that his old friend had kept a tight hold of his axe.

Rollo led his men away and left the camp in stunned silence. Hildr came running from the trees and urged the warriors to help put the store fire out, but Einar could not move. Woebegone, he stood there, staring at Trygve's butchered corpse, wondering how to prevent his people from starving and wrestling with the question of whether it was possible to hate a man as intensely as he hated Rollo the Betrayer.

THIRTEEN

Hundr banged his shield over the rim of Ragnhild's to his left, and Thorgrim did the same on Hundr's right so that their shields overlapped to make the shield wall. Linden wood and iron clattered and clanged all along the line as Hundr's twenty warriors took their place in the third rank amongst Rognvald's, Haesten's, and Ravn's warriors. The army was packed tightly together to make the sturdy war fence, and the acrid smell of sweat, stale breath and old leather filled Hundr's nose. They made the wall more to ward off the enemy rather than to actually invite them to battle. Two hundred Vikings ringed the crest of a hill above the woodland on Hammaburg's south bank, and they faced a vast army. King Louis and his forces had appeared that day, and though Haesten's scouts had warned of the king's approach, there was insufficient time to strike camp and march away from the riverbank before the enemy arrived. The Franks had come over the horizon and through the trees like a relentless tide, slowly but inevitably lapping its way up a beach. They marched in a surging throng of soldiers — first as a mass of moving spears and drab figures, then as a menacing metal-spiked monster eating and crawling its way over the land. Sharp spears, glinting helmets, war banners, horsemen and archers converged for war, casting a vast shadow over the terrain.

"They won't fight," said Ragnhild. Her one eye squinted at the dust kicked up by so many warriors and horses milling about on the riverbank as a thousand Vikings gathered belongings and wrapped up their sailcloth tents to break camp and prepare to march. Hundr blinked away dirt from his own eye and wiped its wetness on his sleeve. He had not yet drawn either of his swords and stared over the rim of his shield at the enemy as they formed up west of the forest on the river's south bank.

"They should," Hundr responded, "but they won't." He and Ragnhild shared the Odin wound – the loss of one eye, and he loved her like a sister. She was the fiercest fighter in Hundr's company, and they had fought side by side for fifteen summers. Odin had sacrificed his eye in Mimir's well and had thrown himself upon his Gungnir spear in return for the gift of wisdom. Then he had hung himself from Yggdrasil, the great tree that binds the universe, to attain the ability to see all that happened across all nine worlds that extended from the tree's mighty boughs and acquire the powerful knowledge of runes. All Hundr had received in return for his lost eye was a lifetime of blindness and pain, but as he watched the army of King Louis marching across the lowlands with their shields, spears and banners, he wished for the ability to gaze toward distant Vanylven and see how Einar fared, and he wished he could peer into

Louis' heart. Did the King want a war of blood, battles, death and pain, or just to drive the Vikings from his lands? Hundr wasn't sure that the Franks actually wanted the fight. They had a reputation for paying Viking leaders to leave their lands unmolested, and Hundr suspected that might have been Haesten's ploy all along.

A trumpet blast screeched out from where the army of the Franks massed in the river valley. Hundr winced at the horrible sound, which was like a duck screaming through a war horn. It was shrill, and every man in the Viking line of battle shook his head at the noise. Another trumpet blared, and Ragnhild cursed in anger.

"If they carry on with those trumpets, I'll charge down there alone and kill the bastards myself," she snapped, and the surrounding warriors laughed. The Viking ranks had a strange sense of calm despite the closeness of an enemy army. It was as though every man knew the Franks would not attack. The armies had come too close too soon, and for whatever reason, be it the will of Tyr or Odin or the will of the Franks' nailed God, none of them had the apprehension or gut-watering fear that usually comes before battle.

Haesten, Rognvald, and Ravn formed their army upon a hill facing the west, with Hammaburg and the river to their north. Haesten had to secure that high ground or find himself pinned and trapped in a curve of the river Elbe, with Louis on one side and the walled city islands on the other. If the King had trapped Haesten in the river's hook, he could have starved the Vikings and worn them down with attacks from across the river and the landward side until Haesten was forced to surrender and beg for his life. But Haesten was not a man to be trapped so easily, so the Vikings held the high ground, allowing for a retreat eastwards along the river and deeper into Saxony. King Louis held the eastern riverbank, which meant that he blocked any retreat towards the Viking fleet, and so whilst Hundr was sure he would not attack that day, being driven away from the ships made his hopes for a quick return to Vanylven seem ever more impossible.

"I hope they do fight," growled Thorgrim. "The Franks don't have the belly for it. They're as soft as Frisian merchants. We should hack our way back to the ships."

"I think maybe the King is spoiling for trouble after all," grumbled Bush, and he pointed to where a force of enemy warriors marched towards the southwest foot of the hill. Five hundred men were massing into marching formation, which was a quarter of King Louis' overall force, according to Hundr's rough count. They came on foot with their streaming red banner whipped by the wind, held aloft on a long spear. King Louis himself rode before them on a prancing white horse, wearing a golden crown atop a shining helmet. Haesten, Rognvald, and Ravn were busy arranging their hasty retreat and leading their forces east, so the camp was all but lifted by the time Louis reached the bottom of the hill.

"Looks like he wants to talk," said Thorgrim, grinning, for Vikings loved the ritual exchange of insults before a fight, priding themselves on conjuring new slurs to spit at the enemy, which they could laugh about when the battle was over. But Hundr doubted that Louis, a noble-born King of East Frankia, Saxony and Bavaria, wanted to call Haesten a whoreson or a piece of toad shit. He came to drive the Vikings from his lands, and Hundr thought that if he were the king, he would try to draw the Vikings down the high ground and entice them to fight, where his greater numbers would crush them into the river.

Haesten, Rognvald and Ravn ignored King Louis and marched eastwards, leaving Hundr and the rearguard shield wall on top of the hill, and the morning wore on without activity. The Vikings could retreat safely behind the hilltop shield wall, and a long line of horsemen, wagons, carts, and marching warriors snaked away to the east and away from the king's army.

"It's getting colder. Might snow soon," said Sigvarth, staring up into the sky, a mass of shifting clouds and little sun. With each passing day, the temperature dropped, and in the far north, that would mean shorter days and the impending arrival of snow. Hundr hoped the gods would delay the season just long enough to keep the sea passable, for he had to return to Vanylven, yet he would do it in winter if necessary.

King Louis rode in front of his warriors, and his white horse churned up the earth as he cantered around the base of the hill. He shouted at his men and drew his sword, pointing it at the Vikings and bellowing words that Hundr could neither hear nor understand.

"He seems keen," remarked Ragnhild.

Hundr frowned as King Louis tried to whip his men into a fury. They began to shout and roar and clash their long spears, and suddenly, Hundr thought they might fight after all. He looked over his shoulder to where Sigrid stood in the rank behind him. Her red-ringed eyes met his, and she just stared at him. Her hair was a choppy fuzz mixed with long hanks of blonde hair where she had hacked it away. Sigrid clutched her axe, and her bow was slung across her back. Hundr still could not summon the words to help her recover from Sigurd's death, and the sorrow of the child's passing was a gulf between them rather than a pain they shared and suffered together.

"You there. He is going to charge us," said Hundr, realising that King Louis had indeed decided to fight. "Warn Haesten. We will hold them here and retreat towards the river. Tell him we will form a marching rearguard for the retreating column." Hundr had called to a young lad who waited behind the shield wall with a dappled pony. He was there to relay any urgent messages between the rearguard and Haesten.

"Yes, lord," replied the young man, slipping as he tried to mount his horse before finally clambering onto its back.

"Wait," Hundr shouted. "Tell Haesten that if he hears three blasts of a war horn, he should send riders to charge into King Louis' flank. Do you understand?"

The lad nodded, wheeled his horse around and galloped down the hillside, away from the shield wall and towards the Viking column.

"Bush, keep your horn ready," Hundr said, and Bush patted the curved horn of creamy white and black, which he kept tied to the back of his belt. "They are going to attack, lads!" Hundr shouted so all the warriors along the Viking shield wall could hear him. "They are mad for our blood, and they're going to march up this hill and try to kill us."

"Let the pig humpers try it," yelled a man with a thick Norse accent, and the Vikings laughed.

"When they come, we must protect the rear of our marching column, so we retreat slowly down the other side of the hill."

"I am Gamli Hrothgrimsson, and I do not run from Frankish blades," said another voice.

"We'll fight them," Hundr shouted, "But we must hold them and march slowly backwards. If we hold here, they will separate us from our army."

"Then I will see you in Valhalla," came the same voice from along the line, and the Vikings cheered that response. Hundr let it go. He had tried to warn them of what must be done, but these were not his men. The only men oathsworn to Hundr on that hill were the twenty he had brought from Vanylven; the rest were Rognvald's or Haesten's men.

"Listen to me," Hundr spoke so that only his twenty could hear him. "I won't die here today. We must return to Einar and the people of Vanylven and put Rollo in his grave. We will retreat. We will hold their charge when it comes and then march slowly, shields towards the army, down that slope with the enemy at our front and our army at our backs."

His men nodded, and Hundr gripped his shield tighter in his left hand, its familiar timber handle comfortable within his calloused palm. The trumpet blew again from below, a long, shrill blast that wailed like a strangled cat.

"That's it," growled Ragnhild. She dropped her shield and took her recurved bow from across her back. She tested the string, pulling it back to her cheek twice, then licked a finger and held it up to get a sense of the wind's strength.

"Don't do it," said Hundr. He knew her too well – she had lost her patience with the trumpeter. Ragnhild shot him a furious look, and Bush laughed like a mischievous child stifling his giggles when he ought to remain quiet. Then Thorgrim laughed, and it rippled along the line as Hundr's men nudged each other and pointed at Ragnhild. She took an arrow from the leather quiver that hung from her belt and laid it upon the string. Below, King Louis capered, urging his men into deeds of bravery, and the trumpeter took five long steps out in front of the

Franks' line of spears. He wore the skin of a strange spotted cat upon his head and raised his long, bronze-coloured instrument to his lips once more. Ragnhild's bow thrummed.

"Eat that, you little bastard," she hissed, and the trumpet sound fell flat as the man died with Ragnhild's arrow in his face. The Vikings erupted into raucous laughter, and King Louis realised he was within bowshot, quickly galloping his fine white horse away from the front line and around to the rear of his warriors. He rode behind them, urging them on to battle, and the Franks roared their own war cries. The murder of their trumpeter gave them the courage they had been searching for, and they came up the hill in organised ranks. They approached with their shields held before them and their spears resting upon shield rims so that they looked like a monstrous hedgehog advancing up the hill. The rest of Louis' army continued to mill about on the riverbank, and he committed no further warriors to the five hundred who came up that hill to attack a Viking shield wall.

Hundr set himself and reached around to the small of his back to draw his seax from its sheath, which hung from his belt by two leather thongs. A sword wasn't much use in the shield wall, in the press of men where opposing armies ram so close together that they can smell each other's stink, meet the eyes of their enemies, and smell their breath before taking their life. There would be the clash of shields, the press of men behind shoving into the front ranks, and within that terrible crush, there was no room to wield a long-bladed sword. Men could rest spears on shield rims and punch the points forward, stabbing aimlessly at the enemy, but a short blade, like the wicked blade of Hundr's seax, could find its way between the shields. It could slide under and around iron rims like an otter's lithe body swimming in a pond, finding the gaps in leather armour or chainmail to rip and tear at an enemy's flesh until he screamed and wailed in pain.

After the pushing, one shield wall would give way. When enough of the front rankers had died or become exhausted, and the rear rankers pushed to the front in rag order, warriors would break the enemy line and hack and slash their way into the opposing shield wall until the enemy broke. And when they did, it was the time for swords and slaughter. So, Hundr held his seax in his right hand and gripped his shield tightly with his left. The enemy came on, singing a war song in their own language, and Haesten's men in the front rank took up one of their own, a rowing song which all Vikings knew, and the entire formation joined in. The Franks slowed as they came up the slope. Their front rankers realised that because they advanced uphill, the Vikings could hack and chop at their heads and shoulders as they tried to reach the high ground. They understood that when they raised their shields to protect against those blows from above, their stomachs and groins became exposed. So, the Franks slowed, the rear ranks shoved the foremost forward, and King Louis emerged again from behind his men to appear at their right flank, swinging his sword and urging them onto valour.

Hoofbeats from the rear caught Hundr's attention, and he turned to see the messenger return on his pony. Lather flecked the beast's sides from the gallop to and from Haesten. The messenger leapt from the saddle and ran to Hundr, shouting from behind the shield wall with a hand cupped to his mouth so that his voice would carry over the din.

"Haesten has your message, my lord," the lad called. "He is ready to ride when he hears the horn blasts."

Hundr nodded his thanks and grinned, for if they could form an organised retreat, then was a chance to slaughter five hundred enemy warriors. The Franks marched again, their king's presence having the desired effect. Hundr could make out Louis' round face beneath his conical helmet and the beards and faces of the growlers in the Frank's front line.

There was a commotion in the Viking rear, and Hundr looked over his shoulder with his good eye to see what caused the disturbance. His head rocked back as men pointed and shouted at a figure clambering onto the messenger's horse. Then, Hundr's mouth dropped open in surprise as he realised the figure was Sigrid. Her roughly cut hair and beautiful face were unmistakable in her shining brynjar. She scrambled onto the horse's back, and the beast wheeled around in a circle, snorting and bucking, but Sigrid held on, sawing at the reins, and Hundr could not understand what she was doing. She clicked her tongue and dug her heels into the horse's flank, setting off at a canter. As she rode along the rear of the shield wall, Sigrid plucked a spear from the hands of a Viking warrior, and then her red-rimmed eyes caught Hundr's.

"I am sorry, my love," she called to him. They were the first words she had spoken since Sigurd had died. Hundr still did not understand. He thought she was running away or riding to join Haesten's marching column. "I must go to Sigurd. He needs his mother. He was too small to die alone. Look after Hermoth, and I will meet you in Valhalla." She screamed like a Valkyrie and urged her mount into a gallop around the flank of the Viking shield wall and raced towards the Franks.

"No, Sigrid, no," Hundr whispered, panic burning in his chest as he realised what she intended. And as she thundered towards Louis, the King of the East Franks, Hundr cried out in horror and pain. He surged forward, desperate to run to her, to stop her. Ragnhild grabbed him, and he shook her off. Then Bush and Thorgrim pinned him, and Hundr roared and shook as he watched his wife, his love, charge towards the King of the Franks. She rode with her spear held overhand, undulating a screeching war cry that sent a shiver down Louis' spine as he saw the Viking warrior woman coming to kill him. He abandoned his bravado and urgently tried to turn his mount away from Sigrid's charge. Twenty Franks peeled away from their shield wall and formed a barrier between Sigrid and King Louis, but she did not slow the horse.

Hundr cried out to her, yet he could not move. His friends held him fast, and the Viking ranks roared their acclaim at Sigrid's brave charge. Sigrid rose in the saddle to launch her spear, and it flew straight and true, but instead of hitting the king, it slammed into his horse's neck. The beast bucked violently, causing Louis to topple, and the Vikings went wild that the King of the Franks had fallen. Sigrid's horse shied away from the enemy warriors and dug its powerful hooves into the earth, throwing Sigrid from the saddle. She fell to the ground, rolled rapidly, and came up snarling with her axe in one hand and a knife in the other.

As the Franks gathered about their king, who rose groggily from the dirt, Sigrid charged at them. She ran headlong into twenty warriors and met her heart-rending end. Sigrid managed to kill two of them before a spear pierced her armpit, and another ran through her thigh. Still, Sigrid swung her axe. Hundr wept at her bravery and the overwhelming sadness which had driven her into a hopeless attack to die a warrior's death. A Frank opened her throat with his sword, and in a wash of bright blood, Sigrid left Midgard to join Sigurd in the afterlife. Hundr sagged, the strength seeping from his body just as Sigrid's lifeblood drained from hers. Visions flashed before his eyes of the day he had first seen her on Orkney, golden-haired and strong-willed. He remembered her hair whipped by the wind at sea and the joy in her blue eyes as their children laughed and played in Vanylven. Yet she was dead now. Sigrid's grief had been too much to bear, and her death took her away from that suffering but left Hundr and Hermoth alone.

"I've never seen anything like that," murmured Thorgrim, his eyes flitting from Hundr to the scene of Sigrid's death.

"Let's get moving, or we'll all die here today," uttered Ragnhild, her face pale at the shock of Sigrid's death.

Hundr found himself trapped in a world between wakefulness and dream. Thorgrim and Bush dragged him away from the fight. He couldn't hear anything but the sound of Sigrid's voice in his head. The Franks charged the Viking lines, and they retreated in perfect order, holding the clash of shields and moving back one pace at a time until they were half down the hill's slope. Hundr was vaguely aware of Bush blowing three blasts on his war horn and of a great cheer as the thunder of hooves rolled along the riverbank when Haesten's horsemen charged.

"Wake up, Lord," Sigvarth said, his bearded face looming before Hundr. But he could not stir himself. His love was dead, gone to join his son in the worlds beyond Midgard. His soul was broken in two, carved open as though by an axe on the battlefield. All that remained for him was little Hermoth, and as they dragged Hundr away from the battle and Haesten led his riders to crush the Franks' attack, Hundr realised he was cursed. Everybody he loved died.

Is this the cost of my reputation? Is this the price Odin takes for my ascent from nothing to becoming who I am today? Must everything I hold dear die or endure pain?

FOURTEEN

"I don't want that woman putting a bloody spell on me," grumbled Einar as he paced back and forth before his cabin. He wrung his hands and stopped, sniffing the foul air coming from his door. He shook his head and carried on five paces, then turned and walked back the other way.

"Stop being so difficult," Hildr tutted, and she hopped in front of Einar to stop him in his tracks. She placed her hands on either side of his face and looked him in the eyes. "We have nothing to eat. Winter is here, there is frost on the water every morning, and soon snow will cover these hills. It will be here for months. We have no home and live in the forest like animals. We need an answer."

"We need an army."

"But we don't have one. Your people are going to starve. Rollo burned all we had and killed Trygve and many of our warriors. If you won't go to Ugattr for fear that he will cast you out, the galdr-woman will help make sure that he won't."

"So, not only do I have to subject myself to this infernal woman's seiðr, but I also have to go begging to Jarl Ugattr?"

"Galdr is runes and songs, the old ways of healing and magic from the days of our ancestors. Seiðr is wicked magic, dark and malevolent. There is a difference, Einar, and you know it."

"I'd rather charge into Vanylven with my men and try to kill the long-shanked bastard." Einar's words were empty, and he spoke of the impossible. His thought cage rattled and swam with the problems he and his people faced. He could not sleep, and Trygve's death had hit Einar hard. Deep down, Einar knew he just had to overcome his warrior's pride and do what must be done.

"We have discussed this many times, my love. You are our leader, and you must do the hard things. You must act so that our people can live and so that we can have our revenge on Rollo."

Einar sighed. He stared into Hildr's blue eyes, and he nodded. Everything she said was true, and Einar could not listen to another child crying because they were hungry. So, he took a deep breath and ducked inside his cabin. Smoke was thick in the dark room. There was a foulness to it, like powdery decay, and Einar's eyes watered as it swarmed his senses. Hundr had submitted himself to the old woman's power when Sigrid struggled to birth the twins, and it had worked then, so Einar knelt in the darkness and readied himself.

"Ah, Lord Einar," came a cracked, dry voice like old leaves in a summer forest. "Drink if you seek wisdom."

A wrinkled face appeared from the smoke, leaning towards Einar and leering at him with a toothless mouth. Spittle ran from the corner of her lips as she cackled, and her spindly gnarled hand appeared, knuckles huge, offering him a horn of foul-smelling liquid.

"Are you sure you can help me, woman?"

Her brows knitted into a frown, and it was a crinkled mocking thing of cunning, cleverness, and malevolent derision. "I cannot tell you what the gods will show you. You have asked for the other worlds to help you save your people, and I will try to send you a vision which will help you on that path. It might show you a vision of doom and destruction or one of hope and happiness. Your path is your own, Einar Rosti, so drink and let us see if the galdr will aid you."

"What is it?" he asked, his head already swimming from the smoke.

"Drink," she replied and would say no more, so Einar took the cup and begrudgingly drank the awful liquid that tasted like death, mould and bitter blood. His head felt instantly light, and Einar sank down so that he lay on his side. The woman laughed again and capered about him, her long, dark stick banging on the ground. Charms hanging from its top shook and clanged together to make rhythmic music. The harsh runes scratched into the dark stick seemed to glow white. They were the Odin runes, and the galdr-woman chanted her nine charms of power.

"You seek power and strength, Einar Rosti," she chimed between verses; her eyes rolled white, and Einar could feel himself slipping.

"Yes," he uttered, and Einar allowed himself to fall under her spell. He drifted away from Midgard as his eyes became heavy and his lids closed.

Einar, who was not Einar, moved about his hall, searching for his favourite weapon. He smiled as his hand curved around the cold whetstone. Dwarfish craftsmen had chipped and knapped its long shaft smooth and carved its giant hammer-like head into the snarling skull of a mighty dragon. Einar ran a monstrous hand over the dragon's stone teeth and the stone of its wicked eyes, and he remembered the cursed Aesir and Vanir he had slain with its hard edges. That memory was not Einar's own, and inside the head which he inhabited, Einar flinched at the landscapes on which the being had fought. He had fought atop icy glaciers and fire-spitting mountains in the eight realms beyond Midgard against monsters with snapping teeth, gods with shining hair and sharp-tipped weapons. The hand was huge, the size of a horse, and Einar reeled, understanding that he was not himself. The hall was enormous, and it was not his own hall at Vanylven but a vast construction as large as Vanylven itself. Its walls were crafted from the timbers of wrecked ships, crushed and lashed together with their curved keels facing upwards and piled prow over stern reaching up to keep the roof in place. The roof arched above him, higher than the largest tree, and that was made from the chariots of champions, of the gods and elves he had killed in battle.

Einar knew his name, for it was his own name. He was still The Brawler, but not Einar Rosti. In this world, he was Hrungnir, which also meant 'the brawler', but here, he was the mightiest and strongest of all the warriors in Jotunheim, the realm of the giants. Einar panicked a little at that realisation, for how could he be another being, especially a hugely powerful giant in mystical Jotunheim? Then he remembered the galdr-woman and her foul potion and understood she had transported him to another realm. Einar fought to manage his panic at that strangeness so that he could allow the vision to show him what it would. His arms were hugely muscled, and his head was bulbous and thick-lipped. Roasted meat and horns of ale filled his table. A hearth fire burned like a yule bonfire, and Hrungnir set himself down on his bench made from the trunks of twenty oak trees and began to eat.

Just as he took a drink of ale, Hrungnir heard a strange sound from beyond his hall. He rose from his table to see who came to pay him a visit or what manner of creature in Jotunheim had disturbed his meal. Hrungnir drew the doors open, and the snow and wind whipped his face and howled into his hall, sending the fire's flames dancing. A horse approached, though it was no usual steed, for this one had eight legs and rode through the air like an eagle on the wing. It landed upon the fjord beyond Hrungnir's hall, where it galloped across the water's surface. Its hooves threw up plumes of water as it rode as though weightless across the tranquil fjord.

"Who is this stranger on a magical horse?" Hrungnir said aloud.

The rider brought his unusual mount to a stop before the hall and leant over the saddle to grin at Hrungnir. The rider was hatchet-faced, and his one eye gleamed like an emerald. His teeth were bright white, his smile was wicked and welcoming, and his stature was lean and tall.

"I wager my own head that my horse can outrun any horse in Jotunheim," intoned the stranger. His voice was simultaneously like the crashing of a waterfall and the sleekit steps of a cat.

Hrungnir's brow furrowed, and he shook his fist at the belligerent stranger who had come to his hall so rude and uninvited.

"I accept your bet," growled Hrungnir, jutting the cliff of his jaw towards the stranger. Hrungnir was the champion of the giants, and who was this sharp-faced stranger with one eye to challenge him in his own hall? Hrungnir had never lost a fight, a challenge to wrestle, nor a race on land or sea, and he was not about to be shamed by this unknown visitor full of bellicose confidence.

Hrungnir marched to his stable and brought forth his steed, a mighty horse fit for a giant. Gullfaxi was his name, golden-mane, and he was the fastest of all the beasts in the vast, dangerous wilderness of Jotunheim. Einar felt the strength of the magnificent horse as he mounted its back. It snorted and pawed at the earth, then set off at a gallop faster than anything Einar had ever experienced. He was Hrungnir, and he clung to Gullfaxi's mane as he pounded the ground with his mighty hooves that could outrun the wind.

The stranger and his eight-legged horse kept pace with Hrungnir and Gullfaxi, and they raced through mud and streams, over steep, rocky hills, across vast mountains, and wove between the trees of the wilderness in a blur of speed. The eight-legged horse burst past Gullfaxi, and her rider whooped for joy as they thundered into the distance. Hrungnir followed, desperate to catch the boastful stranger and win the race. Before Hrungnir realised where he was, he had left Jotunheim and entered Asgard, the realm of the Aesir, who were his mortal enemies. Only when he realised he would never catch the eight-legged horse did the cloak of disguise lift, and Hrungnir instantly recognised the rapid mount as the famed Sleipnir and the stranger was his enemy, Odin himself.

Odin waited for Hrungnir, and with him were Hrungnir's familiar foes, Thor, Tyr, Frey and Njorth, but instead of attacking him with hammer, sword and spear, the Aesir welcomed Hrungnir, and they feasted together to celebrate the great race. The gods granted

Hrungnir a horn fit for a champion, a guest horn which was so curved that he could not set it down and so it was continually refilled, and he drank the honey-sweet ale until he toppled from his feasting bench and belched so loud that all the forests in Midgard shook.

Einar, who was Hrungnir, felt himself drunk and heard the laughter of the gods who sat around him feasting and making merry. As Hrungnir, he stared into the frightening face of Tyr and the open, broad face of Thor. They drank more and more until Hrungnir couldn't control the words that spilt from his mouth. Einar trembled and fought to control the giant whose mind and body he inhabited, but he could do nothing.

"I will kill all of you, Aesir," he boasted, waving his colossal giant's arm around the gathered gods. "I will crush you all like worms. All save beautiful Freya and Sif. You two, I will take back to Jotunheim to be my wives for eternity. I will drink all of your ale, crush your puny heads, and take your women as my own."

Thor rose, his face turned into a frowning terror of sharp cheekbones, blazing eyes and gnashing teeth, and his fury was like a thunderous ocean storm as he slammed his fist down upon the table to shock Hrungnir into silence. Thor reached for his hammer, and Mjolnir shone like the brightest star as the god held it aloft.

"Ha!" Hrungnir called. "Mighty Thor, enemy of all giants on Jotunheim. Would you strike down an *unarmed man who is a guest of your people? All will know that Thor is a coward who spurns his honour-bound duty of guest friendship."*

"Then arm yourself, giant," Thor bellowed. "For nobody threatens my wife and lives to tell the tale."

Sif was Thor's beautiful wife and was herself a giantess. Hrungnir stood to confront the thunder god.

"I challenge you then, Thor, to single combat. Let us fight, you and I, and bring great honour to the victor."

Thor could not refuse the challenge, and the fight was set. Einar felt no fear in the mind of Hrungnir on the day of combat. He marched to the agreed field, which lay on the borders of Asgard and Jotunheim, wearing his heavy stone armour and hefting his stone shield. The battlefield was empty, and Hrungnir waved his whetstone above his head and called for the coward of Asgard to meet his fate. The sky shook, the earth trembled, and thunder split the sky in a flash of dazzling light. Thor roared onto the battlefield, throwing his war hammer, Mjolnir, and Hrungnir slung his whetstone. The two weapons sang past each other as they flew across the plane, and Hrungnir rejoiced as his whetstone hurtled into Thor's skull. He saw victory and was about to crow his might, yet the whetstone smashed on Thor's head, shattered into countless pieces, and those shards became the flints of Midgard. Hrungnir's glory quickened to horror as his weapon broke apart upon the god's brow, and Mjolnir came at him in a blur of iron.

Hrungnir blinked, and Mjolnir slammed into his head, crushing his skull and killing him instantly. Einar felt the pain of that blow as though it were his own head crushed to splinters. But he knew he had harmed mighty Thor and that a shard of that whetstone would remain in Thor's head until the day of Ragnarök.

Einar awoke with a start. He gagged and then vomited a thin string of yellow bile onto the cabin floor. He had been a giant and seen the gods, and his thought cage reeled with the strangeness of it. There had been an Odin trick, a challenge, a feast and single combat. Einar did not know what any of it meant, but as he crawled from the cabin, the galdr-woman cackled and assured him that if he had seen the gods he had their favour. She told him that his spirit had travelled beyond Midgard and into another of the nine realms which stretched from the branches of Yggdrasil.

Hildr met him with a cloak and hurried him away from the cabin. They sat by a fire as Einar told her all he had seen, and the vision shook her. Einar shivered from the foul sickness in his belly and the fearsome knowledge inside his thought cage that he had left Midgard and walked amongst the nine realms. The galdr had worked, but Einar struggled to understand what significance the vision, or his journey to the other world, had for the future of Vanylven or his people.

"It could mean that Rollo has Odin's favour, and that is why he defeated us, just as Odin defeated

Hrungnir in the race?" Hildr said. She stared into the flames, seeking the truth of the vision in her own mind.

"I do not think so," replied Einar. "The galdr-woman said that if I'd seen the gods, I had their favour. I think it's a warning to watch for deep cunning but also not to let pride blind my vision and cloud my judgement."

"What do you mean?"

"All this time, you have been urging me to go to Jarl Ugattr and ask him for food, and I have not done it because I dislike the man. I would not go because I am a warrior. I am Einar the Brawler, and I could not belittle myself in front of that fat pig. Just as Hrungnir was so blinded by Odin's challenge that he accepted a race against mighty Sleipnir, a race he could never win, and he failed to see the right of what he should have done."

"So you will go to Jarl Ugattr?"

"I must, and I should have done it weeks ago. Perhaps we should have all gone to Jarl Ugattr and asked him to house us for the winter instead of living out here in the forest like elves."

"So we shall all march to Ugattr?"

"We shall. All of us will make the journey and throw ourselves upon Ugattr's mercy. We cannot stay here in the woods. Rollo will strike again. He believes Hundr is out here somewhere, and the bastard hates him. Rollo loathes Hundr with the same venom that drips onto Loki's face each day when Sigyn empties the bowl she uses to catch the serpent's drips, which will burn the trickster god until the day of Ragnarök. Rollo will never give up, not now that he is so close to destroying us. He also has a foothold in Norway from which he can harry King Harald and take up their old fight."

"You do not think Rollo will return to his home in Frankia when this is over?"

"Rollo hates King Harald almost as much as he hates Hundr. Harald took everything from him, his lands and his father's jarldom. Rollo is a Duke of the Franks, but he is still a Viking and who knows where his ambition ends? Vanylven is a strong fortress; from there, he can strike up and down the coast with his fleet and his warriors and attack Avaldsnes itself should he wish."

"Harald would stop him. He is the king and has a fleet of his own. Besides, when Hundr returns, we will drive Rollo back to the sea and crush his warriors beneath the fury of our blades."

"So we will. But we must be alive to do it, and even if Hundr returns shortly, we cannot do it without food in our bellies. We will starve to death out here, so let's strike camp and gather our people. For we must march to Jarl Ugattr."

Hildr smiled and sprang to her feet to set about organising the women and children to march. Einar warmed his hands on the fire and belched out some of the galdr-woman's brew, which still churned in his stomach. Einar could see things clearly now since she had worked her galdr or seiðr; Einar wasn't sure which, but the truth of that would play out in the Jarl Ugattr's hall. Only then would Einar know if the crone had woven a charm with her song and rune stick or if it was dark-seiðr that lured him to his death. Ugattr would not welcome Einar and his people. It would be a burden on his winter supplies. Ugattr was a greedy old crust of a bastard, and there was just as much chance that the jarl would slaughter Einar's people as take them in. Ugattr could easily send his warriors out, butcher Einar on the road, and leave his people to rot in the forest. When Hundr and Harald came asking what happened to the people of Vanylven, Ugattr could blame Rollo for the massacre, and nobody would be any the wiser. Despite the uncertainty, Einar would march his people to the old jarl and risk everything, relying on his vision from the gods and believing that his eyes were now open to fate and destiny.

FIFTEEN

Hundr's breath blew from his mouth in great clouds like dragon smoke, and he cuffed at his running nose. He reached down and grabbed Fenristooth's ivory hilt, which was icy to touch, so cold that it almost burned. He wrapped his hands around the grip and loosened the blade in its scabbard. Hundr didn't want to risk the blade sticking in the frost when it was time to kill, and he wanted to kill. He needed it. Haesten, Rognvald and Ravn had led their army in a retreat eastwards away from Hammaburg and the Elbe and had then turned south, aiming to swing their army around King Louis and come about northwest back towards the river and their ships.

They had marched for a week since the fight on the hilltop overlooking Hammaburg's choke point in the Elbe, and it had been a week since Sigrid had died. Since that day, Hundr had led his men and a crack force of the bravest and wildest of Haesten's, Rognvald's, and Ravn's men. They were the rearguard, the men who stayed in the field harrying and hitting the Franks. King Louis' vanguard pursued the Great Viking Army as it trampled across Saxony, foraging, burning farms, and eating and drinking towns dry of food and ale as they tried to stay alive. Winter descended on Saxony, and snow, frost and ice settled upon the land like barnacles and lichen on a ship's hull.

Hundr threw himself into the defensive action. He rode out against the Franks' scouts; he killed and robbed their foraging parties of food and ambushed the vanguard whenever he could. Like the Vikings, the Franks would send warriors out ahead of the army's main body. It was their job to scout, remove obstacles, prepare towns for the marching army, forage and protect the army from attack. Every day since Sigrid's death, Hundr had fought, rode, eaten, and slept in the field. The action meant that he had not had time to think of how his wife had died, how she had sacrificed her life at the altar of her grief. Night was his enemy – when the day's fighting was over, and he was alone beneath his blanket. Then, Hundr's mind had time to reflect on Sigrid, Sigurd, and Hermoth. He would lie awake, questioning if he had been a bad husband and a poor father. He wondered if Sigrid had resented becoming a mother, giving up her dream of being a warrior and a shield maiden like Ragnhild and Hildr. There were no answers to those questions, and sleep came fitfully and with dark dreams each night. Children's laughter mixed with Sigurd's dead face, or the scene of Sigrid hacked to death by Frankish blades would come to him and haunt him. Hundr feared that Sigrid's fetch had remained in Midgard, that she had not travelled to

Valhalla and lingered instead to trouble and haunt Hundr and would do so for the rest of his life.

Hundr slid his sword in and out of his scabbard again, waiting for the enemy to emerge from the trees. He crouched behind a thick hedge of brambles and thorns which separated one farmer's field from another. There were no crops in the ground this time of year. The soil was frozen hard, and Hundr heard the wagons before he saw them. The rumble and creak of their wheels and the whistles and shouts of the herders sang out from the forest before the first riders came from the treeline.

"Here they come," said Ragnhild. She took a bowstring from the pouch at her belt and strung her bow.

"How many?" asked Thorgrim. "My eyes can't see that far."

"Ten guards and the same amount of shepherds and herders," replied Sigvarth.

"Wait until they get close," said Hundr. "Wait until we can smell the cow shit, then attack."

Hundr had thirty men, all crouching behind the hedgerow, and he worried that the mist of their breath rising from the bushes would give them away. The enemy that day was a column of cows and ale being brought from a southern Saxon town north to feed the army. Hundr's men had tracked them and now lay in wait. The supplies would be welcome in camp and help keep the Viking army fed, while for King Louis, the loss would hurt his men and keep them hungry.

"My bloody arse is freezing," muttered Bush, stifling a cough. "How long has it been since we slept in a bed?"

"Too long," replied Thorgrim.

"You know this won't help us, right?" Bush leaned in and whispered to Hundr.

"We hurt the enemy and strengthen our men," Hundr lipped curtly. He spoke more harshly than he intended, but he was growing tired of Bush and the others constantly questioning him. All day, they would ask if he was alright, if he needed anything, or when they would return to Vanylven. Hundr was fed up with it but did not voice those frustrations. They were his warriors, his oathmen, and his friends, and he knew they were worried about him. Sigrid's death had hit him hard – that was plain enough – and Hundr would have acted the same had it been one of their wives who had died so recently and so tragically.

"Being out here like this every day won't help us do what we came here for. Surely, we could just ask Rognvald to take young Prince Erik, and we can be on our way. With Rognvald's men, we could fight our way back to the ships. We could be back in Vanylven before Yule," Bush reasoned.

"We can't just leave Haesten here to die, and besides, the road back to Rognvald's ships is crawling with Franks. We must fight them and march back towards the ships with the army, then we return with Prince Erik."

"It won't help you either," Bush said softly. He fished a scrap of cloth from behind his brynjar and dabbed at whatever he had coughed up.

Hundr clenched his teeth. Bush spoke of his grief, and Hundr did not wish to talk about it. He didn't want to admit that the fighting helped. He could not summon the words to express that it took his mind off Sigrid and Sigurd and the worry for Einar and the folk of Vanylven. Fighting was simple. Hundr sought the enemy. He set ambushes and traps, and he fought and killed. The intricacies of that filled his mind and forced the sadness and sorrow down, barging it away like an enemy in the shield wall.

"Any closer, and they'll see us," warned Ragnhild.

Hundr nodded, and he turned to Agnarr and Jogrimmr, the most trusted of the fighters he had taken from Haesten and Ravn for the rearguard fighting. They were both solid men, grim Vikings who loved battle as much as Hundr and his crew. They nodded their bearded faces to confirm that they were ready, and Hundr pointed north. The two warriors took ten men and skirted along the briar, keeping low as they marched with their axes and knives ready to strike.

The wagons came closer, and the warriors amongst the Franks ranged in front of them. Three were on horseback, armed with shields and swords, and the rest marched with long spears and shields. Hundr took a deep breath before he rose and marched from the hedgerow. The Franks called out in panic when they saw Hundr and his warriors emerge from behind the brambles, and Ragnhild loosed an arrow to take the foremost rider in the neck. The rider coughed and gurgled before tumbling from the saddle, and his horse bolted, dragging the dying man with him so that his blood smeared and dotted the frosted soil like bright berries.

The Franks turned to face their enemy, and Hundr charged them. He gripped Fenristooth and ran across the field, the frozen divots hard and bumpy beneath his boots. Wide-eyed, the Franks stared at him in disbelief. Ragnhild dropped another rider with her deadly arrows, and Hundr twisted around a lowered spear point to cannon his shoulder into the spearman's shield. He turned into the blow, and as he came around, Hundr slashed the blade of his sword across the next warrior's thighs. The Frank cried out in pain, and as he bent over, Hundr brought Fenristooth down overhand to chop into the back of his unprotected neck. The spearman turned and died as Thorgrim swung his double-bladed war axe into his back, crunching ribs and splitting the Frank's heart like a chopped turnip.

Agnarr and Jogrimmr led their men to attack the enemy's rear, and there was a brief clash of arms before the Franks were subdued and the Viking warriors captured the supply wagons and animals. All the Frankish warriors were killed and stripped of anything of value. Hundr and Ragnhild took the two horses and ordered Bush to march the captured supplies back to Haesten and the army whilst they rode to a slant of high ground to the north. The farmland swept up into a hill that fell away into a face of red, chalky rock but would give them a good view across that part of Saxony, which was a low, flat land dotted with forests and farmland. The further south the army marched, farms gave way to heathland, flat and covered by wild grasses and purple heather, and Hundr took Ragnhild to the hilltop to seek more prey, to look for more Franks to kill. There would be scouts and foraging parties thick across the lowlands, reporting back to the main column regularly so that the king could understand where his enemy marched.

The horses cantered up the slope and Ragnhild rode alongside Hundr on a palfrey, its smooth, ambling gait in contrast to Hundr's roan mare, which seemed to want to fight him as he urged her up the hill. Ragnhild reined in at the summit, and Hundr did the same, but where Ragnhild's horse stopped and nuzzled at the frozen grass, Hundr's beast turned in a circle, and he had to haul on the reins to keep the animal still.

"You want to find more prey?" asked Ragnhild, patting her mount's neck and grinning at Hundr's wilder horse and how it annoyed him so.

"Aye, we could fight again today."

"I know Bush clucks about you like an old hen, but he is right. Sooner or later, you will need to mourn for Sigrid."

"I know it," he said, and then before he could say any more, both he and Ragnhild were stunned to silence because snaking towards them from the north was King Louis and his vast army. They spread over the flatlands like a great mass of insects, swarming and shifting, metal glittering and glinting under the cool winter sun. The army was within striking distance, which meant King Louis was close enough to force the Vikings to battle but also vulnerable to being attacked himself. The Franks had the greater numbers, but Hundr dug his heels into his obstinate horse's flanks and thundered towards Haesten, riding hard because he saw a chance to defeat the King of the Franks in battle.

"Fight them?" said Haesten later that day. He drew a hand along his chin beard and stared at Hundr, his sharp face shifting as his mind mulled over the opportunity.

"Why fight when we can turn about them and return to our ships without the need for battle?" asked Rognvald. He sat on a milking stool, devouring steaming hot roast beef. Hundr had found the army at camp and raced to the leaders to tell them how close the enemy had come to their own army.

"For glory," said Ravn, frowning at Rognvald. "If we beat them, we can kill a king, and men will remember our names forever."

"And if we lose?" asked Haesten, yet nobody answered that question.

"If we lose, we die," said Hundr. "Any survivors would have to flee across this frozen wasteland back towards the ships, dogged all the way by the victorious Franks."

Hundr and Ragnhild had ridden hard ahead of his rearguard force to bring the news of the advancing Franks to the army's leaders. Hundr had found them camped by a stream that cut through a swathe of purple heather where the land had changed from verdant farmland to the sandy soil of open heath. The rolling planes in that part of Saxony were heavy with gorse, heather and wild, coarse grass, meaning that there was little to be found by the Viking's foraging parties other than what they could steal from the Franks.

"So, stick to the plan," said Rognvald, dusting a speck of dirt from his fine tunic. "Turn our army northwest tomorrow and march towards the fleet. The Franks are a lumbering mess, whereas we are fast and organised. Why risk battle?"

"The English king beat us at Ethandun," Haesten uttered wistfully, staring away to the north as though he expected to see King Louis marching out before them. "Guthrum came close to crushing Alfred, but then victory became defeat, and they slaughtered our crews in that battle, which was so grim as to be close to the end of days. You were there, Hundr, you saw."

"I was there," Hundr nodded, remembering the terrible battle and how he had marched away from its horror, feeling lucky to have survived.

"If we march away now when we could have fought, men will say that we are raven starvers. That we are shirkers and tremblers."

"Who cares what men say?" tutted Rognvald with a shrug.

"We are *drengr*," said Ravn, clapping his fist to his chest. "Reputation is everything. Who will remember our names when we are dead and gone if we flee from battle? A *drengr* takes the fight; he seeks it out and battles bravely – and in the front rank even if it means his death."

Hundr understood that viewpoint, and he agreed with Ravn. Had he been his younger self, Hundr would have charged headlong into the fight beside the warrior jarl, uninterested in the odds or the outcome, and he would have done it because men would remember his name. Now, however, Hundr had Hermoth to think about, as well as his reputation.

Haesten sighed. "If we shirk the fight, we will lose crews when we reach the fleet. Ships will sail for home and never return. They will return to Kattegat, the Vik and the Skagerrak, and the great army will break up. The jarls and warlords will go back to their fires and tell of the time they almost took Hammaburg and when they almost won a kingdom in England. Their purses and hulls will be as empty as when they left, and men will say that Haesten is not a good ring giver, that he does not have the Odin luck, the battle luck. Then next summer, they will find a new lord to join up with – one who possesses that luck and can lead them to victory, glory and riches."

"So we shall fight, then?"

Haesten tucked his thumbs into his wide belt and smiled mirthlessly. "We should ask your Sami, Jarl Rognvald. See what he augurs for the battle."

"Just so," said Rognvald. "I will ask Bavlos to ask his gods and see if he can tell us if the portents are good or ill."

Rognvald draped an arm over Ravn's broad shoulders and dragged the big man away with him to find Bavlos. Ravn stared at Rognvald's hand as though it were covered in shit, but he followed him anyway, leaving Hundr alone with Haesten.

"Do you believe in the Sami man's seiðr?" asked Haesten once Rognvald and Ravn were out of earshot.

"He has power," Hundr said. "I have seen it… before the battle of Hafrsfjord, and Bavlos once led King Harald Fairhair to the tomb in which he found the Yngling sword in the hands of a *draugr*."

"So he can talk to the gods?"

"His gods, perhaps, but not ours. Bavlos prays to the rivers, trees, the sky, bears, wolves and foxes. He also makes the drink that turns Rognvald from the placid man he is today into a fearsome ulfheðnar."

"Perhaps the little wizard will cast his bones or runes and see a chance for us to fight and become rich. For if we do not find a place to spend the winter here in Saxony, I do not know where to go next."

Hundr stared at the lines and creases in the old warrior's face. They told a tale of a long life at sea and on the edge of a blade. Haesten was an adventurer and a man who had built one of the greatest Viking reputations for himself. He had done more than most men could in twenty lifetimes. But, as Haesten spoke about where to go and what to do, Hundr realised Haesten had nothing. He had no home or family, and Hundr wondered then at the life he had pursued and the dreams that had driven him to leave his home so long ago. Reputation had seemed everything to a small boy shunned by his father and half-brothers in the harsh palace in Novgorod. But when Hundr stared at Haesten amidst the fog of grief over the loss of Sigurd and Sigrid, he wondered whether Haesten actually had what mattered in life. Did the simple churl dwelling in a hovel, farming pigs and wheat, yet sharing his life with a loving wife and children possess more than the great warrior without a place to call home?

Hundr thought of Bush, another fine warrior who had sailed further and seen more of the world than most men could dream of. But he was old and alone, and Bush now talked often of Valhalla. He was concerned for his soul and also what might become of him if he lived. Was Bush's destiny to become an old, toothless shipmaster wandering a port somewhere without a home or anyone to care for him? Would the man who had sailed with Ivar the Boneless, Einar the

Brawler, and The Man with the Dog's Name end up a beggar in a ditch? Hundr shuddered at the thought because that could easily be his destiny. He imagined the Norns cackling and weaving the threads of men's lives at the foot of Yggdrasil and wondered if he would ever have a home of his own or find any sort of happiness. He had been happy with Sigrid, but Vanylven was Einar's home, and everybody whom Hundr had loved was dead, save for little Hermoth.

"What is it, old friend? You seem lost in thought?" asked Haesten.

"My wife died, and I told you of my son's recent passing."

"I heard tell of it. You have my sympathies, but such things are hard to discuss between warriors, are they not?"

Hundr nodded at that truth. "Do you ever wonder what destiny awaits you?"

Haesten smiled. "Of course I do. Only a fool does not fear the future. I think of the men I have killed, the wife and child I lost, and the fortress I once held in Frankia. I think of the time Bjorn Ironside and I took a fleet of long-hulled warships around the curve of far Ispania and traded gold with men whose faces were burned black by the sun. All that remains to me is a glorious death and a place in Valhalla."

"And until then?"

"Until then, I do what I have always done. Fight, take what I can, draw men to my service, and keep them happy with rings and silver. Build a name which men will remember."

"Is that a good life?"

"What do you mean?" Haesten's face curved in on itself as though the question was beyond the realms of comprehension.

"What is our reputation as warriors worth once we are dead?"

"Nothing," said Haesten with a shrug, and he turned and walked away. But then he stopped, seeming to think to himself for a moment, and then glanced back to Hundr with a wolfish grin on his sharp face. "Everything."

Hundr woke early the next morning after a night spent pondering his curse and his fate. A bleak sun had only begun to eek over the flat heath when he pulled on his brynjar and sword and headed out to scout the enemy. Hundr saddled a horse and cantered out into the grey-yellow morning, and as he drew away from the camp, he had to pull his cloak tight about his shoulders to keep out the cold. A frigid wind swept in from the south, with a bite as icy as steel in its whip, and as the tents and standards of the enemy came into view beyond a strange rise of sand dunes in the low heathlands, snow began to fall. It danced and bobbed delicately in the wind. A flurry of white that began as single snowflakes melted the second they hit the frozen ground but quickly became thicker and wilder, blotting out the sky in a sheet of white that wet Hundr's face and concealed the enemy lines from view.

Then the chance hit Hundr like a thunderbolt. The snowstorm hid the enemy, just as any attack would be hidden by the white cloak of falling snowflakes. Hundr wheeled his horse around and galloped back to camp, shedding his melancholy beneath the blanket of snow. He saw a chance of victory, a daring chance to use the snow and attack King Louis and his mighty army. Hundr could win a battle and grasp a chance to sail back to Vanylven, where his people needed him, where Einar needed him. And so, with resolve, he rode to the Viking camp to bring an army to war.

SIXTEEN

Einar and the people of Vanylven reached Jarl Ugattr's lands after four days of hard marching across hills and valleys in the grip of winter's onset. If Einar had marched alone with his warriors, they could have crossed the distance in two days, but the children and the elderly in the company slowed the journey down. They brought their sailcloth tents and as much of their remaining food as they could carry. Each night, they camped in woodland or the lee of a rocky hillside to keep out the chill winds. Children cried, the sick struggled, and Einar marched at the head of the column with Amundr and Torsten whilst Hildr and her newly formed company of archers took up the rear.

Ugattr's lands lay east of Vanylven, along the course of the Nordfjord waterway and where the Innvikfjorden fjord ended. His hall sat between sheer cliffs in a green valley where the glass-like fjord turned into a winding river in a place called Stryn. Einar's column marched silently over a high, pine-covered hillside and descended into the sheltered valley of Stryn. The valley was nestled between snow-capped mountains and steep hillsides thick with dark forest. Stryn itself boasted a high gabled hall and was protected by a ditch, bank, and palisade with a low gate and was only approachable by land from the west. The mountains protected it to the north and east while the south was bordered by water. To approach the town, any attacker or raider would pass countless villages on the journey east, and by the time a fleet of warships reached the end of the fjord, they would find an army of Norse warriors waiting to greet them.

"Looks like a nice place to live," remarked Amundr as Einar called the column to halt.

"If you like goats, ice, and mountain trolls," quipped Einar. The place was green, with a freshwater river bringing cool water down from the mountains. But the hillsides had no farms, only scree and pine trees, and all the folk lived in the valley basin, which meant that whilst Ugattr was safe in his beautiful valley, he was also poor, for Einar could not imagine the area produced much surplus grain or meat to support the jarl, his band of hearth troop warriors and their families who contributed nothing, but whose value was in the strength of their blades. There were trees and goat shit in abundance, though not much wealth that Einar could see save for the three ships which Ugattr's men had dragged up to shore for cleaning and caulking over the winter.

"I like goats," Amundr said in his slow, deep voice. Torsten chortled, and Amundr frowned as if puzzled by his laughter. "They eat anything. Their milk and cheese taste good, and they are easy to keep."

"Can we stop talking about stinking goats, please?" muttered Einar. He pulled off the naalbinding cap and gloves he had worn during the march and searched for his brynjar in the pack he had worn across his back. He unrolled the armour, took off his cloak and shrugged the leather lining and shimmering fish scale plates over his head. Einar slid his axe into the loop at his belt and a long seax blade at the small of his back.

Amundr opened his mouth again, but Torsten punched him lightly on the shoulder and shook his head. Einar ignored the gesture. He knew they were conscious of his belligerent mood, but he was about to beg a fellow jarl for food and a place to house his people over the winter and did not relish the prospect of it. The gates to Stryn were open. It was midway through the afternoon on a grey day, and a bald man came from the gate with his hands on his hips to stare up at Einar's column. The man wore a brynjar and looked over Einar's people for about as long as it would take him to count them. Einar had five score warriors and triple that number of women and children. They were hungry and desperate, and Einar had to persuade Ugattr to give them succour.

"The three of us will go down to the hall," said Einar, glancing at Hildr and Amundr. "The rest will wait here for our return."

Torsten passed the orders back to the warriors and joined the men to form a protective but loosely formed barrier between Stryn and the Vanylven women and children. Torsten wished Einar luck and ensured the warriors' formation did not appear threatening, yet they were ready in case Ugattr decided to take advantage of the easy prey and march his warriors out to butcher them where they stood.

"He won't attack," said Hildr as the three warriors strode down towards where the single man stood before the gates. She went armed with her bow and a quiver of arrows, axe, knife and brynjar. The glint of spears sparkled on the palisade, but there was not a heavy presence of warriors on the walls as far as Einar could see.

"Why not?" asked Einar. "I have met Ugattr before. He is old now, but he was a raider and a slaver in his younger days. With enough men, he could easily cut down our warriors and enslave our women and children – feed them through the winter and sail them to the slave markets in Dublin or Hedeby and make himself a fortune."

"So you don't trust Ugattr, then?" asked Amundr.

Einar resisted the urge to tell the big man to not ask silly questions. "I don't trust anyone."

"Jarl Einar of Vanylven?" said the bald man who stood before Stryn's gate. Einar, Amundr and Hildr stopped in front of him, and he stared at them with a stony expression. His face was long, and he had no hair on his head nor beard upon his face. He had no eyebrows either, so his blue eyes seemed huge and round. A scar cut across his nose, and he was broad across his chest and shoulders.

"I am Jarl Einar. Here to see Jarl Ugattr."

"It is strange for you to visit so late in the year and with so many at your back."

"Who are you?" Einar asked, having already lost his patience with the bald man and his belligerent tone.

"I am Baggi Bjarnisson," said the bald man, proud and with his chin raised.

"Never heard of you. I am Einar Rosti, and I shall speak with my fellow jarl, Ugattr. I have travelled far to pay this visit and am owed the honour of guest friendship. So, are we to bandy words out here all day like fishwives at market, or are you going to show us inside?"

Baggi raised a finger in a flash of anger, but then he took in the size and ferocity of Einar and Amundr and turned on his heel, beckoning them to follow.

"He's a testy little weasel, isn't he?" said Hildr, and Amundr growled.

Baggi led them into a town bustling with folk about their daily business. Stryn was much smaller than Vanylven, and the streets were cramped and slick with mud from the winter rains. A hook-nosed woman crossed Einar's path carrying a basket of eggs, and a young lad hobbled along in front of them, carrying two buckets of sloshing water in a yoke across his shoulders. Ugattr's hall sat on the west of the settlement. It was a long, narrow building with a stag's skull and sprawling antlers set into the gable above green-painted doors. All of Stryn's buildings were roofed with turf rather than the more expensive thatch, and the heavy, earthy smell of burning peat hung about the town like a fog.

Baggi opened the green doors, and Einar, Amundr, and Hildr followed him inside. Two warriors stood guard on the inside, but neither wore brynjars. They wore leather breastplates, held spears in their fists, and stared at Einar as he marched through the door. The hall stretched out long and narrow before him, with raised sleeping platforms on each side and feasting benches in rows along the open central area. A fire roared and crackled at the hall's centre, but there was no smoke hole cut into the roof; instead, the smoke hung and collected in the rafters like a stinking cloud. It seeped slowly out of the earth roof and from the open shutters, but Einar coughed at the cloying lack of air. It was a poor jarl's hall, without the size and grandeur of Vanylven's great hall, and nothing like the iron-wrought walls and doors of the halls Einar had seen in Ireland. A series of stout posts held up the roof, carved from entire tree trunks, which had become blackened by smoke over the years.

At the far end of the hall was a longer feasting bench, with one large chair facing southwards towards the rest of the feasting benches. There was no raised dais, but shields and spears hung from the far wall, as did the skulls of a bear, three wolves and another magnificent stag. Flitches of bacon and other meats hung from the rafters to cure in the dense smoke, and Einar thought it was more like a large

235

hovel than a small hall. As his eyes adjusted to the gloom, he saw women in furs huddled on the side platforms, and children with wild hair and filthy faces stared hungrily at Einar's shining fish scale armour.

"Jarl Ugattr will greet you when he is ready," muttered Baggi, turning to face Einar listlessly.

"Lord," said Einar brusquely.

"What?"

"I am Jarl Einar Rosti, and you will address me accordingly, or we can go outside and make the square. Just you and I between the hazel rods. We can do it now whilst we are waiting."

"Yes, my lord," Baggi blurted, licking his thin lips and backing away from Einar's threat. "I mean no, lord." He stammered, and his eyes flicked from Amundr to Einar, struggling to pay Einar the respect he deserved without agreeing to fight a duel.

Einar curled his lip and allowed Baggi to slink away into a back room through a small door. Einar sat down at a feasting bench with Amundr, and Hildr sat facing him across the tabletop.

"He hasn't even offered us ale or water," said Hildr. "Doesn't bode well."

Einar frowned because Hildr was right. Any jarl, warlord or wealthy merchant across the northlands would greet a guest with food, ale and welcome. It was part of their custom and expected. Einar would greet such visitors warmly in Vanylven and expect to be treated similarly whenever he stopped off at a town or stronghold on the Whale Road. This was the first time a fellow jarl had greeted Einar so coldly, which told him that Ugattr knew of his plight and had, therefore, decided that he did not need to offer any sort of respect or friendship to Einar and his people.

They waited in the hall for so long that Amundr had to ask a woman where he could piss, and still, no food or ale was offered or brought to their table. A weasel-faced steward stoked the fire, and a baby cried in a corner of a raised side platform. A thin dog with a long tail sniffed at Einar's boots and, pissed on the floor rushes by the back wall. Einar was about to bang his fist on the table and seek Ugattr himself when the rear door creaked open, and the small, shambling figure of Jarl Ugattr entered his hall. He was a tiny man, bent and crooked with age, with wisps of grey hair floating from his head as though he was underwater. His bottom gums were toothless, so his chin protruded, and his bottom lip sucked over his top as he limped slowly towards the large chair. He wore a fur cloak, though Einar could not tell which animal it had come from, for the thing was rancid and stank like a rotting corpse. He also wore a wool jerkin that was too tight around his protruding gut, and the bottom half of his belly showed. The flesh jiggled and shook as he walked, as pale and unsightly as a fetch.

Three women trailed after Jarl Ugattr. One was young and lithe, while the other two were older, both sad-faced with dark-ringed eyes and lank, oily hair.

The jarl ignored Einar and slumped in his seat. He grumbled and absentmindedly itched at his patchy beard, which was the colour of a wet, old fleece. Ugattr beckoned to the young girl with his left hand. It resembled a claw because it was missing three fingers, a remnant of a distant fight when the jarl was a younger, less rancid man. The girl reluctantly sat on Ugattr's lap, and his eyes rolled as he fondled her beneath her undyed woollen dress. She stared at Einar with flat, soulless eyes. The weasel-faced steward hurried back into the hall from the front door and set down a platter of meat and a large jug, from which he poured frothing ale into a carved wooden cup.

Ugattr grabbed a slice of pallid meat and sucked it between his missing teeth and gums, then tossed the soppy slice back onto the platter with a slap. He took a pull at his ale, and the liquid ran down his beard to wet his jerkin. Ugattr belched and finally allowed his pale eyes to rest on Einar. Ugattr held Einar's gaze for a moment, and there was certainly no fear in the old man's eyes but no respect, either. He continued to fondle the girl on his lap and turned his head as Baggi came striding in through the rear door.

"Jarl Ugattr, this is Jarl Einar of Vanylven," proclaimed Baggi in a loud voice, extending his arm out towards Einar as though he formally introduced the two lords.

"We have met before," Einar uttered, growing tired of the farce.

Ugattr growled again, and his eyes looked Einar up and down. "What do you want?" he said with a curl of his lip. "Come to beg for more food, I'd wager." His voice was chesty and wet as though thick phlegm sat at the back of his throat.

Einar closed his eyes and took a deep breath, forcing his rising anger down and remembering that he came to Stryn for his people. Without Ugattr's help, they would all die. "Jarl Ugattr," Einar began, bowing his head as an unearned mark of respect. "I come to you as a fellow Jarl and subject of King Harald…"

"Don't give me that, Einar. I've already given you more food than we could spare, and I know that you have lost your lands to a Duke of the Franks. Now, you have brought your people onto my lands, no doubt looking for more charity. Is that not the case, Einar?"

Einar took another deep breath. Ugattr was making a point of not addressing Einar with his title and continued to speak with a disrespectful sneer.

"Yes, an army of Franks forced me out of Vanylven, and my people need food and shelter until such a time as…"

"Well, you won't find it here, Einar. I can tell you that now. Don't think I have forgotten how you came to be Jarl of Vanylven. You and your assassin friend, the Man with the Dog's Name, killed my old friend, the rightful Jarl of Vanylven, and your other friend, the usurper Harald, granted you the land. So, don't come to me now begging for aid. I should drive you out like the filth you are. You are a marauder, a thief and a murderer, and I hope your people die."

Einar's anger rose, and he fought with himself to maintain calm, yet his fists bunched beneath the feasting bench. Amundr rose from his seat in outrage, but Hildr grabbed the giant's arm and dragged him back down.

"We can buy food from you. We have silver to trade for whatever surplus you have…"

"I should take your silver," Jarl Ugattr roared, and spittle flew from his mouth to spatter his plate. He pushed the girl away from him, and she scuttled off into the hall's dark recesses. "I should take everything from you, even your woman there. Yes…" His tongue flickered out as he looked Hildr up and down. "I have heard of your Valkyrie Priestess. Her meat is a bit old and tough for me, but she is pretty, and I could let my men tup her after I've had my fill of her old bones. How about that, Einar? I'll give you a wagon of food, but you must bring all of your women down here and give them to me. I'll take your whore Valkyrie to my bed and then let my hearth troop tup her throughout the winter. Then we shall sell all of your women as slaves. You can leave your weapons and all of your silver, too. That's the bargain. What say you, filth?"

Einar rose slowly, as did Amundr and Hildr. "I came here looking for aid from a fellow jarl, but all I have found is disrespect and insults."

"Don't take that tone with me!" Ugattr bellowed, and a guard slammed the butt of his spear down onto the hard-packed earth floor. The green doors swung open, as did the door at the rear, and warriors streamed into the hall armed with spears and axes. They wore leather armour and came with snarling faces and hungry eyes. The warriors kept on coming, filling the hall with the sound of the tramping boots and the stink of the sweat and sour ale breath. More came until the hall was packed full, and men crowded around Einar until he felt trapped. "I am Jarl here, and I can have your head with a snap of my fingers."

Einar shifted, and a man pushed him so that Einar fell into Amundr. The giant held Einar up, and he surged forward to shove the man back, but a fist cannoned into his head. Amundr charged into them but was beaten back by a dozen punches and kicks.

"Throw them out of my hall!" Jarl Ugattr shouted, and his warriors jostled Einar, Amundr, and Hildr. They cuffed at their heads and viciously kicked and punched them. Einar pushed his way to Hildr and grabbed her. She shrieked and struck out at the warriors who, instead of hitting her, pawed at her body with leering, twisted faces. Einar broke a man's jaw as he grabbed Hildr's breast, and panic burned in his chest as he tried to force his way through the crowd. Ugattr laughed, crowing his power above the din. "Throw the scum into the cold," he cried out, and his men jeered raucously while Einar feared he would die in that backwater hall.

241

"Follow me," Amundr said. The big man cracked his elbow off a man's skull and then picked another up by his throat, shaking him so hard that the man lost consciousness. They fell back from Amundr's size and Einar's anger. Hildr slipped her bow from her shoulder and quickly nocked an arrow to the string. She stretched the bow and aimed the arrow's wicked point at any who came close.

Einar kept moving and was at the green doors in six paces. Ugattr's men pressed close, leering and laughing like a pack of drunken dogs, and all the while, Ugattr cackled, enjoying Einar's humiliation. A fat man with a lopsided face spat on Einar's cheek, laughing as he did so, and Einar flinched at the degrading insult. Amundr pushed the doors open, and they spilt out into the open. Hildr turned and aimed her bow back towards the men inside the hall so that none came forth for fear of taking an arrow to the chest or throat. Einar cursed under his breath, for a horde of women, children, and old folk gathered there and just as their warriors had done in the hall, they shouted and sneered at Einar, Amundr and Hildr. Amundr threw the man he still held to the mud, and the women shrank back from his size, but then a small child with sores at the corners of his mouth picked up a handful of mud and tossed it at Amundr. The mud slapped into Amundr's back, and the giant turned vengefully. He was of the warrior caste, a proud man of reputation who deserved to be treated with respect and honour, not pelted with stinking mud.

"Keep moving," Einar growled, and the three warriors walked as quickly as they could without running. More mud flew from the hands of the mean-faced inhabitants of Stryn, and Einar bit his tongue as a cold, wet clod slapped into the side of his face. They reached the gate, which thankfully was still open, and passed through it as more missiles hit his back and legs. The horde climbed their palisade and hurled insults as Einar retreated up the hill to where his hungry people waited for him by the treeline.

"Snivelling backwater shit-eating turds," Amundr seethed, wiping mud from his face.

"They have forgotten," Einar said quietly, more to himself than anyone else. "I have forgotten."

"Forgotten what?" asked Hildr, her voice trembling from the narrow escape.

Ugattr's people could have easily swarmed and killed them as they left the hall and village, and Einar could only imagine that the reason Ugattr hadn't ordered that slaughter was because he wanted to give his warriors a fight to remember. Ugattr did not wish to curse his hall with murder and instead would send his warriors out in pursuit. They would come from the hall and the walls and hunt Einar's people, and there would be a massacre in a mountain pine forest.

"I lived too soft for too long. Ivar would be ashamed of me. I am Einar the Brawler, Viking Jarl and one-time captain of the warship Seaworm. I was the enforcer for Ivar the Boneless, the most feared killer and Viking warlord in the north, and now I beg

243

a toothless old raven starver for food when I should have taken it by force. Men have forgotten who I am. I have forgotten who I am. It is time to be that man again."

Einar's hand fell to his axe, and he let his fingers touch the cold steel. His thought cage burned with an insatiable desire for retribution against Ugattr's utter disrespect, the fat man who had spat in his face, and the coward who had groped Hildr.

They will suffer for it all, and I, Einar the Brawler, shall take what I need with axe, fire, and war.

SEVENTEEN

Hundr's boots crunched on fresh snow, and as he marched, he kept his one eye on the sun's outline beyond the wall of white flakes so that he knew how to find the enemy. He clenched his teeth to stop them from chattering, and around him, warriors cursed and complained about the bitter cold. The snow fell heavy and thick, and there was an eery silence across the heath as the land grew thicker and heavier with bright white snow.

"I hope you are right about this," intoned Haesten, who marched to Hundr's left. The old warrior carried an axe in his right hand and a shield in his left.

"Who would expect an attack in a snowstorm?" said Hundr. Which was precisely the argument he had used when he had ridden back to camp and urged Haesten, Ravn and Rognvald to attack.

"We could march past the enemy, miss them by a hundred paces, and never know. We could get lost out here."

"Call to Odin and keep a tight hold of your axe. For we are about to slaughter a king's army."

Haesten laughed at that, and on Hundr's right side, Ragnhild cursed the snow as she stumbled on a rock hidden by the cold, white blanket. Half of Ravn's warriors had remained at the Viking camp with Prince Erik and the baggage, but the rest of the Viking army marched towards King Louis and his troops.

"My toes have gone numb," grumbled Thorgrim. He marched like Hundr without a shield. He held his huge double-bladed war axe in two hands and frowned at his snow-sodden boots.

Howling rippled out further down the line, and through the snow, Hundr could just make out the unnerving ulfheðnar capering through the storm with bare chests and painted faces. Rognvald was amongst them. He had drunk Bavlos' brew as soon as they had agreed to attack, and the Jarl of Rogaland was no longer the serene-looking gentleman who wore fine clothes and spoke so eloquently. He had become the vicious, blood-mad wolf man who ran with his pack, and they howled at the snow like animals.

"Look!" Hundr said, pointing to tracks in the snow. There were footprints, almost covered by the heavy storm, yet still visible as sunken divots. "Get ready to charge. Bush?"

"I'm here," piped the old shipmaster, "but my lips might be too cold to blow my horn."

"Then warm them, for as soon as we get a sight of their camp, you are to blow two blasts. Then our army attacks, and we will kill them before they even know we are here." Hundr was confident in his plan, so confident, in fact, that the snowstorm almost seemed Odin sent. Hundr had returned to camp and tried to persuade the leaders to attack, and all had scoffed at the idea, save Haesten. So, Rognvald had asked Bavlos to augur the plan and see what his ancient gods would tell him of the chance to kill an army of Franks. Bavlos had cast off his rancid cloak and drank his foul concoctions. He had danced around a fire and banged his drum with a yellowed thigh bone until his eyes rolled white and foam erupted from his mouth. The seiðr was heavy, and every man who gathered about the Sami shaman's mean fire, which spat and shivered in the snow, clutched the amulet at his neck to ward off the evil spirits.

As Bavlos danced and cast his bones and rune-carved sticks, his dark face had twisted and shifted, crying out that the sky had told him they should attack, that the birds who had not fled south for the winter were hungry for carrion, and the trees told him that the Franks would fall. So, they had marshalled the army and marched into a storm of ice and snow, and Hundr let his desolate anger build and blossom in his chest like a hearth fire. He marched with his two swords drawn, and his dead eye pulsed at the prospect of battle, at the chance to vent his sorrow and anger for the loved ones he had lost. Out there in the snow was an army of enemies for him to cut and slash, to rend and tear and slaughter and lay their souls at the altar of his grief.

"Franks!" shouted a man along the line. Hundr squinted his good eye to peer into the powdery white glare, yet he could see nothing.

"I see them," said Ragnhild, and she pointed her axe ahead. Hundr followed to where the blade pointed, and sure enough, figures shifted there like *draugrs* or elves in the snowstorm's shadow.

"Sound the signal," Hundr ordered, and Bush took his war horn, licked his lips and let two sonorous blasts sing out from the curved horn. The booming sound was like a mighty beast lowing in the wilderness, and the Vikings let out a collective roar. A thousand Viking warriors all shouted their clipped war cry, followed by Haesten leading the battle chant. He beat his axe upon the iron-shod rim of his shield, and after each bang, he bellowed '*Aah-hoo',* and in turn, his men followed so that the Franks would hear a ferocious army of professional warriors coming at them through the storm as though sent against them by their nailed God.

"Odin, hear me," Hundr whispered into the sky. "Hear me, lord of warriors, ripper, and battle screamer. I send you warriors to honour Sigrid and Sigurd, so guide my swords and watch my deeds."

"Valhalla," said Bush, and he grinned at Hundr as he tucked his war horn away and took up his axe. He looked weathered as an old man, his wrinkled, wind-darkened face wet with snow. His paunch wobbled as he advanced, and though it was the shipmaster's greatest desire, Hundr hoped it was not yet Bush's time to join the Einherjar because he needed his friendship in Midgard, and another loss would be too much to bear.

Panic erupted in King Louis' army, and what were distant ghost-like figures now became men. They ran here and there, spears long and waving in the snowstorm as their captains realised an attack descended upon them in impossible circumstances. The Viking line picked up the pace, and Hundr jogged, the weight of his swords familiar and comforting in his hands. Away to his left, the ulfheðnarhowled again, and they sprinted out before the Viking lines, their naked bodies made wet and slick by the snow. Hundr felt their wild rage take hold of him, and he wanted to howl along with them, but he held his tongue. Instead, he burst forward into a headlong charge, and Haesten whooped for joy behind him.

Ragnhild kept pace with him, and, in ten strides, the Franks became clear amongst the snow. A ragged line of warriors held spears at differing angles as they pulled off their night cloaks and tried to don leather armour or grasp their shields. They were fresh from the warmth of their beds, responding to the cry of alarm, and as Hundr ran towards them, the fear on their bearded faces filled his heart with joy. He charged at the biggest of them, a heavy-jawed man with a long spear in his right hand, yet the big man didn't notice until it was too late. Desperately, he opened his mouth to rally his comrades to him, but his effort was in vain. Hundr swerved so that he passed the man on his shield side, then sliced Fenristooth across the man's throat, sending crimson blood to spray onto the snowy ground. Hundr seamlessly blended into the chaos in the blink of an eye, appearing like a nightmarish apparition amongst them.

In the ensuing frenzy, the next Frank died with Battle Fang in his gullet. A spearman lunged desperately at Hundr, yet Ragnhild cracked his skull open with her axe. Thorgrim swung his double-bladed war axe with such power that he swept a spearman's head clean off his shoulders with his first strike, and the Franks cried out in panicked terror. Hundr swept Battle Fang across a Frank's knees and plunged Fenristooth into the man's open mouth as he cried out in agony. The soft silence of the snowstorm became a welter of screaming pain, belligerent war cries, and the thundering clang, bang and crunch of battle. Shields shivered as axes smashed their boards to firewood. Iron weapons met in parry and block, ringing out like dozens of church bells. Men clawed at spilt guts, shimmering purple and blue against the bright snow, and the icy blanket beneath their boots was now a churning mass of liquid pink, and Hundr revelled in it.

A mail-clad Frank came at Hundr brandishing a sword. Hundr rapidly dodged the first strike and let the backswing flash over his head as he ducked beneath it. He bullied the man backwards, lunging with his two swords, and the Frank's long moustache twitched as he zealously tried to match Hundr's sword skill. But he could not match it, for Hundr had forged his skill in Novgorod's training pit and sharpened it in countless battles across the Whale Road. With a lightning-fast motion, he slashed Battle Fang over the Frank's wrist, causing him to yelp and drop his blade. Hundr left him there to die by another man's hand, and he ran into the snarl of tents and darting warriors because the Vikings had punched through the Frank's meagre defensive line and were now amongst them. The battle had turned into a brutal slaughter.

The Franks were taken entirely by surprise. No leader, lord, or king would expect an enemy to attack in such treacherous conditions, and King Louis' army crumbled in panic. Sigvarth ripped a tent open with his axe and dragged a Frank out by his hair so that Ragnhild could cut his throat. Throughout the camp, the Vikings slew and the Franks died. In the thick of it all, a burly great lord emerged from a brightly painted tent. He wore a coat of dazzlingly polished mail and carried a formidable club forged from iron in his meaty fist. He aggressively came at Hundr, swinging the club in a wide sweep. Hundr skillfully evaded it, springing backwards. Two Franks accompanied their lord, and both men carried fine swords. Ragnhild attacked one with her axe, yet the warrior stood his ground and exchanged blows with Ragnhild so that they seemed to dance in the snow as they fought.

The burly man banged into Hundr with his shoulder and punched the haft of his club into

Hundr's face. A thick, gold chain rattled on the Frankish lord's chest as he moved. Hundr lurched away, the iron taste of blood in his mouth. The club came at him through the falling snow, and Hundr raised both of his swords to parry the heavy weapon. The Frank leaned into it, trying to drive Hundr down with his bulk and the weapon's weight, but Hundr turned at the hip, swooping Fenristooth away from the club, and sawed its blade savagely across the Frank's belly. He roared in horror, but his expensive mail held, and as the burly Frank brought his club back to strike again, Hundr dropped to one knee and drove Battle Fang into the man's groin, twisting the blade. Hot blood pumped from the wound as the Frankish lord fell backwards to die, silently writhing in the blood-spattered snow.

"Fight me!" Bush shouted. At the shipmaster's feet lay the second Frank who had charged alongside his burly lord, the ground awash with blood and gore. "Valhalla calls to me. Fight, you bastards!"

The clash of arms and shouts of distress became fiercer to Hundr's left, and he charged towards that noise. He leapt over tent ropes and dodged around hungry-faced Vikings until he came to a mass of men hacking and slashing at one another. There, the Franks had finally organised themselves into a shield wall, protecting a bulk of their warriors attempting to flee across a stream that ran behind them. The water's surface glinted with broken ice, and the Franks leapt into it, gasping at the gelid cold. However, in their hasty retreat, many misjudged the power of its current and were quickly swept away.

The shield wall held, and the Franks fought there with spears and shields, drawing the attention of the Viking horde. They flocked to that fight in a mass of leather, iron, axes, braided beards, and savagery, ready to kill. Ravn was there at the centre, his frame enormous and powerful. He relentlessly beat upon the Frank's shields with his axe, and his men rallied behind him. It was all the Franks could do to hold the Vikings back. Hundr eagerly pushed his way into the fight, enjoying the battle-induced calm that had descended upon him to drown out the sorrow and heartache plaguing his thoughts. Hundr shouldered through the throng of Vikings until he came to the front line, and just as he pushed past a red-headed warrior who wielded a blood-drenched bearded axe, he saw Ravn fighting a great Frankish lord. The man had short black hair and a hard, stern face, and he fought with a spectacular gleaming sword. He was not as burly as Ravn, but what the Norseman had in size and strength, the Frank possessed in skill and sword craft. The Frankish lord's blade whipped from the shield wall like a serpent's tongue, and it ripped out the throat of the warrior beside Ravn. Seizing the opportunity, Ravn hooked his axe over the Frank's shield and dragged him out of the formation.

"Make room, make room!" Ravn roared, and the Vikings immediately fell back, creating a small circle for them to fight in amongst the wild carnage of battle. Ravn beckoned him on, and the Frank attacked

253

with savage speed, charging forward as though he were made of feathers and Ravn of heavy iron. With immense power, the big Viking swung his axe as if to cleave the Frank in two upon impact. But the Frank let go of his shield, grabbed his sword in both hands, and then parried the axe blow with such force that Hundr thought Ravn's axe would shatter the Frankish steel. However, the sword held firm, and the Frank roared in defiance. Stepping back, he swiftly thrust the sword's tip against the top of Ravn's helmet. Then, as fast as lightning, the Frank drew the blade back and slammed the edge on Ravn's exposed ribs, but his brynjar absorbed the cut. Ravn roared in pain and stumbled forward. The Frank kicked out, and his boot connected with the back of Ravn's knee, dropping him to the ground, and it was as though a great oak had fallen.

The Vikings wailed in despair that a Frank had bested their jarl, a man of reputation and ferocity. Svart the Screamer charged from the Viking ranks, screeching like a falcon. Svart ran at the Frank, but he moved with the speed of rushing water, effortlessly sidestepping Svart's attack and opening his throat with a flick of his sword.

The Frankish champion's eyes blazed with triumph, and hope blossomed on the faces of the men behind him. They had been beaten, routed whilst they lay in their beds, but now perhaps there was a flicker of a chance to snatch victory from the jaws of defeat. More of the enemy who had fled into the icy river returned to join the Frank's shield wall. Hundr snarled and stepped forward. The Frankish swordsman drank in his mail and two swords and beckoned Hundr to come and face him.

The two shield walls edged further apart to make more room for the champions to fight. Ravn remained on his hands and knees, gasping for air, and Hundr circled the Frank, who smiled and twirled his sword as his men cheered his prowess. He was a champion in his war finery, and there was no fear in his brown eyes as Hundr advanced with his two swords held low. The Frank lashed out with his blade, though Hundr parried it easily. As he did, the Frank laughed heartily, shaking his head, and said something in his own language that elicited laughter from his men. Hundr responded with a rapid assault, charging him in a blur of sword blades and anger. He swung low and lunged; he slashed and kicked, yet the Frank skillfully evaded every blow until Hundr paused, out of breath and sweating.

The Frank came on, and he was fast, perhaps as fast as Ivar the Boneless himself. Hundr desperately moved away from his fearsome blade, and as he focused on the flashing sword, the Frank's boot lashed out to kick Hundr in the groin. Pain flooded him, and Hundr crumpled. Unable to stay standing, he stumbled and gasped at the stomach-churning clenching in his manhood. The Frank swung his sword around, gesturing at the two Vikings on their knees, and the men in the Frankish shield wall roared and edged forward to support their champion.

The swordsman lifted his blade above his head and turned to Ravn. He was about to sever the jarl's head from his shoulders when Hundr threw himself back, looking up to the sky, and screamed to Odin. He summoned all the pain he had felt when Sigrid and Sigurd had died, and in that torrid crucible of unspeakable agony, the pain in his groin melted away. Hundr leapt forward and, with Fenristooth's blade, caught the Frank's sword on the downward swing. The swords clanged together, and the shock reverberated up Hundr's arm. To his astonishment, Fenristooth shattered under the blow. The ivory-hilted sword gifted to him by the old Jarl of Vanylven had broken in two, and Hundr could not believe that such a finely wrought blade could break. The sword he had wielded in countless fights across the Whale Road had smashed beneath the Frank's steel.

Hundr threw the broken sword at the Frank, and the shattered stump of a blade nicked his cheek as it turned hilt over edge past his head. Hundr followed it up, and as he went, he reached behind him and ripped his seax from the sheath hanging from the rear of his belt. The Frank went to block Battle Fang and then his eyes went wide with shock as he saw the broken-backed seax coming for him. It was too late. Hundr punched the tip of the seax into the champion's eye, twisting the blade. He felt the tip scrape on the skull bone, and when he yanked it free, there was a sucking sound as eye jelly and grey, bloody matter slopped from the terrible wound. Hundr quickly sheathed his seax, seizing the fallen Frank's sword and holding it aloft in triumph. The Vikings erupted in wild whoops and cheers while the Franks bitterly groaned at their defeat.

"You saved my life," Ravn said as he clambered to his feet. "I swear I will repay that debt." Hundr nodded and turned to the Frankish shield wall.

"Kill them all!" he roared and charged into the fence of spears and shields. Ragnhild went with him, as did Bush, Thorgrim, and Sigvarth. Agnarr and Jogrimmr followed them, and the band Hundr had led against the Franks in the field broke the shield wall like it was made of straw. Rognvald's ulfheðnar crew joined the attack from the rear, cutting off the Frank's escape to the river, and the battle in a wind-whipped snowstorm became a great slaughter on a Saxon heath.

Hundr fought like a man possessed as the enemy shield wall broke. He shouted like a wild man, killing and wounding with savage ferocity. He wept for Sigrid and Sigurd as his new sword slashed and drank the souls of the beaten Franks. The sword felt like it was part of him, already an extension of his arm, and he took the lives of any Frank who faced him, each one an offering to Odin and the Aesir for his dead family's safekeeping in the afterlife. The snow became a black-pink slosh of foulness, and Hundr waded through it. He was vaguely aware of Ragnhild, Bush, and the rest of his warriors about him. The men he had led as the army rearguard fought alongside Hundr, and they were brutal fighters all. The bloodshed only ceased when the Vikings grew tired of the relentless killing. Still, many Franks had made it through the river, racing across the white, snow-covered heath away from their dying army.

The battlefield was a mass of blood-churned snow, crawling men clutching at terrible injuries wrought by axe, spear, and sword, and the victorious Vikings who searched the dead to strip them of anything of value. Hundr stood amidst the horror, his brynjar, face, and hair spattered with gore, and he stared up at the white sky, hoping that Odin had indeed witnessed the battle and that the men he had slain were accepted by the god of warriors as a fitting tribute to Sigrid and Sigurd. Ragnhild knelt beside him, wrapping a gash on her forearm with a strip of cloth, and Bush stalked amongst the dead, raging at them, shaking his axe at the corpses.

"Miserable Frank bastards," said Bush as he stepped over a man whose arm was severed at the shoulder. "Not one of you could strike the killing blow." He stared at Hundr with desperate eyes. "I could die in my sleep tomorrow of this cursed cough or from the belly-rotting sickness two years from now. Is Valhalla not my destiny? Am I to be denied an afterlife with Blink, Hrist, Valbrandr, Ivar, and the other heroes we have known?"

Hundr ignored his old friend and left Thorgrim and Sigvarth to assure Bush that if any of them deserved to go to Valhalla, it was him. Hundr examined the sword he had taken from the Frankish champion. It was light and well-balanced but strong enough to shatter Fenristooth. There was writing on the blade, which Hundr could not read. He wiped some of the gore from the steel, and the symbols ULFBERHT were etched deep and clear in the metal. The pommel was a simple half circle of iron, and the cross piece was dotted with small holes. Soft leather wound around the grip, and the sword was long, sharp, and beautifully made. Hundr slid the sword into Fenristooth's old scabbard and picked his way through the dead and dying.

Haesten and his warriors found King Louis' abandoned baggage and tent and inside was a deep chest full of silver coins stamped with the king's image. The Vikings whooped for joy and pranced about the camp, laughing with silk wrapped around their helmets and gold candlesticks in their bloody fists. Hundr stumbled upon two men who had hacked open a barrel of ale, and he took a deep drink as the snow continued to fall. Ravn hailed him from across a stretch of trampled leather tents, and Hundr sighed and went to meet the burly jarl.

"Come, Jarl Hundr," said Ravn. Prince Erik was at his side with a fearful look on his pale face. "We celebrate a glorious victory, and Prince Erik here will make his first kill."

Hundr followed Ravn and Erik, though he still could not summon the energy or will to speak. He was exhausted from fighting, and now that the battle joy had left him, the sadness returned and weighed heavily upon his shoulders as though he wore six brynjars. Ravn strode with a heavy hand on the prince's shoulder and led him to where a group of fifty Franks knelt in the snow. They had been stripped of their armour and weapons, and their heads hung in silent shame. These were the men who had not made it across the river and had instead thrown themselves upon the Viking's mercy. Which, Hundr thought, was unwise. If it were summer, there might have been a sliver of hope that Haesten would let them live to sell them as slaves at the great Viking markets, but in the depths of winter, they were useless mouths to feed, and Hundr did not believe those men would live very long.

"Now," said Ravn in his deep voice. "This one here says he is a count, which is a jarl of sorts. He is a great lord of his people. If you kill him, Prince Erik, your reputation takes seed and begins to flourish. Better to blood yourself now than have it hanging over your head as you grow older. Now, someone give this Count Lothar a stave to defend himself."

A burly Viking warrior dragged a balding man from the group of Franks. He was fat-bellied with a drooping moustache and had been stripped of everything save his undergarments. The Viking thrust a broken spear shaft into his hand, and Count Lothar stared at it with shaking jowls and frightened eyes. The burly Viking sniffed and sneezed, took a knife from his belt, reached behind Count Lothar and cut the sinews behind his left knee. Lothar cried out in pain, and his men kept their heads down, though Hundr noticed that some had begun to tremble at the gruesome spectacle.

"Fight him, Erik. Kill the fat pig, and men will know that Erik of Norway is a killer and a man to fear," said Ravn. He pushed Erik towards the count, and the little prince slid the axe from his belt. It was too big for him, and he held it halfway up the haft in two hands. He licked at nervous lips, and Ravn's men cheered him on. Lothar just stood, hopping on his good leg, bewildered at what was happening. Erik shuffled closer. Evidently, they had trained him to fight, for he twirled the axe around in his wrists and took a long step forward. He swung the axe, and Count Lothar yelped and batted it aside with his piece of wood. The prince came on again, but this time, the axe went low and sliced across the count's thigh so that he tumbled into the black slosh that had once been snow. Erik danced about him and then crashed the axe blade into Lothar's face. The Vikings whooped, and Erik's jaw dropped open in surprise at the bloody mess. The young prince yanked the axe blade free, and the count's blood splattered his little white face. Erik smiled up at Ravn, who grinned broadly.

"Now the boy is a warrior!" Ravn exclaimed, lifting Erik's hand so the Vikings could cheer him. "Erik of the bloody axe is a good name. Look at him, lads!"

"Erik Bloodaxe!" the Vikings cheered, and the prince beamed with pride.

Ravn left the boy with his men and walked over to Hundr with a broad smile on his face.

"So, Jarl Hundr, I owe you a blood debt," he said, clapping Hundr on the shoulder. "When do we set sail for Vanylven?"

EIGHTEEN

Einar stared down through the pine trees at Stryn's walls and its turf-topped homes. Orange glowed from the building's windows as the people kept warm, eating together and drinking ale on a frosty night. Laughter and talk rumbled from Jarl Ugattr's hall, and Einar imagined the old bastard had thrown a sumptuous feast to celebrate his humbling of a famous warrior. Tomorrow, Ugattr would send his warriors out to hunt Einar's people, and Einar could almost hear the warriors boasting of how many Vanylven heads they would take, how many brynjars, swords and axes they would loot, and the women they would take as slaves.

It was bitterly frigid in the forest, and the steam from the mouths of Einar's men rose like billowing smoke within the tall pines. He shivered and then shut the feeling of cold out of his mind, refusing to allow it to cloud his senses. His face was dry and crusty from the mud he had smeared across his skin and brynjar. Einar's men had done the same, and the warriors stood beside him, covered head to toe in mud, so that night embraced them, becoming one with the darkness. They stood armed with shields, axes, and spears, and they were ready to fight to the death, for if they lost, they would die, and their people would starve. The men whispered prayers to the dark and swarthy night goddess Nótt, asking her to keep them hidden and allow them to move through the night shadows like the huldufólk, silent and deadly.

"Are we going to wait until they sleep?" asked Hildr at Einar's elbow. Her eyes shone like candlelight in her mud-darkened face, and there was fervent anger there to match his own.

"No, we go now," Einar said. He could no longer keep his people waiting in the cold and dark. The time for pride-swallowing and patience was over. Einar took his axe and seax from his belt. Amundr was to his left, and Hildr to his right. Torsten was further along the line, marshalling the right flank. Einar raised his axe, pointing the blade towards Stryn, and his warriors moved forward, one hundred warriors armed and ready to kill and take what they needed from Jarl Ugattr and his people. King Harald would be angered that two of his jarls had gone to war. He would have preferred Einar and Ugattr to bring their disagreement to him so that he could decide the best way to resolve their differences. Harald Fairhair would listen to both sides and lay down his law, just as Einar did with the folk under his rule. But Einar's people would be dead by then, and Ugattr had shamed and insulted him, and for that, he would meet his end.

Einar emerged from the forest and led his warriors in a slow march down the valley. There were guards with rushlight torches upon the walls, but Einar did not care. Behind him, men carried pine trunks and stout branches, which they had cut from the forest since Einar had returned. The wood was still thick with bark and wet from the frost. The warriors had lashed them together with belts and jerkins to form makeshift ladders, and Einar would take those ladders and let his men loose upon Ugattr and the people of Stryn. Einar felt young again. He felt just as he had when he had been the captain of the Seaworm when Ivar would send him out on the Whale Road to punish a jarl or warlord who owed Ivar fealty or tribute and had failed in his obligations. In those days, Einar had been a ruthless, pitiless killer, a Viking warrior with a dragonship full of hardened fighters. Those old feelings resurfaced like an apple in a water barrel, and Einar welcomed them. It was time for Ugattr to understand what it meant to cross Einar Rosti.

"Get your archers ready," Einar said, and Hildr paused so that her archers could catch up with her. They had brought the bows and arrows fashioned whilst they'd lived in the woods, and Hildr led them just behind Einar, poised and ready to loose. "Remember, go to the hall first. Ugattr must die." Einar spoke those words loudly, not caring if they carried down the valley towards where Stryn perched beside the shadowy dark borders of the fjord. The river beyond the fjord wound away from the village, and it looked like a black snake slithering towards the stark mountains in the dark. The laughter from inside Stryn's hall cut through all the other sounds to bang around Einar's head like a drum. It was all he could hear, not the crunch of his boots on the frost, or the singing, or the low sigh of chatter, not the dogs barking or the advance of his own warriors. Just the laughter. Ugattr and his men were mocking Einar. He was sure of it. Einar had spent a lifetime at the blade, forging his reputation, and he would not be ridiculed by an old man and his hearth troop of slaving nithings.

The walls loomed as Einar reached the bottom of the hillside, and no alarm had yet been raised. He sucked in huge breaths of night air, letting his vengeful anger grow. A guard's helmet on the walls caught the moonlight, and a moment later, an arrow whipped through the darkness. The figure slumped across the palisade posts, gurgling and dying with Hildr's arrow in his chest. Einar picked up the pace, and his men followed.

"Ready the ladders," Einar called, and he stepped aside to let them run past him. They didn't aim for the gate but the palisade section facing the forest. Einar wanted speed rather than ease of getting his warriors inside Stryn, and of all the fortresses he had stormed or attacked, this was one of the weakest. His men leapt over the ditch, which was too narrow, and their ladders banged against the palisade, which was barely taller than Einar himself. Ugattr's fort was built at half measures by a man who felt wholly secure because his village lay at the end of a winding fjord in Norway's hinterland. It was the last stop before the liveable coast turned into the rugged, remote mountains where nobody save giants, dwarves, and elves could live.

"Me first," Einar said, and he broke into an all-out run. Another guard showed himself on the palisade, and another arrow sang across the walls. The arrow took the man in the shoulder, and he cried out the alarm as Einar's boot met the bottom of the first ladder. His men had laid the timbers so that the two stout logs they had lashed together leant against the palisade at a wide angle, like an oar stretching from the sea to a boat. Einar ran up the twin logs and growled as he reached the summit of the walls. He dropped onto the fighting platform, and a guard came sprinting from the darkness, clutching a sputtering rushlight. Einar advanced on him, and the guard saw a big man swathed in darkness, like a demon from Niflheim. Startled and terrified, the guard let out a scream, losing his grip on the torch and fumbling with his spear. He hesitated, torn between fleeing and defending himself, but Einar's axe swiftly ended his life with a brutal strike to the chest.

Warriors came from buildings half-dressed, staring up at the enemies who surged over the ramparts. Amundr dropped from the fighting platform to land inside Stryn, roaring his hate and defiance at the defenders. Einar dropped beside him, and more Vanylven warriors joined them as they advanced into the town. Two men came charging at them, brandishing spears. Amundr threw his axe at the man on the left with such force that the weapon thudded into the warrior's face and threw him from his feet.

The second warrior paused, allowing Amundr to grab his spear as Einar cut the man's throat with the blade of his axe.

"Death to Stryn!" Einar roared to his men, "Death to Jarl Ugattr!"

As women's screams and men's shouts filled the air, the townsfolk of Stryn rushed out to see what commotion had erupted inside their safe, quiet town. When they emerged from laneways and from behind buildings, they saw Einar and his warriors covered head to toe in black mud, brandishing weapons. The people shrieked and ran away. Einar bared his teeth, his chest heaving with hate. Rollo had driven him to this, and Ugattr had humiliated him. It was time for his enemies to suffer. A warrior burst from a single-storey wattle building, bleary-eyed and holding an axe. Amundr grabbed a spear from a Vanylven comrade behind him, took a stride forward, and hurled the weapon. It wobbled in the air before slamming into the Stryn warrior's stomach, pinning him to his own front door. Einar marched past the wounded man and cracked the blade of his axe across his skull.

"I am Einar Rosti," Einar shouted, shaking his axe and seax. "Who wants to fight with me? Who wants to die?"

Einar and his men strode from the tangle of buildings into a straight, frozen lane leading towards Ugattr's hall. The green doors burst open to let out a cloud of thick smoke, and then the warriors flooded out. Ugattr's hearth troop came from the hall stumbling under the influence of the ale they had supped, and their faces dropped as they saw Einar, Amundr and the Vanylven warriors in their war glory, yet slathered in dried mud so that they looked like the army of the dead. A small, shambling figure shouldered his way to the front of his warriors and squinted into his town at the attackers.

"Ugattr, you stinking coward. Come and fight with The Brawler!" Einar shouted, and he strode towards the hall. His men quickly formed up behind him in a shield wall. Two score warriors had already peeled off from the main force like an eagle spreading its wings, and they secured Stryn's outer streets. A score went west, the rest to the east, and they closed like a fist to push the enemy back towards Ugattr's hall. Einar had given the orders in the depths of the pine forest, and his warriors carried out his plan with ruthless efficiency. More of Ugattr's warriors came running from the streets, causing chaos as they converged in a milling, half-dressed, ill-prepared mess before the hall.

"Any of you bastards who don't want to fight, throw down your weapons now!" Einar bellowed so that the hemmed-in warriors could hear. "Any man with a blade is going to die. No quarter will be given. You scorned me today and spat in my face like a dog. So, any man who wants to fight me in single combat should come forward now."

No man moved. The warriors of Stryn exuded an aura of fear, and it hung around them like dust settling from a shaken rug. An eerie silence fell over the settlement as Einar waited to see if any man in Stryn would take up his challenge, but none did.

"Attack!" Einar roared, and his warriors surged forward. Einar ran into the mass of Stryn warriors, and his axe battered a long-haired man to the ground. He moved like a man half his age. Einar had never possessed the lithe speed of Hundr, but what he lacked in skill and poise, he made up for in sheer brutality. Einar headbutted a man so hard that his nose burst open like an overripe fruit. Amundr fought beside him, and the two men were head and shoulders taller than any man in Stryn. Hildr and her archers clambered onto the earth roofs about the hall to loose their arrows into the enemy, and where there had been silence, there was now screaming, weapons clashing, and suffering as Einar came for his revenge.

The Vanylven warriors moved in unison with their shields overlapped, forcing the enemy back and cutting at them across their iron shield rims. Einar stopped at the foot of Ugattr's hall, and the jarl stared down at him in disbelief. There were fifteen warriors between Ugattr and Einar, and Einar supposed they were the jarl's hearth troop, his chosen warriors whom he kept fed and housed in return for their service. They were professional warriors, the cream of Stryn's fighters, but they did not attack. For a moment, Einar thought of offering them another chance to throw down their weapons and swear an oath to serve him. He could take them into his forces and use them to fight Rollo.

But that would be weak, and I am a killer.

Einar waved his men on, and they hacked into Ugattr's warriors until the steps of his hall ran red with blood.

Einar waited until his warriors had killed the last man, and then they retreated from the hall so that all that lay between Einar and Jarl Ugattr were twenty twitching corpses. Einar stepped through the grizzly mess of torn flesh and lifeless bodies until he came face to face with the jarl. The old man stared up at Einar, rheumy eyes trembling and gnarled hands working over each other like a baker kneading bread.

"You humiliated me," Einar hissed at him. "Now, you will meet your destiny. No Valhalla for you, nor Freya's Fólkvangr. You are destined for Niflheim, where you will wander until the end of days and wish that you had shared your grain and offered us somewhere to stay warm in the winter. Now, join the wraiths and nithingsand meet your doom."

Einar drove the tip of his seax into Ugattr's swollen belly and ripped the blade upwards. He heaved on the hilt and tore the old jarl open like a slaughtered pig. Ugattr tried to grasp Einar's shoulder as he died, but Einar pushed him away contemptuously. The old man died without a blade in his hand, and Einar spat upon the steaming offal that had once been Jarl Ugattr.

"Turn the men folk out into the cold," Einar said. "If they resist, kill them. This place is ours now until we take back Vanylven. All their food and valuables stay with us. The women and children can sleep with the pigs and goats in the barns and haylofts."

His warriors set about that task, and Einar strode inside Ugattr's hall. The feasting benches were still laden with bread, meat and fish, and the fire burned bright. He took a mug of ale, drank deeply, and nodded to himself. With provisions secured, his people would not starve, and all that remained was to await Hundr's return with an army from the king. Einar would keep his people fed and safe, and then he would take back Vanylven and see Rollo dead. Even if he had to send a thousand men to the afterlife to do it.

NINETEEN

The snow stopped falling after the battle of
Lüneburg Heath, and a driving rainstorm blew into
Saxony from the south to wash the slush away and
soak the Viking army as they marched northwest
towards their fleet in the River Elbe. Hundr continued
to lead his force of rearguard fighters because, despite
the great victory over the Franks and Saxons,
hundreds of fugitives from the battle roamed the
countryside in search of food and were desperate to
survive as winter bit hard upon the flatlands. Such
pockets of men were a danger to the marching
Vikings, so Hundr led his small force trailing behind
the Viking marching column in search of those
fugitives. Hundr actively sought confrontations and
skirmishes. The focus kept his mind active as Hundr
tracked the gangs of enemy warriors, defended
against attacks on Viking supplies and foraging
parties, and sprung ambushes to distract his mind
from the tragedy which tore at his soul.

King Louis had suffered a crushing defeat in the
snowstorm on Lüneburg Heath. Frankish prisoners
wept as they told of the catastrophic losses, of how
their brothers and lords had perished in the surprise

Viking attack. King Louis had escaped across the river with his bodyguard, but most of his army had not been so lucky. The loot taken from the king's baggage train had been beyond even Haesten's expectations. The old warlord had laughed for joy when he first set eyes on the piles of silver, gold, and weapons captured from King Louis' camp. Haesten said he had captured cities which yielded less. The Franks had marched with silver and gold to pay their soldiers, accompanied by a vast contingent of bishops and priests to preach the blessings of the nailed God upon King Louis' army. Hundr imagined the priests believed they fought a holy war against a ravaging invader. He remembered from his time spent fighting in England that for worshippers of the Christ, all other religions were abhorrent, and they had little or no tolerance for any god other than the nailed one. Vikings cared little for what other men believed. The Aesir were powerful enough to stand and fight against any gods, and Hundr could not understand the Christ worshippers' intolerance. The prisoners told of four great bishops killed during the battle on the heath, and their tents had yielded fortunes in silver plates, gold candlesticks, staffs, and jewel-encrusted chains and crosses. Haesten's men had also captured a dozen jewel-laden parchments in bound leather, which the priests so prized and contained their runes of power scratched in their Christ language.

The Franks had lost the flower of their nobility in the slaughter. The fighting claimed the lives of eight noblemen, and the surrender resulted in the capture of three more. Haesten had pondered keeping the three surviving lords to ransom back to the king, but he decided it would be too much work to drag them back to the fleet, organise the trade with the Franks, and then feed and care for them until an exchange was made. There was already enough treasure to keep the Viking army happy and enough silver to fill the warriors' purses. So, Haesten had ordered the three noblemen to be killed along with the rest of the surrendered Franks. Little Erik, now called Bloodaxe by the army in gleeful pride, wanted to cut the blood eagle on their backs as a tribute to Odin, but Ravn crucified them instead to settle a debate which had raged between him and Ragnhild. During a night of drinking, Ravn could not believe that crucifixion itself could kill a man, despite Ragnhild insisting otherwise. It turned out that Ragnhild was right. The three men died quickly on the cross, largely because the Vikings drove iron nails through their wrists and ankles, which caused catastrophic injuries. It was a messy business, and even the stoutest of Viking *drengrs* had turned away from the screaming as the dying men sagged on the makeshift crosses.

There was no sign of King Louis in the battle's aftermath, and the Vikings reached the ships on the Elbe with no further engagements other than the rearguard fighting conducted by Hundr and his rangers. His fighters had formed a tight bond. Agnarr, Jogrimmr and other warriors supplemented Hundr's band of twenty. They were men who hungered for regular combat and enjoyed days spent in the field, riding, marching and sleeping rough in the wilderness. They had taken to wearing crow feathers in their helmets, and painted their shields black. The army referred to the warband as the 'Raven Band'. They revelled in the name, and it quickly became a badge of honour.

The Viking fleet remained unmolested in the winter swell of the Elbe, and the guards Haesten had left to protect the precious warships were bored and sullen at missing the battle. Some Franks on horseback came to look upon the dozens of warships but wisely refrained from attacking because the men Haesten had left behind had constructed a fortification sturdy enough to repel most attacks. Haesten's small force had made a simple ditch and bank from the excavated earth and topped it with a ring of brambles and bushes. While it was hastily put together, it would be difficult to attack, and to get to the valuable Viking warships, an enemy would need dozens of warriors. The Viking army stayed for a night by the riverbank, where Haesten threw a feast for the leaders on a dry night, complete with an enormous fire to keep them warm against the evening frost. They ate roasted boar, cheese, pork, and freshly baked bread, and Hundr had a place of honour beside Haesten, Ravn, Rognvald and his captains Hrolfr the Mouse and Hooknose Ymir.

Rognvald had returned to his fine clothes the day after the battle, and any remnants of his mouth-frothing ulfheðnar fury were long gone, yet not forgotten. Previously, the burly Vikings with grizzled beards, tattoos, and scars frowned at Rognvald and talked of his lordly pomposity behind his back. Now, even the fiercest growlers bowed their heads to him with respect. All had witnessed the wild ferocity with which Rognvald and his ulfheðnarfought, and it had been their furious charge into the flanks of the enemy shield wall which had ended the battle. Rognvald had come from the fight with his naked torso sheeted in blood and filth, his eyes terrifyingly wide, and his axe dripping with gore. He had led his ulfheðnar warriors in that last charge, and the Franks crumbled with fear, terrified by the sight of the frenzied fighters. They tried a last desperate run towards the river, only to meet their end.

"There is something special about eating outdoors, don't you think?" Rognvald mused cheerfully, popping a slice of cheese into his mouth and smiling broadly.

"Better to be in a hall by a roaring fire with a wench on my lap," quipped Ravn, and he slapped Hrolfr on the back with such force that he almost fell over.

"Just so," said Rognvald, the sarcasm in his voice barely concealed.

"So, back to Avaldsnes, is it, Jarl Rognvald?" asked Haesten.

Rognvald wore a coiled gold chain around his neck as thick around as a sailing rope. It came from the neck of a dead bishop and had once supported a jewelled cross which would have hung low on the bishop's stomach. Haesten had broken the cross from the chain and handed it to Rognvald as a gift in recognition of his bravery in the battle.

"Back to King Harald in Avaldsnes. Though I do not relish the thought of sailing in winter."

"Hug the coast, sleep on shore each night. Be there in no time," said Ravn, with boar meat juices running down his beard as he took a bite from a rib as long as his forearm.

"And you Jarl Hundr?"

"I have done what Harald asked me to do," replied Hundr, glancing at Ravn before he spoke his next words, conscious of insulting the big man. "We must return Prince Erik to his father." Hundr stared at Rognvald, for the Jarl of Rogaland was Harald's closest advisor, and if any man knew the king's inner thoughts and plans, it was he. "Then I will take the men promised to me and throw Rollo the Betrayer out of Vanylven and send his soul screaming to Niflheim."

"We have the prince, and you shall have the men you need," said Rognvald, and he smiled again, this time lifting his cup of ale and raising it to Hundr. "So long as Njorth does not shipwreck us on the way home."

"King Harald Fairhair will lead his army north to Vanylven in winter to recover your home?" asked Haesten, surprised because fighting in winter was rare. Even though the Vikings had fought against the Franks and Saxons in the snow, their plan had been to winter at Hammaburg and resume their campaign in the spring when roads and fields were easier to march across and food was available to keep the warriors fed. Haesten had only fought because he could not take Hammaburg, and King Louis had brought an army north to cast him out.

"The king will not sail. But I think I shall bring my ships and my ulfheðnarand help you defeat your enemy, Jarl Hundr," said Rognvald.

"You honour me," Hundr responded. "I thought you would long for the warmth of your hall after so much fighting, sleeping and marching in the cold."

"Rollo has long been a thorn in the king's side. He is the last of the old enemy, the only one left who opposed King Harald's rise to become King of all Norway. All the rest are dead or have sworn oaths of loyalty to the throne. The Betrayer sent his burned man to kill Harald, and it was you who killed that assassin. So, I think I will help you destroy Rollo and remove his threat from the tafl board."

"So you bring three ships north?"

"Just so. Three of the crews here are Harald's oathmen. But you shall have three ships and two hundred Rogalanders, including my ulfheðnar, Jarl Hundr."

"I, too, will accompany you to Vanylven," said Ravn. He set his jaw firm and raised a clenched fist, which was bigger than Hundr's pot of ale. "You saved my life, and I will repay that debt by helping you kill this Duke of the Franks. Let us crush his bones together and drive his warriors before us like dogs. I also have three ships and two hundred men to bring, and we shall make great slaughter together. Men will know that Ravn Kjartansson fought beside the Man with the Dog's Name, champion of the Northmen."

Ravn stood and grabbed Hundr's wrist in the warrior's grip. They shook each other's forearms, and Hundr's heart swelled because now he could return to Vanylven with enough warriors to bring Rollo to his knees. Rollo had brought ten ships and seven hundred warriors to Norway, and Hundr would need a similar, but preferably larger, force to throw him out again.

"Jarl Ravn, I welcome your friendship and am proud to fight alongside you. We will make good use of your ships and warriors, as my own ships are trapped in Vanylven's fjord."

"What about you, Lord Haesten?" asked Rognvald. "Where will you and your army spend the winter?"

"I could return to Guthrum in England; he is now known as King Aethelstan. I could stay with him in East Anglia. But I think that would anger King Alfred, so I suppose I shall stay in Frankia. We have beaten the king of the East Franks, but I do not fancy attacking Hammaburg and its river fastness. Many of my men would die in the water or on the high walls. So, I will go south and find a river, then a town, bring my warriors and my silver there, and wait until spring. Then perhaps a city ripe for the taking will present itself." Haesten grinned wolfishly, and Hundr thought that any Frank who saw his hard face at that moment would tremble with fear.

"So we part as friends," said Rognvald.

"We do. And I shall be proud to return Prince Erik to his father, blooded and made man." Ravn smiled and stared at Rognvald across the flames of their campfire. Ravn could have been insulted that Harald sent Rognvald and Hundr to return Prince Erik to Avaldsnes. The king had entrusted Ravn with caring for Erik as his foster son, which was a great honour. But sending Rognvald and Hundr south implied that the king had lost faith in Ravn, and that would cause Ravn to lose face amongst his peers, who were the warriors and lords of Norway. Those men were a hard and unforgiving bunch who would smell any weakness like meat on a fire and flock to pick at the bones of his fall from grace.

"Harald will be delighted to see Erik so hale and grown from a child to a young warrior, already bynamed and with a burgeoning reputation."

Hundr listened as the leaders talked, drank, and celebrated their victory over the Franks, but he could find no joy. His twenty warriors were rich in their share of the plunder, but Hundr took nothing for himself other than the sword he had acquired in battle. He stared into the flames and could not stop his mind from turning to dark thoughts. Memories of Sigrid and Sigurd constantly fought their way to the front of his thoughts, and that melancholy remained with him as the fleet set sail. Hundr and the Raven Band sailed with Rognvald on the Reaver. Their lords freed the warriors who had joined Hundr's twenty from their oaths, and Agnarr, Jogrimmr, and the Raven Band all swore oaths to be Hundr's men and joined his service.

They parted from Haesten at the mouth of the Elbe, and the old wolf followed the coast south whilst Rognvald's and Ravn's ships followed the jagged coast north. There was much free time on board the ship, and that time was Hundr's enemy because whenever he was alone or not busied with a task, his thought cage tortured him with guilt for those he had lost. So, he took his turns at the oar with Rognvald's men and joined in the hard work of raising and lowering the sail, hauling rigging, and responding to the shipmaster's orders whenever they needed to tack and stay as close to the shore as possible. To drift out to sea in winter was to die deep in Njorth's fury, and it took twice as long to make the return journey as it had to reach the Elbe. When the wind grew too fierce, or the shipmasters grew too fearful of gathering clouds or approaching squalls, the fleet would rest in a cove or sheltered shore until the storms passed. That caution allowed them to return to Avaldsnes with no ships lost at sea, a feat which Bush proclaimed was a miracle of Njorth, for the old shipmaster was ever averse to winter sailing.

The fleet entered the Avaldsnes straits, where a throng greeted them with cheers and merry faces. The folk were eager to be reunited with husbands and fathers who had sailed to war and to marvel at the treasure the Vikings had brought back from their adventures.

"I know those hulls," piped Bush, pointing through the mass of masts and prows. Many ships huddled within the safety of Avaldsnes' closeness to the mainland, which shielded them from the dangerous open water. Hundr tried to focus his one eye on the throng of ships, but he could see nothing familiar in the tangle of rigging and timber.

"That's the Sea Falcon," said Ragnhild, and she pointed deep into the harbour.

"If it's the Falcon, then…" Hundr began.

"Asbjorn is here, and there is Harbard's Sword of the Sea."

Hundr's mood lifted immediately at the prospect of reuniting with Asbjorn and Harbard. They were his oathmen and the captains of the Sword and Falcon, both ships of Hundr's fleet. They had spent the previous summer raiding separately to Hundr and the Seaworm to seek silver further south along England's coastline and had not returned to Vanylven before Rollo's attack and Hundr's departure. Though the fall of Vanylven had only happened mere weeks ago, so much had occurred since that fateful day that it felt like he had last sat and talked with his oathmen and captains a lifetime ago.

Hundr followed Rognvald and Ravn from the ships through the crowd and inside the high walls and bustling corridors of Avaldsnes. A steward led them directly to King Harald's hall, where Harald's courtiers and oathmen welcomed them warmly with cheers and shouts of approval at their return. Prince Erik Bloodaxe strutted beside Ravn with his axe held in his little fist. He waved the weapon and showed it proudly to those who had packed into the hall to see him and the warriors. The hearth fire blazed, and the hall was thick with the smells of burning wood, musty floor rushes, and the damp smell of rain-soaked thatch. Hundr's eye searched the hall for any sign of his men but could see none as they reached the raised dais where Harald Fairhair waited for them with a grin splitting his wily face.

"My son is returned to me safe and well," beamed Harald, and the hall went quiet as he spoke. "You have grown taller, my boy, and have become a warrior, I see."

"He was never in danger, Lord King," said Ravn, his voice booming around the hall like a war drum. "You gave a boy to me to foster and teach the ways of war. I return to you Erik Bloodaxe, a warrior who has already killed a Frankish count and bloodied himself in battle."

"Erik Bloodaxe," intoned Harald, nodding appreciatively. "A good name for the heir to the throne. Now, come here, my boy." The prince laughed and ran up the steps to greet his father, and

Harald scooped him up into a bear hug, ruffling his red hair.

"We fought a great battle in a snowstorm against King Louis of the East Franks," said Rognvald, and the people in the hall gasped at the thought of such a death-defying adventure. "I have tales to tell of brave deeds, great slaughter, and a treasure won in a distant land. We killed dukes and counts and powerful holy men dripping in gold."

"We shall hear them all tonight as we feast and celebrate my son's return and your victory. Jarl Hundr, your son Hermoth is safe and well and is eager to see you." Harald beckoned, and little Hermoth came running from behind the dais. He dodged around the legs of the warriors and leapt into Hundr's arms. Hundr held him close and had to fight to hold back the lump in his throat.

"Where are mummy and Sigurd?" Hermoth asked.

"They have gone on another adventure, son. I will tell you of it later when we are alone together," said Hundr. Hermoth looked hale, and Hundr could not release his son. The welcome warmth of his little body penetrated Hundr's brynjar where the sharpest blade could not, and Hundr's love for his son warmed him like a fur cloak about his heart.

"Thank you, Lord King, for taking care of my son."

"And you helped return mine to me. Although it seems, as Jarl Ravn says, he was in little danger after all. I have other news for you, Jarl Hundr. A messenger came to me this past week from Jarl Einar. He has retreated from Vanylven, which is still occupied by our enemy Rollo, and is now with his people at Stryn, where he awaits you."

"Very good, Lord King." That was strange news indeed. Stryn belonged to Jarl Ugattr, who Hundr knew to be a cantankerous old slaver, and he could not imagine Ugattr offering succour and shelter to the people of Vanylven and Einar's warriors without demanding a high price.

"You have fulfilled your part of our bargain, and now I will do the same. You shall have the warriors you requested, and you can sail for Vanylven on the morrow. Indeed, two of your captains arrived in Avaldsnes not long after you departed, and they will be eager to see you."

Hundr bowed to the king in thanks, and then Asbjorn and Harbard came through the crowd and met Bush and Ragnhild warmly before greeting their lord, Hundr, with solemn respect. Asbjorn clasped Hundr's arm in the warrior's grip and pulled him close.

"I am sorry we were late returning from the Whale Road," he said, and there was a catch in Asbjorn's voice. He had fought beside Hundr and Einar for many years, and Hundr considered him a friend. "We got caught up in some trouble in Northumbria. We went to Vanylven when first we sailed across the sea but saw Rollo's Frankish banners on the fjord bridge. So we came south looking for you, lord."

"You did the right thing, and you are here now. We must go north and deal with the Betrayer once and for all."

King Harald Fairhair threw a magnificent winter feast that night, and the Vikings celebrated the famous victory at the battle of Lüneburg Heath. Avaldsnes' great hall was packed to the rafters with warriors, lords, wealthy merchants and courtiers, and they drank finely brewed ale and dined on succulent roast beef and duck, accompanied by intricately patterned bread, honey, butter, and white, soft fish. Ravn told the tale of his fight with the Frankish champion and how the Man with the Dog's Name had saved his life and won a sword worthy of a great champion. Hundr brought forth the Ulfberhtsword and allowed men to pass it around the hall. They marvelled at how light it was to wield and were astonished that it had smashed a good Viking blade in one stroke.

Rognvald told the tale of Jarl Haesten, and all the warriors cheered his name and his deeds, and Hundr was happy to hear his old friend being so well respected. Then talk turned to Rollo. Ravn, Hooknose Ymir, Hrolfr the Mouse, Jogrimmr, and Agnarr swore oaths to defeat the Betrayer. They made the Bragi boast by the fire, and warriors banged the tables with their fists. Bragi was the god of skalds, and men swore to forge epic tales of bravery worthy of the finest skalds. The hall fell quiet as warriors swore to strike ten men down with their axes, to be the first to scale the walls of Vanylven, or to face the Betrayer himself in battle. Hundr made no such boasts. He drank his ale and kept to himself, though many asked him to tell the tale of his famous encounters with Ivar, Eystein, and Halvdan Ragnarsson. He politely refused and sipped his ale until the men became drunk, allowing him to slip away and take his son Hermoth to the room Harald had allocated to Hundr for the night.

Hermoth stared at Hundr with tearful eyes as Hundr told him that Sigrid, much like Sigurd, had passed from Midgard and that he would not see them again until he travelled to the afterlife. Hermoth cried and sobbed, and Hundr did not return to the feast that night. He lay holding his son close, thanking the gods that the boy was alive and well.

The next day, Hundr, Rognvald, and Ravn prepared their fleet to set sail. The king provided barrels of dried fish, freshly brewed ale and oatcakes to keep the army fed as they sailed north to throw Rollo out of Vanylven. Harald offered to keep Hermoth with him whilst Hundr fought, and it honoured Hundr to have his son stay as a foster son with the King of Norway. Eight *drakkar* warships and five hundred warriors sailed from Avaldsnes into the winter sea. Hundr's heart felt lighter even though Hermoth wailed about being left alone, but the lad was better off with King Harald. Hundr sailed into a winter battle and a quest for vengeance, which was no place for a small boy. Besides that, Hermoth was away from his father's curse. Hundr believed that anybody he loved or anyone who grew close to him would die. That was the price Odin took for Hundr's victories. The ships would follow the coast north, just as they had on the journey from the Elbe, but as they left Avaldsnes and the wind picked up, the banner of the one eye flew large and menacing from the sails of the Sea Falcon and the Sword of the Sea, for the Man with the Dog's Name sailed to war. His wife and son were dead. Rollo was the father of all that suffering, and for that, he would pay the ultimate price.

TWENTY

Sweat soaked Einar's body despite the bone-chilling cold. He hefted his shield and moved forward with his warriors on either side of him in the shield wall. Even though his shoulders burned with fatigue from hefting the iron and linden wood shield and his heavy spear, he held fast. Einar barked an order, and the advance halted. He gave another shout, and the wall parted into three sections to allow archers to loose through the gaps. No arrows came, and no enemies died, for this was a practice shield wall, and for the second time that day, Einar pushed his warriors in battle and weapons practice.

It had been two weeks since the attack on Stryn, and Einar's people had taken over the houses, barns, and food inside Jarl Ugattr's town. Einar lived in the hall with Hildr, and it had taken them three days to brush and scrub it free of Ugattr's filth. There were old bones and rotting scraps of food in the dark corners, and the floor rushes hadn't been changed for so long that they were damp and rank with liquid and foul stains. There was a strange feeling about the place, and though Einar knew his people were neither comfortable nor happy in the town they had taken by force, they were dry, warm, and well-fed. Ugattr's stores were full of grain gathered from the few surrounding farms and supplemented by the spoils of the traded furs and pelts his hunters had caught during the summer. There was also salted and smoked pork, beef, lamb and fish, and Einar was no longer worried about his people starving.

Hildr made sure the women and children of Stryn were well cared for. Even though they lived under guard in the stables and barns within the settlement, they always had fire and food. Understandably, they were a surly, resentful bunch and attacked Einar's guards frequently, but Hildr sent women to care for any who fell sick. Indeed, the galdr-woman had saved the life of a child with a cough so gravelly and terrible that it made the town dogs howl. Einar and his warriors had cast all of their menfolk out into the wilderness and killed any who refused to go. Einar had marched out with his men every morning for three days to ensure the warriors who had surrendered after the battle were not lurking in the pine forests or hills surrounding the settlement. It was hard on the women and children because those men would die just as surely as the men who had perished in the attack, but they would never take a place at a feasting bench in Valhalla. Einar had no pity for them, for they had shown none to him or his people when they needed it most.

Ugattr and his men were slavers and had sold countless innocent women and children captured on foreign shores for silver. Ugattr would sail his ships to distant rivers, find an unsuspecting village, slaughter the men and take the rest. Traders from the far south would pay hefty sums for women with blonde hair and blue eyes, and they offered even more for children who would grow into hard-working and compliant slaves. Ugattr had been a filthy bastard, and Einar's men had burned the old jarl and his warriors' corpses outside the settlement without honour or respect.

The practice shield wall closed the gap, and Einar led them forward. He held the position, struck with his spear, and then ordered them back two paces. These were the manoeuvres that won battles – an organised shield wall of professional warriors combining savagery with the skill and discipline to follow orders to ensure the slaughter of the enemy. If Einar's shield wall backed off two paces from the battle line press of shield against shield, the front ranks in the opposing shield wall would stumble forward. The force they shoved against would disappear, and as they took a step forward off balance into that void, Einar's men would strike with spear, axe, and shield, and the front rankers in the enemy line would die. He called a halt, and the men whooped, their cheers a mix of pride in their precise movements and good order and relief that the practice session had come to an end.

Amundr approached with a jug of ale, and Einar took a deep drink.

"They are ready," said the big man, and so they were.

"How many new spears do we have now?" asked Einar.

"We are making ten a day, so we have plenty."

"Start making knives and axes, then."

Amundr nodded and went to inform the work groups of Einar's orders. Every person who had made the journey from Vanylven worked hard each day to prepare to take their town back. The people were proud of where they came from, and from the weakest grandfather to the burliest blacksmith, every single one of them burned with a ferocious desire to win their homes back. So, Einar had set them to work. Each morning, Hildr took groups of women and children into the forests, where they cut and gathered wood for arrows. Each afternoon, they chased chickens, ducks, and geese around to pluck their feathers for the fletchings and used knives to wick small pieces of horn to make the grooved nooks where the bowstrings would fit. She had a company of archers who grew more skilled every day, and Hildr took pride in the accuracy and determined organisation. They gathered sheaves of arrows in Stryn's hall, ready to be put to use when the day came to take their home back.

Torsten worked with the men folk, those who were not warriors but burned with passion to defeat Rollo and his Franks. Some of the men had wives and daughters who had not been lucky enough to escape Vanylven on the day Rollo came, and the fate of those women was enough to drive any man to burn with a white-hot vengeance. So, Torsten taught them to fight. He took fishermen, potters, bakers, smiths, shipwrights, traders and farmers, arming them all with spears and shields. He showed them how to thrust and parry, how to use their shields for defence and attack, and had them raise their weapons and lower them repeatedly to build up the strength in their arms, shoulders, and chests.

Ugattr's dead warriors had yielded leather breastplates, knives, axes, spears, and shields. Torsten distributed those weapons to the newly trained fighters so that they began to look and fight like warriors. Einar was under no illusion of their usefulness in battle, so he would not ask them to stand and trade blows with Rollo's warriors from Frankia. Rollo's men were hardened warriors used to battle, and Rollo had built them into a formidable force. The Betrayer had made himself indispensable to the Franks. He held the lands on their northwest coast, where the wide rivers were so tempting to Viking wolves on the hunt for plunder. Rollo guarded those rivers, and any unsuspecting Vikings who sailed into the wide embrace of their estuaries would find themselves hunted and slaughtered by Rollo and his men. Rollo had risen from nothing, barely surviving the battle of Hafrsfjord, to ascending to great wealth and fame as a duke. He had married a noblewoman of Frankish royal lineage and owned a vast tract of verdant, arable land which would yield immense resources to him every year. He had done well, and Einar hated him with all the intense venom and fire one man could carry against another.

Einar took another drink of the ale and handed it to one of his warriors, who took it gratefully. The men slapped each other's backs and congratulated themselves on their work, and Einar was pleased to see them taking pride in their manoeuvres. They were ready for war, and Einar went amongst them, addressing each warrior by name, offering words of approval for a job well done during the day's training, or recounting the valorous deeds of others from past battles. They were his people, his men, his oathmen, and they looked to Einar for leadership. Determined, he would do his best to right the wrong of the defeat at Vanylven. At that moment, a sudden, great clanging gave Einar pause as he carried his shield and practice spear to where the men gathered them until their next drill.

"Someone's raised the alarm," said a pinched-faced warrior, and then the clanging rang out again. The alarm was little more than a large piece of pig iron hung from a pole, which the warrior on duty would hit with a hammer if there was any sign of trouble.

"Ships in the fjord!" came a voice, and more joined it. A collective cry went up from inside Stryn's walls, and Einar's stomach churned over with a stab of fear. Surely Rollo had not sailed his fleet through the fjords to find him in Stryn? Einar ran with the warriors. He swerved around the earth-roofed buildings and clambered up a ladder to stand upon the palisade. There were indeed ships in the fjord, but as Einar laid eyes on them, his heart soared, and he laughed for joy. Einar punched the man next to him so hard on the shoulder that he fell onto the fighting platform, and the people within Stryn sang out and rejoiced with delight, for two of the ships flew Hundr's banner of the one eye. The rest of the warships flew King Harald Fairhair's snarling wolf sigil, and Einar breathed a sigh of relief because Hundr had returned with an army.

The small jetty, where Stryn's walls opened up facing the water, was thronged with people. The Seaworm, Fjord Bear, Wind Elk, and Sea Stallion were all held inside Vanylven's fjord bridge, and as Einar pushed his way gently through the crowd, he laughed with joy again to see the Sea Falcon gliding in towards the jetty under oars. Hildr was there at the front of the crowd, and Einar draped his arm around her shoulder. She smiled up at him as Einar pulled her close. Hildr had missed Hundr's twins, whom she had helped to nurse and raise, just as she had missed Ragnhild and Sigrid, who were like sisters to her.

Hundr appeared at the Falcon's prow, unmistakable with his one eye and stern face. His hair was pulled back from his face and tied at the nape of his neck. Einar was somewhat surprised because Hundr did not raise his arm in greeting or acknowledge the people on the shore who chanted his name. The ship pulled in carefully beside one of Ugattr's *knarrs,* and the crew used their oar blades to keep the hulls from scraping together. Thorgrim peered over the sheer strake, and Sigvarth Trollhands jumped onto the jetty to tie the ship off securely. The people moved aside to let the crew disembark, and more ships glided towards the shore. They would need to drive their hulls up onto the soft sand along the shore because there was no room on Stryn's small jetty for them all to land safely.

Hundr leapt from the prow and landed with a thud on the weather-darkened timbers. He wore a plain jerkin and trews, for no man sailed in armour unless he faced imminent battle or wished to risk drowning. He looked gaunt, and there was a darkness in his one eye, which made Einar fearful. Hundr was not wearing the patch over his dead eye, and the sunken, puckered scar tissue around the wound was like a bleak cavern in his face. Ragnhild, too, came ashore, and she made straight for Hildr.

"You are returned safe and with an army," said Hildr happily, gesturing at the ships that filled the bay, now bustling with grim-faced warriors. Brightly painted shields adorned the sheer strakes, and men called and shouted orders as they tried to beach the ships and disembark hundreds of men.

"With fell news, though," murmured Ragnhild. Her scarred face pained as she struggled to get the words out. "Better you hear from me now than say something that worsens his humour." Ragnhild flicked her eye towards Hundr and came in closer to Einar and Hildr. "There's no easy way to say this, so I'll just spit it out and say sorry now if my words are harsh or clumsy."

"What is it?" asked Hildr. The joy had drained from her face, and her eyes scoured the ships and warriors coming ashore for faces she recognised and those she missed.

"Sigrid and Sigurd are dead. Sigurd died on the road to Avaldsnes, and Sigrid died in battle against the King of the East Franks. They are gone, and we are all still suffering the pain of it."

"What?" Hildr gasped. Her mouth fell open, and tears welled in her eyes. Einar reeled as though someone had punched him in the face.

"Sigrid and Sigurd are gone?" he stammered. "Where then is little Hermoth?"

"King Harald has taken Hermoth as a foster son until this war is over."

Einar swallowed hard and took a deep breath. He left Hildr and Ragnhild to talk more of the shocking news and went to Hundr's side, laying his hand upon his old friend's shoulder.

"I have heard, and I am sorry," Einar said. It was clumsy, but, of course, it was also impossible to say anything to make Hundr feel better about the numbing loss he had suffered. Hundr stared at him, his dark eye boring deep into Einar's soul. Einar led him away from the jetty, and they walked silently through the town and into Ugattr's hall. The silence wasn't awkward; it was that companionable silence only possible between the greatest of friends. Where each one understands the other and where the need for small talk to fill the silence doesn't exist.

Hundr took a seat next to the fire, and Einar sat opposite him. A steward brought them both a bowl of warm broth and a chunk each of dark bread.

"It has been a long time since summer's end," said Einar. He dipped his bread into the broth and gnawed on the crust. "Rollo killed Trygve. He attacked our camp in the forest. It was a hard fight. After that, we came here."

"Did he die well?" asked Hundr.

"He waits for us in Odin's hall, and we shall drink ale from curved horns with him again one day."

"Is Jarl Ugattr dead?"

"I killed the bastard myself. We asked for his help, and he treated me like a dog."

"Then he got what he deserved." Hundr supped his broth, and his one eye met Einar's. The two men shared a look for a few heartbeats before Hundr stared into the fire. "I should have left my boys here with you."

"That was not their destiny."

"Sigurd is dead, and Hermoth is with King Harald. He is safe with Fairhair. Safer than he ever will be with me."

"Who could care for the lad better than his own father?"

"I am cursed, Einar. Look at my life. I loved Sigrid, and she is dead. She gave up on life. Sigrid charged into the enemy and tried to kill a king. She died bravely, but she welcomed it…she wanted to live amongst us no more. Sigurd is gone, and I am certain that Hermoth is only alive because he is not at my side. Sten died on the walls of Dublin, and I loved him like a father. Saoirse was my first love, and look how she turned out. Had you not taken me on board the Seaworm all those years ago, she would probably be married to Hakon Ivarsson now, a Princess of Northumbria with a brood of Ragnarssons. Odin has taken a high price from me."

"You are not cursed. I am your friend, and no harm has come to me."

"You once called me a luck stealer. Can you really say that your life was not better before you met me? You have been tortured, imprisoned, beaten and wounded."

"But I am also a wealthy jarl, and if I had not met you, I would not have met Hildr."

"When I was a boy, I had to sleep with the animals in the byres and stables. I would pray to the gods to make me into a famous warrior, to let me be a Viking and forge a reputation so that I could show my father and half-brothers that I was more than a half-breed slave, that I was worth something. Odin heard that prayer and brought me reputation, luck, and wealth, but he has taken much in return. I have filled his hall with slain warriors, yet my life is a venom pit of death and suffering."

"You are not cursed!" Einar spoke the words more deliberately this time. "Many children die of sickness in winter. I have experienced it myself, and it is a terrible thing. But Hermoth yet lives, and he needs you. The people of Vanylven need you. Sigrid died in battle, just as she would have wanted. Saoirse chose her own fate when she became the Witch-Queen in Ireland. These things are not your doing. The Norns weave our fates, as you well know. You and I have been friends for fifteen summers, and I am still alive. Those three witches who sit at the foot of Yggdrasil, keeping the roots moist with mud from the great river, have already woven the pattern of our lives, and we cannot change it. They twist our fates together like threads on a loom, and there is no curse in the weft of your life. You have achieved great things, but you have suffered a terrible tragedy. Many fathers and husbands experience the same loss. It is a hard thing but one that must be borne like an axe strike upon a shield. The shield will hold if the man behind it has the strength and will to take the blow and make an attack of his own. Thoughts are waves on the mind sea, and death has turned yours black. That will pass, for you need to be strong for your son who lives. So fill your heart with hate for Rollo, for he is surely the father of all this suffering. Let vengeance be the cure for your curse and your pain."

"I should have…" Hundr's voice trembled, but the words died in his throat. "I could have…" There was a vulnerability in the great warrior that Einar had not seen since the days when Hundr had first joined the Seaworm crew. In those days, he had been a gangly young man, all belligerence and sword skill, but he had also been naïve and alone.

"Nothing you could have done would have made any difference. You were a good husband, and you are a good father. It was just their time to go. That is all there is to it. You must focus on Hermoth. He needs you now more than ever. What sort of man do you want him to grow up to be? Let him have the chance that you never had. He is lucky to be fostered by so great a man as Harald Fairhair. Who else could boast that the first King of all Norway fosters their son? Hermoth will always be able to call Harald his foster father, and that is a great gift indeed. So help me destroy Rollo. Let's build something Hermoth can inherit and secure a place where he can raise his own family. Let us do for him what I could not do for Finn Ivarsson. We all make mistakes, Hundr, and fighting is the only thing either of us has ever been any good at. So, let's take our home back and do it for Hermoth. Strike Rollo down with vengeance and fury in honour of Sigurd and Sigrid, and let the gods see how we honour those who have passed across the Bifrost."

Hundr sighed deeply, but Einar thought he saw the kindling of something in that single, dark eye.

"Rognvald sails with us, and so does Ravn Kjartansson. Rollo still outnumbers us, but we have enough warriors to bring the fight to him and take your jarldom back."

"Rollo must die."

"Rollo must die," Hundr agreed. "But Vanylven is well defended. It will not be easy to take."

"We took it, and so did Rollo."

"True enough. But Rollo had the benefit of surprise on his side, and we will not. When we took the place, we swam the fjord and climbed the towers of the fjord bridge, killed the defenders and removed the rope barrier so that our ships could sail into the harbour and pour our warriors ashore. Rollo was there that day. He climbed the bridge towers with Ragnhild and fought as well as any of our warriors. He will expect us to try that again, and he will be ready. Rollo is no fool, so we must be ready for his surprises and traps."

"The fjord would be too cold to swim this late in the year. Most of the days are now shrouded in darkness. Any man who swims in that water will die."

"So we need to find another way to attack. We could march over the mountain and attack from the landward side. Swarm the palisade from the forest whilst Rollo watches the fjord. He must expect us to retaliate."

"Again, the snow in the high passes could be impassable. Our men could die up there, even though the journey is but a few days. We would need to carry food and shelter for the army to stop the men from freezing to death at night. Rollo has scouts in the woods, or at least he did when we camped there."

"Does he know you are here? Or that I went to Harald?"

"He could, but we have seen no sign of a scout or any sort of raiding party since we came to Stryn. There have been no attacks on our people foraging in the forest or cutting timber. As for him knowing your whereabouts, he knew nothing when we fought at the forest camp. That was why he stopped short of slaughtering us. He wanted to fight you. He hates you. Maybe he has ships or lookouts patrolling the coast; perhaps he saw the fleet flying the wolf and the one eye."

"It must be the sea, then. The passes could indeed be blocked with snow, and Rollo has had time to prepare the forest with traps. Perhaps his men patrol the woodlands still, in case you tried to attack him. Let's talk with Rognvald, Ravn, Ragnhild, and Bush. We need to kill the Betrayer and his Franks. Maybe you are right. Perhaps if I kill Rollo, the gods will grant me peace."

"So let's wash Vanylven in the bastard's blood and offer his warriors' souls to Niflheim. Let's honour the dead with a victory and drive our enemies before us and crush their bones to dust."

TWENTY-ONE

The muscles in Hundr's back stretched as he hauled on the oar. The Sword of the Sea cut through the water like a blade. Men had carved her long, sleek hull from a single piece of oak, and though she was heavy with warriors, she flew across the white-tipped waves like a bird on the wing. The vessel was one of Hundr's fleet and a ship he had captured from an enemy. She was narrow and swift, and though she could not bear as many warriors as the Seaworm, her draught was shallow, which meant she could sail all but the meanest of rivers. The Sword was a Viking *drakkar* and could carry a crew of sixty warriors across the Whale Road to cut deep into foreign lands, navigating the estuaries and rivers to bring axe and sword and the brutality of a Viking raid to towns and villages.

A ship of any sort was expensive to build and keep, and a warship was the sign of a wealthy and successful warrior. Hundr owned five such ships, though Rollo had captured the Seaworm and three of his vessels when he took Vanylven. It took skilled

shipwrights a year to build a *drakkar,* to find the right
oak for the keel and planks, as well as the right pine
for the mast, yard, and oars. Pine roots were essential
for creating the tar, which was mixed with horsehair
to caulk the clinker-built planks, and hemp or seal
hide was necessary for her ropes and rigging. Then
there was the iron for the nails to rivet the planks to
the keel before they painstakingly stuffed the
caulking between each plank to keep out seawater as
the hull flexed under the sea's fury. A constant supply
of fleeces was required so that skilled weavers could
make the heavy sails and repair them each winter.
Fleeces were also needed to make warm clothes,
blankets, and covers for the deck to keep out the
violent squalls which would freeze a man as sure as
ice.

To keep five warships at sea, Hundr had to provide
his crews and warriors with ample warrior rings and
silver. They were his oathmen, and in return for their
duty to fight and die for him, Hundr kept their chests
full of plunder. Vanylven had to produce enough
surplus food to keep the warriors fed and with enough
ale to keep them watered, for ale was safer to drink
than water, which loosened a man's bowels surer than
a mouthful of rotten meat. If the fields and farms of
Vanylven did not produce that surplus, then Hundr
had to use his silver to buy it and keep his army fed.
So, as he stretched his back hauling on the Sword of
the Sea's oar, he appreciated the finely carved
planking and the smooth lines of her prow and sheer
strake. Each of his ships was worth two summers of

raiding and as valuable to Hundr as his weapons and brynjar.

With his hand on the tiller, Einar stood on the steerboard platform and barked orders at the crew. The cliff of his rugged face was set firm, and he stared at the surging sea with grim determination. They had lowered the sails because the wind was unfavourable. The fleet sailed around a jut of rock-covered headland and towards the familiar two sheer cliffs of black and white rock. Between those cliffs was the entrance to Vanylven's fjord, where the rock turned to deep green pines, and the hills rose to taper away high into the mountains beyond. On the edge of the fjord, beneath the evergreen pines and the high snow-capped mountains, Vanylven was nestled in a valley of flatland made green by a river flowing down from the peaks to join the saltwater fjord. Bush called time, and Hundr hauled his oar through the water every time the shipmaster barked, propelling the ship forward at speed towards the fjord.

Hundr's back was to the entrance, and the hills came upon him as he twisted his wrists to lift the oar and lean forward for the next stroke. The oars dripped glistening beads of water like clumps of sparkling jewels, and the crewmen grunted as the oar blades bit again into the rolling sea. The Sword had fourteen banks of oars, which meant over two dozen men hauled her across the Whale Road. As the prow crashed in a surging wave, chill sea water sprayed across Hundr's face, and the salt stung his dead eye like a whip.

On Hundr's port side, Rognvald's three ships raced with urgency, their green sails with the wolf's head banner furled, keeping pace. Shields hung the length of their sheer strakes, just as they did on the Sword of the Sea, and their beast-headed prows snarled with painted teeth and fierce eyes towards their enemies. Ravn's ships sailed on the opposite side. He, too, had brought three fast *drakkar* warships and two hundred of his warriors. The big jarl was clearly visible on the steerboard of the closest ship, bellowing orders to his men and laughing with the joy of being at sea. Ragnhild sailed with Hundr, Einar, Hildr, and Harbard, whilst Bush sailed with Asbjorn, Thorgrim, Amundr, Torsten and Sigvarth on the Sea Falcon. They sailed to war with seven hundred warriors, and Hundr prayed to Odin that it would be enough.

A gust of wind whipped across the deck, followed by a crashing wave which filled the bilge with a surge of water and soaked the crew's faces with its icy spite. They laughed and roared with delight, as ever taking their strange pleasure in the sea's wild fury. Four men bailed the bilge, and that was a constant activity aboard a warship. Hundr had been a bail boy in his time, and the raw-fingered memory of it came back as he cuffed stinging sea water from his dead eye. The fleet came through the cliffs and emerged into the wider fjord. Suddenly, the wet wind vanished, and the water became still and glass-like, so the ships sailed faster, cutting through the fjord water like a knife through soft cheese.

Vanylven was still behind Hundr, for the rowers faced against the direction of travel, and though he could not see the town or its fortifications, they were as familiar to him as the veins on the back of his hand. Two long piers stretched across the water before the town and its harbour. Those piers cut the bay in two, and the fjord bridge contained a gap wide enough for two ships to sail through abreast – the gap was the only way to approach the town from the water. A pair of wooden towers flanked the opening, one at the end of each pier, and a thick, tautly pulled rope spanned the space between. They would lower the rope for friendly ships, but it barred the way for any enemy vessels. Guards would stand in the towers from where they could hurl a rain of spears, arrows and rocks onto the decks of the hostile ships. Hundr recalled how, years earlier, he had assaulted those towers with Ragnhild when he and Einar had helped Rognvald take Vanylven for King Harald.

"Pull, you lazy whores!" Einar bellowed from the steerboard, and Hundr heaved again. A clanging alarm rang out behind Hundr, followed by the repeated trumpet of a war horn. Rollo and his men had seen the fleet of warships approaching and would now set about their defence of Vanylven. Hundr's heart thudded in his chest. His chance for revenge was close – ten more pulls, and he could strike a blow against his great enemy. The crew all wore their armour despite being at sea. They had donned the brynjars or leather breastplates before the fleet had reached Vanylven's outer coastline, and Hundr wore his chainmail, which protected him from neck to knee. He had Battle Fang strapped to his back, and the Ulfberht sword scabbarded at his waist. Ravn's ships surged ahead, the old Viking keen to be the first to strike a blow at the enemy, and from aboard Rognvald's ships came the familiar beat of Bavlos' Sami drums, signalling the time when Rognvald and his fearsome ulfheðnar took their mind-altering war potion.

Hundr pulled again, and the shouts and roars of the Franks echoed across the fjord. He imagined them racing to the fjord bridge to man the towers and piers to ward off the enemy ships. Hundr, Einar, Rognvald, and Ravn had agreed that the best plan was to attack the bridge with full force. There was no room for deep cunning so far into winter. Daylight was fleeting, so their plan was to attack the bridge with everything they had, to overwhelm the defenders and remove the rope barrier. Then, they could enter the harbour and assault the town. Find Rollo and kill the bastard. It was as good a plan as any, and Hundr pulled on his oar once more.

"Prepare to come about!" Einar shouted. As they came closer to the piers, one bank of oarsmen would raise their oars, and the opposite side would continue to pull so that the ship would turn and list as either her port or steerboard side came alongside the pier. Then, the warriors could make the jump from ship to bridge. Hundr ground his teeth, waiting for the order to lift his oar or pull again, depending on where Bush saw a gap for the Sword to make her approach. Suddenly, just as Hundr was about to dip his oar again, a monstrous crunching wrenched the hull. The Sword stopped dead in the water, and a terrible impact threw Hundr backwards from his oar bench. He landed with his heart pounding, sprawled in the bilge along with the rest of the crew, and they were a mass of flailing limbs and clattering weapons. The ship slewed in the fjord, and Einar bellowed from the steerboard like an angered bull.

The hull of the Sword crunched and groaned, and men cried out in terror, springing away from where they had fallen around the mast post. A great plinth of timber had smashed through the ship's planking, and icy fjord water surged through to fill the bilge.

"Bastard's spiked the bay," Einar called, and Hundr followed Einar's finger as he pointed to one of Ravn's ships, which also floundered in the water. Hundr grabbed a rowing bench and hauled himself upright. He ran to port and peered over the side. Beneath the water's surface, he could make out the shimmering form of a fishing boat, her outline shaking and shifting like she was *Naglfar*, the ship made from the fingernails and toenails of the dead on which Loki's monster brood would sail on the end of days at Ragnarök. Rollo had sunk a fishing boat along with her mast, and because the Vanylven men were so familiar with the fjord, they had eyes only for the fjord bridge rather than anything that could lurk beneath the water's surface. The sunken ship's mast post had torn through the Sword's hull like a knife, and all that war rage and preparedness for battle had gone to ruin.

311

Hundr roared and waved at the Sea Falcon, but his friends were within striking distance of the piers and could not hear Hundr's plea. Rollo's men were thick on the fjord bridge, and their weapons bristled like the iron claws of a monstrous sea beast. Ravn saw Hundr's plight from the steerboard of his ship and bellowed at his oarsmen, so the ship came about to rescue Hundr and his crew from the water.

"We are going to drown!" yelled a warrior with a terrified face. He pulled and yanked at his armour, trying desperately to remove its weight before the ship sank and dragged him to the bottom. Fear took hold of the crew in that moment, and Hundr had to fight to master his own thought cage, which threatened to overwhelm him with fears of drowning and being denied an afterlife in Valhalla. He clambered up the deck towards Einar. Ragnhild met him there, and her face was a rictus of impotent fury. There was chaos in the fjord. Two ships were at the fjord bridge, and Rollo's cunning had scuppered another two. The rest of the fleet stopped, gliding aimlessly on the water, their shipmasters unable to decide whether to attack the bridge or to come about and rescue those whose ships were sinking. Their crews peered over the sides with fearful faces, searching the depths for any more sunken fishing boats.

"That snivelling bastard!" Einar cursed, slamming his fist hard on the sheer strake.

Rognvald's ships came about slowly, and her oars bit into the water as they approached cautiously to rescue the stranded crews from their sinking ships. Ravn's ship came alongside the Sword, and her crew reached down with brawny arms to haul the Sword's warriors over the side to safety.

"Please, Odin, no," Hundr whispered. He leant on the sinking ship's sheer strake and looked across the water where the Falcon had come alongside the eastern pier. The rest of the fleet had peeled away from the attack and beat their oars out into the fjord, desperate faces peering over their sides, searching for more obstacles beneath the surface. Rollo's men hurled spears from the pier onto the Falcon's deck, and arrows soared from the towers like a murder of crows descending on the single attacking ship. The Falcon's crew formed up on the deck with their shields raised over them so that the warriors sheltered beneath a roof of iron and linden wood. Spears and arrows clattered from shield bosses and hammered into their boards. The ship scraped alongside the pier, and the shield roof opened for five men to make the daring leap onto the pier, which was thick with enemy warriors. Those brave men did not know that their comrades had broken off the attack. They assumed that hundreds of warriors made the leap simultaneously to hack into Rollo's Franks at multiple locations and overwhelm them.

Hundr grabbed an outstretched hand and clambered onto Ravn's ship from the Sword. All across the deck, Ravn's men heaved the Sword's crew up from the ruined vessel.

"Get us to the pier," Hundr said, grabbing Ravn on his muscular shoulder.

"It's too late. The attack has failed," Ravn replied, his broad face drooping in despair. The brave pride, which usually dripped from Ravn like rain from a thatched hall, had been replaced with reluctant resignation. Hundr stared at him with his good eye and then tore his gaze back to the Falcon. The men who made the first jump battled hard against Rollo's Franks. Steel rang against steel, men shouted their war cries, and others screamed in pain.

"Bush is with them," uttered Ragnhild. She spoke so softly that Hundr could only just hear her.

Hundr ran to the prow and squinted, his one eye unable to make out the old shipmaster in the furious mayhem of the fight on the pier. The Franks shouted, and the few Vanylven men fought. Bush was there, battling for his life and not understanding that the rest of Hundr's army could not reach the fjord bridge.

"Get me to him," wailed Ragnhild, and Hildr held her back because, for a moment, it seemed like Ragnhild would dive into the fjord and swim to Bush's aid.

"That's Torsten as well," said Einar. The Franks pushed back from the fight on the pier, and only two of the Falcon's fighters remained standing. Bush had lost his precious helmet in the fighting, so his head shone bald in the winter sun. Torsten limped, clearly wounded, shouting at his enemies to come and die. Bush barked an order, and the Falcon veered away from the pier. The giant form of Amundr thundered his helpless frustration in the prow, hanging over the side and waving his axe at the enemy. The men on the Falcon did a difficult thing. They rowed away from the pier and left Torsten and Bush to their fate. Asbjorn was the Falcon's captain, and he had proven his bravery countless times, yet now he risked being cursed as a coward to save the lives of the men on his ship. He led his *drakkar* away from the Franks and the fjord bridge, and they wailed in horror as Bush and Torsten remained stranded. There were a hundred or more Franks crammed onto the long pier, and alone without the rest of the fleet, there was no way the crew of the Falcon could attack that pier and live. Asbjorn had abandoned Bush and Torsten, but in doing so, he had saved the Falcon and the lives of sixty men.

The attack had failed, and only Torsten and Bush remained. They seemed so small in between the two massed contingents of enemy warriors, half pressed towards the tower at the end of the pier, and the rest pushed back on the landward side where more Franks bayed and jostled to get closer to the bridge. A figure pushed his way through the press of Franks on the narrow pier, and that man was unmistakable, towering a full head and shoulders above any of his men. It was Rollo, and his warriors cheered his approach. He waved a mighty sword and pointed it out into the bay, shouting words that Hundr couldn't hear over the thunderous acclaim of Frankish warriors. The Betrayer strutted like a champion, and his mail brynjar gleamed brightly. He was a lord of war, and he crowed his victory because Hundr and Einar had failed.

Rollo reached the gap between his warriors, and the Franks fell silent. Torsten let out a bloodcurdling war cry and charged at Rollo, his axe held above and his injured leg trailing behind him. Rollo moved rapidly, and even across the fjord, it surprised Hundr how quickly he moved for a big man. Before Torsten could bring his axe down to strike, The Betrayer's long sword pierced Torsten's belly. Rollo drove the blade through Torsten as though he were made of sand, and the sword's tip punched out of Torsten's back to spray blood over the fjord bridge. Torsten cried out in pain, and Hundr's eye closed of its own accord, his mind flinching at his friend's suffering. Rollo stepped in and lifted Torsten from the bridge by the sword embedded in his torso. Torsten was a big man, renowned for his toughness, and Hundr's eye opened whilst his hands curled into white-knuckled fists. The strength required to haul Torsten from the bridge was immense, and Rollo roared his defiance, the sound of his voice rippling across the fjord like the wind. He tossed Torsten's corpse contemptuously into the water, where it splashed like a boulder.

The Franks cheered, and Rollo waved them to quiet. He circled Bush, and the smaller man turned, axe in hand, to face the Betrayer, surrounded by a sea of foemen.

"I can't just watch him die," Hildr sobbed, and she and Ragnhild held each other, weeping desperately for Bush.

Hundr, Einar, Bush, Hildr, and Ragnhild had met in war-torn England in the year the sons of Ragnar brought their Great Viking Army to destroy Northumbria, East Anglia, and Mercia. That had been fifteen summers ago, and since then, they had formed a tight family bound by the trust and respect required for brothers and sisters of the sword. They had each saved one another's lives countless times, faced death together on distant shores, and had loved and lost friends together across the savagery of the shield wall. To see Bush surrounded by enemies and at the mercy of their greatest foe was too much to bear.

"Die well, old friend," Einar murmured. Of all the warriors who watched Bush face Rollo from the deck of Ravn's ship, Einar had known Bush the longest. They had sailed the Whale Road together from the time they were boys. Back then, they had served the legendary warlord Ragnar Lothbrok and then, later, his son Ivar the Boneless. They had grown up together and grown old together, and Hundr felt helplessly woebegone by the sorrow gripping Einar's heart as he watched his friend from across the water.

"Dog's Name!" Rollo called from the pier. He glanced out at the fjord and pointed his long sword at Bush's chest. "I have your home, and now I have your oathman. Your attack here today was like that of a mewling child. I have bested you again. I am the champion of the Northmen, not you. Twice I have beaten you, and you send this bow-legged turd to do your fighting for you? An old man who can barely hold his axe fights on behalf of the Dog and the

317

Brawler. I am Rollo Ganger, Duke of Frankia, and I am the champion of all Northmen. Now, watch this goat turd die before you sail back to whatever hole you crawled out of. I see the banners of Fairhair in your fleet. The usurper and assassin king picks his sides unwisely. I will deal with him once I have settled with you, Dog."

Bush launched himself at Rollo then, and axe and sword came together with a great ringing sound that would have shaken Asgard itself. The Franks on the pier and the Vikings on the fjord were silent, as though the gods themselves had cast a cloak of peace across the armies while all watched Rollo and Bush fight on Vanylven's fjord bridge. Rollo swung his mighty sword, and Bush ducked beneath the blade. He attacked Rollo with his axe, lunging and swinging, and the big man staggered backwards, dodging and weaving away. Rollo parried one attack with his sword, and Bush punched him in the face. For a fleeting moment, Hundr's chest grew light as he thought Bush's savage attack might just kill Rollo because the axe blade sliced across Rollo's shoulder, and even across the fjord, Hundr saw the scarlet spray of blood.

Rollo roared, charging at Bush again, and Hundr prayed to the gods to give Bush strength. He shuffled and moved, raising his axe and avoiding the onslaught, but Rollo was huge, and it was as though a father fought with his son. Rollo's hand snaked out and caught the haft of Bush's axe. He yanked it wide and stepped in to crash a sickening headbutt into

Bush's face. The shipmaster staggered, and Rollo dragged the blade of his sword across Bush's chest. Bush grunted in pain as the links of his brynjar shattered beneath the keen blade and Rollo's monstrous strength.

"Valhalla!" Bush shouted. The sound pierced Hundr's heart like a knife, for his friend knew that death was upon him; he was about to die with his blade in his fist and with a full heart. He was a warrior. A shipmaster of the Whale Road. Odin would be honoured to have such a Viking join his Einherjar.

Rollo swung his sword in a wide arc, and it sliced through Bush's neck to chop the bald head from his shoulders. The Franks cheered their duke's skill and victory, and Hundr forced himself to remain calm. Rollo had killed Bush and Torsten, and their loss hung over the retreating fleet like a thundercloud of sorrow.

"When we return," Einar growled, "Rollo and every Frank in Vanylven will die. I will make a hill of their corpses and dedicate their souls to Bush. I will take Rollo's skull and use it as a drinking cup and hang his rotten bones above my hall."

The ships rowed away from Vanylven under the shadow of defeat, and with two of their greatest warriors dead. The sorrow was almost too much for Hundr to bear, so much death and so much loss. Fate had ripped loved ones and friends away from him, and as Hundr took his turn at the oar, he wondered if it were possible for a man to feel more pain than he did at that moment. He asked Odin to take Bush and Torsten into Valhalla so that they could seek Sigrid in the great hall where the walls are made of shields and the ceiling of spears, and they would wait for him there where they could drink all night and fight all day. The attack on Vanylven had failed, and Rollo had beaten Hundr once more.

TWENTY-TWO

The Viking fleet limped back to Stryn beneath a pale sky, with the weight of defeat and loss hanging over their heads like an axe blade. People thronged Stryn's small harbour. Folk had flocked there once they had spotted the fleet rowing across the fjord. Expectant cheers had quickly turned to mouths covered with nervous hands and then deep sighs and groans of sorrow as the ships docked and their crews spread the news of the defeat and of Bush and Torsten's death.

It was only mid-afternoon, but the sun was already low in the sky. A sickly, wan light spread across the pine-covered mountains, making the frost-tipped branches glitter like a treasure horde. A dusting of clouds hung still in the sky, and Einar stalked along Stryn's jetty, his thought cage swirling with grief, anger, and shame. People avoided him as he marched through the streets and lanes towards Ugattr's hall. Children stopped playing or ran into their houses to escape his malevolent anger. Women cast their eyes down or turned away from him, and Einar breathed a sigh of relief as he pushed open the green doors and entered the secluded safety the small hall offered from the judgement of his people.

Hildr followed closely behind him, discarding her bow and quiver in a corner, and she kicked a bucket of water across the ground. Ragnhild and Hundr entered shortly after and sat together by the fire. Einar's steward brought them all ale and fussed about preparing a meal. Then Rognvald sauntered into the hall, casting a disapproving look at the meagre surroundings and the meats hanging from the rafters.

"Ugattr did not live well," he said, wiping his hands on the hem of his jerkin and refusing an offered mug of ale. "My stomach is raw from Bavlos' brew, and it will be a while before I can consume anything." The ulfheðnar had worked themselves into their fighting frenzy, encouraged by the Sami war music, but they had wasted their fury as the fleet floundered in the fjord. So, the wolf warriors were a pale and sickly bunch on the return to Stryn, with no war glory to assuage the belly sickness and sore heads that always followed their transformation from men into ulfheðnar.

"How can you be so flippant at a time like this?" snarled Ragnhild. Hundr put his hand over hers to calm her.

"Will being miserable change the fact that Rollo defeated us? Your friends and brothers of the shield wall are dead, but they have gone to glorious Valhalla. There, they sit at feasting tables with heroes of days gone by. They drink golden ale from curved horns and laugh, sharing their tales of adventure and brave deeds. Do not be sad for them. Rejoice that they died in battle and have achieved that which all warriors yearn for – a place in Odin's Einherjar."

"He might seem as soft as a child's blanket," growled Ravn before swiftly downing a cup of ale, clicking his fingers for a refill, and continuing, "but he talks sense. We should celebrate your dead warriors, not mourn them."

Einar paced the hall, seething with anger. "It's not over," he insisted, more to himself than to the others. "We have lost two ships and five men. It's not over."

"We have tried to attack the fjord bridge, and it failed," said Ravn. "Is there another way to take the place?"

"There are the mountain passes, but it's too late to cross them now. Anyone attempting to cross the high trails at this time of year would either die in the heavy snow or be forced back."

A deep cackling sound echoed from a dark corner of the hall, prompting Einar to peer around Ravn's wide frame to see where it came from. Bavlos was huddled by a sputtering rush light, kneeling against a thick post that supported the roof. The Sami shaman chuckled to himself and tickled the belly of a scrawny dog that writhed on its back and wagged its tail.

"What are you laughing at?" Einar demanded, letting his anger get the better of him.

Bavlos looked up, and his bright, clever eyes flashed blue in the gloom. "Forgive me; I mean no insult," he said, raising a gnarled hand to add weight to his apology. "But you southerners know nothing of the white sea. My people live in the snow and ice. Up in your mountains, there has barely been a sprinkling. We could pass through if we wished."

"Even if we could get through," Hundr posited wistfully, "we couldn't march our army that way. We'd need to carry food and weapons for two days, avoid Rollo's scouts in the forest, and then attack Vanylven's walls."

"So are you saying the Betrayer has beaten us?" asked Ragnhild. "Have we surrendered our home to Rollo and his bastard Franks? Did Bush, Torsten, Trygve, and the others all die for nothing?"

Einar flinched at her harsh words, hoping that her reference to others didn't include Sigrid and Sigurd. But Hundr seemed not to notice and instead continued to stare into the fire.

"Our plan of attack was too simplistic. We were like Hrungnir when he was challenged by Odin to race mighty Sleipnir. We allowed our pride and our hate to deceive us when we should have trusted ourselves to cunning and thought," Einar said, and he ran his hand down the spade of his beard. "Rollo would expect an all-out attack on the fjord bridge, and he will probably expect us to try again."

"We must attack again," insisted Hundr, rising from his seat with his one eye blazing. "Our numbers match Rollo's. Each of us has around seven hundred warriors."

"To attack and take any town or city, it is wiser if the attacking force vastly outnumbers the defenders," said Rognvald. Which Einar knew was true, for it was much easier to defend a position from above and beat an enemy back than to scale or take a wall and palisade from below.

"I won't let that bastard defeat me!" Einar bellowed. He shook with rage, no longer able to contain it. "He killed Bush and Torsten. Bush has been my friend since we were boys. We have killed more men, fought more battles, taken more towns and seen more silver than any of you in this shithole of a hall could ever dream of. We have the men, the ships and the will. All we are short of is the cunning to get inside the bloody place."

"What if it can't be done?" said Hildr softly. As a Valkyrie warrior priestess, tenacious courage ran deep within her, and though Einar had lost his temper and was consumed by his desire to crush Rollo, Hildr's thoughts were grounded in the welfare and fate of their people. Which was one of the reasons why Einar loved her so. She was brave but also wise, and though the gods had never granted her the gift of children, Hildr was like a mother to all the people of Vanylven. "If there is no way to throw Rollo and his men out of our home, what do we do? Do we make a life for our people here in this place? Do we build and make Stryn large and strong enough to house those we are responsible for?"

"Rollo won't be happy with just Vanylven," said Rognvald. "He hates you, Hundr, and you, Einar. But more than his hatred for you both is his bitter fury towards King Harald. Rollo believes Harald stole his birthright when he became King of all Norway. It's true that Harald and I took Rollo's father's lands in the war of succession. He is a man denied his birthright, and his whole life is a quest for vengeance for what he believes we stole from him. But such is war, and Viking rule over his land is only as secure as his grip on the haft of his axe."

"You took his lands and those of many others," remarked Ragnhild.

"Just so, but such is the way of our people, no? How many lords and warriors have you killed? Was it not your crews who killed Ketil Flatnose, Eystein Longaxe, and Ivar the Boneless?"

"That is the Viking way," Einar allowed.

"That is our way. We kill the weak, and the strong survive and rule. The way of the Viking is to take what we can from those who do not have the strength to defend it. We are the wolves of the sea and our gods glory in our brutality, for they moulded us in their image."

"What you are saying then," said Hildr, "is that there can be no peace? That we must stop Rollo at all costs?"

"Yes," Rognvald nodded, "because he will never stop. Ravn and I could return to Avaldsnes now, and you could decide to swallow your hate for Rollo and leave him brooding in Vanylven. You can knock down this hovel of a hall and build a greater one, strengthen your walls and build more homes for your people, but in the spring, Rollo will bring his Franks around the coast and attack you again and again, and again until you are all dead. Then he will come for King Harald."

"Rollo wants to be King?" asked Ravn incredulously, his broad face twisting into a frown of disbelief.

"He does not. He wants us all dead, including Harald. But in the end, if he is King Rat, then I am sure he will not refuse the crown?"

"You talk in riddles, Rognvald," huffed Ravn, crossing his arms over his chest. "Speak plainly. Who is King Rat?"

Rognvald sighed. "It is a common enough story in Rogaland, but I will tell it to you now. So, what do you do if you find rats in your hall?"

"Get more cats," said Ragnhild.

"You take a barrel, catch the first rat and throw it in. When you catch the second, for there is never only one rat, throw that one in as well. Do not feed them and leave them for three days. When you return to the barrel, only one rat remains."

"For one has eaten the other?" asked Hildr, scrunching her nose in distaste.

"Just so. Then you catch another and throw that one in and do the same thing. Do this with six rats, and the one left is the strongest. Let the survivor go. Soon, you will have only one rat left. The King Rat. You kill him, and your infestation is no more."

"The King Rat eats the others?"

"Until he is the last survivor, and by then, he has a taste for rat flesh. That is Rollo. He will keep killing until he is the only one left, and to be sure, he already has a taste for jarl flesh."

"I'll take the Raven Band over the mountain," Hundr volunteered, "if Bavlos will come with us and use his Sami craft to guide us through the snow on the high peaks."

"I admire your bravery," said Ravn, "and nobody doubts your courage nor the savagery with which your Raven Band fought in Saxony. But even if you can get through, thirty men is not enough to scale the walls and take Vanylven."

"But it is enough to skirt the settlement in the dark, traverse the fjord bridge, and lower the rope."

"You make it sound simple," Ravn replied. "I am no shirker, but to do that, you must cross the high hills and treacherous snow-filled passes, sleeping in the wilderness for two nights or more. Then, you must approach Vanylven through a forest which we know is crawling with Rollo's scouts. If you survive the mountain and the forest, you must then skirt the palisade and come about the bridge without being seen, cross the pier, and cut the rope. If a Frank sounds the alarm, the entirety of Rollo's warriors will descend upon you, and then it will be your head flashed from your shoulders by Rollo's long sword."

"You forgot to add that we also need to sail our ships around the coast and approach Vanylven in darkness. Then we must cross the fjord, hoping that Hundr has been successful and that the rope is down," said Rognvald, "otherwise, we must turn tail and run again like whipped dogs."

"You are lucky," Bavlos interjected, standing from his crouch and approaching the fire. He grinned at Hundr and then at Rognvald. "For in five days, there will be a new moon, and the night will be at its darkest. That is when the veil between the world of the living and the dead will be at its thinnest, where all that separates Midgard from Niflheim and Valhalla is a sliver of gossamer. In my homeland, it is when we are closest to the trees and the animals, but for you norskrs, it is when your Aesir come so close that you almost reach out and touch them. The new moon is when the trolls and the hudufólk come down from the mountains to steal children…it is when the elves come into our gardens and homes, and when we can ask the dead for help."

"So the sky will be dark in five days?" asked Einar, hope suddenly blossoming in his heart where there had only been despair.

"There will be no moon at all," Bavlos hooted, and he laughed like a madman. "We can ask your glorious dead to aid us in what must be done, and I will take you and your warriors over the white sea, Hundr of the one eye."

"So we shall attack the wretched bastard again, and this time, there can be no failure and no turning back," Einar exclaimed, and he stared at the warriors in his captured hall, letting his fierce gaze rest upon each of them so that they could see and understand his determination.

"We must win or die in the attempt," said Hildr. "For Lord Rognvald is right; there can be no peace with Rollo. Either he dies, or we do. Our people cannot live here in peace. He will hunt and persecute us forever. Rollo must die."

"For Bush and Torsten, for Sigrid, Sigurd, Trygve, and all the others who have perished since Rollo brought his Franks north," Ragnhild intoned, drawing the axe from the loop at her belt. "I will not rest until I have soaked this blade in their blood and had my vengeance."

They swore oaths of vengeful murder, and Einar ordered his servants to fetch more ale and food. Hundr summoned Amundr, Thorgrim, Sigvarth, Asbjorn, and Harbard to join the feast, along with Jogrimmr, Agnarr, Hooknose Ymir, and Hrolfr the Mouse. They drank and ate and celebrated Bush and Torsten's lives. Einar told the tale of how Bush had earned his name, of how he had been shot by an arrow whilst shitting behind a bush on a campaign. The gathered warriors laughed, and each spoke of a brave deed or a fond memory of those who had fallen, all except Hundr, who remained alone by the fire, staring into the dancing flames.

"Should we go to him?" Ragnhild asked Einar as the drinking was in full sway, and Amundr was deep into a belching competition with Ravn.

"Leave him. We grieve for our friends by celebrating their lives and drinking to their glorious ascent to Valhalla. But he has lost a wife and a son, and that is an incomparable grief. Hildr will go to him later when we are all drunk and full of meat and bread. She will listen to him talk about Sigrid and Sigurd, and perhaps he will let his grief out in a different way. But he will fight, as will we all. This could be our last time to cross blades in the shield wall, for Rollo is a stern and cunning enemy. There can be no retreat or surrender in this fight, no quarter asked or given. It is a fight to the death, with either Rollo or us meeting our end. We must hope that the little shaman is right and that he can find a way across the snow because I will attack the piers with my ships even if the rope is not cut when we arrive at Vanylven. We know where Rollo has spiked the fjord, and we can bring our ships to the fjord bridge."

"A fight to the death, then," nodded Ragnhild. She raised her ale and clanked the cup against Einar's so that froth slopped onto the tabletop.

"To the death."

TWENTY-THREE

Hundr led thirty warriors up the pine-covered ridge from Stryn into the mountains. The lofty peaks stood between Stryn's shallow valley and the deeper, cliff-faced mountainsides which swept down towards Vanylven. Thirty warriors and one Sami shaman made the journey, and Bavlos had ensured the Raven Band was well-prepared. Bavlos had gathered the men about him the day following the impromptu feast and bout of drinking to celebrate the lives of Bush, Torsten, and the other warriors who had died since Rollo's arrival in Vanylven.

The warriors carried their helmets, brynjars, and weapons in packs upon their backs, rolled in fleeces and safe from ice and frost. Each warrior also marched with a heavy shield slung across his back and enough food and ale to last the four-day march. In good weather, the journey could be made in two days, but it would take twice as long in the snow. Hundr brought no shield or helmet, for he rarely fought with either unless he was standing in the shield wall. Instead, he carried Ragnhild's bow, three sheaves of arrows, and his pack. Bavlos had directed the warriors and any women folk who could help to gather all the wool and fleeces they could find, and from them, he demonstrated how to make jerkins, trews, coverings for their feet, hats, and tents. Bavlos sought stout leather boots, the largest he could find, and then fitted the insides with a layer of wool to further protect the warriors' feet. The danger of marching in the snow and ice was that feet and hands would freeze and turn black, as was the risk with any of their extremities. Bavlos had laughed as he told the story of his cousin, who had fallen asleep drunk and left his tent flap open. He had awoken to find the tip of his nose blackened along with an ear. Both had to be removed with a knife before the rot spread and killed him.

"He was an ugly bastard anyway," Bavlos had cackled at the end of his gruesome tale, "but you should see him now. He looks like a cross between a toad and a pig."

The Sami showed the women how to make mittens from wool or furs and scarves that would cover the warriors' mouths and noses. They were also tasked with making fleece-lined leather tents, and it all needed to be completed within one day; otherwise, they would not reach Vanylven in time for the new moon. The most cunning of Bavlos' creations were the eye protectors and snowshoes he made for each warrior. Bavlos asked for every person in Stryn to bring whatever items of horn or ivory they possessed. Once the little shaman had a satisfactory pile, he took his knife and showed the warriors how to fashion a thin strip of horn. The length needed to be the width of a man's head and two fingers wide, with two horizontal slits carved at an equal distance into the front. He put the strip on his face and cackled again as the slits made it possible for him to see through the strip of horn. He tied the strip around his head and assured the Raven Band that it was the only way to avoid snow blindness. When a man is deep in the white sea, the glare of the sun from the pure white snow could ruin a man's eyes, so each warrior carefully crafted his own pair of eye coverings to take on the march.

The snow shoes were two pieces of stout wood threaded through with the seal hide ropes the Vikings used for rigging on their warships, and they strapped the entire contraption one on each foot. Hundr marched uphill wearing those shoes, and he marvelled at how he could walk with his armour and his weapons on his back and still not sink into the snow. It was deep as they went higher into the mountains, pure snow, untouched and crisp beneath their boots. The thirty warriors mainly marched in silence. Amundr marched with them, for he knew the way, and Bavlos went with the giant so that they looked like a jotun and a dwarf in their wool and furs marching ahead of the men. Hundr marched alongside Ragnhild, and they also shared a tent in companionable silence on the long, dark nights. She knew of his pain, but her presence without words was a comfort. He was tired of thinking and talking about his grief, and he did his best to concentrate his thought cage on the quest at hand. Jogrimmr and

Agnarr took up the rear, and Thorgrim and Sigvarth marched with the main column, keeping pace and ensuring none of the warriors fell behind. Thorgrim carried his giant double-bladed war axe strapped to his back and waited with any warrior who stopped to piss. It would take an age to remove the furs and woollen clothing, and all knew that to get lost alone in that wintery kingdom was to die.

The march was gruelling. Hundr's thighs burned with fatigue, and his body was sheeted with sweat beneath the heavy but warm clothing. Each night, Bavlos would take dry kindling from his pack and make a smoky fire from pine boughs, and the war band would eat a meagre meal in exhausted silence before collapsing into the tents to fall asleep immediately. No men froze during the march, and Hundr marvelled at how Bavlos found the passes and crags they could traverse as Amundr showed him the way. The passage was treacherous, and Hundr was in no doubt that the mountains would have been impassable but for the Sami man's knowledge. On the third night spent in their tents, Hundr stared up at a black night where the stars shone like jewels in a queen's crown. A shred of moon hung in the sky like a piece of hacksilver, and the high mountain passes were as dark as Midgard at the end of days. Even the snow was as caliginous as the bottom of the sea. Hundr stared up into the bleakness and prayed silently to Odin to bring him strength and power. He prayed to Sigrid and Bush and asked them to harry the Aesir from Valhalla, for he needed their luck and their skill, and as he lay next to Ragnhild swathed in fleeces and furs, he felt Sigrid close to him, and it warmed his heart like a fire. He closed his one eye and heard little Sigurd laugh, just as he would when Hundr would throw him over his shoulder and tickle his underarms. They were wonderful memories, and Hundr slept in the belief that his loved ones would grant him the strength he needed to defeat Rollo the Betrayer.

Hundr woke on the fourth morning to find Bavlos out of his tent and crouched beside a small fire. The shaman used green wood for his flame, and the thick grey smoke twisted and danced into the silent winter sky. Bavlos took handfuls of that smoke and gathered it to him, washing his hair and face in it. He chanted in a deep, undulating voice that seemed to come from the pit of his belly. Bavlos cast his yellowed bone fragments and pieces of wood and horn etched with runes of power, and he opened an eye as he noticed Hundr's approach.

"What does your magic say?" Hundr asked him, his voice muffled by the woollen scarf over his mouth. He adjusted the horn strip across his eyes so that he could see better through the two slits.

"I have asked the snow, the trees and water if they will let us pass today. They say that we shall walk through the forest like ghosts and spirits." Bavlos pointed to a stout little bird with grey feathers and a red bill that resembled blood against the pure snow. "That bird told me we shall reach the edge of the forests outside Vanylven unseen but that there are soldiers in the forest close to the town, and neither my

336

gods nor yours can help us pass the walls without them spotting us."

"If you get me to the forest's edge, shaman," said Hundr, "then you have done your job, and I will make you a rich man."

"I do not desire silver or gold. But when this is over, let me walk with you in the dream world, and I shall heal your pain."

"So be it," Hundr replied, but he wasn't sure if he feared the shaman's strange world, his potions, and his power more than he feared the fight to come.

The Raven Band came down from the mountains on a bright, frosty morning, and it was just as Bavlos said it would be. Thick snow between harsh crags and slopes between sheer rock faces gave way to the pine forest, and as Bavlos led the warriors on a wide descent down the valley to avoid the steepest gulleys, Vanylven came into view. The town poked out where the forest stretched away towards the fjord. Thatched roofs steamed under the pale sun as it warmed the frost away, and hearth fires sent tendrils of smoke into a windless sky. The fjord was still, and it shone the sun's rays back towards a sky the colour of ice on a freshwater pond. The trees became thicker the further down the slope the warband travelled, and Hundr turned to glance over his shoulder at the wisps of white cloud gathered about the snow-covered mountain tops.

Once the men were deep into the forest, they abandoned the snowshoes that had helped them walk through even the deepest snowdrifts. Hundr took off his horn eye mask, and the warband made their way through the forest slope, wearing their wool and fur clothing and carrying their packs upon their backs. There was no sign of Rollo's scouts that high in the forest, no footprints in the snow other than the tracks of animals. The light diminished early in the afternoon, and they made a camp between a cluster of trees but dared not light a fire so close to Vanylven. The smoke from damp twigs or branches would rise above the trees and alert Rollo's scouts to their presence. So, they huddled together inside their stout little tents for the last time and ate a meal of dried meat and the last of their hard-baked biscuits taken from Stryn.

"We wait until the darkness has fallen completely," Hundr told them. The hard-faced warriors with frost in their beards and vengeance in their hearts nodded their understanding. "We make our way down and skirt the walls until we reach the eastern pier. Our priority is to remove the rope that blocks the entrance to the fjord."

"What if we get caught up in trouble?" asked Jogrimmr. He was a big man, not as tall as Einar or Amundr, but taller than Hundr and thickly built across his chest, torso, and legs. Jogrimmr was almost the same width from his shoulders to his feet, and he wore his auburn beard long and loose and combed it to a lustrous sheen. He and Agnarr were two of the warriors who had come to Hundr's service in Saxony, and they were both stout fighters who had proved themselves countless times in the fighting against King Louis' army.

"We can't get caught up. If we meet resistance or they raise an alarm, we keep going. We do not stop to engage Rollo's men. If we must, two of us will peel off at a time to hold the enemy so the rest can continue on. Einar, Rognvald and Ravn will already be on their way around the coast with the fleet, and they will enter the fjord once darkness has fallen. We are lost if we don't open the fjord bridge."

"And if we die?" said Sigvarth with a glint in his eye.

"Then we die," growled Thorgrim as he dragged a whetstone along the blade of his axe. "And I will see you in Valhalla."

They chuckled grimly at that.

"We must succeed, for Bush and Torsten and the others who have fallen," Hundr uttered. He couldn't bring himself to include Sigrid and Sigurd among those who had died because of Rollo's vengeful attack on Vanylven.

"We'll cut the rope," said Ragnhild, "or die trying."

Hundr could not breathe for another day if Rollo lived after that night. The hate inside him burned too fiercely. The Betrayer had taken everything from Hundr. He had cut a hole in Hundr's soul, which could never be repaired, and though Hermoth yet lived, there could be no life for Hundr if he had to share Midgard with Rollo.

Rollo must die.

They huddled in their tents and tried to sleep, but Hundr's thought cage raced with the myriad problems and risks of the attack, so instead, he sat outside swathed in his woollen clothes and his furs and stared up at a small patch of sky visible beneath the snow-heavy pine boughs. He waited for the new moon and for the land to turn blacker than Loki's heart. Hundr took out his Ulfberht sword, sharpened the edge, and then did the same to Battle Fang. He sharpened the wicked blade of his broken-backed seax and laid the three blades out before him.

Bavlos shuffled through the snow and planted himself down next to Hundr. He squinted at him with his dark face scrunched tight, and his beady eyes glared at Hundr's one eye, then also at the weapons.

"Take this," Bavlos said, fumbling inside his robes. His dark, wrinkled hand came out clutching a small, brown clay vial, and he handed it to Hundr.

"What is it?" Hundr asked.

"It is the drink that turns a man into a wild animal. It is the drink of the earth and the forest that can alter a man's mind and turn him into a wolf or a bear. He who drinks this feels no pain or fear and fights with the strength of three men."

"Thank you, Bavlos. Though I do not think that your potion meets the demands of *drengskapr*, the way of the warrior which I follow." Hundr tucked the small clay pot into the pouch at his belt, not wanting to discard its magical powers.

"Let me put a charm on your blades then," said the Sami shaman. "My gods can grant you speed and luck in the fight to come."

Hundr shrugged, for though he did not worship Bavlos' old gods, what harm could it do to have more gods on his side? Especially the ancient Sami gods that men prayed to when the world was young, and the Aesir roamed Midgard like men.

So, Bavlos began his deep-throated chants and banged a smaller version of his war drum, prancing about the two swords and the seax. Hundr closed his eye, allowing Bavlos' strange, guttural chanting to clear his mind. He took deep breaths and imagined himself cutting the bridge rope and cutting Rollo down. Hundr asked Odin to help him with what must be done and to bring him battle luck. Finally, he said a prayer for Sigrid and hoped that she had found the peace in the afterlife which had deserted her in Midgard, and he asked the gods to make sure that little Sigurd was safe and happy. Hundr imagined the lad running through green fields in another of the nine realms that stretched from Yggdrasil's mighty trunk, and a single tear ran down Hundr's cheek.

The sky grew black, and the stars shone bright, but the land was as dark as the day it was first born as the new moon hid the world in a cloak of stygian gloom. Hundr stripped off his woollen clothing and tossed it inside his tent. He unfurled his brynjar coat of chainmail and slid its leather lining over his head. Ragnhild pulled the hem to help the armour slide down over Hundr's shoulders, and he shook himself until the mail was snug to his body like the scaly skin of a dragon. He helped Ragnhild do the same, and she strung her eastern recurved bow, hung a quiver of arrows in a leather bag from her belt, and cast the spare sheaves across her shoulders. Hundr buckled on his belt along with the Ulfberht sword and strapped Battle Fang to his back. His seax hung in a sheath at the rear of his belt. Thorgrim hefted his double-bladed war axe, and Sigvarth raised his hands and prayed to Odin for battle luck. Amundr gathered Jogrimmr and Agnarr to him, and they clashed foreheads together, swearing to fight and die for each other. They were thirty warriors with black-painted shields and raven feathers in the crests of their shining helmets, and they had come to kill.

Bavlos laughed, capering at the chaos of it all, and he said he would follow them to the town later on, hidden from sight by his gods, so Hundr left him there and led his warband down the pine forest's slope towards Vanylven. They marched with shields slung across their backs and brightly honed weapons in their fists. The men were warriors all, blooded in battle and ready to kill. Hundr moved through the trees, and Bavlos' gods had indeed blessed them, for they came upon none of Rollo's scouts until the pines flattened and the hillside slope became the flatland which led down towards Vanylven's landward palisade. Shields clanked against knife handles, and boots crunched in the snow. Hundr wanted to tell his warriors to be quiet and move with stealth, yet they marched as softly as they could for a heavily armed troop of Vikings.

Ragnhild held up a fist as they came about a knot of close pine trees, and she stalked ahead of the warband with an arrow laid across the string of her bow. Hundr crouched and heard a man whistling. It was the first of Rollo's scouts, and Ragnhild disappeared into the darkness. Moments later, the whistling turned into a stifled gurgle as the man died from Ragnhild's deadly arrow. She appeared and waved them on. Hundr followed, and ten paces later, she called a halt again, and another man died. The Raven Band passed his corpse, which lay surrounded by snow. He'd taken Ragnhild's arrow to his eye, and the blood had spattered into the icy whiteness. Hundr and his men stepped over the lifeless body to continue forward. They followed the curve of the forest's edge, keeping it on their left as they moved eastwards around the town, hidden by the forest and the new moon's darkness.

Voices cut through the night, drifting on the cold and through the forest, and Ragnhild waited, kneeling behind a tree and pointing east towards where an orange glow punched through the white and the dark. It flickered and danced, out of place in the harshness of winter and night, and voices laughed and talked there. The warband crept forward, and through the trees, the orange glow showed itself to be an iron brazier around which five men were gathered. The warriors stood swathed in furs, hopping from one foot to the other in the cold, blowing into their hands and warming them on the fire. Two of them wore woollen mittens, but the other three carried bows and so suffered the bite of the cold, for it was their duty to guard any approach from the woods. Only they had failed in that duty because Hundr was there, and beyond their brazier, the palisade joined the edge of the fjord, and all he had to do was get past those men, follow the water's edge, and he would reach the pier which cut westwards into the fjord.

"Should we go around them?" asked Amundr, whispering close to Hundr's ear.

"There is no way around," Hundr replied. "If we go deeper into the forest, we have to come back to follow the shoreline, and they will see us. It's time to fight, but kill the bastards quickly and quietly."

Amundr smiled, his teeth shining white in the night. Hundr motioned for the warriors to spread out in a half circle around the scouts and their brazier, and they moved slowly, boots crunching in the snow as they edged closer to the enemy.

The guards spoke words Hundr could not understand, and the Franks stared into the forest. Thorgrim stepped on a rotten branch hidden beneath the snow, and in the dark of night, the sound of it snapping was like an entire tree falling. The scouts glanced at each other. One took two paces towards the forest and then gasped as an arrow of Ragnhild's punched through his thick fur cloak into his chest.

The remaining four scouts sprang into action. Two men without gloves reached for their bows, and the other two fumbled with their woollen mittens to shake them off so that they could grab their weapons. Ragnhild loosed another arrow, and a gloved man grunted as the shaft thumped into his face. Hundr ran at them and ripped the Ulfberht sword free of its scabbard. The blade was light, and the grip was soft in his palm. One guard reached for his bow and quickly nocked a shaft to the string, so Hundr changed direction and pivoted around a tree trunk. The arrow slammed into the tree, and Hundr manoeuvered to the other side, but Sigvarth moved quicker and threw his axe so that the blade turned head over haft through the air before it crashed into the archer's chest with a wet thud.

Hundr burst from the trees, sweeping his sword over hand, and split the next scout from neck to groin. He toppled, and the red wound gaped as the scout fell and died in the snow. Another of Ragnhild's arrows took the last man's life, and the warband went on, free to march towards the fjord bridge. The fjord water lapped at the shore, the sound rhythmically washing over the shale. Hundr led them on, hoping that somewhere out there, Einar had come with a fleet of ships to bring seven hundred Vikings to take Vanylven.

Hundr's boots crunched into the shore beneath him, and he could make out the pier stretching from the east coast into the water. It had been so easy. There couldn't be more than ten men on the fjord bridge to look out into the night water, and victory seemed so close that he could reach out and touch it. But then a voice called out from the palisade, and another joined it. Then, more voices shouted, and there was a loud iron clanging from deep within Vanylven. A wall guard had noticed the dead scouts in the brazier's glow, and what all had seemed so easy became red war and slaughter.

TWENTY-FOUR

Hundr turned to the palisade, which reared up like a solid black mass in contrast to the shining surface of the fjord. Torches bobbed up and down upon its summit as guards raced along the fighting platform, shouting and searching for their enemies. They saw dead men in the glow of a brazier between the walls and the forest and knew they were under attack. Bearded faces appeared over the parapet, followed by more shouting. A Frank cast a spear from the palisade, arcing through the air and splashing in the fjord three paces from Hundr's feet.

"Go quickly," he said. The Raven Band marched double time, falling short of running because the weight of their weapons and mail made doing so difficult. The warriors grabbed the shields from their backs and filled their hands with axes or swords, and Ragnhild loosed three arrows at the walls to keep the guards at bay.

"They are going to charge us from the town," said Ragnhild. "I'll hold them here."

There was a gate in the wall facing out towards the forest. From that gate, a path cut through the trees and wound its way south where merchants, farmers, and other folk who visited Vanylven from the landward side could access the town. Hundr thought Rollo would send warriors from that gate to pursue the men who had killed his guards. Ragnhild could hold them there with her bow, but she would be quickly overwhelmed.

"No, we keep going together," said Hundr, and the thirty warriors of his warband hurried along the water's edge towards the pier. Behind them, Vanylven awoke like a kicked wasp's nest. What had been a quiet night for the men inside the settlement now erupted into a maelstrom of shouted orders. Wood and iron banged and clanged, and the wall gate screeched open as the Franks surged to meet the threat. Hundr hurried at the head of his warriors, and the pier came into view ahead of them, stretching out into the glassy water like the Bifrost Bridge, which connects Midgard to Asgard. Shapes moved on the bridge, a torch came from the tower at the end of the pier, and suddenly Hundr had enemies behind and in front. A figure came from the forest, lumbering from the gloom like a jotun, and Ragnhild loosed an arrow to send the man sprawling. Hundr's heart pounded in his chest, and his breath came ragged from dashing along the water's edge in his heavy brynjar. The shouting from behind drew closer, and boots thundered from Vanylven towards the fjord bridge.

As they came within twenty paces of the bridge, four men stood before its timber steps, men with shields and spears who had made a small shield wall to protect the pier against attack.

"We have to break them, fast," said Hundr, and he glanced over his shoulder. A mass of warriors ran along the shore. They had come quickly, and some held flaming torches, illuminating their short hair and desperate faces. Most came without breastplates and clutched only a spear or a knife as they raced to stop Hundr from reaching the fjord bridge. A spark of fear struck in Hundr's belly, for if he did not get onto the narrow bridge quickly, his warband would be trapped between two enemies. They would die on the shore and leave Einar and the fleet stranded in the water. So, it was a race for survival between Hundr's warriors, who had to lower the fjord rope, and the Franks, who feared that if the rope came down, a fleet of murderous Vikings would descend upon them like a nightmare.

Amundr bellowed a war cry, and before Hundr had the chance to turn back towards the pier, the giant was already running at full pelt towards the small shield wall on the pier's steps. He ran with his axe and shield as though they weighed no more than a sack of feathers, and Hundr followed. Ragnhild loosed arrow after arrow into the warriors who came from the town. Agnarr and Jogrimmr stood with her, feet planted and ready to meet the enemy. One of the four Franks in the shield wall threw a spear, and Amundr darted to one side as it flew over his shoulder. He crashed into their shields in four long strides with all the force of a charging bull. Enemy shields cracked and scattered, and Amundr rolled on the ground, falling from the monstrous impact. Hundr flew into the gap and sliced his sword across the throat of a stunned Frank, and in a rapid turn, he gouged open the belly of a second enemy before Thorgrim hit another Frank so hard that his double-bladed war axe embedded itself into the man's torso like a damp log. He wrenched it free, and the final Frank attempted to flee, but as he turned, he ran into Amundr. The big man punched the edge of his shield into the Frank's face with a sickening crunch, and suddenly, the entrance to the bridge was free.

Hundr leapt up the steps and slid Battle Fang back into her sheath at his back. He slipped the Ulfberht sword into her scabbard and drew his seax. The pier was narrow, wide enough for only two men to walk abreast, so there was no room for swordplay. Any fighting on the bridge would be up close and nasty, with no room to dance or swing a blade, only brutal stabbing and bloody combat. At least a dozen Franks were running towards him from the tower, and Amundr, Thorgrim and Sivgarth went to meet them. Ragnhild came up the steps to the pier and turned to loose another arrow at the approaching horde. The Raven Band followed her, their boots thudding on the timber laths from which the pier was constructed. Agnarr and Jogrimmr took up the rear, and the two men turned as they came up the steps.

"We'll hold them here, my lord," said Agnarr.

Hundr wanted to tell them to come, to follow him across the bridge, but he knew Agnarr had the right of it. There would be no time to kill the men who came from the towers and cut the rope before the enemy approaching from the town swarmed them from behind. The rope spanning the gap between the two towers was incredibly thick and comprised a series of hemp ropes twisted and coiled together to make one great rope, strong enough to fetter Fenris Wolf until the end of days. To cut it or release it would take time.

"Let these Frankish whores come and fight with a Viking. I will stand and die here, Lord Hundr," added Jogrimmr, with iron will in his voice and pride on his face.

"When I drink ale tonight in Valhalla, I shall boast that I fought alongside the Man with the Dog's Name and the heroes there will be envious of my deeds."

Hundr nodded. He wanted to tell the two warriors how brave they were and thank them for their sacrifice, but there was no time, so instead, he raised his fist to his chest in salute and then turned to run along the fjord bridge. Behind him, Agnarr and Jogrimmr sang a rowing song together, a war song for brave men, and they hefted their shields, holding firm against the onrushing enemy. Weapons clashed there, men screamed, and Ragnhild let two more arrows fly into the mass of enemies on the shore before she came running behind Hundr.

Ahead on the pier, Thorgrim and Sigvarth had already engaged the Franks who came from the tower at the end of the bridge. Hundr reached that struggle, but he was at the back of his warriors, and though he could hear the fighting, he could not get through the press of his men to make a difference. Agnarr and Jogrimmr held the enemy who came from the landward side, but they could not do so for long against such overwhelming odds. Hundr's sense of urgency boiled over, and he cursed. Placing one hand on Ragnhild's shoulder and another on the back of the warrior in front of him, he clambered up onto the handrail spanning the length of the pier and ran along it. The fjord stretched away below him, and to fall into that icy water in his brynjar would mean certain death. Nevertheless, he had to remove the fjord rope, so determinedly, he ran across the thin, treacherous handrail. The flashing blades came closer, faces peered up at him in surprise, and Hundr ran with his seax in his hand and desperation in his heart.

Thorgrim's twin axe blades flashed in the starlight, and Hundr was close to the combat, but as he put his right foot down on the rail, it slipped, causing his leg to shoot out from under him. Hundr gasped and instinctively used his left foot to launch himself forward. He flew off balance and crashed through Sigvarth and Thorgrim to cannon into the Franks standing between the Raven Band and the bridge tower. Men grunted and cried out, and Hundr landed awkwardly with his legs splayed, and his seax fell from his grip. A boot kicked him in the ribs, while another connected with the side of his head, a hand pressed down on the back of his neck, and he could smell the garlic stench of an enemy's breath as he spat a curse. There was a thud and the slap of metal in meat above him, and hot liquid spilt over Hundr's face, filling his mouth with the ferrous taste of blood. He surged upwards, refusing to die, and his hand found the antler hilt of his seax. He drove the wicked point into a man's thigh and ripped it upwards, tearing flesh and savagely scraping on bone.

The Franks fell back, and as Hundr rose into the space, only three of them remained. He burst past their frightened faces as Amundr grabbed one of the short-haired enemies by his breastplate and threw him from the bridge with a loud splash. Hundr left his warband to deal with the remaining Franks, and he waved Amundr on to join him as he raced towards the tower and the bridge rope. Hundr rushed into the tower, and in his haste, he accidentally kicked over a small table laden with bread and cheese. He quickly located the wheel used to wind the fjord rope and attempted to turn it by hauling on a handle that stuck out from its edge, but the thing barely moved.

"Help me!" he called, and Amundr joined him. With the giant also heaving on the rope, it shifted, but then the wheel groaned and stopped dead. Thorgrim joined them, and they heaved again. The wheel creaked, stiff with salt water and cold, but it turned, and the great rope finally gave way. Its thick coils lowered as Hundr, Amundr, and Thorgrim hauled on the wheel.

"They are coming, hurry!" shouted Ragnhild from above. She had climbed the tower to loose more arrows into the enemy who had overcome Agnarr and Jogrimmr and advanced up the bridge in a surge of desperation. Those men knew that if Hundr and his warriors succeeded, more enemies would come from the fjord and wild sea beyond, so they charged up the pier to fight for their lives. The Franks crashed into the Raven Band, and that crunch of iron, wood, flesh and steel was sickening. Men died and shouted in terror, the darkness enveloped by the sound of war. Hundr heaved again, and the rope plopped into the water.

"Keep turning it until it's as low as it can go," Hundr ordered. If they left the rope resting too close to the waterline, it would crush the hull of any approaching ship, so it had to be lowered deep below the surface. "Then smash the wheel."

Hundr climbed up the ladder to join Ragnhild as she drew her bow. It thrummed against the power of its horn and sapwood construction to send an arrow hurtling towards the enemy.

"It's done," he said. Ragnhild dropped to her knees and fished inside her pack. She pulled out a handful of dry tinder, scraps of brittle wood, leaves, and a large ball of fluff which had come away from the woollen clothing Bavlos had made. Hundr took a flint from the pouch at his belt, grabbed his seax, wiped the blood from the blade on his trews, and then scraped the blade down the flint until sparks flew. He repeated that three times until the kindling caught fire. Ragnhild took an arrow from her quiver, which she had already wrapped with a rag soaked in caulking pitch from Stryn. The arrow ignited, and she aimed high, pulled the bowstring back to her cheek and loosed the missile high into the sky.

The fire crackled and rose into the darkness, and there was a collective gasp from the men who fought on the pier. A great roar went up from the black night beyond the fjord, the bloodcurdling sound of seven hundred Vikings as they saw the signal and knew it was time to bring their warships and savagery to Vanylven. The Franks on the fjord bridge pier paused, faces staring out into the darkness. Half of Hundr's warband had died defending the tower, and for ten heartbeats, the only sound was the chop of Amundr and Thorgrim's axes hammering into the rope wheel.

From out in the new moon's blackness, a drum boomed deep and loud, slowly echoing around the fjord and mountains beyond, and then the pace quickened. Each time the war drum boomed, the Vikings out in the void let out a clipped roar, all seven hundred warriors shouting simultaneously with the drums. Then, from the dark came the first snarling dragon head rearing up from the water, oars splashing vigorously and surging the ship towards the gap between the two fjord bridge piers. Another beast-headed prow appeared, and then more. Ravn's broad frame stood in the first ship's prow. He barked an order, prompting his men to cast a volley of spears and arrows at the Franks on the bridge, who cried out in agony as the projectiles struck their mark. Ravn held his axe up as he spotted Hundr on the tower, and Hundr gritted his teeth because the fjord rope was down and the way into Vanylven's harbour was open.

"Board the ships!" Hundr ordered. The Franks on the pier, who had been so determined to kill the Raven Band, fled from the carnage as yet more arrows slammed into their ranks, the iron tips tearing and ripping at their flesh.

"War!" bellowed a familiar voice, and the Sea Falcon came from the darkness like one of the Loki brood on the day of Ragnarök. Einar stood at the prow, his broad, hard face stern and staring at the gap. "War!" Einar yelled again. The crew shouted their defiance along with him. The Raven Band made the small jump from the bridge to the decks of the warships as they glided through the gap, and Hundr waved to Rognvald as his warships sailed through, but the Jarl of Rogaland did not see him. Rognvald was stripped to the waist and deep in his ulfheðnar trance, along with his other wolf warriors, who gnashed and capered about the deck in hungry anticipation of blood and violence.

"Let's go," Ragnhild said as she clambered down the tower ladder. Hundr followed her, and as the Falcon came through the gap, she made the leap onto the ship's deck. Hundr quickly glanced behind, ensuring that he was the last of the Raven Band to leave the pier. All that remained on the bridge were corpses and the smashed rope wheel. With resolve, Hundr jumped, landing with a thud in the Falcon's bilge. As he rose, the crew stared with wide eyes at his blood-soaked face, and Hundr raised his seax to the sky.

"Death to the Betrayer!" he shouted, and the crew took up the call.

Einar loomed giant and malevolent in the prow, and as the harbour came into view, he leaned over to let his axe blade drag in the water. Warships and Viking fury had finally come for Rollo and his Franks, and they came from the darkness like monsters on the wing. The enemy was thick on the harbour jetty with spears and shields, but there was terror in their eyes as the wrath of hundreds of Vikings bore down upon them, thirsty for vengeance and blood.

TWENTY-FIVE

Einar sucked in a gulp of salty air as he leant over the *drakkar's* prow with one hand hooked around the curved timber carved into the shape of a falcon's neck. The joins of his fish scale brynjar stretched and shifted on the supple leather lining, and the armour shone like the stars. Hildr had scrubbed the brynjar with sand, which meant that Einar sailed to battle like a resplendent lord of war. He relished dragging his axe blade in the night-black water, just as he used to do when raiding in the Seaworm. Those were the old days, before he was a jarl – when he was simply Einar the Brawler. Einar's heart soared as the bearded axe blade sliced into the fjord and sprayed his face and beard with icy water.

"War!" he shouted at the top of his lungs, delighting in the crew's enthusiastic echo of the chant. He hauled himself up and turned, looking for Bush at the steerboard to share his excitement at the fight to come. But, of course, Asbjorn was there instead, and Einar felt a moment of sadness for his dead friend. The Falcon sliced through the fjord like a knife, and Asbjorn leant on the tiller as she came through the gap in the bridge and into the harbour, so the *drakkar* banked away to make room for the next ship to enter. Hundr joined Einar at the prow, his scar-ravaged face already sheeted in blood. Ragnhild was there, too, as were Thorgrim, Amundr, and Sigvarth.

"You did it then?" Einar beamed.

"The rope is down," Hundr replied.

"A hard fight?"

"A stroll in the night."

Einar laughed and clapped his friend on the shoulder. The oars bit into the fjord, and the ship sped towards the shore. Ravn and Rognvald were ahead, and five more warships were coming behind. "We must succeed this time. Rollo cannot live."

"We approach too quickly. There are ships in the harbour," said Hundr, pointing his seax towards the shore. The jetty was lined with a horde of Franks, and the harbour was filled with ships. The Seaworm was there somewhere, as were Hundr's other captured ships, obscured amidst the vessels Rollo had brought north from his home in Frankia.

"We go in full force, no quarter," Einar growled, and he meant it. He didn't care that there was no space to bring the Falcon alongside the jetty. His warriors had to get from the deck to the harbour, and Einar did not intend to glide softly in under a hail of arrows and spear points. "Pick up the pace. Three more pulls." The crew followed his orders, and the warship moved faster. The Falcon prow aimed straight for the closest jetty where Franks were as thick as flies on shit. Einar drove them towards where the fighting would be heaviest, where the most dangerous men could fight, kill, and burnish their reputations bright with the blood of their enemies. A ship's length to the east, Rognvald's *drakkar* was almost at the harbour, and to the west, Ravn's warriors roared and cheered as their warship flew towards the jetty. The Franks launched a barrage of spears and arrows at Ravn's deck, and from the Falcon's steerboard, Asbjorn counted down the oar pulls.

"Three!" Asbjorn shouted, and the crew grunted from the effort of propelling the ship with all their might. "Two!" The oar blades cut through the water to give the vessel even more momentum. "One! Raise oars!" The oars bit and then rose, and the crew scrambled to safely stow the oar blades in their crutches. To throw them or leave them loose on deck was to create confusion and obstacles at their feet when they were about to fight for their lives.

"Shields!" Einar shouted. The crew immediately responded in unison, and seventy shields scraped and banged as the warriors moved their strong, calloused hands from their oar shafts to grab the handles of the linden wood iron-shod shields.

Hundr realised what Einar intended and braced himself in the prow's curve, and Einar hoped Bush would not be angry with him in Valhalla because he was about to ruin a good ship. Einar laughed, and Hundr looked at him strangely, but everything was now so simple with the smooth wooden prow beneath his hand as the snarling carved beast's head stormed towards the enemy. All the suffering Einar and his people had endured since the day Rollo brought his venom to Vanylven, all the pain and death brought down upon Hundr, all of Einar's friends and comrades who had died, the starving and cold of the forest, the shame of defeat, the humiliation in Ugattr's hall, it all now came down to this moment. It all boiled down to something Einar was as familiar with as the haft of his axe or the curve of Hildr's neck. Violence. Hildr and her Valkyrie sister Ragnhild loosed arrows at the enemy from the deck, bows thrumming and arrows whistling, and Einar could see the eyes of his enemies, their short hair and clipped beards and the shine of their spear points.

"Brace yourselves!" Einar called and sank down to join Hundr in the prow's curve. The Falcon slammed into a Frankish ship, its momentum and weight driving the enemy vessel away from the harbour. The prowsmashed into the jetty with a deafening crunch, the shattering of timber and the screams of the enemy. Einar held on tight, and the impact threw his warriors from the rowing benches or toppled them from where they clung onto the mast or rigging ropes. The Falcon reared up on the jetty as it tore through the planking. Splinters flew, and Franks cried out in pain and terror. Einar grabbed the halyard rope and hauled himself to standing. Desperate Frankish eyes peered up at his broad, rugged face. One wailed like an infant as the

361

prow had crushed his spine upon impact; more flailed in the water, and the rest edged back from the vast ship, as large as a building and terrifyingly powerful. Einar had driven the Falcon right up onto the jetty, and Ragnhild and Hildr loosed their deadly shafts into the enemy. The Franks in the front tried to push at the men behind them to flee, and the Franks in the rear shoved them back towards the towering Viking *drakkar*.

Further along the harbour, Ravn and Rognvald had brought their ships to bear, and axe-wielding warriors poured from the bows so that the crunch, crash, and screaming sound of war echoed around the mountains.

"For those we have lost…and for Vanylven," Einar said, and he clasped forearms with Hundr. The two friends stepped onto the Falcon's prow strake and leapt over the side. The Franks had been ready to meet an attack with sharp spears, arrows and shields, but in the carnage of the Falcon's crash into the jetty, they had lost all formation and discipline. Einar and Hundr flew from the warship, screaming their war cries and brandishing axes and swords. Einar landed on top of a fat man, who screamed as Einar drove him down onto the planks. He scrambled like a landed fish, eyes closed and teeth clenched hard. Einar headbutted him savagely twice. The gristle of the Frank's nose burst, and as Einar stood up, he stamped on the Frank's throat with his boot.

"Come and fight with Einar," he snarled, then launched himself at his enemies, swinging his bearded axe with vengeful fury. Hundr fought at Einar's side, his new sword bright and dazzling as it carved into the enemy and drove them backwards. A spear point came at Einar, and he caught the shaft with his left hand, dragging the attacker towards him. The men yelped, and Einar chopped his axe into the side of the spearman's head before kicking him into the water. An enormous enemy charged with glaring eyes and a sword in his hand, and an arrow sang from the Falcon's deck to pierce the big man's eye. He dropped to the jetty, and the Franks edged away from the fury of the Northmen. Amundr, Sigvarth, and Thorgrim made the jump, and Thorgrim whooped for joy as he drove an enemy to his knees with a vicious sweep of his double-bladed war axe. Amundr barged his way past Einar and charged into the Franks. The giant went unarmed and simply used his size and unnatural strength to punch, shove, and kick the Franks from the jetty into the water, where their breastplates would drag them down to drown in the shallows.

Einar followed the giant, and more of the Viking fleet reached the harbour. A terrible howl cut through the clang of iron and the shouts of the fighting men, sending a shiver down Einar's neck. It was Rognvald with his band of ulfheðnar, unleashed amongst the Franks, and though he couldn't see them, Einar knew they would wreak terror amongst the enemy. The Franks fell back, running towards the streets and lanes of Vanylven, and Einar charged after them. The battle for the harbour was over, and Einar had won, but now the real fighting would begin. There would

363

be no shield wall or pitched battle in the fight for the town. It would be small-scale, savage encounters in front of butcher shops or beside forge bellows. Men would hide and die in houses or find themselves cornered in alleys. Einar had fought in towns and cities before, and there was no room for generals or battle strategy. It was just savagery and brutal hacking and slashing between people's homes, and Einar was ready for it.

The Vikings charged after the Franks, and the enemy had no time to close the gate which led from the town down into the harbour. Ravn and his warriors were already through that gate, and Einar followed the big jarl through the gateway. Thorgrim and Sigvarth were with Einar, as was Asbjorn, but as he passed beneath the open gate, Einar lost sight of Hundr, Hildr, and Amundr in the press of warriors. The Vikings burst into the town. Men hurtled into the snarl of streets, dark beneath the new moon and thick with winter mud between houses topped with damp, grey thatch. Einar followed the backs of Ravn's men along a street of single-storey wattle houses, and then he turned left into a narrow alley that ran between those buildings and the fishermen's warehouses. Einar's boots splashed through the mud, which was snow turned to slush and mixed with the earthen streets to form a boot-high slopping mess underfoot. He ducked under a low beam sticking out from the warehouse and emerged into the square where the fishermen would sell their catch early in the morning. A brazier of burning logs lit that square, casting the surrounding buildings in shifting shadows, and a dog ran into the darkness with a fearful whine.

Einar paused, his heart leaping because, across that square, a group of bare-chested Vikings fought with a few of Ravn's men. They were berserkers, Rollo's Norse berserkers, armourless, fighting with strange, wild eyes and reckless abandon. More of them flooded into the square, and the handful of Ravn's men died beneath their axe blades. A broad-chested man with a huge head and thick shoulders like boulders fought at the centre of the wild men. He wore a bearskin over his head, draping down his back, and the bear's teeth crowned his head to give the warrior a feral air. Blood spattered his face and torso, and Einar recognised Kveldulf the berserker, the bear warrior who had killed Ulf and had wrought so much terror amongst Einar's people in their forest camp.

"I hate berserkers," Einar said, and he strode into the square. The berserkers growled and hopped around like madmen as they noticed Einar, Thorgrim and Sigvarth across the open space. "You," Einar pointed his axe at Kveldulf. "Come and die." Einar reached behind him and whipped his seax free of his sheath so that he went to fight with that wickedly short blade in his left hand and his axe in his right. He was old, and his best years were behind him, but he was still Einar Rosti, unafraid and raring to fight the bear-man.

Kveldulf grinned, his tombstone teeth flat and grim in his wide mouth. He waved his berserkers back, and they frothed and romped at the edges of the square as Kveldulf came on. He wielded an axe and charged at Einar, suddenly and rapidly sprinting across the square in his battle madness. Einar went to meet him, and just as they were about to collide in furious battle, Kveldulf's boot skidded in the mud, and his leg slewed sideways so that he fell to one knee. Einar surged forward and smashed his knee into the berserker's face. He pivoted at the waist to bring his axe around in a backhand and was sure that he would cut the bastard's head from his shoulders, but Kveldulf had recovered and blocked Einar's axe with the haft of his own weapon.

Kveldulf growled like the beast he wore upon his head and drove Einar backwards. His strength was astonishing, and as Einar pushed back against his enemy's weapon, the two men came close. The rancid stench of Kveldulf's breath was inescapable, tinged with decay and the powdery stink of whatever foul mind-altering brew he drank to turn into the bear. Einar brought his seax around and sliced the edge across Kveldulf's ribs, and he twisted away in pain. The other berserkers barked and cried in sympathy for their wounded leader, but Kveldulf came on again as though the cut was nothing. He hacked and stabbed at Einar with his axe, and Einar fell back under the crazed onslaught. He ducked under a wild swing, yet Kveldulf raked his face with the nails of his left hand. The scratches burned, and Einar's breath laboured as he tried desperately to keep the berserker at bay. Kveldulf did not let up his furious attack, and Einar's shoulders tired as he parried the relentless assault. An axe swing slipped between Einar's weapons and scraped the length of Einar's brynjar before Kveldulf punched Einar full in the face. Einar staggered, and in that moment, Kveldulf swung again, connecting with Einar's axe close to where his hand gripped the haft and forcefully ripped the weapon from him.

Kveldulf roared in triumph, and his berserkers joined in raucously. Einar felt the lurching twist of fear in his stomach. Death was close. If Kveldulf kept on coming, then his strength, youth, and madness would drive Einar down until the berserker hacked him to pieces. But Einar refused to die. He had suffered too much, and his hunger for vengeance burned brighter than Kveldulf's madness, so Einar threw himself at his enemy and drove him to the ground. They rolled in the mud, beating and scratching at each other in the filth and the darkness. Einar stabbed furiously with the point of his seax, puncturing Kveldulf's legs and stomach with dozens of short, quick punches of the broken-backed blade. Kveldulf grabbed Einar's hair and tried to force him away, but Einar reached up with his free hand, hooked his finger into Kveldulf's mouth, and ripped it savagely like a fishhook.

Kveldulf bucked and twisted to get away from Einar's ferocity; his ruined cheek flapped open, and his naked stomach and chest ran slick with dark blood. His teeth gnashed, and he squealed and yelped at the pain, his altered mind unable to call upon the pride of a *drengr* to keep him from mewing in terror. Einar stabbed him again in the belly, but this time, he pushed the blade deeper, and Kveldulf let go of Einar's hair to punch him on the side of the head. Einar crashed a headbutt into Kveldulf's face and mashed his head back into the mud, driving his forehead into the berserker's eye socket until the bones crunched and crushed beneath his skull. He roared in Kveldulf's face, and the berserker flailed in the mud, twisting in Einar's grip like a pig in shit, his body awash with blood and filth. The bear's head and fur had slipped from Kveldulf, and as he turned, Einar grabbed him around the skull and yanked him backwards, exposing his muscular neck. Then, in a single, swift motion, Einar seized his chance and cut Kveldulf's throat with one brutal sweep of his seax.

Blood spurted violently, and a foul gust of air whistled from the berserker's open throat. Einar let the dying man flop to the earth before rising to bellow his triumph to the sky. He called upon Odin, Bush, Sigrid, Ulf, Trygve, Torsten, and the rest to witness his deeds.

"Einar, look!" came a voice behind him, its urgency snapping him from his reverie. Thorgrim gestured across the square where one of Kveldulf's berserkers was charging towards Einar, yet Einar had only his seax in hand. The crazed man sprinted with wild abandon, and Einar turned to Thorgrim, who tossed his double-bladed war axe so that the weapon flew high. The berserker drew close, roaring and screaming in his madness, and Einar dropped his seax to catch Thorgrim's axe just in time. In one fluid motion, he caught the haft and swung the mighty weapon, driving its blade deep into the berserker's chest to send him crashing on top of his dead captain's corpse. The rest of Kveldulf's berserkers charged then, and Einar, Thorgrim and Sigvarth were alone in the square. Twenty bare-chested enemies were coming for blood, and Einar thought he would surely die. Yet, suddenly, an ethereal howl split the air.

Rognvald came running from an alley with his wild ulfheðnar close behind him. They crashed into Kveldulf's berserkers, and it was a mad welter of bear against wolf as two forces driven to savage fury by the gods and their mind-altering potions ripped and tore at each other. Rognvald, usually so calm and refined, chopped a berserker's head clean from his shoulders and danced in the dead man's blood.

"Time to go," said Einar. He rolled his aching shoulders, bending to pick up his axe and seax. "Rollo must die."

TWENTY-SIX

Hundr ran through the tangle of Vanylven's laneways with his Ulfberht sword in his hand and vengeance in his heart. It was chaos in the darkness, where the only light came from open window shutters or braziers full of burning logs outside a tavern or where Rollo's men had gathered to patrol the walls. He came across Ravn and his warriors battling in a wide street opposite a blacksmith's forge, and the jarl fought at the front of his men like a *drengr* of legend. Hundr veered away from that fight. He hunted bigger prey. Amundr lumbered behind him as they made their way towards the Vanylven centre, where Einar's hall stood proudly in a vast square courtyard and where Hundr hoped to find Rollo.

The shock of the Viking fleet landing with such ferocity had all but broken Rollo's warriors, forcing them into a wild battle inside the settlement. Despite the Franks being driven back into the streets, there were still hundreds of enemy soldiers within Vanylven's walls, ready to defend their lives. Hundr did not know how the battle fared as he dashed through the streets. In one lane, Vikings slaughtered a group of Franks, but in another street, fifty Franks advanced in organised fashion with shields and spears upon a dozen of Rognvald's fighters, and that fight could only end with a small Frankish victory. But Hundr could not stop to help or worry about how the battle swayed. The warp and weft of the conflict were already in the hands of the Norns, and Hundr trusted his warriors and those of his allies to overcome Rollo's men. He had a personal battle to fight with Rollo the Betrayer, and his desire for that battle was an overwhelming burning fire inside him. It churned and boiled like molten iron, and Hundr ran through the ebb and flow of the fight for Vanylven with a solitary focus. Vengeance.

A ruddy-faced Frank burst from a rickety doorway, but Hundr shouldered him out of the way, and the man cried out behind him as Amundr hit him with his axe.

"Not that way," Amundr panted, and Hundr paused. The big man shook his head and leant forward with his hands on his knees, sweat dripping down his face. A group of spear-armed Franks jogged across the lane Hundr had been about to join, and they headed west, away from Vanylven's main square. "They aren't going to the square," Amundr said with a shrug when Hundr raised his eyebrow to question how Amundr knew the Franks would come that way. "They are coming from it."

Rollo was a cunning bastard and not a man to just sit back and let defeat wash over him. He would fight until his last breath, and as another company of Franks crossed the street, it hit Hundr like a hammer.

"We are driving his men towards the town centre," Hundr exclaimed, "and Rollo is sending his men to the edges of the settlement, where he will attack our flanks and rear. He still has the numbers to win the fight and would pin us in the main square just as we planned to do to him."

"So what do we do?"

"Kill Rollo. Cut the head off his army, and the rest will surrender."

"But what if they don't?"

Hundr clapped the big man on the shoulder and stared deep into his eyes.

"You saved my sons' lives when Rollo attacked Vanylven. I can never thank you enough for that. Trust me now, fight with me. I can feel in my soul that we will win this fight. Are you with me?"

Amundr smiled, and his eyes flickered over Hundr's scarred face and ravaged eye.

"To the death, my lord," he nodded. The battle raged across Vanylven; screams and war cries rose above the buildings to meld with the ring of steel upon steel and the crash of shields, but a moment passed between Hundr and Amundr that conveyed their deep bond of friendship, trust, and comradeship. Hundr knew he could trust the giant implicitly, and he would gladly die defending Amundr's back.

Hundr set off again and turned left into a lane of two-storey, narrow houses built of wattle, painted with bright doorframes and window shutters. He stopped in his tracks because a force of twenty Franks came charging towards him with shields raised and spears levelled. There were too many to fight, so Amundr kicked a door in and smashed it from its hinges as he drove his shoulder through it. Hundr followed him, and they darted around a low table and stools. The Franks chased them through the doorway, shouting and cursing in their own language. Rollo's warriors had commandeered the house, like most of those in the town, and it was a mess of broken ale jugs and stale, rotting floor rushes.

"There's no way out," said Amundr in alarm as he reached the rear wall. But then he tested the wattle filling between the houses' wooden wall posts and set his jaw. "Hold them off as long as you can." Amundr hefted his axe and hacked into the wall, dislodging great clumps of dry wattle with every strike. Hundr turned and slashed the point of his sword across the eyes of a Frank who lunged at him, and the man staggered away screaming. The next assailant ran onto the sword's tip, and Hundr had to rip it free of the man's guts before the blade became tangled in his innards. The small room was dark and dingy, and the nauseating stink of blood and voided bowls filled the enclosed space. The Franks huddled at the door, wanting to attack but wary of their wounded comrades who writhed and screamed in pain. They looked from Hundr's blood-soaked sword to his terrifyingly scarred face with the ruin of his dead eye and chose not to attack.

"I'm through," Amundr shouted, and the house groaned and creaked as he shoved his mighty frame through the gap he had cut with his axe. Hundr followed, and as he burst through the wall, he found himself surrounded by the enemy in Vanylven's main square.

The square was lined with Franks. On one side, Ravn fought with his warriors in a brutal battle against three ranks of organised Franks, while on the other, Harbard and Asbjorn's crews fought desperately to force the enemy back. But Hundr estimated that only half of Rollo's warriors were in the square. He stood from the ruins of the building's wall, and Amundr quickly filled the hole with debris. A great groan went up from the Vikings beyond the town. Hundr assumed that Rollo's men had completed their circuit of the walls and now attacked the Vikings' rear, pinning them between the courtyard and the harbour.

"There he is," said Amundr, and Hundr stared above the press of warriors to see Rollo standing on the steps to Einar's hall. He wore a knee-length brynjar and held an enormous sword with its point resting on the ground, his hands on the crossguard. Five burly Franks, big men with white crosses painted on their black leather breastplates, formed Rollo's personal guard, who stood before him. A feral, sinister smile adorned the Betrayer's face as he watched his cunning plan unfold. They had scattered flaming torches around the courtyard to provide a dim, eerie light in the darkness. Hundr found himself on one side of the square without an entrance because its long wall was the rear of a row of houses. The Franks bunched where the streets met the square courtyard, so he was free to charge at Rollo, but if he did, countless foes would cut him down, so Hundr paused, caught in a precarious position and unable to sway the battle in his favour. The square was swarming with hundreds of Franks, preventing the Vikings from battling through, yet more came from the rear, and Hundr could only imagine the viciously intense fighting in the streets.

A clay pot exploded ten paces from where Hundr and Amundr stood and then another across the square. Hundr looked upwards and saw barely discernable figures moving on the rooftops in the darkness. More pots smashed, and black pine caulking tar, which smelled bitter and acrid, oozed from the broken shards. The pots came down like rain, smashing amongst the Franks, who peered up into the dark night to see who pelted them. A flash of light on the thatch of Einar's hall caught Hundr's attention, quickly followed by another. At that moment, an undulating high-pitched scream erupted, and its familiarity was like summer's bird song to Hundr's desperation. It was Ragnhild, and across the rooftops around the square, archers sparked flints, and the folk Hildr had trained loosed flaming arrows down at the enemy. The other Vanylven residents threw missiles and roared their hate at Rollo's men. The incendiary arrows slapped into the backs and shoulders of the Franks, and the flames sputtered out. But then one hit a pot shard, igniting the tar, and flames whooshed along the enemy line as though a dragon blew its fiery breath across the courtyard.

More pots flew from the rooftops, and the fire grew in intensity, spreading through the enemy ranks and unleashing a cacophony of anguished screams as the fire consumed their legs and bodies. A man ran across the square, screeching like a pig and patting frantically at his hair, which had caught fire, and the square became ringed with flames. Dozens of arrows thrummed from the rooftops where Ragnhild, Hildr, and the archers rained down death upon the Franks. Hundr shielded his face from the wall of heat as the flames blocked the courtyard from the streets.

"Rollo is in there!" Amundr called, shouting to be heard above the crackle of the fire and screaming of burning Franks. He glanced at Hundr and then burst through the flames, axe in hand, to brave the fire and kill their enemy. Hundr tried to follow, but he could not bring himself to charge into the blaze. However, Rollo was beyond the raging flames and separated from all but his personal guard, so Hundr shouted Odin's name and charged. The fire licked at his skin as he ran through it, and there was a moment of gut-churning fear as the flames singed the hairs on his arms and beard. But as Hundr emerged on the other side, he was unscathed, and before him, Amundr faced off against Rollo's five bodyguards.

"Dog!" Rollo bellowed above the chaos, and he pointed his long sword at Hundr. "Leave the brute and kill the one-eyed bastard!" he ordered his guards. They skirted around Amundr and came towards

Hundr. Amundr let them pass and strode forward, axe in hand, to fight Rollo.

"No," Hundr whispered. He had come too far to die like this. The five Franks were all big men with shields, helmets, spears, and swords. To fight those five chosen champions was to die. Rollo was a killer and a great warrior in his own right, so the men he selected as his personal hearth troop would be brutal fighters. Each man towered over Hundr, and with their armour, helmets and swords, they would bully Hundr, trap him between them, and then hack him to pieces with their blades. Even so, Hundr could not give up. His mind conjured images of Sigrid's sacrifice and Sigurd's cold little body; then, his thoughts shifted to Bush, Torsten, and all of his fallen men, allowing an overwhelming surge of incandescent rage to overtake him. Suddenly, he remembered Bavlos had charmed his weapons and given him the berserker potion should he require the wild fury and unbridled violence it could unleash. Hundr took the small clay vial in his hand and bit the stopper from its lid. The mouldy fungal foulness of its contents made him retch, and he raised the drink to his lips but suddenly cast it away without drinking a single drop. Hundr trusted the gods, the Norns, and his skill to guide his hand against his mortal enemy. "No, no, no," Hundr said again, and he sheathed his sword and pulled his heavy brynjar over his head. The five huge Franks paused and stared at one another in disbelief as Hundr stripped away his armour and then his boots so that he stood before them in only his trews. Hundr grasped his two swords and closed his one eye, asking Odin for battle luck and Bavlos' ancient gods to honour their shaman's charms.

The blazing fire raged around the courtyard, enveloping the surrounding houses and buildings, creeping up timber posts and hissing on the winter-damp thatch. The battle raged on behind that wall of flame, but within the courtyard, there was only Hundr and the five champions. Beyond them, Amundr and Rollo came together. The two giant men moved with speed and power, which belied their size, but Hundr had to fight five men. So, with dogged fortitude, he flexed his hands around the leather-bound grips of his swords and broke into a run. The huge Franks came for him, faceless and terrifying in their iron helmets. They tried to bunch together and come in tight formation, but in stripping away his armour and everything of any weight, Hundr became something different. He was fast and lithe, at one with the new moon and the darkness, and the Ulfberht sword was light and deadly.

Hundr darted to his left, then feinted to his right. The closest warrior swung his sword, yet it was as though he moved underwater, and Hundr flew like a bird. He ducked beneath the sword and sliced the Ulfberht sword across the Frank's shins. The champion let out a metallic cry inside his helmet, and Hundr rolled past him, using the falling man's body as a shield. The next attacker fumbled around his toppling comrade, and Hundr whipped Battle Fang forth, opening his throat so that blood spurted and poured down the dying man's breastplate.

Hundr kept moving. A blade cut down his back like a red-hot whip, but he surged to his right, ignoring the man behind, and a huge Frank loomed up before him with his shield raised. Hundr jumped, bringing Battle Fang down hard on the shield rim before driving it downwards. A startled face framed in cold metal appeared behind the shield, and Hundr plunged the tip of the Ulfberht sword into the man's mouth, ripping his face open. Suddenly, an enemy blade viciously slashed at his left thigh. Hundr fell to his back and rolled over just as the next champion attacked him with his sword raised high, trying to chop the blade down and smash Hundr's chest to ruin. But Hundr flicked the Ulfberht's tip up, and as the Frank came on, his weight drove his body onto the sword, and Hundr twisted away, tearing his blade free of the champion's guts. He rose, grimacing at the pain in his leg and back, surrounded by the four men who lay dead or dying inside the flame-lit courtyard. The last champion roared and charged behind his shield, yet Hundr skipped away, limping but just avoiding the bigger man. The Frank turned and swung his shield, and the iron rim thudded into Hundr's shoulder, sending him spinning. He ducked, and the Frank's sword sang over his head.

Hundr stabbed down with Battle Fang, and the sword point pierced the Frank's boot, pinning his left foot to the ground. He howled in pain and lunged his sword, but Hundr leapt away from its point. The Frank pulled at his trapped and bleeding foot, shaking his head whilst waving his sword to keep Hundr away. Hundr circled him, quick and deadly, the tiny stones and grit of the frozen ground scratching the soles of his bare feet. As Hundr continued to circle around him, the Frank twisted to defend himself but couldn't free his foot from where Battle Fang pinned it. In desperation, the Frank dropped his sword and shield and forcefully wrenched Battle Fang free of his foot, but he was too late. Hundr drove the Ulfberht sword into the man's spine and ruthlessly thrust the blade through bone and gristle.

Across the courtyard, Amundr was down. He bled from wounds in his arm, shoulder, and leg, and he stared up at Rollo, who stood over him with his long sword poised to strike.

"Rollo!" Hundr shouted, loud enough to be heard above the roar of the fire and the clashing din of battle.

Rollo turned from Amundr and grinned. His eyes took in his defeated champions, and they glittered with a look of cunning as he raised his sword, pointing it at Hundr.

"So we meet at last, Dog," drawled Rollo, and he moved towards Hundr, striding lithely on the balls of his feet. Given his considerable height and breadth, Rollo wore a brynjar big enough to fit two men, and his sword surpassed Hundr's Ulfberht in both width and length, extending an entire forearm's length beyond it.

"I wish you were there that day when I came to your fortress in Frankia, and I wish we had fought and settled it all then, once and for all," said Hundr wistfully. There had been so much suffering, and so many good people lost in their feud.

"You attacked my home, and now I have taken yours. You are Fairhair's spineless pup, and now you shall meet your pathetic end. But know this before you die – I shall destroy Harald Fairhair for what he took from me."

"I should have left you chained in Ketil Flatnose's hall. I wish I had."

"But you didn't. You freed me, and you took Flatnose's daughter, as well as his hoard. You and Harald took everything from me, but look at me now. I am Duke of Frankia, and my son William will marry into the royal family. I have land, men, ships and power. What do you have?"

"She died, Rollo. After you came here to Vanylven, Sigrid died, and so did my son."

Rollo's face dropped a little, the corners of his mouth turning down.

"My blood feud is with you, not them. I did not wish for your son to die." Rollo's head twitched as though he understood some measure of Hundr's loss, but then his mask of fury returned, and his mouth set firm in a thin, straight line.

"And yet they are dead!" Hundr yelled as he raised his sword, the tip banging against Rollo's blade. Lightly, he took a step backwards, his bare feet crunching on the earth and his naked torso warmed by the flames.

Rollo roared in anger, and his sword snaked out in a vicious lunge. Hundr parried the blade with his sword, and the power of Rollo's strike shook the bones in Hundr's arm. He stepped in to brutally punch Rollo in the eye and then spun away as Rollo's sword swept around and missed him by a hand's breadth. Hundr winced as the pain in his leg and back throbbed. Rollo attacked with his sword, swiftly raising the weapon above his head and bringing it down with all of his strength in a ferocious two-handed strike. Hundr raised his own sword just in the nick of time, and the two blades clashed together, ominously resounding like a bell to proclaim the end of days. The shock of the blow shook Hundr's shoulders and arms, forcing him to roll away backwards and rapidly sidestep another wild swing of Rollo's sword.

Rollo sucked in mouthfuls of air, already tiring from the weight of his blade and his heavy armour. Hundr set his jaw determinedly and absorbed the pain of his wounds. He danced around Rollo's sword and sliced the Ulfberht blade across Rollo's arm. Rollo gasped in pain as the weapon cut his skin below the sleeve of his brynjar, and he tried to raise his sword, but he was slow, while Hundr was fast. Hundr swung his blade down, and the edge chopped into Rollo's hand at the grip of his sword, cutting three fingers away in a splash of vivid scarlet. Rollo took a heavy step backwards, and Hundr whipped his sword around, reversing his grip so that the blade slashed across Rollo's face. Blood sheeted his mouth and beard, and Rollo moved like a pregnant sow, slow and laboured. He was an enormous man; with his sword and armour, he could effortlessly break a shield wall or crush a champion to offal. But Hundr was fast and unarmoured, and he possessed sword skill drilled into him from the time he could walk in distant Novgorod. The Ulfberht blade felt like a wand in his hand, part of him, and so light that it was like lifting his own arm.

Furious, Rollo screamed with hatred, and he ran forward, driving his sword overhand once more, his good hand gripping both the hilt and his other bloody, mangled fist. Rollo put everything into that strike, aiming to cleave the Dog's Name in two, but Hundr braced himself and brought the Ulfberht up to meet the monstrous sword where the blade became hilt and tang. The swords clashed, and Rollo's blade shattered on the Ulfberht sword, just as Fenristooth had broken when Hundr had fought the Frankish champion at the battle of Lüneburg Heath. Rollo's face contorted in horror as the shards of his sword caught the red-orange firelight, and Hundr twisted his wrists and dragged his sword blade across Rollo's throat. The bigger man coughed and choked, carmine blood pulsing from the thin, wicked cut on his neck to wash the front of his brynjar. Rollo dropped heavily to his knees, and Hundr peered into his dying eyes.

"I lost the love of my life and my beautiful son because of you," Hundr uttered. He pulled the sword hilt from Rollo's hand, tossing it aside, and then he swept his sword once over Rollo's head to condemn him. "I curse you, Rollo the Betrayer. I send you to spend the afterlife in Nástrǫnd, on the corpse shore, where the serpent Níðhöggr will gnaw on your corpse until the end of days."

Hundr stepped backwards and let out a great shout, all pain and grief in the guttural animal bellow. It came from deep in his stomach, and Hundr drove the tip of his sword into Rollo's eye. It punched through jelly, blood, brain and skull to burst through the back of his enemy's head, and Hundr ripped the blade free. Hundr sagged to his knees, and all of his anger and rage flew from him like a bird on the wing. His wounds suddenly throbbed and wracked him with pain. His greatest enemy was dead, and he had his revenge.

TWENTY-SEVEN

"Gather them by the shore," said Einar. His warriors led a shame-faced, bedraggled line of Franks away from the square along the mud-churned road which sloped down towards the fjord. Einar wiped his eyes and face on the back of his hand, and it came away blackened with soot. The vicious battle had raged through the night, with pockets of Rollo's Franks fighting for their lives in the curve and twist of Vanylven's streets. Once word spread of their duke's death, however, they surrendered with clasped hands in desperate prayer to their nailed God. So, two hundred enemy survivors knelt beside the fjord's lapping shore. A sallow sun rose in a dirty sky, stained by the smoke billowing from burned buildings around Vanylven's main square.

After the fighting was over and most of the Franks had surrendered, Einar, Ragnhild, and Hildr led their forces in the effort to put out the flames. The pine tar fire had caught the wall timbers and thatch of those buildings close to the main square, but the winter dampness and night frost had thankfully held it at bay so that the flames had not spread across the town. The people made a chain of hands from the flaming courtyard down to the fjord and passed buckets of water along the line. They doused the fire until it sputtered, turning from fierce fire to black, smoking ruins. Luckily, only the buildings around the courtyard were damaged, and Einar's hall escaped unscathed. The shame-faced Franks who marched away from Einar across the square were the last of the enemy, and Einar had never been so tired. His eyes stung from the smoke, and every muscle and bone in his body ached from the fighting.

"We must treat the wounded," said Hildr. Ash had turned her golden and greying hair black, but her eyes remained bright and keen. "You included."

"I'll live," Einar replied. He had taken wounds in the fighting, especially in the brutal battle with Kveldulf, but so had many others, and he was their jarl, their leader. He had to be strong and lead the way with the repairs and rebuild of his town.

"What shall we do with the prisoners?"

"Put them on their ships and send them home. Don't give them any food or water. We shall need everything here to feed our own people. They can leave as they came and find their own way home to Frankia."

Einar left her and walked to where Hundr sat with Amundr on the steps to the great hall. Both men had taken serious wounds in the fighting, but they sat in companionable silence, staring at the smoking ruins around them.

"I will fetch Ragnhild to tend to your scratches," Einar said, looking down upon their terrible cuts and gashes.

"Scratches?" piped Amundr, and he laughed.

"It's over," Einar said as he sat beside Hundr.

"Rollo is dead, but we have lost much to rid ourselves of him," murmured Hundr. His scarred face looked drawn and pale, and for the first time, Einar thought his friend could finally grieve for his dead family.

"So let's rebuild. Then we can bring Hermoth home where he belongs."

"I must also go to Bavlos. The shaman would walk with me in the dream world. I might find Sigurd there…" Hundr's voice trailed off, and he grimaced at the pain of his wounds. Hundr smiled wanly and sat back to watch tendrils of smoke drift up to the winter sky. The Betrayer was dead, and that fight was over. Einar's people had reclaimed their homes and had enough food to survive the winter. Rognvald would return to King Harald with an enemy removed from the tafl board, and Ravn had repaid his blood debt to Hundr. Hundr was right, though; they had lost much to rid themselves of their fearsome enemy. Many good friends and loved ones had perished, and Einar would celebrate their lives with feasts and tributes to the gods. Then, when days drew longer and the snow melted in the high places, it would be time to take to the Whale Road once more in pursuit of reputation and glory.

MAILING LIST

If you enjoyed this book, why not join the authors mailing list and receive updates on new books and exciting news. No spam, just information on books. Every sign up will receive a free download of one of Peter Gibbons' historical fiction novels.

https://petermgibbons.com/

ABOUT THE AUTHOR

Peter Gibbons

Peter is the winner of the 2022 Kindle Storyteller Literary Award, and an author based in Kildare in Ireland, with a passion for Historical Fiction, Fantasy, Science Fiction, and of course writing!

Peter was born in Warrington in the UK and studied Law at Liverpool John Moores University, before taking up a career in Financial Services and is now a full time author.

Peter currently lives in Kildare Ireland, and is married with three children. Peter is an avid reader of both Historical Fiction and Fantasy novels, particularly those of Bernard Cornwell, Steven Pressfield, David Gemmell, and Brandon Sanderson.

Peter's books include the Viking Blood and Blade Saga and The Saxon Warrior Series. You can visit Peter's website at www.petermgibbons.com.